James Maidment, James Paterson, John Kay

Kay's Edinburgh Portraits

a series of anecdotal biographies chiefly of Scotchmen - Vol. 1

James Maidment, James Paterson, John Kay

Kay's Edinburgh Portraits
a series of anecdotal biographies chiefly of Scotchmen - Vol. 1

ISBN/EAN: 9783337410087

Printed in Europe, USA, Canada, Australia, Japan

Cover: Foto ©Andreas Hilbeck / pixelio.de

More available books at **www.hansebooks.com**

KAY'S EDINBURGH PORTRAITS

A Series of

Anecdotal Biographies Chiefly of Scotchmen

Mostly Written by

JAMES PATERSON

Author of the "History of Ayrshire," "Contemporaries of Burns,"
etc., etc.

And Edited by

JAMES MAIDMENT, Esq., Advocate

Editor of the "Book of Scottish Pasquils," etc.

Popular Letterpress Edition
IN TWO VOLUMES.—VOLUME I.

LONDON: HAMILTON, ADAMS, & CO.
GLASGOW: THOMAS D. MORISON
1885.

EDITORIAL PREFACE.

–

THE great and continued interest felt in the celebrated but rather mis-named work, known as *Kay's Edinburgh Portraits*, has suggested the desirableness of issuing a popular letterpress edition for reading simply. Hitherto it has only been within the reach of the really wealthy, notwithstanding the fact that the greater part of the book is such as to render it unusually attractive to readers in general. No Scotchman, wherever resident, if at all interested in the lives and actions of his fellow-countrymen, can turn over the leaves of the work in question, without feeling delighted with the charmingly written biographies contained therein.

The title of the book, though, is somewhat misleading. It suggests too much of the idea of local biography, which certainly is a mistake, as the great majority of the best lives contained in the volumes are decidedly of general interest; and it is safe to say that, as Anecdotal Biographies, there is no work at all to be compared with the one in question, so far as regards the field of Scottish literature. Hitherto the idea before the public has rather been that the biographies are an appendage to the portraits, which, as regards priority of execution, is indeed the case; but as concerning merit, the reverse may be taken for the fact. The *engraved* portraits are exceedingly interesting, but what we may call the *pen* portraits are surpassingly so, and that to a much wider class. It is unfortunate that the publisher of the original work in 1842 did not give the chief writer of the biographies the acknowledgment that was his due, especially as the duties of biographer had been discharged with such exceptional ability and painstaking devotion.

But at that time neither Paterson the author, nor Maidment the editor, had attained to the literary distinction which afterwards fell to their lot, as the result of their enthusiastic labours. This non-acknowledgment in the case of Paterson is another illustration of a literary genius not being fully appreciated by his contemporaries. The same remark holds true with regard to the artist Kay, as well as with the author Paterson.

The present issue is, of course, meant for the general reader—not for the collector. As will be apparent, it contains every biography of real moment to the class signified, forming a collection of what may well be described as the very best Anecdotal Biographies ever written of these our countrymen. In order to render the book thoroughly interesting from beginning to end, those sketches that were so very short as to give little more than a few dry facts regarding the life and death of individuals of little concern,

are omitted. But the present issue contains everything really
of value or interest to the general Scottish reader. That the
biographies are much more interesting than the portraits
there can be little doubt, the more especially as the latter
are to a considerable extent what may be termed caricatures, whereas the former are true to the life. At the
same time the issue of this edition may increase the interest
in the engravings, and may result in some cases in a desire
to possess or examine the large work.

With reference to the writer of the most of these sketches,
less is known by the public than should be the case,
considering all he has done. Mr. James Paterson was for
over forty years a diligent writer on Scottish National
Antiquities, Family History, and Biography. Unambitious
of personal celebrity, he acquired his information by painstaking research and laborious investigation. The information so obtained he presented to the public in a variety
of well-written and most useful publications, and he had,
to an unusual extent, that rare and desirable faculty of
writing on whatever subjects he took up in a peculiarly
interesting and strongly descriptive style. Of his writings
several occupy an exceptionally high place as works of
authority, while all are held in esteem. Somewhere about
twenty volumes—all relating to Scottish affairs—came
from his pen, a few of which may be mentioned. In
addition to the great majority of the biographies in *Kay's
Portraits*, he wrote the *History of the County of Ayr*, a

work involving an immense amount of original research, and particularly rich in the department of Family History. Also, *The Life and Adventures of James the Fifth; The Origin of the Scots and the Scottish Language; The History of the Regality of Musselburgh; A Memoir of James Fillans, Sculptor; Wallace and his Times; The Contemporaries of Burns; The History and Genealogy of the Family of Wauchope-Merschell;* and a considerable number of others.

It may be well to add that the responsible duties of general editor of the biographies contained in Kay's Portraits were discharged by the celebrated antiquary, James Maidment, Esq., Advocate, who has since become so distinguished in the field of Scottish poetical literature, as the Editor of *Scottish Ballads and Songs,* the *Book of Scottish Pasquils 1548-1715,* and other works. Paterson tells us that Mr. Maidment added to the MSS. submitted to him many curious notes of the highest import. In the present issue, these notes instead of being put at the foot of the page, and thus constantly and awkwardly breaking the continuity of the narratives, are inserted in the body of the work, in their respective and appropriate places—altogether a better arrangement for the reader.

CONTENTS OF VOLUME I.

KAY'S EDINBURGH PORTRAITS.

JOHN KAY,

Caricaturist, Engraver, and Miniature Painter.

THE following sketch of the life of John Kay was written by himself, with the view, it is believed, of being prefixed to a collection of his works which he had projected :—

" JOHN KAY was born in April, 1742, in a small house a little south from Dalkeith, commonly called Gibraltar. His father, Mr. John Kay, was a mason in Dalkeith, as well as his two paternal uncles, James and Norman Kay. His mother, Helen Alexander, was heiress to many tenements in Edinburgh and Canongate, out of which she was tricked by the circumvention of some of her own relations.

" She had still so much confidence in these relations, however, that upon the death of her husband in 1748, she boarded her only son John, then only six years of age, with one of them, who used him extremely ill, and not only neglected, but beat and starved him. While he lived with these savages in Leith, he ran various risks of his life from accidents without doors, as well as from bad usage within ; and there is every reason to believe that they really wished his death, and took every method to accomplish it except downright murder. On one occasion he was blown into the sea from the Ferry-boat Stairs, and on another he fell into the water on stepping across the joists below the Wooden Pier, but recovered himself both times, by grasping the steps on the one occasion, and the joists on the other. But he ran a still greater risk of drowning upon a third occasion, when, happening to be seated on the side of a ship in the harbour, he was accidentally pushed overboard, and being taken up for dead, remained in that condition for some time, till one of the sailors, anxious to see him, in his hurry trampled upon his belly, which immediately excited a groan, and produced respiration and articulation. He might have died, however, that same evening, had not other people taken more care of him than his barbarous relations did.

" About this time he gave strong proofs of an uncommon genius for drawing, by sketching men, horses, cattle, houses, etc., with chalk, charcoal, or pieces of burnt wood, for want of pencils and crayons. But under the government of his cousins, no propensity of this kind was either attended to or encouraged. And, though he himself wished rather to be a mason, the profession of his father and uncles, yet, by some fatality or other, it happened that he was bound apprentice to one George Heriot, a barber in Dalkeith, about the age of thirteen or little more.

"With this honest man he learned his business, and served six years, during which time, although he did every kind of drudgery work, he was perfectly happy in comparison of the state of tyranny under which he had so long groaned at Leith. When his time was out he came to Edinburgh, where he wrought seven years as a journeyman with different masters, after which he began to think of doing business for himself; but not having the freedom of the city, he was obliged to purchase it from the Society of Surgeon-Barbers, of which corporation he accordingly became a member the 19th December 1771, upon paying about £40 sterling.

"This business he carried on with great success for several years, being employed by a number of the principal nobility and gentry in and about Edinburgh. Among other genteel customers, he was employed by the late William Nisbet, Esq., of Dirleton, who not only employed him in town, but also took him various jaunts through the country with him in his machine; and at last became so fond of him, that for several years before he died, particularly the two last (1783 and 1784), he had him almost constantly with him, by night and by day.

"The leisure time he had on these occasions, while he lodged at Mr. Nisbet's house, afforded him an opportunity, which he took care not to neglect, of gratifying the natural propensity of his genius, by improving himself in drawing; and Mr. Nisbet having approved of his exertions, and encouraged him in the pursuit, he executed at this time a great number of miniature paintings—some of which are still in the possession of the family of Dirleton, and the greater part in his own.

"It should have been mentioned earlier in the order of chronology, that our hero married, so early as the twentieth year of his age, Miss Lilly Steven, who bore him ten children, all of whom died young except his eldest son, William, who was named after Mr. Nisbet, and who seems to inherit his father's talent for drawing. Mrs. Kay died in March, 1785, and after living upwards of two years a widower, our hero married his present wife, Miss Margaret Scott, with whom he now lives very happily.

"Mr. Nisbet, of Dirleton, previous to his death, sensible that, by occupying so much of Mr. Kay's time, he could not but hurt his business, although he sent money regularly to Mrs. Kay, had often promised to make him amends by settling a genteel annuity upon him. This, however, from his debilitated habit of body, was delayed from time to time, till death put it out of his power. But, to the honour of his heir, he was so sensible of Mr. Kay's good offices to his father, as well as of his father's intentions, that he voluntarily made a settlement of £20 per annum for life upon him.

"After the death of his patron, our author attempted to etch in aquafortis, and having published some of his Prints executed in this way, he met with so much unexpected success, that he at last determined to drop his old profession altogether, which he did accordingly in 1785.

" Our author has drawn himself, in the Print, sitting in a thoughtful posture, in an antiquated chair, (whereby he means to represent his love of antiquities,) with his favourite cat (the largest it is believed in Scotland) sitting upon the back of it; several pictures hanging behind him; a bust of Homer, with his painting utensils on the table before him, a scroll of paper in his hand, and a volume of his works upon his knee."

Mr. Kay continued from the above period till about the year 1817 to exercise his talents in engraving. For a period of nearly half a century, few persons of any notoriety who figured in the Scottish capital have escaped his notice, and he has occasionally indulged himself in caricaturing such local incidents as might amuse the public. In this way he has formed a collection altogether unique; and we concur with Mr. Chambers in thinking, that " it may with safety be affirmed that no city in the empire can boast of so curious a chronicle." It is right, in addition to this, to mention that his etchings are universally admitted to possess one merit, which of itself stamps them with value, namely, that of being exact and faithful likenesses of the parties intended to be represented.

The emoluments derived from his engravings and painting miniature likenesses in water colours, together with the annuity from the Dirleton family, regularly paid by Sir Henry Jardine, rendered him tolerably independent.

He had a small print-shop on the south side of the Parliament Square, in which he sold his productions, and the windows of which, being always filled with his more recent works, used to be a great attraction to the idlers of the time. It was, with the rest of the old buildings in the square, destroyed by the great fire in November, 1824.

In his outward appearance he was a slender, straight old man, of middle size, and usually dressed in a garb of antique cut, of simple habits, and quiet unassuming manners. He died at his house, No. 227 High Street, Edinburgh, 21st February, 1826, in the eighty-fourth year of his age. His widow survived him upwards of nine years; her death took place in November, 1835. The son alluded to by Mr. Kay in his biography predeceased his father.

THE DAFT HIGHLAND LAIRD.

JAMES ROBERTSON, of Kincraigie, in Perthshire, was a gentleman by birth. He was a determined Jacobite, and had been engaged in the Rebellion of 1745, for which he was confined in the Tolbooth of Edinburgh.

It was during this incarceration that the Laird exhibited those symptoms of derangement which subsequently caused him to obtain the *soubriquet* of the " Daft Highland Laird." His lunacy was first indicated by a series of splendid entertainments to all those who chose to come, no matter who they were.

His insanity and harmlessness having become known to the authorities, they discharged him from the jail, from which, however, he was no sooner ejected than he was pounced upon by his friends, who having cognosced him in the usual manner, his younger brother was, it is understood, appointed his curator or guardian. By this prudent measure his property was preserved against any attempts which might be made by designing persons, and an adequate yearly allowance was provided for his support. A moderate income having in this way been secured to the Laird, he was enabled to maintain the character of a deranged gentleman with some degree of respectability, and he enjoyed, from this time forward, a total immunity from all the cares of life. When we say, however, that the Laird was freed from all care and anxiety, we hazarded something more than the facts warranted. There was one darling wish of his heart that clung to him for many a day, which certainly it was not very easy to gratify. This was his extreme anxiety to be hanged, drawn, and quartered, as a rebel partisan of the house of Stuart, and a sworn and deadly foe to the reigning dynasty. He was sadly annoyed that nobody would put him in jail as a traitor, or attempt to bring him to trial. It would have been a partial alleviation of his grief, if he could have got any benevolent person to have accused him of treason. It was in vain that he drank healths to the Pretender—in vain that he bawled treason in the streets; there was not one who would lend a helping-hand to procure him the enjoyment of its pains and penalties.

The Laird, although he uniformly insisted on being a martyr to the cause of the Chevalier, seemed to feel that there was something wanting to complete his pretensions to that character—that it was hardly compatible with the unrestrained liberty he enjoyed, the ease and comfort in which he lived, and the total immunity from any kind of suffering which was permitted him; and hence his anxiety to bring down upon himself the vengeance of the law.

Failing, however, in every attempt to provoke the hostility of Government, and thinking, in his despair of success, that if he could once again get within the walls of a jail, it would be at any rate something gained; and that his incarceration might lead to the result he was so desirous of obtaining, he fell on the ingenious expedient of running in debt to his landlady, whom, by a threat of non-payment, he induced to incarcerate him. This delightful consummation accordingly took place, and the Laird was made happy by having so far got, as he imagined, on the road to martyrdom.

It was a very easy matter to get the Laird into jail, but it was by no means so easy a one to get him out again. Indeed, it was found next to impossible. No entreaties would prevail upon him to quit it, even after the debt for which he was imprisoned was paid. There he insisted on remaining until he should be regularly brought to trial for high treason. At last a stratagem was resorted to to induce him to remove. One morning two soldiers of the Town-Guard appeared in his apartment in the prison, and informed him that they had come to escort him to the Justiciary Court, where the Judges were assembled, and waiting for his presence, that they might proceed with his trial for high treason.

Overjoyed with the delightful intelligence, the Laird instantly accompanied the soldiers down stairs, when the latter having got him fairly outside of the jail, locked the door to prevent his re-entering, and deliberately walked off, leaving the amazed and disappointed candidate for a halter to reflect on the slippery trick that had just been played him.

The Laird after this having, it would seem, abandoned all hope being hanged, betook himself to an amusement which continued to divert him during the remainder of his life. This was carving in wood, for which he had a talent, the heads of public personages, or of any others who became special objects of his dislike, and in some cases of those, too, for whom he entertained a directly opposite feeling; thus, amongst his collection were those of the Pretender, and several of his most noted adherents.

These little figures he stuck on the end of a staff or cane, which, as he walked about, he held up to public view. His enemies, or such as he believed to be such, were always done in a style of the most ridiculous caricature. The Laird exhibited a new figure every day of the year, and as this was expected of him, the question, " Wha hae ye up the day, Laird ? " was frequently put to him, when he would readily give every information on the subject required.

When the print to which this notice refers was first exhibited, the Laird retaliated by mounting a caricature likeness of the limner on his staff; and when asked for the usual information demanded in such cases, " Don't you see it's the barber ? " he would reply; " and wasn't it a wise thing of him, when drawing twa daft men, to put a sodger between them ? " On another occasion, meeting the Honourable Henry Erskine one day as he was about to enter the Parliament House, of which the Laird was a great frequenter, the former inquired how he did : " Oh, very weel ! " answered the Laird ; " but I'll tell ye what, Harry, tak' in Justice wi' ye," pointing to one of the statues over the old porch of the Parliament House, " for she has stood lang i' the outside, and it wad be a treat for her to see the inside, like other strangers ! "

He was of a kindly and inoffensive disposition, and, in keeping with this character, was extremely fond of children, and of those young persons generally who treated him with becoming respect. For these he always carried about him in his pocket a large supply of tops, *peeries*, and *tee-totums*, of his own manufacture, which he distributed liberally amongst them ; while to adults he was equally generous in the articles of snuff and tobacco, giving these freely to all who chose to enter into conversation with him. The Laird was thus a general favourite with both young and old.

He resided on the Castlehill, and was most frequently to be seen there, and in the Grassmarket, Lawnmarket, and Bow-head.

He wore a cocked Highland bonnet, as represented in the picture, which is an admirable likeness, was handsome in person, and possessed of great bodily strength. He died in July 1790. He retained to his dying hour his allegiance to the House of Stuart; and, about two years before his demise, gave a decisive instance of it, creating a disturbance at Bishop Abernethy Drummond's chapel, in consequence of the reverend gentleman and his congregation, who had previously been Nonjurants, praying for King George III.

JAMIE DUFF,

An Idiot.

JAMIE DUFF was long conspicuous upon the streets of Edinburgh as a person of weak intellects, and of many grotesque peculiarities. He was the child of a poor widow who dwelt in the Cowgate, and was chiefly indebted for subsistence to the charity of those who were amused by his odd but harmless manners. This poor creature had a passion for attending funerals, and no solemnity of that kind could take place in the city without being graced by his presence. He usually took his place in front of the *saulies* or ushers, or, if they were wanting, at the head of the ordinary company; thus forming a kind of practical burlesque upon the whole ceremony, the toleration of which it is now difficult to account for. To Jamie himself, it must be allowed, it was as serious a matter as to any of the parties more immediately concerned. He was most scrupulous both as to costume and countenance, never appearing without crape, cravat, and weepers, and a look of downcast woe in the highest degree edifying. It is true the weepers were but of paper, and the cravat, as well as the general attire, in no very fair condition. He had all the merit, nevertheless, of good intention, which he displayed more particularly on the occurrence of funerals of unusual dignity, by going previously to a most respectable hatter, and getting his hat newly tinctured with the dye of sorrow, and the crape arranged so as to hang a little lower down his back.

By keeping a sharp look-out after prospective funerals, Jamie succeeded in securing nearly all the enjoyment which the mortality of the city was capable of affording. It nevertheless chanced that one of some consequence escaped his vigilance. He was standing at the well drawing water, when lo! a funeral procession, and a very stately one, appeared. What was to be done? He was wholly unprepared: he had neither crape nor weepers, and there was now no time to assume them; and moreover, and worse than all this, he was encumbered with a pair of "*stoups!*" It was a trying case; but Jamie's enthusiasm in the good cause overcame all difficulties. He stepped out, took his usual place in advance of the company, stoups and all, and, with one of these graceful appendages in each hand, moved on as chief usher of the procession. The funeral party did not proceed in the direction of any of the usual places of interment. It left the town: this was odd! It held on its way: odder still! Mile after mile passed away, and still there was no appearance of a consummation. On and on the procession went, but Jamie, however surprised he might be at the unusual circumstance, manfully kept his post, and with indefatigable perseverance continued to lead on. In short, the procession never halted till it reached the seaside at Queensferry, a distance of about nine miles, where the party composing it embarked, coffin and all, leaving the poor fool on the shore, gazing after them with a most ludicrous stare of disappointment and amazement. Such a thing had never occurred to him before in the whole course of his experience.

Jamie's attendance at funerals, however, though unquestionably proceeding from a pure and disinterested passion for such ceremonies, was also a source of considerable emolument to him, as his spontaneous services were as regularly paid for as those of the hired officials; a douceur of a shilling, or half-a-crown being generally given on such occasions.

We come now to view the subject of our memoir as a civic dignitary —as Bailie Duff—a title which was given him by his contemporaries, and which posterity has recognized. The history of his elevation is short and simple. Jamie was smitten with the ambition of becoming a magistrate; and at once, to realise his own notions on this subject, and to establish his claims to the envied dignity in the eyes of others, he procured and wore a brass medal and chain, in imitation of the gold insignia worn by the city magistrates, and completed his equipment by mounting a wig and cocked hat. Jamie now became a veritable bailie; and his claims to the high honour—it gives us pleasure to record the fact—were cheerfully acknowledged.

At one period of the Bailie's magisterial career, however, his pretensions certainly were disputed by one individual; and by whom does the reader imagine? Why, by a genuine dignitary of corresponding rank—a member of the Town Council! This person was dreadfully shocked at this profanation of things sacred, and he ordered his brother magistrate, Duff, to be deprived of his insignia, which was accordingly done. City politics running high at this time, this odd, and it may be added absurd, exercise of power, was unmercifully satirized by the local poets and painters of the day.

It may not be without interest to know that this poor innocent manifested much filial affection. To his mother he was ever kind and attentive, and so anxious for her comfort, that he would consume none of the edibles he collected till he had carried them home, and allowed her an opportunity of partaking of them. So rigid was he in his adherence to this laudable rule, that he made no distinction between solids and fluids, but insisted on having all deposited in his pocket.

The Bailie at one period conceived a great aversion to silver money, from a fear of being enlisted; and in order to make sure of escaping this danger, having no thirst whatever for military glory, he steadily refused all silver coin; when his mother, discovering that his excessive caution in this matter had a serious effect on her casual income, got his nephew, a boy, to accompany him in the character of receiver-general and purse-bearer; and by the institution of this officer, the difficulty was got over, and the Bailie relieved from all apprehension of enlistment.

He was tall and robust, with a shrinking, shambling gait, and usually wore his stockings hanging loose about his heels, as will be shown by a full-length portrait of him done by Kay at an after period. He never could speak distinctly, though, it was remarked, that, when irritated, he could make a shift to swear. He died in 1788.

FRANCIS M'NAB, Esq.,
Of M'Nab.

SCOTLAND, about the close of the eighteenth century, contained few men of greater local notoriety than the herculean Highlander, whom Mr. Kay has represented in the act of reeling along the North Bridge, a little declined from the perpendicular. "The Laird of M'Nab," as he was commonly called, represented his clan at a time when the ancient peculiarities of the manners and ideas of a Highland chief were melting into an union with those of a Lowland gentleman. A strong dash of the primitive character, joined to much natural eccentricity, tended to make him a wonder in the midst of the cultivated society of his day. To complete the effect of his singular manners, his person was cast in one of nature's most gigantic moulds.

A volume, and that not a small one, might be filled with the curious sayings and doings of this singular gentleman ; but unfortunately the greater part of them, for reasons which may be guessed, could not, with any degree of propriety, be laid before the public.

The Laird was remarkable, above all things, for his notions of the dignity of his chieftainship. A gentleman, who had come a great distance to pay him a visit, either ignorant of, or forgetting the etiquette to be observed in speaking to or of a Highland chieftain, inquired if *Mr.* M'Nab was within ?—"Mr." being a contemptible Saxon prefix, applied to every one who wears a passable coat, and well enough probably in the case of those ignoble persons who earn their bread by a profession, but not at all fit to be attached to the name of a Highland chief. The consequence of this error of the Laird's visitor was, that he was refused admittance—a fact the more astonishing to himself, as he distinctly heard the Laird's voice in the lobby. In explanation of his blunder, he was told by a friend that he should have inquired, not for *Mr.* M'Nab, but for the *Laird* of M'Nab, or simply M'Nab, by way of eminence. Acting on this hint, he called on the following day, and was not only admitted, but received with a most cordial and hearty welcome.

Of the Laird's literary attainments, some anecdotes have found their way into the jest-books. In one of these he is represented as laying the blame of certain orthographical errors with which he was charged on one occasion to the badness of his pen, triumphantly asking his accuser, " Wha could spell with sic a pen ? "

Of a piece with this, and indicating a somewhat similar degree of intellectual culture, was his going to a jeweller to bespeak a ring, similar to one worn by a friend of his which had taken his fancy, and which was set either with the hair of Charles Edward or some other member of his family, the latter circumstance of course constituting its chief value. "But how soon," said the jeweller, whom he was for binding down to a day for the completion of the work, "will you send me the hair?"—"The hair, sir!" replied M'Nab fiercely; "Py Cot, sir, you must give me the hair to the pargain!"

In cases, however, where the Laird is exhibited in the exercise of his own native wit, he by no means cuts the ridiculous figure he is made to do in such stories as the above. The Laird was a regular attendant on the Leith races, at which he usually appeared in a rather flashy-looking gig. On one of these occasions he had the misfortune to lose his horse, which suddenly dropped down dead. At the races in the following year, a wag who had witnessed the catastrophe rode up to him and said, "M'Nab, is that the same horse you had last year?"

"No, py Cot!" replied the Laird, "but this is the same whip;" and he was about to apply it to the shoulders of the querist when he saved himself by a speedy retreat.

On the formation of the Local Militia in 1808, M'Nab being in Edinburgh, applied for arms for the Breadalbane corps of that force, but which he ought to have called the 4th Perthshire Local Militia. The storekeeper not recognising them by the name given by M'Nab, replied to his application that he did not know such a corps.

"My fine little storekeeper," rejoined the Laird, highly offended at the contempt implied in this answer, "that may be; but, take my word for it, we do not think a bit the less of ourselves by *your* not knowing us."

M'Nab was proceeding from the west, on one occasion, to Dunfermline, with a company of the Breadalbane Fencibles, of which he had the command. In those days the Highlanders were notorious for incurable smuggling propensities; and an excursion to the Lowlands, whatever might be its cause or import, was an opportunity by no means to be neglected. The Breadalbane men had accordingly contrived to stow a considerable quantity of the genuine "peat reek" into the baggage carts. All went well with the party for some time. On passing Alloa, however, the excisemen there having got a hint as to what the carts contained, hurried out by a shorter path to intercept them. In the meantime, M'Nab, accompanied by a gillie, in the true feudal style, was proceeding slowly at the head of his men, not far in the rear of the baggage. Soon after leaving Alloa, one of the party in charge of the carts came running back and informed their chief that they had all been seized by a posse of excisemen. This intelligence at once roused the blood of M'Nab. "Did the lousy villains *dare* to obstruct the march of the Breadalbane Highlanders!" he exclaimed, inspired with the wrath of a thousand heroes; and away he rushed to the scene of contention. There, sure enough, he found a party of excisemen in possession of the carts. "Who the devil are you?" demanded the angry chieftain. "Gentlemen of the excise," was the answer. "Robbers! thieves! you mean; how dare you lay hands on his Majesty's stores? If you be gaugers, show me your commissions." Unfortunately for the excisemen, they had not deemed it necessary in their haste to bring such documents with them. In vain they asserted their authority, and declared they were well known in the neighbour-

hood. "Ay, just what I took ye for; a parcel of highway robbers
and scoundrels. Come, my good fellows," (addressing the soldiers
in charge of the baggage, and extending his voice with the lungs of a
stentor,) "Prime!—load!—" The excisemen did not wait the completion of the sentence; away they fled at top speed towards Alloa, no
doubt glad they had not caused the waste of his Majesty's ammunition.
"Now, my lads," said M'Nab, "proceed—your whisky's safe."

This original character, but kind, single-minded man, died unmarried
at Callendar, in Perthshire, on the 25th June, 1816, in the eighty-
second year of his age.

ANDREW BELL,
Author and Engraver.

ANDREW BELL, a very odd-looking gentleman, was an engraver; and
however flattering the representation of his person may be considered,
it is nevertheless perfectly correct—his nose to a hair's-breadth, and
the angle of his legs to a point. Mr. Bell began his professional career
in the humble employment of engraving letters, names, and crests on
gentlemen's plate, dog's collars, and so forth; but subsequently rose
to be the first in his line in Edinburgh. His success, however, can
scarcely be attributed to any excellence he ever attained as an engraver,
but rather to the result of a fortunate professional speculation in which
he engaged. This was the publication of the "Encyclopædia Britannica," of which he was the proprietor to the amount of a half, and to
which he furnished the plates. By one edition of this work he is said
to have realised twenty thousand pounds.

Mr. Bell did not possess the advantage of a liberal education, but
this deficiency he in some measure obviated in after life by extensive
reading, and by keeping the society of men of letters, of which aids to
intellectual improvement he made so good a use that he became remarkable for the extent of his information, and so agreeable a companion that his company was in great request.

Mr. Bell was a true philosopher: so far from being ashamed of the
unnecessary liberality of nature in the article of nose, he was in the
habit of making it the groundwork of an amusing practical joke.

He carried about with him a still larger artificial nose, which, when
any merry party he happened to be with had got in their cups, he used
to slip on, unseen, above his own immense proboscis, to the inexpressible horror and amazement of those who were not aware of the trick.
They had observed, of course, at the first, that Mr. Bell's nose was
rather a striking feature of his face, but they could not conceive how
it had so suddenly acquired the utterly hideous magnitude which it
latterly presented to them.

Mr. Bell was also remarkable for the deformity of his legs, upon
which, however, he was the first person to jest. Once, in a large company, when some jokes had passed on the subject, he said, pushing out

one of them, that he would wager there was in the room a leg still more crooked. The company denied his assertion and accepted the challenge, whereupon he coolly thrust out his other leg, which was still worse than its neighbour, and thus gained his bet.

Mr. Bell was the principal proprietor of the " Encyclopædia Britannica." The second edition of this work began to be published in 1776. At the death of Mr. M'Farquhar, the other proprietor, in 1793, the whole became the property of Mr. Bell. It is well known that he left a handsome fortune, mostly derived from the profits of this book. By the sale of the third edition, consisting of 10,000 copies, the sum of £42,000 was realised. To this may be added Mr. Bell's professional profits for executing the engravings, &c. Even the warehouseman, James Hunter, and the corrector of the press, John Brown, are reported to have made large sums of money by the sales of the copies for which they had procured subscriptions. After Mr. Bell's death, the entire property of the work was purchased from his executors by one of his sons-in-law, Mr. Thomson Bonar, who carried on the printing of it at The Grove, Fountainbridge. In 1812, the copyright was bought by Messrs. Constable & Co., who published the fourth, fifth, and sixth editions, with the Supplement by Professor Napier. The work still continues to maintain so high a reputation in British literature, that a new and stereotyped edition, with modern improvements, and additions to its previously accumulated stores, is now publishing by Messrs. Adam & Charles Black.

Mr. Bell was in the habit of taking exercise on horseback. The animal he rode was remarkably tall; and Andrew, being of a very diminutive stature, had to use a small ladder to climb up in mounting it. The contrast between the size of the horse and his own little person, together with his peculiarly odd appearance, rendered this exhibition the most grotesque that can well be conceived; but such was his magnanimity of mind, that no one enjoyed more, or made greater jest of the absurdity than himself.

Mr. Bell left two daughters. One of them was married to Mr. Paton, ropemaker, Leith; and the other to Mr. Thomson Bonar, merchant in Edinburgh.

Mr. Bell acknowledged he was but a very indifferent engraver himself; yet he reared some first-rate artists in that profession. He died much regretted, at his own house in Lauriston Lane, at the advanced age of eighty-three, on the 10th May, 1809.

LORD KAMES,
Of the Court of Session.

HENRY HOME, Lord Kames, well known by his numerous works on law and metaphysics, was a judge of the Courts of Session and Justiciary.

He was born in the county of Berwick, in the year 1695, and was descended of an ancient but reduced family. But it was to his own exertions, his natural talent and profound legal knowledge, that he was indebted for the high rank and celebrity he subsequently attained; for his father was in straitened circumstances, and unable to extend to him any such aid as wealth could afford.

His lordship was early destined for the profession of the law, in which he wisely began at the beginning, having started in his career as a writer's apprentice, with a view of acquiring competent knowledge of the forms and practical business of courts. After long and successful practice at the bar, he was raised to the bench, and took his seat 6th February, 1752.

Lord Kames possessed a flow of spirits, and a vivacity of wit, and liveliness of fancy, that rendered his society exceedingly delightful, and particularly acceptable to the ladies, with whom he was in high favour. He is accused of having become in his latter years somewhat parsimonious; what truth may have been in the accusation we know not.

Notwithstanding the general gravity of his pursuits, his lordship was naturally of a playful disposition, and fond of a harmless practical joke, of which a curious circumstance is on record.

A Mr. Wingate, who had been his private tutor in early life, but who had by no means made himself agreeable to him, called upon him after he had become eminent in his profession, to take his opinion regarding the validity of certain title-deeds which he held for a sum of money advanced on land. The lawyer, after carefully examining them, looked at his old master with an air of the most profound concern, and expressed a hope that he had not concluded the bargain. The alarmed pedagogue, with a most rueful countenance, answered that he had; when Mr. Home gravely proceeded to entertain him with a luminous exposition of the defects of the deeds, showing, by a long series of legal and technical objections, that they were not worth the value of the parchment on which they were written. Having enjoyed for some time Wingate's distress, he relieved the sufferer by thus addressing him—"You may remember, sir, how you made me smart in days of yore for very small offences; now, I think our accounts are closed. Take up your papers, man, and go home with an easy mind; your titles are excellent."

Lord Kames, so eminent as a judge and an author, was also an amateur agriculturist of considerable reputation; and his "Gentleman Farmer" was long held as a complete *vade mecum* on the subject of farming. Among other contemplated improvements, he entertained a notion of the practicability of concentrating the essence of manure, so as not only to render the substance more productive, but the mode of application less laborious. Conversing one day with a tenant, and seeing the immense quantity of ordinary manure he was laying on a field, Lord Kames observed that he could make the full of his *snuff-box* go as far in producing a crop. "Gif ye do that," said the doubting farmer of the old school, "I'll engage to carry hame the crap *in my pouch!*"

Being on one occasion at Stirling, in his official capacity as a Lord of Justiciary, Kames invited Mr. Doig, a teacher there of deserved

LORD KAMES   HUGO ARNOTT   LORD MONBODDO

[*To face page 21*]

FRANCIS M'NAB, Esq.,

reputation, to sup with him. In the company of one so famous as the celebrated Judge, it was natural that the teacher should display his conversational acquirements to the utmost advantage. Old Kames was highly amused by the facetious talents of his guest, and for a time guardedly maintained a proper degree of etiquette; but a fresh sally of pleasantry breaking down all formality, out at last came his familiar expression—"Eh, man, but ye're a queer b—h!" The pedantry of the teacher was perhaps a little alarmed—"Thank you," said he; "I've often been termed a *dog* (Doig) before; but this is the first time I've ever been called a *b—h !*"

When Lord Kames was a young advocate at the bar, the Jesuitical Lord Lovat, who was notorious for his insincerity, had observed his talents; and conceiving that he might, in the course of events, become serviceable to his views, resolved upon making him his friend. Lovat then lived in a villa somewhere about the head of Leith Walk, and often observed young Home pass up and down between Edinburgh and Leith. Presuming upon very slight acquaintance, his lordship one day ran out, and, clasping the advocate in his arms, began to administer some of those compliments, which he used to call his *weapons*—"My dear Henry," he cried, "how heartily do I rejoice in this rencontre. How does it come to pass that you never look in upon me? Almost every day I see you go past my windows, as if for the purpose of inflaming me with a more and more passionate desire for your company. Now, you are so fine-looking—so tall, and altogether so delightful in your aspect, that unless you will vouchsafe me some favour, I must absolutely die of unrequited passion." "My Lord," cried Home, endeavouring to extricate himself from his admirer's arms, "this is quite intolerable; I ken very weel I am the coarsest and most black-a-vised b—h in a' the Court o' Session. Hae dune—hae dune!" "Well, Henry," said Lovat, in an altered tone, "you are the first man I have ever met with who had the understanding to withstand flattery." "My dear Lord," said Home, swallowing the compliment with avidity, and returning the embrace, "I am rejoiced to hear you say so."

Amongst his lordship's singularities, which were not a few, was an unaccountable predilection for a certain word, more remarkable for its vigour than its elegance, which he used freely even on the bench, where it certainly must have sounded very oddly. This peculiarity is pointed out in the amusing poem, entitled the "Court of Session Garland," by James Boswell—

> "Alemoor the judgment as illegal blames—
> 'Tis equity, you *b—h*,' replies my Lord Kames."

About a week before his death, which was the result of extreme old age, feeling his end approaching, he went to the Court of Session, addressed all the judges separately, told them he was speedily to depart, and bade them a solemn and affectionate farewell. On reaching the door, however, he turned round, and, bestowing a last look on his sorrowing brethren, made his exit, exclaiming, "Fare ye a' weel, ye b—hes!"

Not more than four days before his demise, a friend called on his lordship, and found him, although in a state of great languor and debility, dictating to an amanuensis. He expressed his surprise at seeing him so actively employed. "Ye b—h," replied Kames, "would you have me stay with my tongue in my cheek till death comes to fetch me!" A day or two after this, he told the celebrated Dr. Cullen that he earnestly wished to be away, because he was exceedingly curious to learn the nature and manners of another world. He added —"Doctor, as I never could be idle in this world, I shall willingly perform any task that may be imposed on me in the next."

During the latter part of his life, he entertained a dread that he would outlive his faculties, and was well pleased to find, from the rapid decay of his body, that he would escape this calamity by a speedy dissolution. He died, after a short illness, on the 27th of December 1782, in the 87th year of his age.

His lordship lived in the *self-contained* house at the head of New Street, fronting the Canongate, east side, a house which was then considered one of the first in the city.

The works of Lord Kames are—"Remarkable Decisions of the Court of Session, from 1706 to 1728," folio; "Essays upon several Subjects in Law," 1732; "Decisions of the Court of Session, from its first institution till the year 1740," 1741—two volumes were afterwards added by Lord Woodhouselee, and a Supplement by M'Grugar; "Essays on several Subjects concerning British Antiquities," 1747; "Essays on the Principles of Morality and Natural Religion, in Two Parts," 1751, 8vo; "The Statute Law of Scotland, abridged, with Historical Notes," 1757, 8vo; "Historical Law Tracts," 1759, 8vo; "The Principles of Equity," 1760, folio; "Introduction to the Art of Thinking," 1761, 12mo; "Elements of Criticism," 1762, 8vo, 3 vols.; "Remarkable Decisions of the Court of Session, from 1730 to 1752," 1766, folio; "Gentleman Farmer," 1772, 8vo; "Sketches of the History of Man," 1773, 2 vols., 4to; "Elucidations respecting the Common and Statute Law of Scotland," 1777, 8vo; "Select Decisions of the Court of Session, from 1752 to 1768," 1780, folio; and "Loose Hints upon Education, chiefly concerning the Culture of the Heart," 1781, 8vo.

HUGO ARNOT, Esq.,

Advocate.

HUGO ARNOT, Esq., was, in as far as his person is concerned, a sort of natural curiosity. He was of great height, but sadly deficient in breadth; yet an intelligent friend, who has contributed some information to this work, and who knew him well, complains that the limner has made him "*really too solid!*" If this be so, it is an error which is corrected in another likeness of him. Mr. Arnot's person was, in truth, altogether an extraordinary and remarkable one, and it was in consequence the source of many jests and witticisms.

Mr. Arnot was the son of a merchant and ship proprietor at Leith, where he was born on the 8th December, 1749. His name was originally Pollock, but he changed it in early life to Arnot, on the occasion of his falling heir, through his mother, to the estate of Balcormo, in Fife. He was bred to the law, and became a member o fthe Faculty of Advocates in the year 1772. A severe asthma, however, which was greatly aggravated by almost every kind of exertion, proved a serious obstruction to his progress at the bar, where, but for this unfortunate circumstance, there is little doubt that his talents would have raised him to eminence.

Mr. Arnot published in 12mo, London, 1776, "An Essay on Nothing, a Discourse delivered in a Society," which was favourably received. In 1779, appeared his "History of Edinburgh," which makes, perhaps, as near an approach to classical excellence as any topographical publication which has ever appeared in Scotland. The merit of this work is sufficiently expressed in the fact of its not having been thrown into the shade, either in respect of information or composition, by any subsequent production. In 1785, Mr. Arnot published a "Collection of Celebrated Criminal Trials, with Historical and Critical Remarks," which added considerably to the reputation of its author.

Prior to the publication of this curious work, Arnot quarrelled with the booksellers; and in December, 1784, he advertised the book to be published by subscription, adding, "Mr. Arnot printed, a few days ago, a prospectus of the work, that the public might form some idea of its nature, and he sent it to be hung up in the principal booksellers in town; but they have thought proper to refuse, in a body, to allow the prospectus and subscription papers to hang in their shops. The prospectus will therefore be seen at the Royal Exchange Coffee House, Exchange Coffee House, Prince's Street Coffee House, and Messrs. Corri and Sutherland's Music Shop, Edinburgh, and Gibb's Coffee House, Leith."

Mr. Arnot, in his day, enjoyed an unusually large share of local popularity, proceeding from a combination of circumstances—his extraordinary figure, his abilities, his public spirit, his numerous eccentricities, and his caustic wit and humour. The reverse of Falstaff in figure, he resembled that creature of imagination in being not only witty himself, but the cause of wit in others. The jest of Henry Erskine, who, meeting him in the act of eating a spelding or dried haddock, complimented him on looking so like his meat, was but one of many which his extraordinary tenuity gave rise to.

Going alongst the North Bridge one day, Mr. Arnot, who was of so extremely *nervous* and irritable a disposition, that he appeared, when walking the streets, as if constantly under the apprehension of some impending danger, was suddenly surrounded by about half-a-dozen unruly curs in the course of their gambols. This was a trying situation for a man of his weak nerves; but he wanted only presence of mind, not courage, and the latter, after a second or two, came to his aid. It rose with the occasion, and he began to brandish his stick; striking right and left, in front and in rear, with a rapidity and vigour that kept the enemy at bay, and made himself, in a twinkling, the centre of a canine circle. The resolution, however, which had come so opportunely to his assistance on this occasion, in the end gave way.

Perceiving a break in the enemy's lines, he bolted through, turned again round, and thus, keeping the foe in front, retreated, still flourishing his stick, till he got his back against a wall, where, though it does not appear that he was pursued by the dogs, he continued the exercise of his cudgel for some time with unabated vigour, as if still in contact with the enemy, to the great amusement of the bystanders, amongst whom recognising a young man whom he knew, he roared out to him in a voice almost inarticulate with excessive agitation—" W——l, you scoundrel! why did you not assist me when you saw me in such danger?"

The man whom nervous disease placed in this grotesque attitude was originally of an intrepid mind, as is sufficiently proved by several incidents in his early life. One of them was his riding to the end of the Pier of Leith on a spirited horse, when the waves were dashing over it in such a way as to impress every onlooker with the belief that he could not fail to be swept into the sea.

Another, was his accepting the challenge of an anonymous foe, who took offence at a political pamphlet he had written. This person called on him to meet him in the King's Park, naming the particular place and time. Mr. Arnot repaired to the spot at the appointed hour; but, though he waited long, no antagonist presented himself.

In his professional capacity he was guided by a sense of honour and of moral obligation, to which he never scrupled to sacrifice his interests. He would take in hand no one cause, of the justice and legality of which he was not perfectly satisfied. On one occasion, a case being submitted to his consideration, which seemed to him to possess neither of these qualifications—" Pray," said he, with a grave countenance, to the intending litigant, "what do you suppose me to be?" "Why," answered the latter, "I understand you to be a lawyer." "I thought, sir," said Arnot, sternly, "you took me for a scoundrel!" The man withdrew, not a little abashed at this plump insinuation of the dishonesty of his intentions.

On another occasion he was waited upon by a lady not remarkable either for youth, beauty, or good temper, for advice as to her best method of getting rid of the importunities of a rejected admirer, when, after telling her story, the following colloquy took place:—

" Ye maun ken, sir," said the lady, "that I am a namesake o' your ain. I am the chief o' the Arnots."

" Are you, by Jing?" replied Mr. Arnot.

" Yes, sir, I am; and ye maun just advise me what I ought to do with this impertinent fellow?"

" Oh, marry him by all means! It's the only way to get quit of his importunities."

" I would see him hanged first!" replied the lady, with emphatic indignation.

" Nay, Madam," rejoined Mr. Arnot; "marry him directly, as I said before, and, by the Lord Harry, he'll soon hang himself!"

The severe asthmatic complaint with which he was afflicted, subjected him latterly to much bodily suffering. When in great pain one day from difficulty in breathing, he was annoyed by the bawling of a man selling sand on the streets.

" The rascal! " exclaimed the tortured invalid, at once irritated by the voice, and envious of the power of lungs which occasioned it, " he spends as much breath in a minute as would serve me for a month."

The following anecdote is told of Hugo Arnot and Mr. Hill, afterwards Professor of Humanity (Latin), who was then tutor to the Lord Justice-Clerk's son. Arnot met him returning from the Grassmarket on one occasion when three men were executed there, and inquiring where he had been, Mr. Hill replied that " he had been seeing the execution." " What," said Hugo, " you, George Hill, candidate for the Professor's Chair of *Humanity!* " " Yes," said Mr. Hill. " Then, by ——," continued the indignant Hugo, " you should rather be Professor of *Barbarity;* and you are sure of the situation, for it is in the gift of my Lord Justice-Clerk! "

Mr. Arnot's celebrated " Essay on Nothing," so full of quaint humour itself, and the subject of several good sayings by his contemporaries, is now, perhaps, only familiar in name to the generality of readers. As a specimen of the *nervous* style of the author, the following quotation from the preface may not be unassuming :—" I do not communicate this treatise, says Hugo, " to promote *directly* piety, morality, meekness, moderation, candour, sympathy, liberality, knowledge, or truth ; but *indirectly,* by attempting to expose and to lash pride, pedantry, violence, persecution, affectation, ignorance, impudence, absurdity, falsehood, and vice. Besides the stilts of Preface and Dedication, I intended to have procured some recommendatory verses, which may be called ' Passports for begging civility and favour from the *Christian reader.*' But, as I know no person living (at least in the British realms), who is endued with any share of poetic fire ; and, besides, am persuaded, if there were any such, none of them would be so fool-hardy as to recommend this performance, I hope, instead of these, the reader will accept the following verses, written in praise of this performance by myself. This practice, I assure him, has by no means novelty to recommend it, although it has not hitherto been openly avowed :—

" Three sages in three learned ages born,
Three different polished stages did adorn.
In dreams and prophecies the first excelled ;
With pies and tarts the next his pages swelled ;
His high-dressed dishes praised in loud bombast ;
But I, In Nothing, have them all surpass'd."

The publication of the Essay occasioned the following epigram, by the Hon. Andrew Erskine, brother to the musical Earl of Kelly :—

" To find out where the bent of one's genius lies,
Oft puzzles the witty, and sometimes the wise ;
Your discernment in this all true critics must find,
Since the subject's so pat to your body and mind."

The Hon. Henry Erskine was once disputing with Arnot about the disposition which the Deity manifests in the Holy Scriptures to pardon the errors of the flesh—the metaphysician insisting for a liberal code, and the wit taking a rather more confined and Calvinistic view

of the case. At last, on Arnot avowing his resolution to live in the
hope of pardon, Erskine readily conceded that great allowance is made
for the *flesh;* but, affecting to be doubtful in the peculiar case of his
friend, he replied—

> " Though bawdy and blasphemy may be forgiven,
> To flesh and to blood, by the mercy of Heaven ;
> Yet I've searched the whole Scriptures, and texts I find none,
> Extending that mercy *to skin and to bone.*"

Mr. Arnot's tenuity of person, as a subject of satirical remark, was
not entirely confined to the learned. One day as he was standing in
Creech, the bookseller's shop, an old woman—a hawker of fish from
Musselburgh—came in to purchase a Bible. To quiz the old lady a
little, Hugo said he wondered she could trouble her head reading such
a nonsensical, old-fashioned book as that. Horror-struck at his
blasphemous remark, the old woman eyed Hugo in silence a few
seconds, measuring him from head to foot with inexpressible amazement. At length she exclaimed—" Gude hae mercy on us! Wha
wad hae thocht that ony human-like cratur wad hae spoken that way.
But *you,*" she added, with an expression of the most perfect contempt
—" a perfect *atomy!*"

Mr. Arnot was long afflicted with a nervous cough. He came into
Creech's shop one day, coughing and wheezing at a tremendous rate.
Casting his eye on Mr. Tytler, of Woodhouselee, who happened to be
present, he observed to him, " If I do not soon get quit of this ——
cough, it will carry me off like a *rocket.*" Mr. Tytler replied, " Indeed,
Hugo, my man, if you do not mend your manners, you will assuredly
take quite a *contrary direction.*"

Mr. Arnot had a habit of ringing his bell with great violence—a
habit which much annoyed an old maiden-lady who resided in the floor
above him. The lady complained of this annoyance frequently, and
implored Mr. Arnot to sound his bell with a more delicate touch; but
to no purpose. At length, annoyed in turn by her importunities,
which he believed to proceed from mere querulousness, he gave her to
understand, in reply to her last message, that he would drop the bell
altogether. This he accordingly did; but in its place substituted a
pistol, which he fired off whenever he desired the attendance of his
servant, to the great alarm of the invalid, who now as earnestly
besought the restitution of the bell, as she had requested its discon-
tinuance.

Mr. Arnot died on the 20th November, 1786, in the 37th year of his
age, exhibiting, in the closing scene of his life, a remarkable instance
of the peculiarity of his character, and, it may be added, of his fortitude. For several weeks previous to his death, he regularly visited
his appointed burial-place in South Leith Churchyard, to observe the
progress of some masons whom he had employed to wall it in, and
frequently expressed a fear that his death would take place before they
should have completed the work.

LORD MONBODDO,

Of the Court of Session.

JAMES BURNETT (LORD MONBODDO). This learned, ingenious, and
amiable, but eccentric man, was one of the judges of the Court of
Session. He was the eldest surviving son of James Burnett, Esq. of
Monboddo, in the County of Kincardine, where he was born in the
year 1714.

His lordship received his initiatory education chiefly at the school
of Laurencekirk, and afterwards was sent to King's College, Aberdeen,
where he distinguished himself by his proficiency in ancient literature,
the study of which, in after life, became his ruling passion, and
engrossed his attention to the entire exclusion of the productions of
modern talent.

Having been early destined for the bar, he proceeded, after completing his literary education at Aberdeen, to Groningen, where he
studied Civil Law for three years. At the end of this period he came
to Edinburgh, where he happened to arrive on the forenoon of the day
which concluded with the public murder, as it might be called, of
Captain Porteous. When about to retire to rest, his lordship's curiosity
was excited by a noise and tumult in the streets, and, in place of going
to bed, he slipped to the door half undressed, and with his nightcap
on his head. He speedily got entangled in the crowd of passers-by,
and was hurried along with them to the Grassmarket, where he became
an involuntary witness of the last act of the tragedy. This scene
made so deep an impression on his lordship, that it not only deprived
him of sleep during the remainder of the night, but induced him to
think of leaving the city altogether, as a place unfit for a civilized
being to live in. From this resolution, however, he was subsequently
diverted, on hearing an explanation of the whole circumstances
connected with the proceeding. His lordship frequently related this
incident in after life, and on these occasions described with much force
the effect which it had upon him.

Lord Monboddo passed his Civil Law examinations upon the 12th
of February, 1737, and being found duly qualified, was admitted a
member of the Faculty of Advocates. In 1767 he was appointed a
Lord of Session, and assumed the judicial designation by which he is
now best known. It is a remarkable circumstance, that the seat on
the bench occupied by his lordship was enjoyed by only three persons
(himself being one) during the long period of one hundred and
ten years.

Lord Monboddo's patrimonial estate was small, not producing during
the greater part of his life more than £300 a-year; yet of so generous
and benevolent a disposition was he, that he would not raise his rents,
nor dismiss a poor tenant for the sake of augmentation. It was his
boast to have his lands more numerously peopled than any portion of
equal extent in his neighbourhood.

When in the country, during the vacation of the Court of Session, he wore the dress of a plain farmer, and lived on a footing of familiarity and kindness with his tenantry that greatly endeared him to them.

His lordship's private life was spent in the enjoyment of domestic felicity and in the practice of all the social virtues. Though his habits were rigidly temperate, there were few things he so much delighted in as the convivial society of his friends. He was a zealous patron of merit, and amongst those who experienced his friendship was the poet Burns.

Notwithstanding the amiable character of Lord Monboddo, and his many excellent qualities, he was not a little remarkable for his eccentricities, and for the strangeness and oddity of some of his opinions and sentiments. The most remarkable of these, as recorded by himself in his celebrated work on the Origin and Progress of Language, is the assertion that "the human race were originally gifted with tails!" It was in allusion to this extraordinary discovery, that Lord Kames, to whom he would on a certain occasion have conceded precedency, declined it saying, "By no means, my lord, you must walk first that I may see your tail!"

The work of his lordship above alluded to was severely handled in the *Edinburgh Magazine and Review*, by Dr. Gilbert Stuart, its editor, a severity which is said to have occasioned the downfall of that publication by the general offence which it gave. To this work Hume, the historian, was a contributor.

Many peculiarities also marked his lordship's conduct in his official capacity, for he brought them even into court with him. Amongst these was his never sitting on the bench with his brethren, but underneath with the clerks, a proceeding which is said to have been owing to the circumstance of their lordships having on one occasion decerned against him in a case when he was pursuer for the value of a horse, and in which he pleaded his own cause at the bar. This statement relative to the cause which induced his lordship to take his seat at the clerk's table, is somewhat doubtful; the deafness under which he laboured affords a much more satisfactory reason. The first time he sat there was upon occasion of the decision of the Douglas cause, when having been originally the leading counsel on behalf of Archibald Douglas (afterwards Lord Douglas), he felt a delicacy in giving his opinion from the bench, and preferred delivering it at the clerk's table. His speech in favour of the paternity is admitted to have been the most able one on that side of the question. Generally speaking, he was not inclined to assent to the decisions of his colleagues. On the contrary, he was often in the minority, and not unfrequently stood alone. He was nevertheless an eminent lawyer, and a most upright judge, and had more than once the gratification of having his decision confirmed in the House of Peers, when it was directly opposed to the unanimous opinion of his brethren.

It has been already mentioned that an exclusive admiration of classic literature, which extended to everything connected with it, formed a prominent feature in his lordship's character. This admiration he carried so far as to get up suppers in imitation of the ancients. These he called his *learned* suppers. He gave them once a-week, and his guests generally were Drs. Black, Hutton, and Hope, and Mr. William

Smellie, printer, including occasionally the son of the gentleman last mentioned, the present Mr. Alexander Smellie.

His lordship was in the habit for many years, during the vacations, of making a journey to London, where he enjoyed the society of some of the most eminent men of the period, then residing there, and frequently had the honour of personal interviews with the king, who took much pleasure in conversing with him. During one of his visits to London (May, 1785), he was present in the King's Bench, when, owing to a false rumour that the court-room was falling, the judges, and lawyers, and visitors, made a rush to get out, his lordship took it very coolly, as the following anecdote, extracted from one of the journals of the day, evinces:—"In the curious *route* of the *lawyers' corps*, it is singular that the only person who kept his seat was a venerable stranger. Old Lord Monboddo, one of the Scots judges, was in the Court of King's Bench, and being short-sighted, and rather dull in his hearing, he sat still during the tumult, and did not move from his place. Afterwards being asked why he did not bestir himself to avoid the ruin, he coolly answered—'that he thought it was an *annual ceremony*, with which, as an *alien* to our *laws*, he had nothing to do!'"

These journeys his lordship always performed on horseback, as he would on no account even enter a carriage, against the use of which he had two objections: First, that it was degrading to the dignity of human nature to be dragged at the tails of horses, instead of being mounted on their backs ; and second, that such effeminate conveyances were not in common use amongst the ancients.

He continued these annual equestrian journeys to London till he was upwards of eighty years of age. On his last visit, which he made on purpose to take leave of all his friends in the metropolis, he was seized with a severe illness on the road, and would probably have perished on the way-side, had he not been overtaken accidentally by his friend Sir John Pringle, who prevailed upon him to travel the remainder of the stage in one of these vehicles for which he entertained so profound a contempt. Next day, however, he again mounted his horse, and finally arrived in safety and in good spirits at Edinburgh.

His lordship was very partial to a boiled egg, and often used to say, "Show me any of your French cooks who can make a dish like this."

Lord Monboddo died on the 27th May, 1799, at the advanced age of eighty-five.

His character is thus summed up in the first four lines of an epitaph written on him by James Tytler, an unfortunate son of genius who had experienced his benevolence :—

> "If wisdom, learning, worth, demand a tear,
> Weep o'er the dust of great Monboddo here ;
> A judge upright, to mercy still inclined,
> A gen'rous friend, a father fond and kind."

LORD GARDENSTONE,

Of the Court of Session.

MR. FRANCIS GARDEN, judicially denominated Lord Gardenstone, was distinguished as a man of some talent and much eccentricity. Born in 1721, the second son of a Banffshire gentleman, he chose the profession of an advocate, and was admitted a member of Faculty upon the 14th of July, 1744. On the 3rd of July, 1764, he was raised to the Bench. He is here represented in the latter part of life, as he usually appeared in proceeding from his house at Morningside (the one next the Asylum), to attend his duties in the Court. Kay has endeavoured to represent him as, what he really was, a very timid horseman, mounted, moreover, on a jaded old hack, which he had selected for its want of spirit, preceded by his favourite dog Smash, and followed by a Highland boy, whose duty it was to take charge of his Rosinante on arriving at the Parliament House.

In early life, Mr. Garden participated largely in the laxities of the times. He was one of those ancient heroes of the bar, who, after a night of hard drinking, without having been to bed, and without having studied their causes, would plead with great eloquence upon the mere strength of what they had picked up from the oratory of the opposite counsel. In 1745, being in arms as a loyal subject, he was despatched by Sir John Cope, with another gentleman, to reconnoitre the approach of the Highland army from Dunbar. As the two volunteers passed the bridge of Musselburgh, they recollected a house in that neighbourhood where they had often regaled themselves with oysters and sherry, and the opportunity of repeating the indulgence being too tempting to be resisted, they thought no more of their military duty till a straggling Highland recruit entered and took them both prisoners. John Roy Stuart made a motion to hang them as spies; but their drunkenness joined so effectually with their protestations in establishing their innocence, that they were soon after liberated on parole.

In his more mature years, Lord Gardenstone distinguished himself by a benevolent scheme of a somewhat unusual kind. Having, in 1762, purchased the estate of Johnstone, in Kincardineshire, he devoted himself for some years to the task of improving the condition of those who resided upon it. The village of Laurencekirk, then consisting of only a few houses, was taken under his especial patronage. He planned a new line of street, offered leases of small farms, and of ground for building on extremely advantageous terms, built a commodious inn for the reception of travellers, founded a library for the use of the villagers, and established manufactures of various kinds. By some of his operations he lost largely, but this did not in the least abate his philanthropy, or for a moment interrupt the career of his benevolence. The manufacture of a very elegant kind of snuff-box, the hinges of which are styled "invisible," such as those made in Cumnock, Ayrshire, is still carried on in the village to a considerable extent.

His lordship's labours in this good work were crowned with the success they merited. His village grew rapidly, and before his death had attained a degree of importance and prosperity that exceeded his most sanguine expectations. Of the delight which Lord Gardenstone took in this benevolent project, a singularly pleasing expression occurs in a letter which he addressed to the inhabitants of Laurencekirk. "I have tried," he says, "in some measure a variety of the pleasures which mankind pursue, but never relished anything so much as the pleasure arising from the progress of my village."

In his lordship's anxiety to do everything in his power to invest his favourite village of Laurencekirk with attractions for strangers, he erected a handsome little building adjoining the inn as a museum, and filled it with fossils, rare shells, minerals, and other curiosities. Considering the facility of access, it is not surprising that these should from time to time disappear; not unfrequently the unsuspecting proprietor was imposed upon, by having his curiosities stolen, and sold over again to himself! In this building there was also kept an album, or commonplace book, in which visitors were invited to record whatever they thought fit, and, as might be expected, many of the entries were not of the choicest description. The apartment was likewise adorned by portraits of a number of the favourite original inhabitants of the village. The inn itself was kept by a favourite servant of his lordship's, who rejoiced in the refreshing patronymic of "Cream," a kind-hearted and worthy man.

In the year 1785, his lordship succeeded, by the death of his elder brother, Alexander Garden of Troup, to the possession of the family estates, which were considerable. His acquisition of this additional wealth, was marked by another circumstance, which strikingly evinces the natural generosity of his disposition. He remitted to the tenants all the debts due to him as heir to his brother.

On his accession to the family property, his lordship set out on a tour to the Continent, where he remained three years, traversing in this time great part of France, the Netherlands, Germany, and Italy. The results of his observations during this tour (which was made in part with the view of gratifying curiosity, but chiefly with that of improving his health, which was much impaired), he gave to the world in two volumes, entitled, "Travelling Memorandums made in a Tour upon the Continent of Europe in the year 1792." A third volume of this work was published after his death. About the same time he published "Miscellanies in Prose and Verse," a collection of light fugitive pieces, partly of his own composition, and partly of others, the boon companions of his youth. The best of these, however, are attributed to Lord Gardenstone himself.

Among the eccentricities of Lord Gardenstone, was an attachment to the generation of pigs. He had reared one of these animals with so much affectionate care, that it followed him wherever he went like a dog. While it was little, he allowed it even to share his bed during the night. As it grew up, however, which no doubt it would do rapidly under such patronage, this was found inconvenient; and it was discarded from the bed, but permitted still to sleep in the apartment, where his lordship accommodated it with a couch composed of his own clothes, which he said kept it in a state of comfortable warmth.

His lordship consumed immense quantities of snuff; requiring such a copious supply, that he carried it in a leathern waistcoat-pocket made for the purpose, and used to say that if he had a dozen noses he would give them all snuff. His use of this article was so liberal, that every fold in his waistcoat was filled with it; and it is said that from these repositories the villagers, when conversing with him, frequently helped themselves, without his knowledge, to a pinch.

In his dress his lordship was exceedingly plain, a circumstance which gave rise to an incident highly characteristic of him, which occurred at one time when he was returning from London.

Observing some young bucks taking inside tickets for the coach in which he was about to travel, he took his for the outside. On arriving at the end of the stage, where the passengers were to breakfast, his lordship, who had been shown into an inferior room, while his better-dressed fellow-travellers were conducted to the best, called the waiter, and desired him to carry his compliments to the young gentlemen, on whose philanthropy it was his object to make an experiment, and to request that they would permit him to have the honour of breakfasting with them. To this message precisely such an answer was returned as his lordship expected. It was that the gentlemen above stairs kept no company with *outside* passengers. Lord Gardenstone made no reply, but desired the waiter to bring him a *magnum bonum* of claret, and to send the landlord to share it with him, concluding with an order to get a post-chaise and four ready for him immediately. These commands, which very much amazed both mine host and his man, having been in due time complied with, his lordship paid his bill and departed, giving orders previously to his coachman so to manage as to arrive at the stage where his former fellow-travellers would dine, precisely at the same time with them, that they might witness the respect which should be paid to him by the landlord, to whom he was known. All this the young bucks accordingly saw, and having set on foot some inquiries on the subject, they soon discovered their mistake. With the view of atoning for their incivility, they now sent a polite card to Lord Gardenstone, begging his pardon for what had happened in the morning, which they attributed to their ignorance of his quality, and requesting it, as a particular favour, that he would *honour them with his company to dinner.* To this polite card his lordship returned a verbal answer, that "he kept no company with people whose pride would not permit them to use their fellow travellers with civility."

The latter years of this amiable man's life were spent in the discharge of the duties of his office of a judge; and the very last act of his public beneficence was the erection of the ornamental building that encloses St. Bernard's Well, in the neighbourhood of Edinburgh.

His lordship died at Morningside, near Edinburgh, on the 22nd of July, 1793, in the 72nd year of his age.

Dr. JAMES GRAHAM   Miss DUNBAR

[To face page 37.

JOHN ROBERTSON
(Second Illustration.)

Dr. GLEN

Vol. I., Plate III.]

DR. GLEN,

Edinburgh.

DR. GLEN was a gentleman who enjoyed considerable celebrity in his day, at once for the amount of his wealth and the tenacity with which he held it. He had made a fortune abroad in the practice of his profession; and, in his latter years, returned to his native country —*not* to enjoy it. He was twice married. On the second occasion he had attained the discreet age of seventy; and it is said that, amongst the other soft and captivating things which the venerable lover whispered into the ear of the young lady on whom his choice had fallen, to induce her to receive his addresses, was the promise of a carriage. To this promise the Doctor was faithful. The carriage was got—but no horses. "That's more than I bargained for," said the Doctor; "I promised a carriage, and there it is; but I promised no horses, neither shall you have them." And here again the Doctor was as good as his word. The consequence was a quarrel with his young wife, aggravated by certain attempts, on her part, to revolutionize his house. The result may be anticipated—three weeks after the marriage a separation took place by mutual consent, the husband settling a sufficient aliment on his affectionate spouse.

There is another anecdote of the Doctor's happy talent for saving, but of so incredible and absurd a character, that, assured as we are of its truth, we have some hesitation in mentioning it. It is said that, on the death of his wife—the first, we presume—he adopted the ingenious expedient of attempting to procure a *second-hand* coffin to hold her remains, for lessening the funeral expenses on this melancholy occasion.

At a very advanced period of life, the Doctor was prevailed upon by a friend, but by what process of reasoning is not known, nor can be conjectured, to enter the society of Freemasons—a step which not a little surprised every one who knew him, or was aware of his penurious habits. How much was their surprise increased, when they found the Doctor entering, as he did, into all the spirit of the association, whether in its business or its pleasures, with an ardour and enthusiasm unequalled by the youngest member! The Doctor became, in truth, in so far at least as the circumstance of his connection with the brethren was concerned, a totally changed man. He headed deputations, presided at lodges, and became, in short, the leading spirit of the fraternity. The members of the Lodge of St. Andrew's, to which he belonged, and which was at this juncture rather barren of funds, early saw, in the Doctor's new-born passion, a very pleasant and rational prospect of effecting an improvement in their exchequer. Without loss of time they flattered the Doctor's vanity by electing him their Master, and ere long they succeeded in obtaining from him no less a sum, it is said, than one hundred pounds sterling.

The Doctor was a regular attendant at church, and always contributed to the plate. That his charity on such occasions might be duly appreciated by those who were in attendance, instead of throwing in his halfpence in the usual careless way, he piled them up into one solid massive column of copper, and gently placing the pillar down, left it, a conspicuous monument of his benevolence.

One act of public spirit, however, does mark the Doctor's life, and if his motive in performing it, as was uncharitably reported at the time, was vanity, one cannot help being struck with the ingenuity which directed him on the occasion. He presented the governors of the Orphan Hospital with a bell! His fame was thus literally sounded throughout the city; yet, lest any should have been ignorant of the gift, he took care when in company, on hearing it ring, to advert to its fine tone, and thus lead the way to a narrative of his generosity.

Being once troubled with sore eyes, after in vain trying the prescriptions of several physicians, he applied to Dr. Graham, who cured him in a very short time, for which he expressed great gratitude. Wishing to make him some remuneration, he consulted some of the young members of the Faculty; and, as the most genteel way of doing what he wished, they recommended him to invite the Doctor and a few of his own friends to dinner in Fortune's (the most fashionable tavern at that time), and provide himself with a handsome purse, containing thirty guineas or so, and offer it to the Doctor, which they assured him he would not accept. They accordingly met, and after a few bottles of wine had been drunk, the old Doctor called Dr. Graham to the window, and offered him the purse, which he at once accepted, and, with a very low bow, thanked him kindly for it. The Doctor was so chagrined that he soon left the company, who continued till a pretty early hour enjoying themselves at his expense.

The father of Dr. Glen was a native of the west of Scotland, and had three sons, all of whom were prosperous in the world. One of these gentlemen was appointed governor of one of the West India Islands, where he amassed a large fortune, of which he left £30,000 to his niece, the daughter of the third brother, who ultimately succeeded to the reversion of the Doctor's property. This amiable lady was subsequently married to the late Earl of Dalhousie, father to the present noble Earl.

Dr. Glen enjoyed, by purchase, an annuity from the city of Edinburgh, of which he lived so long to reap the benefit, that the magistrates gave up all hopes of his ever dying at all, and began to consider him as one of the perpetual burdens of the city. He, however, died in 1786.

DR. JAMES GRAHAM,

Edinburgh.

DR. JAMES GRAHAM was born at the head of the Cowgate, Edinburgh, 23rd June, 1745. His father, Mr. William Graham, saddler in Edinburgh, was born in Burntisland in 1710. He married, in 1738, in Edinburgh, Jean Graham (born 1715), an English lady; they had issue three daughters and two sons. The eldest daughter was married to a Mr. Smith; the second to the celebrated Dr. Arnold of Leicester, Fellow of the Royal College of Physicians, Edinburgh; and the third to Mr. Begbie, town smith. James was the eldest son; both he and his younger brother William studied medicine. The two brothers, in their early years, were not unfrequently mistaken for one another, from their strong family likeness, and from following the same profession. William, after practising some time as physician, abandoned medicine entirely, and entered into holy orders. He was an Episcopalian, and married the celebrated writer, Mrs. Catherine Macaulay, sister to Alderman Sawbridge; she died at Binfield, in June, 1791. Mr. William Graham was alive in July, 1836, being eighty-one years of age. He then resided in Loicestershire, where he was deservedly held in high estimation.

Dr. James Graham, after having finished his studies in Edinburgh, went to England, and began business in Pontefract, where in the year 1770 he married Miss Mary Pickering, daughter of a gentleman of that place, by whom he had a son and two daughters. His eldest daughter was married to the late Mr. Stirling, minister of Dunblane, a very accomplished lady, who is still alive. The other daughter died in the apartments of the Observatory on the Calton Hill, of consumption, about four years before her father; his son is still alive.

After residing some time in England, Dr. Graham went to America, where he figured as a philanthropic physician, travelling for the benefit of mankind, to administer relief, in the most desperate diseases, to patients whose cases had hitherto puzzled the ordinary practitioners. Having the advantage of a good person, polite address, and agreeable conversation, he got into the first circles, particularly in New England, where he made a great deal of money. He then returned to Britain; and, after making an excursion through England, during which, according to his own account, he was eminently successful in curing many individuals, whose cases had been considered desperate, he visited Scotland, and was employed by people of the first quality, who were tempted to put themselves under his care by the fascination of his manner, and the fame of his wondrous cures. So popular was he, that he might have settled in Edinburgh to great advantage, but he preferred returning to England. He fixed his abode in the metropolis, where he set on foot one of the most original and extravagant institutions that could well be figured, the object of which was for " preventing barrenness, and propagating a much more strong, beautiful, active, healthy, wise, and virtuous race of human beings, than the present puny, insignificant, foolish, peevish, vicious, and nonsensical race of Christians, who quarrel, fight, bite, devour, and cut one another's throats about they know not what."

The " Temple of Health," as he was pleased to term it, was an establishment of a very extraordinary description, and one in which all the exertions of the painter and statuary—all the enchantments of vocal and instrumental music—all powers of electricity and magnetism—were called into operation to enliven and heighten the scene. In a word, all that could delight the eye or ravish the ear—all that could please the smell, give poignancy to the taste, or gratify the touch, were combined to give effect to his scheme—at least, such was his own account.

Of his numerous puffs on the subject, one may be selected by way of a specimen :—

> "TEMPLE OF HEALTH AND HYMEN, PALL-MALL, NEAR THE KING'S PALACE.
>
> "If there be one human being, rich or poor, male, female, or of the doubtful gender, in or near this great metropolis of the world, who has not had the good fortune and the happiness of hearing the celebrated lecture, and of seeing the grand celestial state bed, the magnificent electrical apparatus, and the supremely brilliant and unique decorations of this magical edifice, of this enchanting Elysian palace!—where wit and mirth, love and beauty—all that can delight the soul, and all that can ravish the senses—will hold their court, this, and every evening this week, in chaste and joyous assemblage! let them now come forth, or for ever afterwards let them blame themselves, and bewail their irremediable misfortune."

In this way his numerous auditors were properly prepared for his lectures, which were delivered in the most elegant and graceful manner. The following letter—his own production, perhaps, from a periodical work of the time—descriptive of his Temple and lectures, is curious :—

> "TO THE EDITOR OF THE 'WESTMINSTER MAGAZINE.'
>
> "*Audi alteram partem.*
>
> "SIR,—I have heard many persons exclaim against Dr. Graham's Hymeneal Lectures, and reprobate him in the most oprobrious terms; but having not been myself to see his Temple of Hymen, I thought it unjust to censure, or join in condemning that which I had never seen, or him whom I had never heard. Curiosity (a passion remarkable in the people of England) prompted me to go with an intimate friend and pay a visit to the Doctor, whom I found attended by about forty gentlemen, who were intent on listening to his connubial precepts. I gave attention, and determined to judge impartially of what I heard as well as saw, and the following is the result of my unprejudiced observations :—
>
> "His rooms are fitted up in a very elegant and superb manner, far beyond anything I ever saw, and must have cost him a very considerable sum of money. A statue of Beauty, or *Venus de Medicis*, is the only object that appeared to me censurable, as likely to excite unchaste ideas. His lecture is well adapted to the subject he treats on, and is interspersed with many judicious remarks, well worthy the attention of the Legislature, to prevent prostitution and encourage matrimony. The nature of the subject naturally obliges him to border on what is generally termed indelicacy; but he always endeavours to guard his audience against imbibing sentiments in any respect repugnant to virtue, chastity, and modest deportment; he earnestly recommends marriage as honourable in all, and as strongly execrates prostitution and criminality; wherein then is he to blame?
>
> "BOB SHORT.
>
> "December, 1781."

In Spring 1783, Dr. Graham again paid a visit to his native city, and for the first time gave his fellow-citizens a lecture, which the Magistrates of Edinburgh deemed improper for public discussion, and accordingly endeavoured to suppress by the arm of power. The Doctor immediately published "an appeal to the public," in which he attacked the Magistrates, and particularly the Lord Provost, John Grieve, Esq. For this, the Procurator-Fiscal raised a criminal complaint in the Bailie Court against him, and as his real prosecutors were his judges—the result was, his being mulcted in £20, and imprisoned till the fine was paid. He suffered, however, no very tedious imprisonment, as his supporters collected the money amongst themselves. He also continued to give his eccentric lectures as long as the public curiosity lasted; and to induce people to hear his lectures, the admission being three shillings, he promised each person a book worth six shillings—viz., a copy of his lectures! The admission was reduced subsequently to two shillings, and lastly to one. The following advertisement was circulated by him in December 1783:—

"DOCTOR GRAHAM desires to inform the Ladies and Gentlemen of Edinburgh, that at the earnest desire of many respectable persons, he proposes to favour them on Monday evening next, the 27th instant, and the three following evenings, with A LECTURE on the simplest, most rational, and most effectual means of preserving uninterrupted bodily Health, and the most delightful mental sunshine or serenity to the very longest period of our Mortal Existence: Teaching them how to build up the human Body into a fair and firm Temple of Health, and to repose the Soul on the all-blessing Bosom of that pure, temperate, rational, and Philosophical Religion!—which alone is accepted of God!!! and truly useful to all his Creatures. The Lecture being therefore at once Medical, Moral, and Religious; the Technical Terms and nonsensical jargon of the followers of the Medical Trade or Farce being avoided, and the whole treated in a plain, practical, and useful manner, DR. GRAHAM trusts it will prove perfectly satisfactory, and of the highest importance to the health and happiness, temporal and eternal, of every sober and intelligent person who honours him with their company; as the precepts and instructions proposed to be delivered in this long and pathetic Lecture cannot fail, if duly practised, to preserve them in health, strength, and happiness, through the course of a long, useful, and truly honourable life *here;* and to prepare them for the enjoyment of eternal felicity *hereafter.*

"The Lecture will be delivered on MONDAY EVENING next, the 27th, and the three following evenings, precisely at Seven o'clock, in St. Andrew's Chapel, foot of Carrubber's Close, next to the New Bridge.

"Admission only One Shilling.

"Ladies are requested to come early, in order to be agreeably accommodated with seats, as the Lecture will begin *exactly at* Seven o'clock.

"N.B. Dr. G. has not the least intention of lecturing any more for several years in Edinburgh than the above four nights; and if the Chapel is not pretty full the two first nights, he will not repeat the lecture as proposed the two last nights, viz. on Wednesday and Thursday; and as the shilling paid for admission can only defray the various expenses, Dr. G. hopes that the inhabitants of Edinburgh will esteem these lectures as very great and important favours conferred upon them.

"December, 1783.

"All Dr. G.'s books and pamphlets are to be had at the Doctor's house, and at Mr. Brown's, bookseller, Bridge Street."

While his Temple of Health was in its glory, it cannot be doubted that such an exhibition, lauded as it was on all hands in the most extravagant terms, must have produced a great deal of money in such a city as London, where every species of quackery is sure to meet with support and encouragement; but Doctor Graham, instead of realising a fortune, deeply involved himself by the great expense he was put to in maintaining the establishment in proper splendour. In his own expenditure he was very moderate; for he not only abstained from wine, spirits, and all strong liquors, but even from animal food—and, consistently with this mode of life, he recommended the same practice to others; and whilst confined in the Jail of Edinburgh, for his attack on the civic authorities, he preached—Sunday, August 17, 1783—a discourse upon Isaiah, xl. 6, "All flesh is grass;" in which he strongly inculcates the propriety of abstinence from animal food. In this odd production, of which two editions were afterwards published, he says, "I bless God! my friends! that he has given me grace and resolution to abstain totally from flesh and blood—from all liquors but cold water and balsamic milk—and from all inordinate sensual indulgences. Thrice happy! supremely blessed is the man who, through life, abstains from these things; who, like me, washes his body and limbs every night and morning with pure cold water—who breathes continually, summer and winter, day and night, the free open cool air—and who, with unfeigned and active benevolence towards everything that hath life, fears and worships God in sincerity and in truth."

In addition to the peculiarities pointed out by the Doctor in his discourse, he dissented in many other respects from the ordinary usages of mankind. He wore no woollen clothes; he slept on a hair-mattress, without feather-bed or blankets, with all the windows open; he said, and perhaps with some degree of truth, that most of our diseases are owing to too much heat:—and he carried his cool regimen to such an extent, that he was in terms with the tacksman of the King's Park, for liberty to build a house upon the top of Arthur's Seat, in order to try how far he could bear the utmost degree of cold that the climate of Edinburgh affords; but, though the tacksman was willing, the noble proprietor would not listen to the project.

Amongst other eccentric plans recommended to his patients was that of earth-bathing,—which was neither more or less than burying them alive up to the neck in the earth, in which position they were to remain for ten or twelve hours. He tried this extraordinary remedy upon himself and one of his daughters, and actually induced his brother-in-law to follow their example. Other persons were also found simple enough to submit to this new species of temporary sepulture.

In 1787, this singular being appeared in a new character, as a special delegate from Heaven to announce the Millennium. He not only styled himself "The Servant of the Lord, O. W. L." *i.e.*, "Oh, Wonderful Love," but attempted to begin a new chronology—dating his bills such a day of the first month of the New Jerusalem Church; but before the coming of the second month the prophet was, by order of the Magistrates, put under restraint, not indeed in prison, but in his own house, from whence he, some months afterwards, removed to the north of England. His religious frenzy appears to have lasted some time; and we learn from the following extract, copied from the *Whitehaven Packet*, that a year afterwards his mind still wandered :—

"WHITEHAVEN.—Tuesday morning, Dr. James Graham was sent off to Edinburgh in the custody of two constables. This unfortunate man had, for some days past, discovered such marks of insanity as made it advisable to secure him."—*August 22, 1788.*

Whether he ever got entirely quit of his religious fancies, is uncertain; and in a very complete and curious collection of tracts, advertisements, &c., by, or relative to, Dr. Graham, occurring in the late Mr. John Stevenson's sale catalogue for 1825, there is a "manuscript written expressly for Dr. Graham, *regarding his religious concerns,* by Benjamin Dockray, a Quaker at Newtown, near Carlisle, in 1790," which would seem to indicate that his mind, on that head, was not at that date entirely settled.

His death took place somewhat suddenly, in his house, opposite to the Archer's Hall, upon the 23d June, 1794—it was occasioned by the bursting of a bloodvessel. He was buried in the Greyfriars' churchyard, Edinburgh. His widow survived him about seven years, and died at Ardwick, near Manchester, in the year 1801.

His circumstances, during the latter period of his existence, were far from affluent. To one of his publications, however, he was indebted for an annuity of fifty pounds for life; for it happened that a gentleman in Geneva, who had perused it, found his health so much improved by following the advice of its author, that, out of gratitude, he presented him with a bond for the yearly payment of that sum.

With all his eccentricities, he had a benevolent and charitable disposition, and his conduct towards his parents was exemplary. Even when in his "high and palmy state," he paid them every attention. Whilst in Edinburgh, he took them every morning in his carriage, which was one of the most splendid description, for an airing, attended by servants in gorgeous liveries; and these worthies—old-fashioned Presbyterian Whigs of the strictest kind—were infinitely gratified by the "pomp and vanities" with which they were surrounded.

It would be very difficult to give an exact catalogue of Dr. Graham's works. Such as we have seen are annexed. The list is far from complete.

.I. The General State of the Medical and Chirurgical Practice exhibited; shewing it to be inadequate, ineffectual, absurd, and ridiculous. London, 1779. 12mo. This passed through several editions; and an abstract was published at the small charge of sixpence.—II. Travels and Voyages in Scotland, England, and Ireland—including a Description of the Temple of Health, and Grand Electrical Apparatus, &c., which cost upwards of £12,000. London, 1783. 12mo.—III. Private Medical Advice to Ladies and Gentlemen—to those especially who are not blessed with Children—sealed up, price One Guinea, alone, at the Temple of Health and of Hymen. The whole comprised in eight large folio pages.—IV. The Christian's Universal Prayer—to which are prefixed a Discourse on the Duty of Praying, and a Short Sketch of Dr. Graham's Religious Principles and Moral Sentiments.—V. Hebe Vestina's Celebrated Lecture; as delivered by her from the Electrical Throne, in the Temple of Health, in London. Price 2s. 6d.—VI. A Discourse delivered on Sunday, August 17, 1783, in the Tolbooth of Edinburgh, by Dr. James Graham, of the Temple of Heath in London, while he was, by the most cruel and most unlawful stretch of power, imprisoned there for a pretended libellous Hand-bill and Advertisement, which was said to be published by him, against the Magistrates of that City. Isaiah, chapter xl., verse 6—"All flesh is grass." Edinburgh, 1783. 4to.—VII. The Principal Grounds, Basis, Argument, or SOUL, of the New Celestial Curtain (or Reprehensory) Lecture, most humbly addressed to all Crowned Heads, Great Personages, and Others, whom it may concern. By James Graham, M.D. London, 1786.—VIII. A New and Curious Treatise of the Nature and Effects of Simple Earth, Water, and Air, when applied to the Human Body: How to Live for many Weeks, Months, and Years, without Eating anything whatever, &c. By James Graham, M.D. London, 1793.

FRANCIS GROSE, ESQ.,

Antiquary.

THE Print of the celebrated antiquary, Captain Grose,

"A fine fat fodgel wight, of stature short, but genius bright,"

represents him in the act of copying an inscription from an ancient ruin, and was done during his visit to Edinburgh in 1789.

He was exceedingly corpulent, and used to rally himself with the greatest good humour on the singular rotundity of his figure. The following epigram, written in a moment of festivity, by the celebrated Robert Burns, the Ayrshire bard, was so much relished by Grose, that he made it serve as an excuse for prolonging the convivial occasion that gave it birth to a very late hour:—

"The Devil got notice that Grose was a-dying,
So whip! at the summons, old Satan came flying;
But when he approach'd where poor Francis lay moaning,
And saw each bed-post with its burthen a-groaning,
Astonished confounded, cries Satan, '——,'
I'd want him, ere take such a ———— load.'"

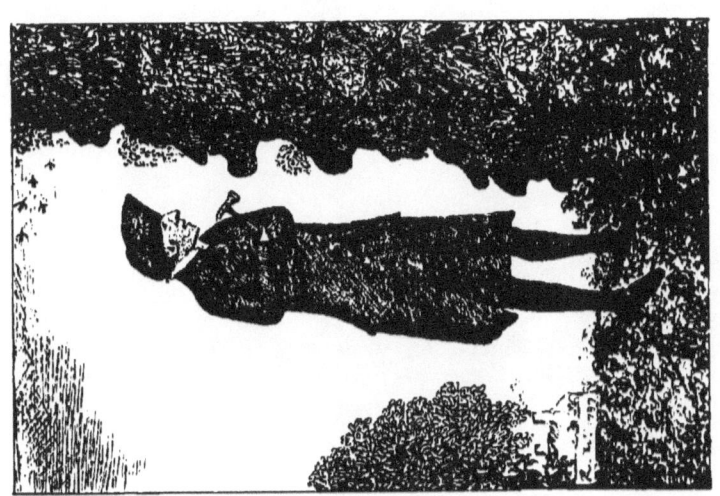

FRANCIS GROSE, Esq.

Vol. I., Plate IV.]

Dr. JAMES HUTTON

[To face page 44.

It may be noticed that Grose acknowledges his obligations to the poet in the following terms, in his *Antiquities of Scotland :*—" To my ingenious friend, Mr. Robert Burns, I have been variously obligated: he not only was at the pains of making out what was most worthy of notice in Ayrshire, the county honoured by his birth, but he also wrote expressly for this work, the pretty tale annexed to Alloway Church." This " pretty tale " is Burns' inimitable " Tam o' Shanter."

Captain Grose was born in the year 1731, and was the son of Mr. Francis Grose of Richmond, jeweller, who fitted up the coronation crown of George the Second, and died in 1769. By his father he was left an independent fortune. In early life he entered the Surrey militia, of which he became Adjutant and Paymaster; but so careless was he, that he kept no vouchers either of his receipts or expenditure. He used himself to say he had only two books of accounts, viz., the right and left hand pockets. The results may be easily anticipated, and his fortune suffered severely for his folly. His losses on this occasion roused his latent talents; with a good classical education, a fine taste for drawing, encouraged by his friends, and impelled by his situation, he commenced the "Antiquities of England and Wales," the first number of which was published in 1773, and the fourth volume completed in 1776. In 1777 he resumed his pencil, and added two more volumes to his English Views, in which he included the islands of Guernsey and Jersey, in 237 views, with maps of the counties, besides a general one. The work was reprinted in eight volumes in 1787.

The success of this work induced Grose to illustrate in a similar manner "The Antiquities of Scotland." This publication, in numbers of four plates each, commenced in the beginning of 1789, and was finished in 1791, forming two volumes, with 190 views, and letterpress. Before the plates of the latter numbers were out of the engraver's hands, the author " turned his eyes to Ireland, who seemed to invite him to her hospitable shore, to save from impending oblivion her mouldering monuments, and to unite her, as she should ever be, in closest association with the British Isles. The Captain arrived in Dublin in May, 1791, with the fairest prospect of completing the noblest literary design attempted in this century." Such are the words of Dr. Ledwich, to whom Grose had applied for assistance, and by whom the work was completed, in two volumes, in 1795. But, while in Dublin, at the house of Mr. Hone, Grose was suddenly seized with an apoplectic fit, and died, in the fifty-second year of his age, upon the 12th of May, 1791. The following epitaph proposed for him, was inserted in the *St. James's Chronicle*, May 26:—

> Here lies Francis Grose:
> On Thursday, May 12, 1791,
> Death put an end to
> His *views* and *prospects*.

Upon occasion of his marriage, Grose took up his residence in Canterbury, where he remained several years, during which period his wit and vivacity made him many friends. No one possessed more than himself the faculty of setting the table " in a roar," but it was never at the expense of virtue or good manners. He left several sons and daughters; one of the latter married Anketil Singleton, Esq., Lieut.-Governor of Sandguard Fort. His son, Daniel Grose, F.A.S., Captain of the Royal Regiment of Artillery, was, after several campaigns in America, appointed Depute-Governor of the new settlement at Botany Bay, 1790.

Besides the works above noticed, he published—"A Treatise on Ancient Armour and Weapons; illustrated by plates taken from the original armour in the Tower of London, and other arsenals, museums, and cabinets." Lond. 1785. 4to. A Supplement was added in 1789.—"A Classical Dictionary of the Vulgar Tongue." Lond. 1785. 8vo.—"A Guide to Health, Wealth, Honour, and Riches." Lond. 1785. 8vo. This is a most amusing collection of advertisements, principally illustrative of the extreme gullibility of the citizens of London. A very humorous introduction is prefixed.—"Military Antiquities, respecting a History of the English Army, from the Conquest to the Present Time." 2 vols. Lond. 1786-88. 4to. With numerous plates. This work was published in numbers.—"The History of Dover Castle. By the Rev. William Darrell, Chaplain to Queen Elizabeth." 1781. In 4to, the same size as the large and small editions of the Antiquities of England and Wales; with ten views engraved from drawings by Captain Grose.—"A Provincial Glossary; with a Collection of Local Proverbs and Popular Superstitions." Lond. 1788. 8vo.—"Rules for Drawing Caricatures; the subject illustrated with four copperplates; with an Essay on Comic Painting." Lond. 1788. 8vo. A second edition appeared in 1791, 8vo, illustrated with twenty-one copper-plates, seventeen of which were etched by Captain Grose.— After his demise, was published "The Olio; being a collection of Essays, Dialogues, Letters, Biographical Sketches, &c. By the late Francis Grose, Esq., F.R.S. and A.S.; with a portrait of the author. Lond. 1796. 8vo.

There are dissertations by him in the Archæologia, the one "On an Ancient Fortification at Christchurch, Hants," and the other "On Ancient Spurs."

Although the verses written by Burns during Captain Grose's peregrinations through Scotland collecting its antiquities are sufficiently well known, we cannot refrain from concluding this article with them:

> Hear, Land o' Cakes, and brither Scots,
> Frae Maidenkirk to Johnny Groats,
> If there's a hole in a' your coats,
>   I rede you tent it;
> A chiel's amang you takin notes,
>   And, faith, he'll prent it.

> If in your bounds ye chance to light
> Upon a fine, fat, fodgel wight,
> O' stature short, but genius bright,
>   That's he, mark weel—
> And wow! he has an unco slight
>   O' cauk and keel.

> By some auld, houlet-haunted biggin,
> Or kirk deserted by its riggin,

It's ten to ane ye'll find him snug in
>> Some eldrich part,
Wi' deils, they say, —— safe's! colleaguin'
>> At some black art.

Ilk ghaist that haunts auld ha' or chamer,
Ye gipsy-gang, that deal in glamor,
And you deep-read in hell's black grammar,
>> Warlocks and witches,
Ye'll quake at his conjurin hammer,
>> Ye midnight ——.

It's tauld he was a sodger bred,
And ane wad rather fa'n than fled;
But now he's quat the spurtle-blade,
>> An' dogskin wallet,
And taen the——*Antiquarian trade*,
>> I think they call it.

He has a fouth o' auld nick-nackets,
Rusty airn caps, an' jingling jackets,
Wad haud the Londians three in tackets
>> A towmond gude,
And parritch pats, an' auld saut-backets,
>> Before the flood.

O' Eve's first fire he has ae cinder;
Auld Tubal Cain's fire-shool and fender;
That which distinguished the gender
>> O' Balaam's ass;
A broom-stick o' the witch o' Endor,
>> Weel shod wi' brass.

Forbye, he'll shape you aff fu' gleg,
The cut o' Adam's philibeg,
The knife that nicket Abel's craig
>> He'll prove you fully,
It was a fauldin jocteleg,
>> Or lang kail-gully.

But wad ye see him in his glee,
For meikle glee and fun has he,
Then set him down, and twa or three
>> Gude fellows wi' him;
And *port, O port!* shine thou a wee,
>> And then ye'll see him!

Now, by the powers o' verse and prose!
Thou art a dainty chiel, O Grose!
Whae'er o' thee shall ill suppose,
>> They sair misca' thee,
I'd tak the rascal by the nose
>> Wad say, Shame fa' thee.

DR. JAMES HUTTON,

Author of the "Theory of the Earth."

DR. HUTTON was an ingenious philosopher, remarkable for the unaffected simplicity of his manner, and much esteemed by the society
in which he moved. In his dress he very much resembled a Quaker,
with the exception that he wore a cocked hat. He was born in the
city of Edinburgh, on the 3d June, 1726, and was the son of a merchant there, who died in the infancy of his son. He was educated at
the High School; and, after going through the regular course at that
seminary, he entered the University of Edinburgh in 1740. The
original intention of his friends was, that he should follow the profession of a Writer to the Signet; and, with this view, he for some time
pursued the course of study enjoined by the regulations of that Society,
and accordingly attended the Humanity (or Latin) Class for two
sessions. It would appear, however, that the early bent of his genius
was directed towards chemistry; for, instead of prosecuting the study
of the law, he was more frequently found amusing the clerks and
apprentices in the office in which he had been placed, with chemical
experiments. His master, therefore, with much kindness, advised
him to select some other avocation more suited to his turn of mind;
he, accordingly, fixed on medicine, and returned to the University.
Here, during three sessions, he attended the requisite classes, but did
not graduate. He repaired to Paris, and spent two years in that city.
On his way home he passed through Leyden, and there took the degree of Doctor of Medicine, in the month of September, 1749.

Meanwhile he had formed, in London, an intimate acquaintance
with Mr. John Davie. They entered into a co-partnership, and
engaged in the manufacture of sal-ammoniac from coal-soot, which
was carried on in Edinburgh for many years with considerable success. From his peculiar habits he had little chance of getting into
practice as a doctor of medicine, and he appears to have relinquished
the idea very early. He determined to betake himself to agriculture:
for this purpose he resided for some time with a farmer in the county
of Norfolk; and, in the year 1754, bringing a plough and a plough-
man from England, he took into his own hands a small property
which he possessed in Berwickshire. Having brought his farm into
good order, and not feeling the same enthusiasm for agriculture which
he had previously entertained, he removed to Edinburgh about the
year 1768, and devoted himself almost exclusively to scientific
pursuits.

In 1777, Dr. Hutton's first book, entitled, "Considerations on the
Nature, Quality, and Distinctions of Coal and Culm," was given to
the world. He next published an outline of his "Theory of the
Earth," in the first volume of the "Transactions of the Royal Society
of Edinburgh." Dr. Hutton had, during a long course of years,
accumulated a variety of facts in support of his theory—having undertaken journeys not only through Scotland, but also through England
and Wales, and different parts of the continent of Europe. In the
same volume he published another paper, entitled, "A Theory of

Rain." This theory met with a vigorous opposition from M. de Luc, and became a subject of controversy, which was conducted with much warmth.

In 1792 he published " Dissertations on different subjects in Natural Philosophy," in which his theory for explaining the phenomena of the material world seems to coincide very closely with that of Boscovich, though there is no reason to suppose that the former was suggested by the latter.

Dr. Hutton next turned his attention to the study of metaphysics, the result of which he gave to the public in a voluminous work, entitled, " An Investigation of the Principles of Knowledge, and of the Progress of Reason from Sense to Science and Philosophy." 3 vols. 4to. Edinburgh, 1794. While engaged in its publication he was seized with a dangerous illness, from which he never entirely recovered. In 1794 appeared his " Dissertation upon the Philosophy of Light, Heat, and Fire," 8vo. In 1796, his " Theory of the Earth " was republished in 2 vols., with large additions, and a new Mineralogical system. Many of his opinions were ably combated by Kirwan and others.

Professor Playfair, who had adopted the leading doctrines of the Doctor's theory, published, in 1802, a work entitled, " Illustrations of the Huttonian Theory of the Earth." A short time before his death the Doctor wrote a work on Agriculture, which was intended to form 4 vols. 8vo. The MS. was recently in existence.

A second Print represents Dr. Black and Dr. Hutton, who were for a long series of years most intimate and attached friends, conversing together. Their studies and pursuits were in many respects intimately connected, and upon different subjects of philosophical speculation they had frequently opposite opinions, but this never interrupted the harmony of their personal friendship. They were remarkable for their simplicity of character, and almost total ignorance of what was daily passing around them in the world. An amusing illustration of this will be found in the following anecdote :—

Several highly respectable literary gentlemen proposed to hold a convivial meeting once a week, and deputed two of their number, Doctors Black and Hutton, to look out for a suitable house of entertainment to meet in. The two accordingly sallied out for this purpose, and seeing on the South Bridge a sign with the words, " Stewart, vintner, down stairs," they immediately went into the house and demanded a sight of their best room, which was accordingly shown to them, and which pleased them much. Without further inquiry, the meetings were fixed by them to be held in this house ; and the club assembled there during the greater part of the winter, till one evening Dr. Hutton, being rather late, was surprised, when going in, to see a whole bevy of well-dressed but somewhat brazen-faced young ladies brush past him, and take refuge in an adjoining apartment. He then, for the first time, began to think that all was not right, and communicated his suspicions to the rest of the company. Next morning the notable discovery was made, that our amiable philosophers had introduced their friends to one of the most noted houses of bad fame in the city ! !

These attached friends agreed in their opposition to the usual vulgar prejudices, and frequently discoursed together upon the absurdity of many generally received opinions, especially in regard to diet. On one occasion they had a disquisition upon the inconsistency of abstaining from feeding on the testaceous creatures of the land, while those of the sea were considered as delicacies. Snails, for instance—why not use them as articles of food? They were well known to be nutritious and wholesome—even sanative in some cases. The epicures, in olden time, esteemed as a most delicious treat the snails fed in the marble-quarries of Lucca. The Italians still hold them in esteem. The two philosophers, perfectly satisfied that their countrymen were acting most absurdly in not making snails an ordinary article of food, resolved themselves to set an example; and, accordingly, having procured a number, caused them to be stewed for dinner. No guests were invited to the banquet. The snails were in due season served up; but, alas! great is the difference between theory and practice—so far from exciting the appetite, the smoking dish acted in a diametrically opposite manner, and neither party felt much inclination to partake of its contents; nevertheless, if they looked on the snails with disgust, they retained their awe for each other; so that each, conceiving the symptoms of internal revolt peculiar to himself, began with infinite exertion to swallow, in very small quantities, the mess which he internally loathed. Dr. Black at length broke the ice, but in a delicate manner, as if to sound the opinion of his messmate:—"Doctor," he said, in his precise and quiet manner, "Doctor, do you not think that they taste a little—a very little queer?" "———— queer!————queer, indeed!—tak them awa', tak them awa'!" vociferated Dr. Hutton, starting up from table, and giving full vent to his feelings of abhorrence.

Dr. Hutton's health had begun to decline in 1792; and, as before mentioned, he was seized with a severe illness during the summer of 1793, which, after some intervals of convalescence, terminated at last in his death, upon the 26th March, 1797, having written a good deal in the course of the same day. He died, like his friend Dr. Black, a bachelor.

DR. JOHN BROWN,

Author of "The Brunonian System of Medicine,"

Is represented with the ensign of the Roman Eagle Lodge, which used to be carried at public processions before the Master, a situation which he long held.

The miniature scene in the background describes what had frequently happened, namely, the Doctor at a bowl of punch, with Mr. Little of Libberton, Mr. John Lamont, surgeon, and Lord Bellenden, heir to his Grace the Duke of Roxburghe, playing on the fiddle—an accomplishment in which he excelled—for the entertainment of the company. His Lordship, who was remarkable for his free, generous, and hospitable disposition, in 1787 married Miss Sarah Cumming of Jamaica, a lady paternally of Scottish, but maternally of African descent. The other two gentlemen in conversation at the back of this convivial group, are Dr. William Cullen and Dr. Alexander Hamilton, Professor of Midwifery; the gentleman in white clothes, to the left, is Dr. James Graham, already described.

Dr. John Brown was born in the parish of Buncle, in the county of Berwick, of parents more respectable for decency of character than dignity of rank. Discovering early marks of uncommon talents, his parents were induced, after having fruitlessly bound him as an apprentice to a weaver, to change his destination. He was accordingly sent to the grammar-school of Duns, where, under Mr. Cruickshanks, an able teacher, he studied with great ardour and success. His application, indeed, was so intense, that he was seldom without a book in his hand. It is said that Brown submitted, in his youth, to be a reaper of corn, to procure for himself the means of improvement. With the price of such labour he put himself to school, where his abilities attracted the attention of his master, and procured him the place of assistant. His revolt from the loom, according to this account, must have been attended with highly honourable circumstances.

The years of Brown's grammar education appear to have been, in no common degree, well-spent and happy; and he continued at school until he had nearly attained the age of twenty. In the summer of 1757, his reputation as a scholar procured him the appointment of tutor to a family of some distinction in the neighbourhood of Duns, where, however, he did not long continue an inmate. Upon relinquishing this situation he repaired to the University of Edinburgh, where, after going through the usual course of philosophy, he entered upon his theological studies: he attended the lectures of the professors, diligently applied to the study of the authors recommended by them, and proceeded so far as to deliver in the public hall the usual academical exercise prescribed prior to ordination as a clergyman of the Scottish Establishment. At this point he stopped, and relinquished the profession of divinity altogether: the sequel will sufficiently explain his motives for this change. Its immediate consequence was his retreat from Edinburgh to Duns. Here he engaged himself as usher to the school which he had lately quitted; and in this capacity he officiated a whole year, in the course of which one of the classes in the High School at Edinburgh becoming vacant, Brown appeared as a candidate, but proved unsuccessful.

When Brown renounced divinity, he turned his thoughts to the study of medicine; and in order to defray the necessary expense attendant upon this new pursuit, he became what in college parlance is termed a "grinder," or preparer of Latin translations of the inaugural dissertations which medical students are bound to publish before taking their degree as Doctors in Medicine. His attention was first directed to this employment by accident. Application being made to one of his friends to procure a person sufficiently qualified to turn an essay of this kind into tolerable Latin, Brown was recommended, and performed the task in a manner that exceeded the expectations both of the friend and the candidate. When it was observed how much he had excelled the ordinary style of such compositions, he said he had now discovered his strength, and was ambitious of riding in his own carriage as a physician. This occurred towards the close of 1759.

Brown next turned his attention to the establishment of a boarding-house for students, a resource which would enable him to maintain a family. His reputation for various attainments was, he thought, likely to draw round him a number sufficient to fill a large house. With this prospect he married in 1765 Miss Euphemia Lamont, daughter of Mr. John Lamont, merchant in Edinburgh, by whom he had twelve children. His success answered his expectations, and his house was soon filled with respectable boarders; but he lived too splen-didly for his income; and it is said that he managed so ill, that in two or three years he became bankrupt. Towards the end of 1770, he was miserably reduced in circumstances, but he nevertheless continued to maintain his original independence of character. He seemed to be happy in his family; and, as far as could be observed, acquitted him-self affectionately both as a husband and a parent. He still attended the medical classes, which, according to his own account, he had done for ten or eleven years.

From the celebrated Cullen he early received the most flattering marks of attention. This speculist, like Boerhaave, and other men of genius in the same station, was accustomed to watch the fluctuating body of students with a vigilant eye, and to seek the acquaintance of the most promising. Brown's intimate and classical knowledge of the Latin language served him as a peculiar recommendation; and his circumstances might induce Cullen to believe that he could render this talent permanently useful to himself. Taking, therefore, its possessor under his immediate patronage, he gave him employment as a private instructor in his own family, and spared no pains in recommending him to others. A close intimacy ensued. The favoured pupil was at length permitted to give an evening lecture, in which he repeated, and sometimes illustrated, the morning lecture of the professor, for which purpose he was entrusted with Cullen's own notes. This friendship, however, was not of permanent duration.

When the theoretical chair of medicine became vacant, Brown gave in his name as a candidate. On a former occasion, of a nature some-what similar, he had disdained to avail himself of recommendations, which he might have obtained with ease; and, though his abilities were far superior to those of the other candidates, private interest then prevailed over the more just pretentions of merit. Such was his sim-plicity that he conceived nothing beyond pre-eminent qualifications necessary to success. The Magistrates and Council of Edinburgh were the patrons of this professorship, and they are reported, derid-ingly, to have inquired who this unknown and unfriended candidate was, and Cullen, on being shown the name, is said to have exclaimed, "Why, sure this can never be our Jock!"

Estranged from Dr. Cullen, Brown gradually became his greatest enemy, and shortly afterwards found out the New Theory, which gave occasion to his publishing the "Elementa Medicinæ," in the preface to which work he gives an account of the accident that led to this dis-covery. The approbation his work met with among his friends, encouraged him to give lectures upon his system. Though these lec-

tures were not very numerously attended by the students, owing to
their dependence upon their professors, he had many adherents, to
whom the sobriquet of "Brunonians" was attached. It is unnecessary
to enter upon all the angry disputes that subsequently arose. Suffice
it to say that the enmity of his medical opponents, his own violence,
and the pecuniary embarrassments he laboured under, ultimately compelled him to leave Edinburgh for London in 1786. During his residence in Edinburgh, Dr. Brown was elected President of the Medical
Society in 1776, and again in 1780.

Observing that the students of medicine frequently sought initiation
into the mysteries of Freemasonry, our author thought their youthful
curiosity afforded him a chance of proselytes. In 1784 he instituted
a meeting of that fraternity, and entitled it the "Lodge of the Roman
Eagle." The business was conducted in the Latin language, which
he spoke with uncommon fluency. "I was much diverted," observes
Dr. Macdonald, "by his ingenuity in turning into Latin all the terms
used in Masonry."

In lecturing, Dr. Brown had too frequently recourse to stimulants.
He usually had a bottle of spirits—whisky generally—on one side, and
a phial of laudanum on the other. Whenever he found himself lan-
guid preparatory to commencing, he would take forty or fifty drops of
laudanum in a glass of whisky, repeating the quantity for four or five
times during the course of the lecture. By these means he soon waxed
warm, and by degrees his imagination became dreadfully excited.
Before leaving Edinburgh, he was so miserably reduced in his circumstances as to be committed to prison for debt, where his pupils attended
his lectures. His liberation from jail was principally attributable to
the exertions of the eccentric but amiable Lord Gardenstone.

Shortly after his arrival in London, the peculiarity of his appearance
as he moved along—a short, square figure—with an air of dignity, in
a black suit, which made the scarlet of his cheeks and nose the more
resplendent—attracted the notice of certain "*Chevaliers d'Industrie,*"
on the look-out for spoil in the street. They addressed him in the
dialect of his country: his heart, heavy as it must have been from the
precariousness of his situation and distance from his native land,
expanded to these agreeable sounds. A conversation ensued, and the
parties by common consent adjourned to a tavern. Here the stranger
was kindly welcomed to town, and, after the glass had circulated for
a time, something was proposed by way of amusement—a game at
cards, or whatever the Doctor might prefer. The Doctor had been
too civilly treated to demur; but his purse was scantily furnished,
and it was necessary to quit his new friends in search of a supply.
Fortunately he applied to Mr. Murray the bookseller, who speedily
enlightened him as to the quality of his companions.

A London sharper, of another denomination, afterwards tried to
take advantage of the Doctor. This was an ingenious speculator in
quack medicines. He thought a composition of the most powerful
stimulants might have a run, under the title of "Dr. Brown's Exciting
Pill;" and, for the privilege of the name, offered him a sum in hand,
by no means contemptible, as well as a share of the contemplated
profits. Poor Brown, needy as he was, to his honour indignantly
rejected the proposal.

By his sojourn in London, Brown did not improve his circumstances: he persisted in his old irregularities, projecting at the same time great designs, and entertaining sanguine expectations of success; but, on the 7th of October, 1788, when he was about fifty-two years of age, he was seized with a fit of apoplexy, and died in the course of the night.

SIR JAMES HUNTER BLAIR, BART.,

Lord Provost of Edinburgh,

Is here represented with his robes on, and holding a plan of the South Bridge in his hand. From Kay's own authority we learn, that "he etched this Print by express commission, for which he received a guinea for the first impression, and at the rate of half-a-guinea for another dozen."

Sir James was the second son of Mr. John Hunter, merchant in Ayr, and was born in that town on the 21st day of February, 1741. His father acquired considerable property in land and money, and left his children, who were still young at his death, in easy circumstances. In the year 1756, Sir James was placed as an apprentice in the house of the brothers Coutts, bankers in Edinburgh. It was at this time that his friendship commenced with Sir William Forbes, who was then a fellow-clerk in the bank. Sir William, in a letter, written after the death of Sir James, observes, "our friendship terminated only with his life, after an intimacy which few brothers can boast of, during thirty-one years, in which long period we never had a difference, nor a separation of interest."

After the death of Mr. John Coutts, the principal partner of the house, Sir William and Mr. Hunter were admitted to a share of the business in 1763, and gradually rose to the head of the copartnery.

In December, 1770, he married Jane, eldest daughter of John Blair, Esq. of Dunskey, in the county of Wigton. This lady's father, at his death, left no fewer than six sons, four of whom were alive at the time of their sister's marriage, but all having died, she succeeded, in 1777, to the family estate. Sir James on this occasion assumed the name of Blair, and was afterwards, in the year 1786, created a Baronet of Great Britain.

On the estate which had thus unexpectedly devolved to him, he commenced a plan of most extensive and judicious improvements. He nearly rebuilt the town of Portpatrick; he repaired and greatly improved the harbour; established packet-boats of a larger size on the much-frequented passage to Donaghadee in Ireland; and lastly, while the farmers in that part of Scotland were not very well acquainted with the most approved modes of farming, he set before them a successful example of the best modes of agriculture, the greatest service, perhaps, which can be performed by a private man to his country.

In September, 1781, he was called, without any solicitation on his part, to represent the city of Edinburgh in Parliament; and at the

Sir J. HUNTER BLAIR

Rev. ALEX. CARLYLE, D.D.

The preserver of the Church from Fanaticism

Vol. I., Plate V.]

[To face page 54.

general election in summer 1784, he received the same honour; but before the end of the first Session he resigned his seat, to the surprise of many, in favour of Sir Adam Fergusson, Bart., as he found his professional avocations required an attendance quite incompatible with his Parliamentary duties.

At Michaelmas, 1784, in compliance with the urgent request of the Town-Council, he was elected Lord Provost of Edinburgh; and he speedily evinced his public spirit by setting on foot various projects for the improvement of the city, among the not least important of which was the rebuilding the College. The access to Edinburgh from the south, on account of the narrowness and steepness of the lanes, was not only very incommodious but even hazardous; and, accordingly, it had been proposed to open a communication between the High Street and the southern parts of the city and suburbs by means of a bridge over the Cowgate. This scheme, although its great importance was abundantly obvious, appeared so expensive, and was attended with so many other difficulties, that every previous attempt had proved unsuccessful, and it required all the address and influence of the Lord Provost to carry it into execution.

In order to defray the great expense, Sir James devised means which, to men of less discernment or knowledge in business, appeared very inadequate to the purpose. His scheme was this: The property which lay in the line of the intended communication, and to a considerable distance on each side of that line, was to be purchased at its real value at the time; and after the communication was opened, such parts of the ground thus purchased as were not to be left vacant, were to be disposed of for the purpose of erecting buildings, according to a plan prepared for the purpose. Sir James conceived that the sale of these areas, in consequence of the great improvement of their situation, would raise money sufficient, not only to pay for the first purchase of the property, but also to defray the expense of building the bridge, and whatever else was necessary for completing the communication. But lest there should be any deficiency, and in order to afford security for borrowing the money which might be requisite, the trustees for carrying on the work were to be empowered to levy a sum not exceeding 10 per cent. of the valued rents of the houses in Edinburgh and the environs; and to remove all cause of complaint, he proposed that if any of the owners of the property to be purchased should not agree with the trustees, the price of their property should be fixed by the verdict of a jury, consisting of fifteen persons, to be chosen by lot out of forty-five proprietors of houses or lands in the city or county, named by the Sheriff in each particular case.

These proposals were published in November, 1784, and met with the same reception which has often attended schemes of still greater importance, and more extensive utility. They were censured and vigorously opposed. A man of less ardour and public spirit would have yielded to the discouragements which Sir James experienced on this occasion. Fortunately he was of such a temper that they served only to stimulate his exertions, without rendering him less prudent in his measures. His perseverance surmounted every opposition. An Act of Parliament was obtained for carrying into execution not only the plan which has been mentioned, but likewise several others, of great importance to the city; and on the 1st day of August, 1785, the work was begun by laying the foundation-stone of the bridge which now connects, by an easy and spacious communication, the suburbs on the south with the rest of the city.

The foundation of the new bridge was laid with great solemnity by the Right Hon. Lord Haddo, Grand-Master Mason of Scotland, in presence of the Lord Provost and Magistrates, a number of the nobility and gentry, and the master, officers, and brethren of all the Lodges of Freemasons in the city and neighbourhood.

In the foundation-stone were cut five holes, wherein the Substitute Grand-Master put some coins of his Majesty George III., and covered them with a plate, on which was engraven an inscription in Latin, the translation of which is as follows :—

" By the blessing of Almighty God, in the reign of George III., the " father of his country, the Right Hon. George Lord Haddo, Grand- " Master of the most ancient fraternity of Freemasons in Scotland, " amidst the acclamations of a Grand Assembly of the Brethren, and " of a vast concourse of people, laid the first stone of this bridge, in- " tended to form a convenient communication between the city of " Edinburgh and its suburbs, and an access not unworthy of such a " city.

" This work, so useful to the inhabitants, so pleasing and convenient " to strangers, so ornamental to the city, so creditable to the country, " so long and much wanted and wished for, was at last begun with " the sanction of the King and Parliament of Great Britain, and with " universal approbation, in the Provostship of James Hunter Blair, " the author and indefatigable promoter of the undertaking, August " the first, in the year of our Lord 1785, and of the era of Masonry " 5785, which may God prosper."

Sir James lived only to see the commencement of the great works which he had projected. In spring, 1787, he went to Harrowgate for the recovery of his health, but without the appearance of any alarming complaint. The waters had not the success which he expected. In the month of June his indisposition was much increased, and terminated in a fever. He died on the 1st day of July, 1787, in the 47th year of his age. His remains were conveyed to Edinburgh, and deposited in the Greyfriars' churchyard.

In private life, Sir James was affable and cheerful, warmly attached to his friends, and anxious for their success. As a magistrate, he was upright, liberal, and disinterested. His talents were of the highest order—to an unwearied application, he united great knowledge of the world, sagacity in business, and soundness of understanding; and he died unusually respected.

Hunter Square and Blair Street were named after Sir James, whose estates and titles are inherited by Sir David Hunter Blair, Bart., who held the late Patent of Printer to her Majesty for Scotland.

THE REV. ALEXANDER CARLYLE, D.D.,
Of Inveresk.

DR. CARLYLE (born January 26, 1722, died August 25, 1805) is memorable as a member—though an inactive one—of the brilliant fraternity of literary men who attracted attention in Scotland during the latter half of the eighteenth century. His father was the minister of Prestonpans. He received his education at the Universities of Glasgow, Edinburgh, and Leyden. While he attended these schools of learning, his elegant and manly accomplishments gained him admission into the most polished circles, at the same time that the superiority of his understanding, and the refinement of his taste, introduced him to the particular notice of men of science and literature. At the breaking out of the insurrection of 1745, being only twenty-three years of age, he thought proper to enrol himself in a body of volunteers, which was raised at Edinburgh to defend the city. This corps was dissolved on the approach of the Highland army, when he retired to his father's house at Prestonpans, where the tide of war soon followed him. Sir John Cope having pitched his camp in the immediate neighbourhood of Prestonpans, the Highlanders attacked him early on the morning of the 21st of September, and soon gained a decisive victory; Carlyle was awoke by an account that the armies were engaged, when, in order to have a view of the action, he hurried to the top of the village steeple, where he arrived only in time to see the regular soldiers flying in all directions to escape the broadswords of the Highlanders.

Having gone through the usual exercises prescribed by the Church of Scotland, he was presented, in 1748, to the living of Inveresk, near Edinburgh. In this situation he remained for the long period of fifty-seven years. His talents as a preacher were of the highest order, and contributed much to introduce into the Scottish pulpit an elegance of manner and delicacy of taste, to which this part of the United Kingdom had been formerly a stranger, but of which it has since afforded some brilliant examples. In the General Assembly of the Church of Scotland, Dr. Carlyle acted on the *moderate* side, and, next to Dr. Robertson, was one of the most instrumental members of that party in reducing the government of the Church to the tranquillity which it experienced almost down to our own time. It was owing chiefly to his active exertions that the clergy of the Church of Scotland, in consideration of their moderate incomes, and of their living in official houses, were exempted from the severe pressure of the house and window tax. With this object in view he spent some time in London, and was introduced at Court, where the elegance of his manners, and the dignity of his appearance, are said to have excited both surprise and admiration. He succeeded in his efforts, though no clause to that purpose was introduced into any Act of Parliament. The ministers were charged annually with the duty, but the collectors received private instructions that no steps should be taken to enforce payment.

Public spirit was a conspicuous part of the character of the Doctor. The love of his country seemed to be the most active principle of his heart, and the direction in which it was guided at a period which seriously menaced the good order of society, was productive of incalculable benefit among those over whom his influence extended. He was so fortunate in his early days as to form an acquaintance with all those celebrated men whose names have added splendour to the literary history of the eighteenth century. Smollett, in his "Expedition of Humphry Clinker," a work in which fact and fiction are curiously blended, mentioned that he owed to Dr. Carlyle his introduction to the literary circles of Edinburgh. After mentioning a list of celebrated names, he adds—"These acquaintances I owe to the friendship of Dr. Carlyle, who wants nothing but inclination to figure with the rest upon paper."

Dr. Carlyle was a particular friend of Mr. Home, the author of *Douglas*, and that tragedy, if we are not misinformed, was, previous to its being represented, submitted to his revision. It is even stated, although there appears no evidence of the truth of the assertion, that Dr. Carlyle, at a private rehearsal in Mrs. Ward's lodgings in the Canongate, acted the part of *Old Norval*, Dr. Robertson performing *Lord Randolph*—David Hume, *Glenalvon*, and Dr. Blair!! *Anna*— *Lady Randolph* being enacted by the author. He exerted, as may be supposed, his utmost efforts to oppose that violent opposition which was raised against Mr. Home by the puritanical spirit, which, though by that time somewhat mitigated, was still far from being extinguished in this country; and successfully withstood a prosecution before the Church courts for attending the performance of the tragedy of *Douglas*.

Dr. Carlyle rendered an essential service to literature, in the recovery of Collins' long lost "Ode on the Superstitions of the Highlands." The author, on his death-bed, had mentioned it to Dr. Johnson as the best of his poems, but it was not in his possession, and no search had been able to discover a copy. At last, Dr. Carlyle found it accidentally among his papers, and presented it to the Royal Society of Edinburgh, in the first volume of whose Transactions it was published; and by the public in general, as well as by the author himself, it has always been numbered among the finest productions of the poet.

It is much to be regretted that Dr. Carlyle favoured the world with so little from his own pen, having published scarcely anything except the Report of the Parish of Inveresk, in Sir John Sinclair's Statistical Account, and some detached pamphlets and sermons. To his pen has been justly attributed "An Ironical Argument, to prove that the tragedy of *Douglas* ought to be publicly burnt by the hands of the hangman."—Edinburgh, 1757, 8vo, pp. 24. It is understood that Dr. Carlyle left behind him, in manuscript, a very curious Memoir of his time, which, though long delayed, we have now reason to believe will soon in part be given to the world.

With the following description of the personal appearance of Dr. Carlyle, when advanced in years, the proprietor of this work has been favoured by a gentleman to whom the literature of his country owes much:

"He was very tall, and held his head erect like a military man— his face had been very handsome—long venerable gray hair—he was an old man when I met him on a morning visit at the Duke of Buccleuch's at Dalkeith."

ANGELO TREMAMONDO, ESQ.,
Riding-Master,

As his almost unpronounceable name indicates, was a native of Italy. He came to Edinburgh about the year 1768, and was the first public teacher of riding in Scotland, having been appointed "Master of the Royal Riding Menage," for which he had a salary from Government. The people of Scotland are proverbial for a hatred to long names; so in their hands Angelo dwindled down to plain "*Ainslie*," and Tremamondo was unceremoniously discarded. "Ainslie" lived in Nicolson Square, and was reputed to be wealthy. Having accidentally got a small piece of steel into one of his eyes, nearly all the physicians in Edinburgh were consulted, but without effect. At last Tremamondo was directed to Miller, the famous occulist, who succeeded in restoring him to his sight; but, unfortunately for the Italian, he succeeded also in becoming his son-in-law very soon after. The Doctor, perhaps, loved Miss Tremamondo well enough, but it afterwards appeared he had likewise "cast an eye" on her papa's purse; and, thinking that the old fellow did not "tell out" fast enough, a lawsuit was the unhappy consequence. Like all other lawsuits, where there is anything like a fat goose to be plucked, it was carried on for a length of time with various success. Kay's MS. mentions that, when Tremamondo received the first summons from his friend of the lancet, he was transported into a regular tornado of passion. He tore down a picture of his daughter which hung in the parlour, and, dashing it in pieces, threw it into the fire. While the old Italian and his son-in-law were thus pulling and hauling, the daughter, like a too sensitive plant, died of a "broken heart." Tremamondo died at Edinburgh, in April, 1805, aged eighty-four.

Of the Riding-Master's early history, very little is known; but from a work published by his nephew in 1830, entitled "Reminiscences of Henry Angelo," we are made acquainted with the fact of his having an elder brother of the same profession, and who resided principally in London.

In these reminiscences Angelo the younger speaks very highly of his father, Dominico Angelo Malevolti Tremamondo—not only was he the best "master of equitation," but one of the most "scientific swordsmen of the day;" and so well proportioned in lith and limb, as to be equally fitted for a "gallant in love, or a hero in war."

Angelo the elder was a native of Leghorn. His father being a wealthy merchant there, intended him for the counting-house, but the ledger had no charms for the handsome Tremamondo, who determined to push his fortune by other means. He accordingly visited various parts of the Continent, and soon found his way to Paris, at that time if not now the gayest and most polite city in the world; and so effectually did Tremamondo cultivate every external accomplishment, that he became proverbially one of the most elegant men of the age, "the gayest of the gay."

Not long before he left Paris, a public fencing-match took place at a celebrated hotel, at which were present the most renowned professors and amateurs of the science. Tremamondo was persuaded by the Duc de Nivernois to try his skill. No sooner had he entered the lists than a celebrated English beauty, Miss Margaret Woffington, the well-known actress, presented him with a bouquet of roses, which, as we are told, he placed on his breast with the most exquisite gallantry, and, addressing the other knights of the sword, exclaimed, " This will I protect against all opposers." Tremamondo fenced with the best of them, but none could disturb a single leaf of his bouquet.

While in Paris, Tremamondo had formed an acquaintance with a French officer, who boasted much of his fencing abilities. Motives of jealousy induced him to waylay our hero one night, who happened to be only armed with a *couteau de chasse*, a small sword usually worn in undress. Tremamondo, acting on the defensive for some time, at last made a home-thrust at the officer, who fell, and there was every reason to think he was mortally wounded. The officer was taken home. Next day Tremamondo visited him, and although he found him in bed gasping, he did not think there was enough of alteration in the officer's countenance for so serious an injury. He immediately suspected there had been deception, and, throwing the bed-clothes suddenly off, discovered the officer's *cotte de maille*. The officer ashamed at his cowardly conduct, and dreading the stigma, implored secrecy and forgiveness.

Shortly after our hero's arrival in London, he married Miss Masters, whose father had commanded the Chester man-of-war. About the year 1758, he was engaged by the Princess Dowager of Wales, " to teach the young princes the use of the small sword, and subsequently to teach them to ride in the menage."—" During this time," continues Angelo the younger, " my father frequently took me thither, when he attended his royal pupils, and I rarely came away without a pocketful of sweetmeats." At an interview with the King, on which occasion Tremamondo displayed the various styles of riding on his favourite horse Monarch, among others that of riding the "great horse," his Majesty was pleased to declare that Angelo was the most elegant horseman of his day; and it was in consequence of this interview that the King persuaded Mr. West, the celebrated artist, when he was commissioned to paint the picture of the "Battle of the Boyne," to make a study of Tremamondo for the equestrian figure of King William. He also sat to the sculptor for the statue of King William, subsequently set up in Merrion Square, Dublin.

While in London, Tremamondo was challenged to a trial of skill with a Dr. Keys, reputed the most expert fencer in Ireland. The scene of action was in an apartment of the Thatched House Tavern, where many ladies and gentlemen were present. When Tremamondo entered, arm-in-arm with his patron, Lord Pembroke, he found the Doctor without his coat and waistcoat, his shirt sleeves tucked up, and displaying a pair of brawny arms—the Doctor being a tall athletic figure. After the Doctor had swallowed a bumper of *Cogniac*, he began the attack with great violence. Tremamondo acted for some time on the defensive, with all the grace and elegance for which he was renowned, and after having planted a dozen palpable hits on the breast of his enraged antagonist, he made his bow to the ladies, and retired amid the plaudits of the spectators.

Angelo the younger relates another anecdote of his father, which he calls "a fencing-master's quarrel." Shortly after Tremamondo's appointment as fencing-master to the Prince of Wales and the Duke of York, a Mr. Redman, an Irishman, who had been formerly patronised by the royal family, was continually abusing Tremamondo for a foreigner, and for having supplanted him. They met one day in the Haymarket, where words ensued, and then blows—the Irishman with a shillelah, and the Italian with a cane. On this occasion also, Tremamondo was victorious, having broke his opponent's head; but next day, to wipe off the disgrace of having fought like porters, he challenged his rival to meet him with swords, but Redman answered that he would put him in "the Crown Office," and immediately entered an action against him in the King's Bench, which ended in Tremamondo having to pay £100 damages, and £90 costs.

So much for the gallant Dominico Angelo Malevolti Tremamondo. We find little more recorded of him than that he was acquainted with almost all the celebrated characters of his day, whether of the "sock and buskin," or the gymnastic "art of equitation." He was generous in the extreme, and Angelo the younger had an opportunity at his father's well-replenished table of forming a most extensive and interesting acquaintance.

Old Dominico died at Eton in 1802, aged eighty-six, and was so much in possession of his faculties that he gave a lesson in fencing the day before his death.

ADAM SMITH, LL.D.,
Author of the "Wealth of Nations."

ADAM SMITH, LL.D., was born at Kirkaldy, on the 5th of June, 1723, a few months after the death of his father, who was Comptroller of the Customs of that town. His mother was Margaret Douglas, daughter of Mr. Douglas of Strathenry. His constitution was very delicate, and required all the care and attention which a kind parent could bestow. She is reported to have treated him with unlimited indulgence; but this produced no injurious effects upon his disposition, and during the long period of sixty years, he was enabled to repay her kindness by every token which filial gratitude could inspire. A singular incident happened to him when about three years old. Whilst with his mother at Strathenry, where she was on a visit, he was one day amusing himself at the door of the house, when he was stolen by a party of vagrants, known in Scotland by the name of tinkers— *Anglice*, Egyptians or Muggers. Fortunately he was immediately missed, and his uncle pursuing them, found them located in Leslie Wood, where he was rescued from their hands.

At a proper age young Smith was sent to the parish school of Kirkaldy, then taught by Mr. David Miller, a teacher, in his day, of considerable repute. In 1737, he repaired to the University of Glasgow, where he remained till 1740. Being elected as an exhibitioner on Snell's foundation, he went to Baliol College, Oxford, and resided there for seven years. Mr. Snell's foundation is perhaps one of the largest and most liberal in Britain. In the year 1688, he bequeathed an estate in Warwickshire for the support of Scottish students at Baliol College, Oxford, who had studied for some years at the University of Glasgow, in which the patronage is vested. They now amount to ten, and may remain at Oxford for ten years.

Dr. Smith had been originally destined for the Church of England, but not finding the ecclesiastical profession suitable to his taste, he abandoned the path that had been chalked out for him, returned to Kirkaldy, and lived two years with his mother. He fixed his residence in Edinburgh in 1748, and during that and following years, under the patronage of Lord Kames, he read Lectures on Rhetoric and the Belles Lettres. In 1751, he was elected Professor of Logic in the University of Glasgow, and in the subsequent year was removed to the Professorship of Moral Philosophy in the same seminary. He remained in this situation thirteen years, and frequently was wont to look back to this period as the most useful and happy of his life.

In 1755, "The Edinburgh Review" was projected, and to this work—which only reached two numbers, and is now remarkable for its scarcity—he contributed a review of Dr. Johnson's Dictionary, and a letter addressed to the editors, containing observations on the state of literature in the different countries of Europe. The "Theory of Moral Sentiments" appeared in 1759, and the same volume contained a dissertation on the origin of languages, and on the different genius of those which are original and compounded. Towards the end of 1763, he received an invitation from the Right Hon. Charles Townshend, to accompany Henry Duke of Buccleuch on his travels, and the liberal terms of the proposal made, added to the strong desire he had felt of visiting the Continent of Europe, induced him to resign his Professorship at Glasgow. Before he left that city, he requested all his pupils to attend him, and as each name was called over he returned the several sums he had received as fees, saying, that as he had not completely fulfilled his engagement, he was resolved his class should be instructed that year *gratis*, and the remainder of his lectures should be read by one of the senior students.

After leaving Glasgow, he joined the Duke at London early in 1764, and set out for Paris in the month of March. In this first visit to Paris they only spent ten or twelve days, and then proceeded to Toulouse, where they fixed their residence: they next undertook a pretty extensive tour through the south of France to Geneva, and about Christmas 1765, revisited Paris, where they resided till October 1766, when the Duke returned to London.

For the next ten years Dr. Smith lived chiefly with his mother in Kirkaldy, and his time was entirely occupied by his studies. In the beginning of 1776, he gave to the world the result of his labour, by the publication of his "Inquiry into the Nature and Causes of the Wealth of Nations." About two years after the appearance of this work, he was appointed one of the Commissioners of his Majesty's Customs in Scotland, a preferment bestowed upon him through the

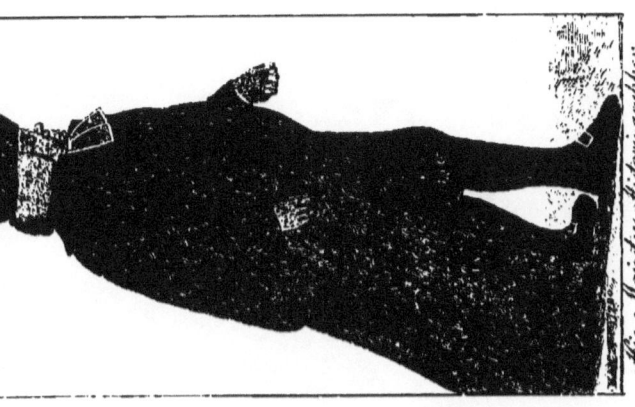

His Majestys Historiographer.

The Rev. WM. ROBERTSON, D.D.

[*To face page* 62.]

The Author of the Wealth of Nations

ADAM SMITH, LL.D.

Vol. I., Plate VI.]

interest of the Duke of Buccleuch. When he obtained this appointment he offered to resign the annuity of £300 per annum, which had been granted him for superintending the Duke's education and travels, an offer which was immediately declined. The greater part of the two years preceding his appointment he lived in London in a society too extensive and varied to afford him any opportunity of indulging his taste for study, although much of it was spent with some of the most distinguished literary characters, as may be seen by the following verses by Dr. Barnard, addressed to Sir Joshua Reynolds and his friends :—

> " If I have thoughts and can't express 'em,
> Gibbon shall teach me how to dress 'em,
> In words select and terse ;
> Jones teach me modesty and Greek,
> Smith how to think, Burke how to speak,
> And Bendire to converse."

In 1778, Dr. Smith removed to Edinburgh, with the view of attending to the duties of his new office, where he passed the last twelve years of his life, enjoying an affluence more than equal to all his wants. He now and then revisited London. The last time he was there, he had engaged to dine with Lord Melville, then Mr. Dundas, at Wimbledon ; Mr. Pitt, Mr. Grenville, Mr. Addington, afterwards Lord Sidmouth, and some other of his lordship's friends were there. Dr. Smith happened to come late, and the company had sat down to dinner. The moment, however, he came into the room, the company all rose up ; he made an apology for being late, and entreated them to sit down. " No," said the gentlemen, " we will stand till you are seated, *for we are all your scholars.*" His mother died in extreme old age in 1784. His own health and strength gradually declined (for he began very early to feel the infirmities of age) till the period of his death, which happened in July, 1790. A few days previous to this he gave orders to destroy all his manuscripts, excepting some detached Essays, which were afterwards published, having been entrusted to the care of his executors, Dr. Joseph Black and Dr. James Hutton, with whom he had long lived in habits of the most intimate friendship. Although Dr. Smith's income for the latter years of his life was considerable, he did not leave much fortune, owing to the hospitality and generosity of his nature. No man ever did more generous things. His library, which was a valuable one, it is understood is still preserved entire. It had devolved to his nephew, the late Lord Reston, and is now in possession of his widow.

VINCENT LUNARDI,
The Celebrated Aeronaut.

THIS celebrated aeronaut visited Scotland in the month of September, 1785. His first ascent took place at Edinburgh, on the 5th of October following, from Heriot's Hospital Green. The Print, which is allowed to be an excellent likeness of Lunardi, represents him as he appeared ready to ascend. His dress was of scarlet, with blue facings.

Several aerial attempts had been made at Edinburgh, with partial success, in 1784, by Mr. Tytler, but the previous fame of Lunardi created an unparalleled excitement in Scotland, so that an immense concourse of people of all classes were assembled to witness what had hitherto been deemed almost an impossibility. "In the Green of Heriot's Hospital," it is said, "the company was numerous and genteel, and the concourse of people on the different eminences were immense. It is calculated that above 80,000 spectators assembled on this occasion, which put a stop to almost all business for a great part of the day, and most of the shops were shut. At twelve o'clock a flag was displayed from the Castle, and a gun (which had been brought from Leith Fort), was fired from the Green when the process of filling the balloon began. At half-past two it was completely inflated." All the arrangements being completed, Mr. Lunardi gave the signal at ten minutes to three, when the balloon ascended in a S.S.E. direction, "in the most grand and magnificent manner," amid the acclamations of the people. He passed over the city at a great height, waving his flag as he proceeded. According to Lunardi's own account, "the balloon, after rising, took a north-east direction, and, near to the Island of Inchkeith, came down almost to the sea; he then threw out some ballast, and the balloon rose higher than before. A current of wind carried him east to North Berwick; a different current then changed his course, and brought him over between Leven and Largo. After this, a S.S.W. breeze brought him to the place where he descended," which was on the estate of the Hon. John Hope, a mile east from Ceres. "When the balloon was at its highest elevation (about three miles), the barometer stood at eighteen inches five-tenths. Mr. Lunardi at this time felt no difficulty in respiration. He passed through several clouds of snow, and lost sight at times both of sea and land. His excursion took about an hour and a half; and it would appear he passed over upwards of forty miles of sea, and about ten of land." On his descending, Mr. Lunardi was first welcomed by Mr. Robert Christie, and next by the Rev. Robert Arnot, who came running, with a crowd of people after him. He was accompanied to Ceres by a body of gentlemen who soon collected, where he was "received by the acclamations of a prodigious multitude, his flag being carried in procession before him, and the church-bell ringing in honour of such a visitant." At the manse of Ceres he drank a few glasses of wine, and both there and at the house of Mr. Melville he received the compliments of a great many ladies and gentlemen. The same evening he started for Cupar, having been invited by the authorities, where the most enthusiastic reception awaited him. After having been next day entertained at dinner, and presented with the freedom of the burgh, he proceeded to St. Andrews, to which place he had been invited by the Club of Gentlemen Golfers, where he was made a citizen, and had, by diploma, the honour of " Knight of the Beggar's Benison " conferred upon him.

Such is a brief account of Lunardi's first aerial trip in Scotland. Brilliant it certainly was, and it is as unquestionable, that although half a century has since elapsed, it has not been surpassed. Many anecdotes are told of the surprise and terror of the peasantry on first beholding the balloon. Some reapers in a field near to Ceres were dreadfully alarmed—judging from so uncommon an appearance, and the sound of Lunardi's trumpet—that the end of all things was at hand. Certain it is, however, that the Rev. Mr. Arnot, who was previously aware of Lunardi's ascent, required considerable persuasion to convince the people that they might approach the object of their terror without fear of supernatural injury.

Mr. Lunardi's next adventure took place at Kelso, on the 22d of October. In this flight he did not ascend above a mile, keeping constantly in view of the earth. After the lapse of nearly an hour and a half, he anchored in Doddington Moor, when some people getting hold of the ropes, he was carried to Barmoor in Northumberland, where he descended. The aeronaut had been invited to Kelso by the gentlemen of the Caledonian Hunt. While here, he was much delighted with the races, and in one of his letters alludes to a match between the Duke of Hamilton and Robert Baird, Esq., who rode their own horses; he likens the contest to the ancient Olympic Games. "He dined on Saturday with Sir James Douglas, of Springwood Park, and supped with the gentlemen of the Caledonian Hunt. On Sunday he was entertained by Sir James Pringle at Stitchel; on Monday, by Lord Home at Hirsel; and same evening by the ancient Lodge of Freemasons." He is stated also to have taken "much notice of the two Miss Halls of Thornton, Miss Wilkie of Doddington, and Miss Car of Newcastle," who, no doubt, were highly gratified by his condescension!

Glasgow was next visited by the aeronaut, where he ascended from St. Andrew's Square on the 23rd of November. A crowd of nearly 100,000 persons had assembled to witness his flight. The balloon took a north-east direction for about 25 miles; the wind then changing, he was carried south-east until he descended near Alemoor, in Selkirkshire, having passed over a distance of 125 miles in two hours. Lunardi thus describes his descent:—"When I came in sight of the heathy hills, I heard a voice call, 'Lunardi, come down!' quite plain, and I knew not who it was. I saw at a distance sheep feeding, but could not see a human being. I called aloud several times through the hill, and after a minute, or seventy seconds, I could hear the echo of my words returned as loud as they were pronounced, but I never had repeated 'Lunardi, come down,' though I heard these words several times repeated, on which I answered through the trumpet, 'Hallo, hallo,' with a great voice. I heard the words, 'Lunardi, hallo,' repeated, and being now quite free from interruption of clouds, I could see distinctly some people on horseback. At last I hastened my descent between two hills, where I came down as light as a feather. Two trembling shepherds came to me, an old man and a boy, whom I encouraged by calling to them, 'My dear friends, come hither.' They crossed the water and came up to me." At this time Mr. and Mrs. Chisholm, of Stirches, happened to be returning on horseback from a visit, who very kindly received Mr. Lunardi, at whose suggestion Mrs. Chisholm boldly took possession of the car, resigning her horse to the aeronaut, and while some shepherds held on by the ropes, the party thus proceeded a distance of nearly three miles. Lunardi spent the night at Stirches, and dined next day with the magistrates of Hawick, who presented him with the freedom of the town.

Mr. Lunardi made a second ascent from Glasgow on the 5th of December, and, as on the former occasion, he was witnessed by a vast concourse of people. His ascent was very majestic; but he did not proceed to a great distance, having alighted at Campsie, about twelve miles distant, where he was received by the Rev. Mr. Lapslie, minister of that place, who transmitted an account of his descent to one of the Glasgow journals.

The fifth ascent of Lunardi in Scotland, and the second at Edinburgh, again occurred at Heriot's Hospital Green. He made offer of the profits of this second exhibition for the benefit of the Charity Workhouse, but the directors politely declined accepting his offer, on the ground that, however desirous they might be to promote the interests of the institution, they were unwilling that any one should *risk his life* for its benefit. On Tuesday, the 20th December, Lunardi took his flight a few minutes before one o'clock. On this occasion he was dressed in the uniform of the Scots Archers, having been previously admitted an honorary member of that body, as well as having had the freedom of Edinburgh conferred upon him. He was also provided with a cork jacket, as on the former occasion, furnished by Dr. Rae, together with other precautionary means of safety, in case of an immersion in the German Ocean. These, as it happened, were not without their use. On this occasion, says our informant, Lunardi was positively assured, from the direction of the wind, that he would be driven into the German Ocean. "Me don't mind that—somebody will *pick* me up." Fortunately for him, somebody did *pick* him up. The balloon ascended with great rapidity, taking a more easterly direction than formerly, and was seen by means of a telescope, about two o'clock, in rather a perilous situation, about two miles north-east of Gullanness. Not far from this place, it appears the balloon had descended so low as to immerse the car in the water, when some fishermen observing the occurrence, immediately proceeded to his rescue. Owing, however, to the rapidity with which the car was dragged, nearly three quarters of an hour elapsed before they were able to render any assistance ; and when they came up, Lunardi was breast deep in the water, and benumbed with cold. They were then five or six miles from land. He would have cut away the balloon, but seeing the fishermen approaching, he was unwilling to lose it by doing so. On leaving the car for the boat, however, the balloon, being thus lightened, rose with great force, carrying every appendage with it in its flight. Mr. Lunardi was then taken to Mr. Nisbet's, of Dirleton, where he spent the evening. In a letter dated that night to the magistrates of Edinburgh, he speaks lightly of his danger, expresses regret at losing the balloon, but was hopeful that the people would be satisfied with his conduct. Fortunately, the balloon was picked up next day by the May cutter, about 12 miles off Anstruther.

Lunardi then returned to England, exhibiting his aerial ingenuity in the provincial towns (having been in London some time previous to his arrival in Scotland). A very unfortunate occurrence took place on his ascending at Newcastle:—A Mr. Heron having hold of one of the ropes, incautiously twisted it round his arm, and not being able to disentangle himself in time, he was lifted up to a considerable height, when the rope giving way, he fell, and was killed on the spot. Mr. Heron was on the eve of marriage, and at the time the accident occurred the lady of his affections was by his side.

Mr. Lunardi again visited Edinburgh the year following (1786), and ascended the third time from Heriot's Hospital Green, on the 31st of July. On this occasion a lady (Mrs. Lamash, an actress) was to have accompanied him, and had actually taken her seat in the car; but the balloon being unable to ascend with both, Lunardi ascended alone. In consequence of little wind, he came down about two miles distant. On his return to the city in the evening, he was carried through the streets in his car by the populace, and received other demonstrations of admiration.

Very little is known of Mr. Lunardi's personal history, save that he was a native of Italy, and some time Secretary to the then late Neapolitan ambassador. In 1786, he published an account of his aerial voyages in Scotland, which he dedicated to the Duke and Duchess of Buccleuch. This small volume, although proving him to be a man of education, and some talent as a writer, throws very little light upon his history. It consists of a series of letters addressed to his "guardian, Chevalier Gerardo Compagni." These letters were evidently written under the impulse of the moment, and afford a connected detail of his progress in Scotland. They are chiefly interesting at this distance of time, as showing the feelings and motives of one, who, whether his "labours were misdirected" or not, obtained an extraordinary degree of notoriety. In short, the volume is amusing in this particular, and adds another proof to the many, that few, very few, seek the advancement of society, or of the sciences, for humanity's sake alone. Fame is the grand stimulus. A portrait of the author is prefixed, which corresponds extremely well with Mr. Kay's sketches of him. Lunardi must have been at that time a very young man.

The young adventurer, on his arrival in the Scottish capital, is much pleased with its ancient and romantic appearance. He expresses himself with great animation on all he sees around him, and apparently with great sincerity. As a specimen of the man and his opinions, we are induced to make one or two extracts. In the first letter, after describing his arrival, he says:—

"I have apartments in Walker's Hotel, Prince's Street, from whence I behold innumerable elegant buildings, and my ears are saluted with the sounds of industry from many others similarly arising. Hail to the voice of labour! It vibrates more forcibly on the chords of my heart than the most harmonious notes of music, and gives birth to sensations that I would not exchange for all the boasted pleasures of luxury and dissipation."

These sentiments would have done credit to one less gay and youthful than Lunardi. In another letter he says, "I am now happy in the acquaintance of the Hon. Henry Erskine, Sir William Forbes,

and Major Fraser." True to his clime, however, the letters of
Lunardi betray in him all the volatility and passion ascribed to his
countrymen. At one moment he is in ecstacy, the other in despair.
He had chosen George's Square for his first display, and had contracted with Isaac Braidwood of the Luckenbooths, who had actually
begun to enclose the area, when an order from the Magistrates stopped
farther proceedings. The vexation and despair of the aeronaut at
this manifestation of hostility is indescribable. He writes:—" I
understand a *lady* has been the underhand prompter! Hold, I beg
pardon of the fair sex; they are my best friends, and I prize their
approbation beyond the highest honour fame can give! And shall a
female Machiavel of *fifty* be ranked with them? Forbid it, politeness—forbid it, humanity—forbid it, truth!"

He subsequently obtained the use of Heriot's Hospital Green, advertised his ascent, but another disappointment occurred, and another
paroxysm ensued. The waggoner from Liverpool had deceived him
as to the time of his arrival—his apparatus for filling the balloon
would not be forwarded till after the day advertised. " What shall I
do?" he writes to his guardian; " Numbers of people will come from
Aberdeen and Glasgow, and they must be disappointed! *Maledictus
homo quis confidit in homine!* Oh! what a frame of mind I am in!"
And there follows the confession—" Fame and glory, ye objects of my
pursuits, ye destroy my peace of mind, yet are ye still dear to me."

To help him out of this dilemma, one Mr. Chalmers, a plumber,
engaged to make him two vats or cisterns, in sufficient time for his
purposes, but when the day appointed arrived, Chalmers had not fulfilled his promise, coolly saying he could not get them done. Such
repeated disappointments were enough to make the most " phlegmatic mortal " mad. " My patience forsook me," says Lunardi; " I
loaded him with invectives, but they were thrown away upon the
phlegmatic mortal; he quietly maintained his *sang froid.*"

Mr. Erskine having directed the aeronaut to a Mr. Selby, another
plumber, who quickly set to work upon the vats, our hero is again
transported from the depths of despair to happiness. " I am now in
a happy frame of mind," he writes, " for conversing with the ladies,
two hundred of whom have called this morning "—(at the Parliament
House, where the balloon was exhibiting).

For the honour of the " Land of Cakes," we cannot refrain from
quoting the following eulogium on our countrywomen, at the close of
last century:—

" Happy mortal! you exclaim; and well you might, could you
form any idea of the SCOTTISH BEAUTIES! Their height, in general,
approaches to what I would call the majestic, adorned with easy
elegance; their figures are such as Grecian artists might have been
proud to copy. But to describe their faces. The pencil of Titian,
or Michael Angelo, could scarce have done them justice! No perfume
shop supplies the beautiful colour that glows on their cheeks and lips:
it is the pure painting of health, and pictures forth minds as pure.
Nature has made them lovely, and they have not suffered art to spoil
her works. I have endeavoured to give you some idea of their personal charms, but their mental ones are far more striking. Grace

without affectation—frankness without levity—good humour without folly—and dignity without pride—are the distinguishing character-istics."

This is no doubt the language of poetic feeling; but however enthusiastic an admirer of the fair sex the young Italian may have been, he shows himself not incapable of appreciating the duties of social sober life. In another letter he says :—

"The people of distinction in Scotland are blest with elegance and happiness, and know not that insatiable ambition, which, while it swallows up every other comfort and endearment of life, never fails to prove the bane of human bliss; their enjoyments are chiefly those of the domestic kind—a virtuous and lovely wife—the education and company of their children." Truly may we add, in the language of Burns—

" From scenes like these old Scotia's grandeur springs."

Judging of Lunardi from his letters while in Scotland, he seems to have been a youth of a warm temperament—amiable in his feelings—of a poetical vein; but extremely vain and ambitious; and, like many of his countrymen, volatile and irritable. Young and handsome, he was not only an admirer of the ladies, but was in turn himself admired. The marked attention on the part of the fair sex seemed too powerful for the youthful aeronaut's good sense—his conceit became intolerable.

Once when in company, being called on for toast, he gave—"Lun-ardi, whom the ladies love." This instance of bad taste and audacious conceit might have been the burst of an unguarded moment, but it had the effect of disgusting all who heard him.

In compliment to the aerial stranger, the Scottish ladies wore what they called " Lunardi bonnets," of a peculiar construction, and which for some time were universally fashionable. They were made of gauze or thin muslin, extended on wire, the upper part representing the balloon. Burns, in his " Address to a Louse," alludes to this head-dress in the following words :—

" I wadna been surprised to spy
    You on an auld wife's flanin toy;
Or aiblins some bit duddy boy—
        Ou's wyliecoat;
But Miss's fine *Lunardi!* fie,
        How daur ye do't?"

Lunardi died of a decline, in the convent of Barbadinus, at Lisbon, on the 31st of January, 1806.

- - --- —

JAMES TYTLER,
Chemist.

MR. JAMES TYTLER was born at the manse of Fearn, of which place his father was minister. James received an excellent provincial education; and afterwards, with the proceeds of a voyage or two to Greenland, in

the capacity of medical assistant, he removed to Edinburgh to complete his knowledge of medicine, where he made rapid progress not
only in his professional acquirements, but in almost every department
of literature.

At an early period he became enamoured of a sister of Mr. Young,
Writer to the Signet, whom he married. From this event may perhaps be dated the laborious and poverty-stricken career of Tytler.
His means, at the very outset, were unequal to the task of providing
for his matrimonial engagements, and from one failure to another he
seems to have descended, until reduced to the verge of indigence.

He first attempted to establish himself as a surgeon in Edinburgh ;
and then removed to Newcastle, where he commenced a laboratory,
but without success. In the course of a year or two he returned to
Leith, where he opened a shop for the sale of chemical preparations ;
and here again his evil destiny prevailed. It is possible his literary
bias might have operated as a drag upon his exertions. These repeated failures seem to have destroyed his domestic happiness. His
wife, after presenting him with several children, left him to manage
them as best he could, and resided with her friends, some time in
Edinburgh, and afterwards in the Orkneys.

Previous to this domestic occurrence, Tytler had abandoned all his
former religious connexions, and even opinions ; and now finding himself thrown upon his literary resources, he announced a work entitled,
" Essays on the most important subjects of Natural and Revealed
Religion." Unable to find a bookseller or printer willing to undertake
the publication of his Essays, Tytler's genius and indefatigable spirit
were called forth in an extraordinary manner. Having constructed a
printing-press upon a principle different from those in use, and having
procured some old materials, he set about arranging the types of his
Essays with his own hands, and without previously having written
down his thoughts upon paper. Mr. Kay states in his MS., that
twenty-three numbers of the Essays were issued in this manner, and
were only interrupted in consequence of other engagements entered
into by the author.

Mr. Tytler was known by his previous literary contributions, but his
fame was increased by the publication of his Essays, which were admired not only for the clearness of their reasoning, but for the extraordinary manner of their production.

The attention of the booksellers being thus directed towards him,
he was engaged in 1776 as a contributor, or rather as editor of the
second edition of the *Encyclopædia Britannica*, a work which, under
his management, was enlarged from three to eight volumes quarto.
Subsequently, he was much employed by the booksellers in compila-
tions and abridgments ; the most important of which was the *Edinburgh Geographical Grammar*. Besides conducting various periodicals,
he published a translation of the four Eclogues of Virgil into English
verse ; and from his own press, in a similar manner to his Essays,
issued the first volume of a general *History of all Nations*.

At the commencement of the " balloon mania," Tytler's genius took
a new flight. In 1784, he issued proposals to ascend in a fire-balloon,
when a considerable sum was immediately subscribed to enable him

to proceed with the experiment. He accordingly constructed a balloon of about forty feet in height, and thirty in diameter, with stove and other apparatus; but although he had contemplated ascending during the week of the races (early in August), it was not till the 27th of that month that he succeeded in making a decisive attempt. On this occasion he rose to the height of three hundred and fifty feet. The scene of the experiment was at Comely Gardens, near the King's Park. Although he succeeded in demonstrating the principle of a fire-balloon, all his attempts were short of success. When Lunardi visited Scotland in 1785, he was of course much interested in the aeronaut's success, and hence Mr. Kay has, with much propriety, associated him with the "fowls of a feather." In the volume published by Lunardi in London (which we have elsewhere noticed), giving an account of his Scottish aerial voyages, we find a poetical address to that gentleman by Mr. Tytler, commencing—

" Etherial traveller ! welcome from the skies—
Welcome to earth to feast our longing eyes."

This effusion was no doubt in compliment to the successful aeronaut ; but as Tytler, in a long note, is careful to explain the principle of his "fire-balloon," and the causes of failure, it is to be presumed that the author was influenced by a desire to set himself right in the opinion of Lunardi and the public. In this note Tytler attributes his ill success, in the first instance, to the want of proper shelter, and the smallness of the stove, which could not supply enough of heat. In the second, his friends were alarmed at the idea of " dragging into air" a cumbrous iron apparatus, and therefore, although Tytler gave directions to have the stove enlarged, they deceived him by actually making it less. By this time the public were highly dissatisfied, and he states that he was vilified in the newspapers—denounced as a coward and a scoundrel—and pointed to as one deserving magisterial surveillance. " I bore it all," says poor Tytler, " with patience, well knowing that one successful trial would speedily change the public opinion." Accordingly, on the third occasion, he did not trust to his friends ; he had the stove enlarged nearly a foot, and with great hopes of success proceeded to the trial. So early as five o'clock in the morning the balloon was inflated, and when he took his seat it rose with much force; but having come in contact with a tree, the stove was broken in pieces, while the adventurer himself narrowly escaped injury. This disaster put an end to the speculation, although not to the spirit of the projector, who remained firmly convinced of the practicability of his invention.

Tytler's first wife being dead, he married, in 1779, a sister of Mr. John Cairns, flesher in Edinburgh, by which union he had one daughter. On the death of his second wife in 1782, he was wedded, a third time, to Miss Aikenhead in December following, by whom, says Mr. Kay's MS., "he has two daughters (twins) so remarkably like each other, though now four years of age, that they can hardly be distinguished from each other, even by their parents, who are often obliged to ask their name, individually, at the infants themselves." Kay also mentions, and while he does so, admits his own belief in the practicability of the invention, that he (Tytler) " is at present engaged in the construction of a machine, which, if he completes it according to his expectations, will in all probability make his fortune." This machine was no less than "the *perpetuum mobile*, or an instrument which, when once set a-going, will continue in motion for ever!"

Kay farther adds—"He has just completed a chemical discovery of a certain water for bleaching linen, which performs the operation in a few hours, without hurting the cloth." This was a practical and beneficial discovery; but like the other labours of Tytler, however much others may have reaped the benefit, it afforded very little to himself.

To add to, or rather to crown the misfortunes of the unlucky son of genius, he espoused the cause of the "Friends of the People," in 1792, and having published a small pamphlet of a seditious nature, was obliged to abscond. He went to Ireland, where he finished a work previously undertaken, called "A System of Surgery," in three volumes. Immediately afterwards he removed to the United States, where he resumed his literary labours, but died in a few years after, while conducting a newspaper at Salem. His family were never able to rejoin him.

THE REV. WILLIAM ROBERTSON, D.D.,

Author of the "History of Scotland."

THIS eminent divine resided within the old College, at the south gate, nearly on the spot where the centre of the library now is. He was born in the year 1721, in the manse of Borthwick, of which parish his father, also called William, was then minister, but who was afterwards presented to the Old Greyfriars' Church, Edinburgh. His mother was Eleanor, daughter of David Pitcairn, Esq., of Dreghorn; by the father's side he was descended from the Robertsons of Gladney, in Fife, a branch of the ancient house of Strowan. Dr. Robertson received the first rudiments of his education at Dalkeith, under Mr. Leslie; and in 1733, when his father removed to Edinburgh, he commenced his course of academical study, which he completed at the University of Edinburgh in 1741. In the same year he was licensed to preach by the Presbytery of Dalkeith; and, in 1743 was, by the Earl of Hopetoun, presented to the living of Gladsmuir, in East Lothian. Soon after this, his father and mother died within a few hours of each other, when six sisters and a younger brother were left almost wholly dependent on him. He immediately took them home to his humble residence at Gladsmuir, where his stipend amounted to little more than £60 a-year, and devoted his leisure hours to the superintendence of their education. After seeing them all respectably settled in the world, he married, in 1751, his cousin Mary, daughter of the Rev. Mr. Nisbet, one of the ministers of Edinburgh.

In the Rebellion of 1745, when Edinburgh was threatened by the Highlanders, he hastened into the city, and joined a corps of Volunteers raised for its defence; and when it was resolved to deliver up the city without resistance, he, with a small band, tendered his assistance to General Cope, who lay with the Royal army at Haddington—an offer which the General (fortunately for the Doctor and his party) declined. He then returned to the sacred duties of his parish, where he was much beloved ; and soon afterwards began to display his talents in the General Assembly of the Church of Scotland, where he became the object of universal attention and applause. It was about this time that Dr. Robertson so ably defended his friend Mr. Home, the author of the tragedy of *Douglas*, from the proceedings adopted against him in the clerical courts.

The first publication of Dr. Robertson was a sermon, which was preached by him before the Society for Propagating Christian Knowledge, in 1755 ; and to it may be attributed the unanimity of his call to the charge of Lady Yester's Church in Edinburgh, to which he was translated in 1758. In February, 1759, appeared his "History of Scotland during the Reigns of Queen Mary and James VI." The effect of this work produced was instantaneous and extraordinary—congratulatory letters of praise, from the most eminent men of the time, poured in upon him ; and it is said that the emoluments derived from it exceeded £600. Preferment immediately followed, which changed at once the whole aspect of his fortunes ; for in the same year he was appointed Chaplain to the Garrison of Stirling Castle, in the room of Mr. William Campbell. Next year he was nominated one of his Majesty's Chaplains for Scotland ; in the year following (1761), on the death of Principal Goldie, he was elected Principal of the University of Edinburgh, and translated to the Greyfriars' Church. Two years afterwards he was appointed by the King Historiographer for Scotland, with a salary of £200 a-year.

In 1779, Dr. Robertson published, in three volumes 4to, a "History of the Reign of Charles V.," which still further increased the reputation of its author. For the copyright he received no less than £4500, the largest sum then known to have been paid for a single work ; and which, according to the calculation of the Rev. Dr. Nisbet, of Montrose, amounted exactly to twopence-halfpenny for each word in the work.

Dr. Robertson, in 1778, gave to the world his "History of America," in two volumes quarto, a work which was well received at the time, and which still continues to be popular. On this occasion he was elected an honorary member of the Royal Academy of History in Madrid, who appointed one of their members to translate the work into Spanish ; but, after it was considerably advanced, the Spanish Government interfered and prevented it.

In the year 1781, he was elected one of the Foreign Members of the Academy of Sciences at Padua, and, in 1783, one of the Foreign Members of the Imperial Academy of Sciences at St. Petersburg.

In 1791 appeared his last work, also in quarto, entitled, "Historical Disquisitions concerning the Knowledge which the Ancients had of India, and the Progress of Trade with that Country, prior to the Discovery of the Cape of Good Hope."

The Doctor's powerful and persuasive eloquence had gained him an influence in the General Assembly which intimately and conspicuously associated his name with the Ecclesiastical affairs of Scotland. He was a long time leader of the Court party in our Ecclesiastical Parliament, and as a speaker, it is said, he might have ranked with the first names in the British Senate. He retired from the business of the Church Courts in 1780, but still continued his pastoral duties, preaching when his health permitted, till within a few months of his death, which took place at Grange House, near Edinburgh, on the 11th June, 1793.

His colleague Dr. John Erskine, in a sermon preached after his death, said, " Few minds were naturally so large and capacious as Dr. Robertson's, or stored by study, experience, and observation, with so rich furniture. His imagination was correct, his judgment sound, his memory tenacious, his temper agreeable, his knowledge extensive, and his acquaintance with the world and the heart of man very remarkable."

Dr. Robertson is said to have excited the enmity of Dr. Gilbert Stuart, in consequence of his assumed opposition to the appointment of that clever but vindictive personage, to one of the Law Chairs in the University. Whether the Principal really interfered is not certain, but Stuart believed he had done so, and that was quite sufficient to induce him to take every means in his power to annoy his imagined enemy. The " View of Society in Europe," is in direct opposition to the luminous introduction to Dr. Robertson's "History of Charles V.," and the " History of Scotland, from the Reformation to the Death of Queen Mary," is an undisguised and virulent hypercritical attack on the " History of Scotland " by the same eminent writer, and does no great credit to the talents of Dr. Stuart. The Empress Catherine of Russia was so delighted with Dr. Robertson's works, that she presented him with a handsome gold enamelled snuff-box, richly set with diamonds, through Dr. Rogerson, which is still in possession of the family.

Dr. Robertson left three sons and two daughters. The eldest son was a Lord of Session. He lived in Charlotte Square, and died about the year 1836. The second son, Lieutenant-General James, who distinguished himself under Lord Cornwallis, resided, in 1841, at Canaan Bank, near Edinburgh. The third son was also in the army, but, having married the heiress of Kinloch-Moidart, he retired, and afterward lived almost entirely upon his estate. The eldest daughter married Patrick Brydone, Esq. of Lennel House, author of a " Tour through Sicily and Malta," one of whose daughters became Countess of Minto ; and another, the wife of Admiral Sir Charles Adam, K.B. The youngest daughter married John Russell, Esq., Writer to the Signet.

A COCK-FIGHTING MATCH

Between the Counties of Lanark and Haddington.

THIS affair was decided in the unfinished kitchen of the Assembly Rooms, in 1785 ; on which occasion the gentlemen cock-fighters of the county of East Lothian were the victors. Among the audience

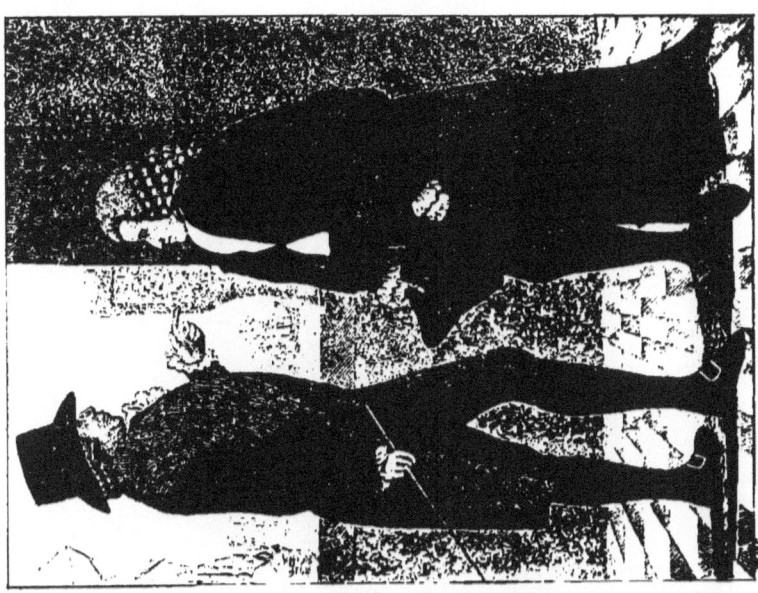

"Thus we poor Cocks, exert our skill & brav'ry
For idle Gulls, and Kites, that trade in Knav'ry"

A COCK FIGHTING MATCH
Between the Counties of Lanark and Haddington.

Vol. I., Plate VII.

HENRY VISCOUNT MELVILLE. Rt. Honble. ROBERT DUNDAS

[To face page 74]

will be recognised likenesses of the principal individuals of this fancy at the time. Kay, in his MS. notes, particularly points out those of Sir James Baird of Newbyth, William Hamilton, Esq. of Wishaw (afterwards Lord Belhaven), —— MacLeod, Esq. of Drimnin, Lord North the caddy, the noted Deacon Brodie, and several other eminent cockers. The two figures in the pit represent the persons employed by the different parties; the one was an Edinburgh butcher, the other an Englishman.

In allusion to this contest Kay observes, "It cannot but appear surprising that noblemen and gentlemen, who upon any other occasion will hardly show the smallest degree of condescension to their inferiors, will, in the prosecution of this barbarous amusement, demean themselves so far as to associate with the very lowest characters in society."

Cock-fighting prevailed to a great extent among the Romans, who most likely adopted it among other things from the Greeks, with this addition, that they used quails as well as the common gamecock. With the Romans cock-fighting is presumed to have been introduced into Britain, although the first notice we have of it is by Fitz-Stephen, in his Life of the famous Thomas a-Becket, in the reign of Henry II. There were several enactments made against the practice in the reigns of Edward III. and Henry VIII., but it is well known that the cockpit at Whitehall was erected by royalty itself, for the more magnificent celebration of the sport: it was again prohibited during the Protectorship of Cromwell in 1654, and afterwards by the Act 25th Geo. III. Notwithstanding the efforts made to put it down, this disreputable amusement continued in all parts of England to be practised with the utmost wantonness almost to the present time.

In Scotland, cock-fighting was for many years an ordinary recreation. In 1705 William Machrie, fencing-master in Edinburgh, published "An Essay upon the Royal Recreation and Art of Cocking. Edinburgh, printed by James Watson in Craig's Closs. Sold by Mr. Robert Freebairn in the Parliament Closs, 1705." 12mo. This tract, which is now exceedingly scarce, is dedicated to the nobility and gentry of Scotland, who are told that "the sport of cock-fighting is improv'd to a great height; 'tis as much an art as managing of horses for races or for the field of battle; and tho' it has been in vogue over all Europe, yet 'twas never esteem'd nor practis'd but by the nobility and gentry. It was kept up only by people of rank, and never sunk down to the hands of the commonality, where the art of managing this fierce and warlike bird had been either lost or slighted." Some verses, signed "T. C.," are prefixed, from which we learn that

> "The sword has always flourish'd, and the bow,
> So long neglected, claims its birthright now,
> And our *cock-matches* owe their rise to you."

From which it may be inferred that this species of amusement had been introduced into Scotland by Machrie, who terms it "a very Innocent, Noble, and highly *Heroick* Game!"

The style of this curious publication is highly inflated, and the attempt to confer dignity upon this wretched and cruel sport is ludicrous enough. After very minute researches into the antiquity of the " Royal recreation," the history of the cock and its habits, the proper mode of treatment, etc., the author concludes—" I am not asham'd to declare to the world that I have a special veneration and esteem for those gentlemen within and about this city who have entered on society for propagating and establishing the royal recreation of cocking (in order to which they have already erected a Cockpit in the Links of Leith), and I earnestly wish that their generous and laudable example may be imitated to that degree, that (in cock-war) village may be engaged against village, city against city, kingdom against kingdom—nay, the father against the son, until all the wars in Europe, wherein so much Christian blood is spilt, be turned into that of the innocent pastime of Cocking."

From the date of Machrie's work until recently, the practice of cock-fighting seems to have been pretty general, especially in Edinburgh, where a regular cock-pit was erected, and liberally supported for many years. On turning over the files of the Edinburgh journals, the names of gentlemen still alive are to be found, who now, it is to be presumed, would not be disposed to consider their former " cocking" propensities with much complacency. An attempt was made two or three years since to revive the " Royal recreation " in a certain city in the west, but it was very properly put down by the magistracy.

HENRY VISCOUNT MELVILLE.

The Right Honourable HENRY DUNDAS, Viscount Melville and Baron Duneira, was second son of Robert Dundas of Arniston, Lord President of the Court of Session, by Anne, daughter of Sir William Gordon of Invergordon, his lordship's second wife, and was born on the 28th April, 1742.

To prevent any misconception, it may be right to mention that there were two Presidents of the Court of Session bearing the name of Robert Dundas. The first, who was born on the 9th December, 1685, and died on the 26th August, 1753, was the father of Lord Viscount Melville. The second, who was born on the 18th July, 1713, and died, in the 75th year of his age, on the 13th December, 1787, was the eldest son of the preceding judge by his first marriage with Elizabeth, daughter of Robert Watson, Esq. of Muirhouse, and in this way was the "half-brother" (to use a Scoticism) of Lord Melville.

After completing his education at the University of Edinburgh with the usual course of legal study, he was admitted a Member of the Faculty of Advocates in the year 1763.

At this period it has been said, that, after paying the expense of his education and admission to the Faculty, Mr. Dundas had just sixty pounds remaining of his patrimony.

Mr. Dundas began his splendid public career in the comparatively humble capacity of an assessor to the Magistrates of Edinburgh. The office of one of his Majesty's Depute-Advocates was then conferred upon him; and subsequently he was appointed Solicitor-General for Scotland.

To these situations he recommended himself by his superior talents, which were early displayed, and which obtained for him the highest consideration of the Bench and Bar. But the ambition of Mr. Dundas was directed to higher objects than were to be attained even by the most brilliant success at the Scotch bar, where the only honour that would follow the most successful exertion of talent, would be a seat on the bench. He accordingly resolved to try his fortunes in the sister kingdom, and with this view, in the year 1774, successfully contested the county of Mid-Lothian with the Ministerial candidate. He, however, afterwards joined the party then in power—became a zealous and able supporter of Lord North's Administration—and was, as a reward for his services, appointed Lord Advocate of Scotland in 1775. Two years afterwards, he obtained the appointment of Keeper of his Majesty's Signet for Scotland.

Mr. Dundas had now obtained a high reputation as a statesman; and from his knowledge of public business, and intimate acquaintance with the condition of the country, was considered so desirable an auxiliary by those in power, that no change of Ministry seriously interfered with his advancement, every new Administration being equally anxious with its predecessors to secure his services. Thus, on the promotion of Lord Shelburne to the Premiership (1782), Mr. Dundas was appointed Treasurer of the Navy. This situation, however, he resigned on the formation of the celebrated Coalition Administration. He was again restored to office by Mr. Pitt, of whom he was latterly one of the steadiest and ablest supporters.

During this interval, Mr. Dundas had rendered himself remarkable in Parliament for his intimate acquaintance with the affairs of India, and was twice appointed chairman of committees appointed for the purpose of legislating for this immense territory. But it was as Treasurer of the Navy that Mr. Dundas's services were of the greatest benefit to his country. In this department he effected a total reformation; substituting order and economy for perplexity and profusion—securing greater promptitude in the payment of the seamen's wages—carrying through Parliament various measures calculated to improve their condition and to increase their comforts—and removing a fruitful source of fraud against the families of sailors, by procuring an Act for preventing the successful use of forged instruments. He it was, also, who introduced the bill which empowers seamen to make over their half-pay to their wives and families. Such were some of the benevolent and judicious improvements which Mr. Dundas introduced. He held the office of Treasurer of the Navy till 1800. In the Session of 1784, Mr. Dundas introduced a bill for restoring the estates forfeited on account of the Rebellion of 1745—a measure not less remarkable for its policy than for its liberal and generous spirit.

In 1791, Mr. Dundas was appointed Principal Secretary of State for the Home Department, having been previously nominated President of the Board of Control.

Amongst the public measures that originated with Mr. Dundas about this period of his career, was the formation of the Fencible regiments, the Supplementary Militia, the Volunteer Corps, and the Provisional Cavalry. With him also originated the improved system of distributing the army throughout the country in barracks and garrisons. The singular ability and judgment which marked Mr. Dundas's superintendence on military affairs, suggested the propriety of appointing him Secretary of State for the War Department, and he was nominated to this office accordingly, in the year 1794. In 1800, he was appointed Keeper of the Privy Seal of Scotland, and his son succeeded him as Keeper of the Signet. He held the offices of Secretary of State, and President of the Board of Control, till his resignation along with Mr. Pitt in 1801.

While in the House of Commons, Mr. Dundas represented first the county, and afterwards the city, of Edinburgh. For the former he sat from 1774 till 1787, and for the latter from 1787 till 1802, when he was elevated to the Peerage by patent dated December 21st of that year, by the title of Viscount Melville of Melville, in the county of Edinburgh, and Baron Duneira, in the county of Perth.

Neither the important services which Lord Melville had rendered his country, nor his well-known disinterested and generous nature, could protect him from a prosecution—persecution we had nearly said —instituted ostensibly on the grounds of public justice, but which was carried on with a spirit of bitterness, that, to say the least of it, was calculated to create serious doubts as to the purity of the motives of those with whom it originated.

On the 8th of April, 1805, his lordship, who had previously held for a short time the appointment of First Lord of the Treasury, was accused in the House of Commons, by Mr. Whitbread, of having misapplied or misdirected certain sums of public money, with a view to his own private advantage and emolument. Articles of impeachment having been preferred, his lordship was brought to trial before his Peers in Westminster Hall, on the 29th of April, 1806. The result was a triumphant acquittal (12th June following) from all the charges. In truth, the utmost extent of any blame imputable to him was, that he had placed too much confidence in some of the subordinates in his office.

After his acquittal, Lord Melville was restored to his place in the Privy Council, from which he had been removed pending his trial, but he did not again take office. From this period he lived chiefly in retirement, participating only occasionally in the debates of the House of Lords.

His lordship died very unexpectedly in the house of his nephew, Lord Chief Baron Dundas, in George Square, on the 29th May, 1811; having come to Edinburgh, it is believed, to attend the funeral of his old friend Lord President Blair, who had died suddenly a few days before, and was at the moment lying in the house adjoining that in which Lord Melville expired.

His lordship was distinguished in his public life by a singular capacity for business, by unwearied diligence in the discharge of his numerous and important duties, and, as a speaker, by the force and acuteness of his reasoning. In private life his manners were affable and unaffected, his disposition amiable and affectionate. A striking instance of the kindliness of his nature is to be found in the fact, that to the latest period of his life, whenever he came to Edinburgh, he made a point of visiting all the old ladies with whom he had been acquainted in his early days, patiently and perseveringly climbing, for this purpose, some of the most formidable turnpike-stairs in the Old Town. In his person he was tall and well-formed, while his countenance was expressive of high intellectual endowments.

The city of Edinburgh contains two public monuments to Lord Melville's memory. The one a marble statue by Chantrey, which stands in the large hall of the Parliament House; the other a handsome column, one hundred and thirty-five feet high, situated in the centre of St. Andrew's Square. This noble pillar is surmounted by a statue of his lordship, fifteen feet in height.

Lord Melville married first, Elizabeth, daughter of David Rennie, Esq., of Melville Castle, and by her had one son (the present Viscount) and three daughters. This marriage having been dissolved in 1793, he married, secondly, Jane, sister to James Hope, third Earl of Hopetoun, but by her (who remarried, in 1814, Thomas Lord Wallace) he had no issue.

THE RIGHT HONOURABLE ROBERT DUNDAS,

Lord Chief Baron of the Court of Exchequer.

THE Right Hon. ROBERT DUNDAS of Arniston, Lord Chief Baron of the Court of Exchequer, was eldest son of the second Lord President Dundas, and was born on the 6th of June, 1758. He was educated for the legal profession, and became a member of the Faculty of Advocates in the year 1779; immediately after which, he was appointed Procurator for the Church of Scotland.

On the promotion of Sir Ilay Campbell to the office of Lord Advocate, Mr. Dundas, then a very young man, succeeded him as Solicitor-General; and on the elevation of the former to the Presidency, the latter was appointed to supply his place as Lord Advocate, being then only in the 31st year of his age.

This office he held for twelve years, during which time he sat in Parliament as member for the county of Edinburgh. On the resignation of Chief Baron Montgomery, in the year 1801, he was appointed his successor. His lordship held this office till within a short time of his death, which happened at Arniston on the 17th June, 1819, in the sixty-second year of his age. At this period his lordship resided in St. John's Street, Canongate.

The excellencies which marked the character of his lordship were many, and all of the most amiable and endearing kind. In manner, he was mild and affable; in disposition, humane and generous; and in principle, singularly tolerant and liberal—qualities which gained him universal esteem.

As presiding judge of the Court of Exchequer, he on every occasion evinced a desire to soften the rigour of the law when a legitimate opportunity presented itself for doing so. If it appeared to his lord-ship that an offender had erred unknowingly, or from inadvertency, he invariably interposed his good offices to mitigate the sentence. By the constitution of this court it was assumed that the king could not be subjected in expenses: thus when a party was acquitted—no unfre-quent occurrence—he had to bear his own costs, which were always very considerable—but the Lord Chief Baron, whenever he thought that the party had been unjustly accused, invariably recommended to Government that he should be repaid what he had expended, and his recommendations were uniformly attended to.

"It was in private life, however," says his biographer, "and within the circle of his own family and friends, that the virtues of this excel-lent man were chiefly conspicuous, and that his loss was most severely felt. Of him it may be said, as was most emphatically said of one of his brethren on the bench, he died, leaving no good man his enemy, and attended with that sincere regret which only those can hope for who have occupied the like important stations, and acquitted them-selves as well."

GENERAL SIR RALPH ABERCROMBY, K.B.

SIR RALPH ABERCROMBY was the son of George Abercromby of Tulli-body, in Clackmannanshire. He was born, in 1734, in the old mansion of Menstrie, which at that period was the ordinary residence of his parents. The house, which is in the village of Menstrie, although not inhabited by any of the family, is still entire, and is pointed out to strangers as the birthplace of the hero. After going through the usual course of study, he adopted the army as his profession; and, at the age of twenty-two, obtained in the year 1756 a commission as Cornet in the 3rd Regiment of Dragoons.

During the early part of his service he had little opportunity of displaying his military talents, but he gradually rose, and in 1787 had attained the rank of Major-General. After the breaking out of the French revolutionary war, Sir Ralph Abercromby served in the cam-paigns of 1794 and 1795, under the Duke of York, and by his judicious conduct preserved the British army from destruction during their disastrous retreat through Holland. He commanded the advanced guard, and was wounded at the battle of Nimeguen.

After the return of Sir Charles Grey from the West Indies, the French retook the islands of Guadaloupe and St. Lucia, made good their landing on Martinique, and hoisted their national colours on several forts in the islands of St. Vincent, Granada, &c., besides possessing themselves of booty to the amount of 1800 millions of livres. For the purpose of checking this devastation, the British fitted out a fleet in the autumn of 1795, with a proper military force. Sir Ralph was entrusted with the charge of the troops, and at the same time appointed Commander-in-Chief of the Forces in the West Indies. Being detained longer than was expected, the equinox set in before the fleet was ready to sail, and, in endeavouring to clear the Channel,

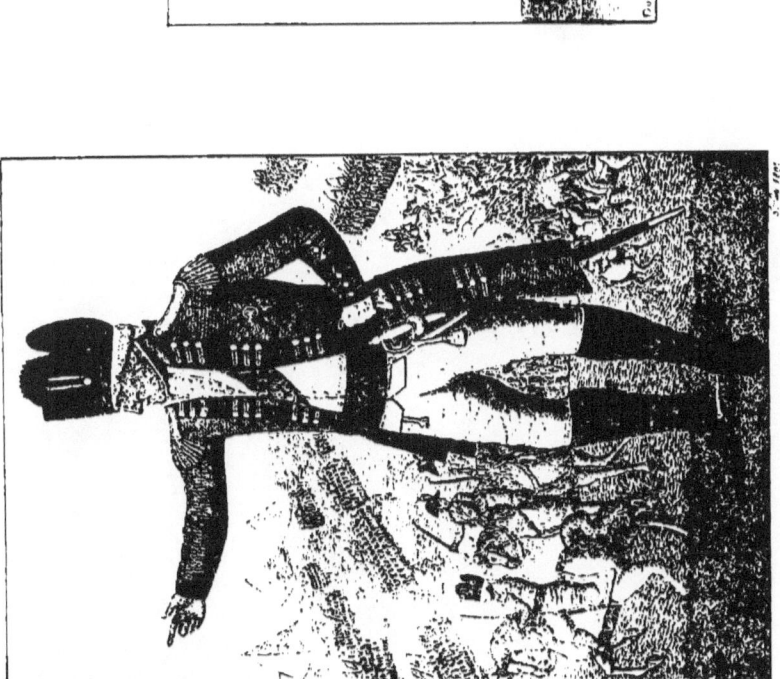

La. Ram. Eternal providence! What is thy name.
My name is Norval: and my name he bears.

Mrs. SIDDONS at the Edinburgh Theatre.

Sir RALPH ABERCROMBY, K.B.

several of the transports were lost. The remainder of the fleet reached the West Indies in safety, and by the month of March, 1796, the troops were in a condition for active duty. The General succeeded in driving the French from all their possessions, and, assisted by part of a new convoy from Britain, was enabled to capture the island of Trinidad from the Spaniards.

Sir Ralph next made an attack upon the Spanish island of Puerto Rico, which proved unsuccessful, but without by any means tarnishing his previously well-earned laurels. On his return to this country in 1797, he was received with every demonstration of public respect. He was presented by his Majesty with the Colonelcy of the Scots Greys—invested with the honour of the Order of the Bath—rewarded with the lucrative governments of Fort-George and Fort-Augustus, and, on the 26th of January, he was raised to the rank of Lieutenant-General in the Army.

Sir Ralph was next appointed to the chief command in Ireland, where the flame of civil war was threatening to burst forth. After visiting a great portion of the kingdom, and restoring in a great degree the discipline of the army, which, in the Commander's own words, had become, from their irregularities, "more formidable to their friends than their enemies," the General was removed by the Marquis Cornwallis, who united the offices of Lord-Lieutenant and Commander-in-Chief in his own person, much to the satisfaction of Sir Ralph, who was anxious to leave Ireland. He was then appointed Commander of the Forces in Scotland.

In 1798, Sir Ralph was selected to take charge of the expedition sent out to Holland, for the purpose of restoring the Prince of Orange to the Stadtholdership, from which he had been ejected by the French. In this expedition the British were at the outset successful. The first and well-contested encounter with General Daendell, on the 27th of August, near the Helder Point, in which the Dutch were defeated, led to the immediate evacuation of the Helder, by which thirteen ships of war and three Indiamen, together with the arsenal and naval magazine, fell an easy prey to the British. The Dutch fleet also surrendered to Admiral Mitchell, the sailors refusing to fight against the Prince of Orange. This encouraging event, however, by no means spoke the sentiments of the mass of the Dutch people, or disconcerted the enemy. On the morning of the 11th of September, the Dutch and French forces attacked the position of the British, which extended from Petten on the German Ocean to Oude-Sluys on the Zuyder-Zee. The onset was made with the utmost bravery, but the enemy were repulsed with the loss of a thousand men. Sir Ralph, from the want of numbers, was unable to follow up this advantage, until the Duke of York arrived as Commander-in-Chief, with a number of Russians, Batavians, and Dutch volunteers, which augmented the allied army to nearly thirty-six thousand.

An attempt upon the enemy's positions on the heights of Camperdown being agreed upon, on the morning of the 19th September the allied forces successfully commenced the attack. The Russians made themselves masters of Bergen; but commencing the pillage too soon, the enemy rallied, and attacked the Russians—who were busy plundering—with so much impetuosity, that they were driven from the town in all directions. This untoward circumstance compelled the British to abandon the positions they had stormed, and to fall back upon their former station. Another attack on the stronghold of the enemy was made on the 2nd of October. The conflict lasted the whole day, but the enemy abandoned their positions during the night. On this occasion Sir Ralph Abercromby had two horses shot under him. Sir John Moore was twice wounded severely, and reluctantly carried off the field; while the Marquis of Huntly (the late Duke of Gordon), who, at the head of the 92nd regiment, was eminently distinguished, received a wound from a ball in the shoulder.

The Dutch and French troops having taken up another strong position between Benerwych and the Zuyder-Zee, it was resolved to dislodge them before they could receive reinforcements. A day of sanguinary fighting ensued, which continued without intermission until ten o'clock at night, amid deluges of rain. General Brune having been reinforced with six thousand additional men, and the ground he occupied being nearly impregnable, while the arms and ammunition of the British, who were all night exposed to the elements, were rendered useless, retreat became a measure of necessity. Upon this the Duke of York entered into an armistice with the Republican forces, by which the troops were allowed to embark for England, where they arrived in safety.

In the month of June, 1800, General Abercromby was appointed Commander-in-Chief of the troops ultimately destined for Egypt. Owing to casualties unnecessary to mention, the armament did not reach the place of its destination till the 8th of March, 1801, on which day the troops disembarked in Aboukir Bay, notwithstanding the strenuous efforts of the French to prevent them.

On the 13th March, Sir Ralph attacked the French in their position, and succeeded, after a keen contest, in forcing them to retreat to the heights of Nicopolis. An attempt to take these heights, which were found to be commanded by the guns of the fort, proved unsuccessful. The British took up the position formerly occupied by the enemy, with their right to the sea, and their left to the canal of Alexandria, thus cutting off all communication with the city. On the 18th the garrison of Aboukir surrendered.

General Menou, the French commander, having been reinforced, attempted to take the British by surprise, and suddenly attacked their positions with his whole force. The enemy advanced with much impetuosity, shouting as they went, but they were received with steady coolness by the British troops. The field was contested with various success, until General Menou, finding that all his endeavours proved fruitless, ordered a retreat, which from the want of cavalry on the part of the British, he was enabled to accomplish in good order. This battle, which proved decisive of the fate of Egypt, and left an impression not easily to be defaced of British courage and prowess, was dearly gained by the death of Sir Ralph himself. Early in the morning, he had taken his station in the front line, from the exposed nature of which, and at a moment when he had dispersed all his staff on various duties, the enemy attempted to take him prisoner. Two of the enemy's cavalry dashing forward, and " drawing up on each side, attempted to lead him away prisoner. In this unequal contest he received a blow on the breast; but with the vigour and strength of arm for which he was distinguished, he seized on the sabre of one of those who struggled with him, and forced it out of his hand. At this moment, a corporal of the 42nd Highlanders, seeing his situation, ran up to his assistance, and shot one of the assailants, on which the other retired." From this perilous situation, the General was relieved by the valour of his troops, when it was discovered that he had been wounded in the thigh. He was repeatedly pressed by the soldiers to have the wound attended to; but he treated it as a matter of no moment, and continued to give directions on the field until victory became certain by the retreat of the enemy. The intense excitement of action being thus over, Sir Ralph at last fainted from loss of blood; and although the wound was immediately examined, every attempt to extract the ball proved unsuccessful. He was carried on a litter aboard the Foudroyant, where he died on the 28th March.

The death of General Abercromby was looked upon as a national calamity. A monument was ordered to be erected to his memory by the House of Commons; and his Majesty, as a mark of further respect, confirmed the title of Baroness on his lady, and the dignity of Baron to the heirs-male of his body. On the recommendation of his Majesty, a pension of £2000 per annum was voted to the Baroness, and to the two next succeeding heirs.

The capital of his native country was not backward in acknowledging the honour reflected by so worthy a son. At a meeting of the Magistrates and Town Council of Edinburgh, it was resolved that a monument to the memory of Sir Ralph Abercromby should be erected on the wall of the High Church; and a very liberal collection was made in all the churches and chapels for the relief of the families of the " brave men who had fallen in Egypt." In honour of his memory, also, the Edinburgh Volunteer Brigade, on the 2nd of June, performed a grand military spectacle at the Meadows. They were dressed in " deep funeral uniform," while the bands performed " plaintive pieces of music, some of which were composed for the occasion." The crowd of spectators, as may be supposed, was immense, and the scene is said to have been " solemn and impressive."

Sir Ralph married Anne, daughter of John Menzies, of Fernton, in the county of Perth, by whom he had four sons and two daughters. His eldest son, George, on the death of his mother, 17th February, 1821, became Lord Abercromby of Aboukir and Tullibody, and married, 27th January, 1799, Montague, third daughter of Henry, first Viscount Melville, by whom he had issue one son and two daughters. His second son, John, G.C.B., died unmarried, in the year 1817. The third son, James, married in 1802, Mary Ann, daughter of Egerton Leigh, Esq., by whom he has issue one son, Ralph (born 6th April, 1803), now Minister at Turin. The fourth son, Alexander, C.B., is a Lieutenant-Colonel in the army.

LAUCHLAN M'BAIN,

A Well-Known Vendor of Roasting-Jacks.

LAUCHLAN M'BAIN was a native of Old Meldrum, Aberdeenshire, where he served his apprenticeship as a tailor. He afterwards became a soldier, and at one time served in the 21st, or Royal Scots Fusiliers. It is not said whether he had been at the inglorious affair of Preston-pans, but he hesitated not to state that he was one of the victors at Culloden. At what period he obtained his discharge is unknown; but, unfortunately for him, his retirement from the army was not accompanied by any pension. Upon the cessation of his military duties, he came to Edinburgh, where he settled down in civil life, by becoming a manufacturer of fly-jacks and toasting-forks. In this vocation Lauchlan soon acquired notoriety, and became one of the characters of "Auld Reekie." Those who recollect him, and there are many, still remember the fine modulations of his sonorous yet musical voice, as he sang the "roasting, toasting" ditty; and, like Blind Aleck of Glasgow, he was "the author of all he made, said or sang."

Lauchlan was unquestionably a favourite with the populace; but as the most universally esteemed are unable to elbow through the world without sometimes giving offence, so it happened with the honest vendor of roasting-jacks. His professional chant, as he frequently winded his way up the back-stairs leading from the Cowgate to the Parliament Square, became exceedingly annoying to the gentlemen of the long robe, who, though anxious to abate the nuisance, were unable legally to entangle their tormentor in the meshes of the law. Lauchlan, sensible that these visits might be turned to account, was most assiduous in paying them, and never failed, when the judges were sitting, to exert his stentorian lungs under the windows of the Court-house. This he did with such success, that at length both judges and practitioners, having lost all patience, collected amongst them a sum of money, which they deemed sufficient to purchase an exemption in future from these provoking visitations. Lauchlan pocketed the fee, and promised faithfully not to let his voice come within hearing of the Court in future. He no doubt intended to keep religiously by the letter of his agreement, but at the same time mentally calculated upon the *éclat*, if not the profit, of outwitting a whole court of lawyers. Accordingly, next day he was seen at the usual spot with a huge bell, to which he gave full effect by a scientific movement of the arm that would have done credit to the most experienced city-bellman. Many wondered at the sudden change in Lauchlan's mode of announcing his presence; but he explained this by facetiously remarking, that "having sold his *own* tongue to the judges, he was under the necessity of using another." The ingenuity of Lauchlan was rewarded by an additional *douceur*, coupled with the condition, which he scrupulously kept, that in future there was to be an absolute cessation of his visits in that quarter.

In the course of his peregrinations, Lachlan offended a well-known civic dignitary, Bailie Creech, one of the chief booksellers in Edinburgh, whose shop formed the east end of the Luckenbooths. The Bailie felt his dignity lessened by the contemptuous manner in which the Veteran of Culloden treated his instructions not to bawl so unharmoniously in front of his premises. At last, resolving to compel obedience, he summoned Lauchlan to *compear* before the magistrates. On the day of trial the defender fearlessly entered the Council Chamber, where Creech sat in judgment. After the complaint had been preferred, and a volley of abuse discharged by the angry Bailie, old Lauchlan, with an air of well-assumed independence, produced his discharge, and asserted the right which it gave him to pursue his calling in any town or city in Great Britain, save Oxford and Cambridge. The northern Dogberry was dreadfully vexed that in this way his mighty preparation had come to nothing; and, after advising with the ordinary assessor in the Bailie Court, the well-known *James Laing*, he found himself compelled to dismiss the complaint. No sooner had Lauchlan regained the "crown o' the causey," than a universal shout from the "callants" announced the defeat of the Bailie; while the victor, taking his station on the debateable ground in front of the shop, commenced with renewed vigour the obnoxious *cry* of "R—r—r—roasting, toasting jacks." This was repeated so often, that even the penurious Mr. Creech was compelled to *purchase* a cessation of hostilities.

Notwithstanding all his popularity, however, poor Lauchlan found himself, at an advanced age, possessor of more fame than fortune. It is possible that his own tippling propensities, and consequent want of economy, may have had some share in producing this disastrous result. On one occasion the late Mr. Smith, lamp-contractor for the city of Edinburgh, was the means of saving the poor fellow's life, having found him fast asleep, in a cold wintry night, among the snow near the Meadow Cage.

Finding old age and frailty stealing upon him, Lauchlan made an unsuccessful application, in 1805, to the Marquis of Hastings, then Earl of Moira, who was at the time Commander-in-Chief of the Forces in Scotland, to obtain a pension in consequence of the long period of his service. Starvation or the Workhouse were now the veteran's only alternatives. His philosophy preferred the latter, and the interest of some friends procured him admission to the Charity Workhouse. One would have thought his weatherbeaten hulk had at length found a quiet haven—but no! *genius*, it has been remarked, is always *young*, and the adventurous spirit of the warlike son of Mars could not subside into inglorious quiescence. Old Lauchlan, at the age of ninety-six, was turned out of barracks for an amour! The tender-hearted old nurse of the establishment—some twenty years younger than himself—had shown him kindness during an illness, ministering to his wants, and sometimes sitting at his bedside, receiving with greedy ears his stories

> " Of moving accidents by flood and field,
> Of hairbreadth 'scapes in the imminent deadly breach."

One day—one unpropitious day—an evil eye beheld the simple pair; and such proceedings not being in accordance with the rules of the establishment, they were both expelled. What could a man of spirit do in such a dilemma? Marriage could alone testify his gratitude to the gentle fair, and his resentment of a harsh world's cruelty.

In a second Print of the vendor of roasting-jacks, done in 1815, the contrast in the "altered gait" of the two figures, is a striking illustration of the progress of time. He is here represented as again employed in the disposal of his roasting-jacks; but, alas! the best of his days were over. Like other geniuses, he found he had outlived his reputation; and the useful implements in which he dealt hardly enabled him to beat off the wolf from his door. His wife continued to cling to him through all his adversity, and, it is said, helped to cheer the gloomy winter of his age and fortunes. Lachlan appears, however, to have again obtained admission to the Workhouse; for, in a notice of his death, it is stated that he died there on the 3rd October, 1818, aged 102.

MRS. SIDDONS,

At the Edinburgh Theatre.

EVERY one who has turned over the leaves of a dramatic biography is acquainted with the usual statements relative to the life of Mrs. SIDDONS—how she first appeared at Drury Lane Theatre, in the year 1775, as the representative of *Portia*, and towards the end of the season degenerated into a walking Venus in the pageant of the *Jubilee* —how she returned to the Bath Theatre the year following—how, a few years afterwards, she reappeared in London with extraordinary success, and, after a brilliant career, finally retired from the stage in July, 1812. Her biographers, however, have never indulged the world with anything like a detailed account of her first appearance on the Edinburgh stage, which occurred on the 22d May, 1784. During her engagement, "the rage for seeing her was so great, that one day there were 2557 applications for 630 places;" and many even came from Newcastle to witness her performances. Her engagement was owing to a few spirited individuals, who took all risk on themselves, the manager of the Edinburgh Theatre being afraid of hazardous speculations. The *Edinburgh Weekly Magazine*, in its report of her appearance, mentions that "the manager had taken the precaution, after the first night, to have an officer's guard of soldiers at the principal door. But several scuffles having ensued, through the eagerness of the people to get places, and the soldiers having been rash in the use of their bayonets, it was thought advisable to withdraw the guard on the third night, lest any accident had happened from the pressure of the crowd, who began to assemble round the doors at eleven in the forenoon."

The plays she acted in were as follow:—May 22, Venice Preserved; 24, Gamester; 26, Venice Preserved; 27, Gamester; 29, Mourning Bride; June 1, Douglas; 3, Isabella; 5, Jane Shore; 7, Douglas; 9, Grecian Daughter (for her benefit); 10, Mourning Bride; 11, Grecian Daughter (for benefit of the Charity Workhouse).

On the 12th she set out for Dublin, where she was engaged to perform twenty nights for £1000.

In speaking of her appearance in *Douglas*, the *Courant* observes, " We have seen Mrs. Crawford in the part of Lady Randolph, and she played it perhaps with more solemnity and as much dignity as Mrs. Siddons, but surely not with so much interesting sensibility. It would far exceed our limits to point out or describe the many beauties that charmed us in the representation of this piece. Mrs. Siddons never once disappoints the spectator; but from the moment of her appearance she interests and carries along his admiration of every tone, look, and gesture. While the discovery of her son gradually proceeds, she suspends the audience in the most pleasing interesting anxiety.

" During the beautiful narration of Old Norval, when he says—

> ' Red came the river down, and loud and oft
> The angry spirit of the water shriek'd,' &c.,

she kept the audience by her looks and attitude in the most silent anxious attention, and they read in her countenance every movement of her soul. But when she breaks out—

> ' Inhuman that thou art !
> How could'st thou kill what waves and tempests spared ? '

they must be of a flinty nature indeed who burst not into tears.

" When she discovers herself to her son—

> ' My son ! my son !
> I am thy mother, and the wife of Douglas,'

we believe there was not a dry eye in the whole house."

Mrs. Siddons played eleven nights exclusive of the charity one. She shared £50 a-night for ten nights, and at her benefit drew £350, besides a sum of £260, with which a party of gentlemen presented her. From the subscribers she received an elegant piece of plate, on which was engraved—" As a mark of esteem for superior genius and unrivalled talents, this vase is respectfully inscribed with the name of SIDDONS.—Edinburgh, 9th June, 1784."

The poetical epistle which follows, showing the ferment into which her presence threw the town, is clever, and worthy of preservation :—

EPISTLE FROM MISS MARIA BELINDA BOGLE AT EDINBURGH, TO HER FRIEND, MISS LAVINIA LEETCH, AT GLASGOW.

I HEAR with deep sorrow, my beautiful Leetch,
In vain to come here you your father beseech ;
I say in all places, and say it most truly,
His heart is as hard as the heart of *Priuli;*
'Tis composed of black flint, or of Aberdeen granite,
But smother your rage--'twould be folly to fan it.

Each evening the playhouse exhibits a mob,
And the right of admission 's turn'd into a job.
By five the whole pit used to fill with subscribers,
And those who had money enough to be bribers ;
But the public took fire, and began a loud jar,
And I thought we'd have had a Siddonian war.

The Committees met, and the lawyers' hot mettle
Began very soon both to cool and to settle :
Of public resentment to blunt the keen edge,
In a coop they commented that sixty they'd wedge ;
And the coop's now so cramm'd it will scarce hold a mouse,
And the rest of the Pit's turn'd a true public-house.
With porter and pathos, with whisky and whining,
They quickly all look as if long they'd been dining ;
Their shrub and their sighs court our noses and ears,
And their twopenny blends in libation with tears :
The god of good liquor with fervour they woo,
And before the fifth act they are "*a' greeting fou.*"
Though my muse to write satire's reluctant and loth,
This custom, I think, savours strong of the Goth.

As for Siddons herself, her features so tragic
Have caught the whole town with the force of their magic :
Her action is varied, her voice is extensive,
Her eye very fine, but somewhat too pensive.
In the terrible trials of *Beverley's* wife
She rose not above the dull level of life.
She was greatly too simple to strike very deep,
And I thought more than once to have fallen asleep.
Her sorrows in *Shore* were so soft and so still,
That my heart lay as snug as a thief in a mill :
I have never as yet been much overcome
With distress that's so gentle, and grief that's so dumb ;
And, to tell the plain truth, I have not seen any
They get, like the tumble of *Yates* in *Mandane ;*
For acting should certainly rise above Nature ;
But, indeed, now and then she's a wonderful creature.
When *Zara's* revenge burst in storms from the tongue,
With rage and reproach all the ample roof rung.
Isabella, too, rose all superior to sadness,
And our hearts were well harrow'd with horror and madness.
From all sides of the house, hark the cry how it swells !
While the boxes are torn with most heart-piercing yells,—
The Misses all faint, it becomes them so vastly,
And their cheeks are so red, that they never look ghastly :
Even ladies advance to their grand climacterics
Are often led out in a fit of hysterics ;
The screams are wide-wafted, east, west, south, and north,
Loud Echo prolongs them on both sides the Forth.

You ask me what beauties most touchingly strike ?—
They are beauteous all, and all beauteous alike,
With lovely complexions that time ne'er can tarnish,
So thick they're laid o'er with a delicate varnish ;
Their bosoms and neck have a gloss and a burnish,
And their cheeks with fresh roses from Raeburn they furnish.

I quickly return, and am just on the wing,
And some things I'm sure that you'll like I will bring—
The sweet Siddons' cap, the latest dear ogle ;
Farewell till we meet.   Your true friend,
                                        MARY BOGLE.

Edinburgh, June 7, 1784.

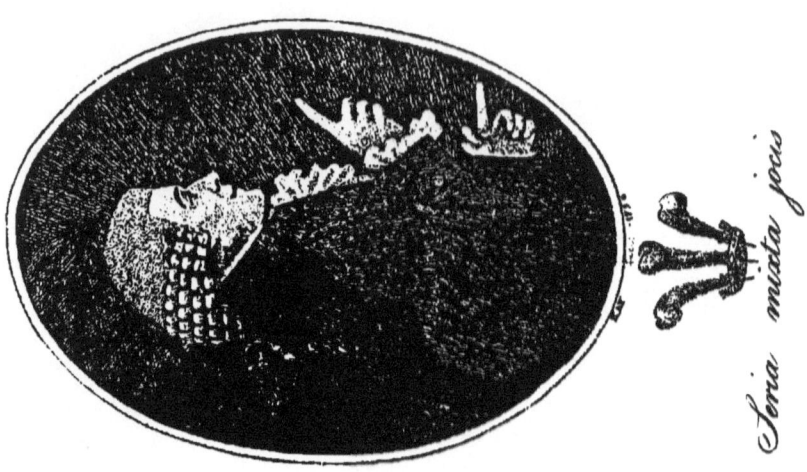

Seria mixta jocis

The Hon. HENRY ERSKINE

[To face page 89

TXP 1731

The Rev. HUGH BLAIR D.D.

During the summer season of the following year Mrs. Siddons again honoured Modern Athens with her presence, and created as great a sensation as she had done the year preceding. The receipts during her engagement were:—1785, July 12, Grecian Daughter, £95; July 14, Macbeth, £125; July 16, Fair Penitent, £126; July 18, Isabella, £154; July 20, Douglas, £130; July 23, Carmelite, £128; July 25, Venice Preserved, £130; July 26, Carmelite, £84; July 27, Which is the Man? £84; July 28, Isabella, £139; July 29, Suspicious Husband, £15; July 30, Jane Shore, £115; August 1, Earl of Warwick, £123; August 2, Mourning Bride, £107; August 3, Provoked Husband, £125; August 6, Gamester, £200; August 8, Douglas, £137; August 9, Earl of Warwick, £60 16s.

On the 12th August, Mrs. Siddons made her first appearance in Glasgow in the character of *Belvidera*.

THE REV. HUGH BLAIR, D.D.,
Of the High Church, Edinburgh.

THE author of the "Lectures on Rhetoric and Belles Lettres," and of five volumes of universally admired Sermons, whose life and writings have done so much credit to the Scottish pulpit, was born at Edinburgh in 1718. His father was a merchant, and grandson to Robert Blair, an eminent Presbyterian "Scots Worthy" of the seventeenth century.

Young Blair commenced his academical studies in 1730; and having been prevented by constitutional delicacy of health from participating much in the pastimes peculiar to youth, his devotion to the acquisition of knowledge became the more close and effective. His first striking demonstration of talent was exhibited in an "Essay on the Beautiful," written while a student of logic, and when only in his sixteenth year, which, as a mark of distinction, was ordered by Professor Stevenson to be publicly read at the end of the session.

In 1741, he was licensed by the Presbytery of Edinburgh; and his sermons being distinguished at the very outset for correctness of design, and that peculiar chastity of composition which so much distinguished his after productions, his talents as a preacher soon became the topic of public remark. His first charge was the parish of Collessie in Fife, presented to him by the Earl of Leven in 1742; but the very next year he was recalled to the metropolis, by being elected one of the ministers of the Canongate Church. Here, in 1745, on the breaking out of the Rebellion, he preached a sermon warmly in favour of the Hanoverian line, which was afterwards printed, and it is said had the effect of strengthening the loyalty of the people.

Blair continued in the Canongate eleven years, during which period he had the satisfaction of attracting an immense congregation from all quarters of the city, and found himself daily acquiring popularity. In 1754 he was called to the pastorship of Lady Yester's Church by the Town Council of Edinburgh; and again by the same body, in

1758, he was translated to one of the charges in the High Church. About the same period, the degree of D.D. was conferred upon him by the University of St. Andrews. In 1759, Dr. Blair commenced the delivery of those lectures on " Rhetoric and the Belles Lettres," afterwards given to the public in a printed form, and which have since continued to hold precedence as a standard work on literary composition. The lectures were undertaken with the concurrence of the University; and so popular did they at once become, that in 1761 the Town Council procured from Government an endowment of £70 a year towards instituting a rhetorical class in connexion with the College, of which Dr. Blair was appointed Professor. Hitherto, except in the case of one or two sermons on particular occasions, which were printed, the Doctor had not appeared as an author before the world. The deep interest which he took, however, in the exertions of Macpherson to recover the traditional poetry of the Highlands, led him to publish, in 1763, " a Critical Dissertation on the Poems of Ossian," which was held by the advocates for their authenticity, to be one of the finest specimens of " critical composition in the English language."

Dr. Blair was the *first* person who introduced the poems of Ossian to the notice of the world; first, by the " Fragments of Ancient Poetry " which he published; and next, by setting on foot an undertaking for collecting and publishing the entire poems. He used to boast of this, but he little dreamed that the lapse of a few years would produce so general a change in public opinion as to the authenticity of these remarkable productions.

Although his style of pulpit oratory had become an object of very general imitation among the young clergy, and although he had been repeatedly urged to favour the world with some of those productions which had captivated so many hearers, it was not till 1777 that he was induced to think of publishing. In that year he transmitted the MS. of his first volume of sermons, through the medium of Mr. Creech, to an eminent publisher in London (Mr. Strachan), with a view to the disposing of the copyright. Strachan, presuming probably on a very general feeling of aversion then existing in the public mind towards clerical productions, sent a discouraging answer to Dr. Blair. In the mean time the MS. had been handed to Dr. Johnson for perusal, who, after Strachan's unfavourable letter had been despatched to the north, sent a note to the publisher, in which he says, " I have read over Dr. Blair's first sermon with more than approbation; to say it is good, is to say too little." This judgment, strengthened by a conversation afterwards held with Dr. Johnson, soon convinced Mr. Strachan of the error he had committed. He therefore wrote a second time to Dr. Blair, inclosing Johnson's note, and agreeing, in conjunction with Mr. Cadell and Mr. Creech of Edinburgh, to purchase the volume for one hundred pounds. The MS. was first submitted to the perusal of Mr. Creech, who was so highly taken with it, that he made an offer off-hand to the author of one hundred guineas. Dr. Blair was so much struck with the amount, as to be almost incredulous of the verity of Mr. Creech's offer. " Will you indeed!" was his exclamation. The popularity of these sermons exceeded all anticipation; so much so, that the publishers presented the author with two additional sums of money, by way of compliment. Not long after its first publication, the volume attracted the notice of George III. and his consort—a portion of the sermons, it is said, having been first read to their Majesties in the royal closet by the eloquent Earl of Mansfield. So highly did their Majesties esteem the merits of the author, that a pension of £200 was settled upon him. The Doctor afterwards published other three volumes of sermons, all of which met an equally flattering reception, and were translated into almost all the European languages.

Upon occasion of the publication of Dr. Blair's Lectures, Logan the poet addressed a letter to Dr. Gilbert Stuart, at that time editor of the "English Review and Political Herald," from which the following beautiful extracts have been taken :—

" Dr. Blair's Lectures are to be published some time in spring. I need not tell you that I am very much interested in the fate and fame of all his works. Besides his literary merit, he hath borne his faculties so meekly in every situation, that he is entitled to favour as well as candour. He has never with pedantic authority opposed the career of other authors, but has, on the contrary, favoured every literary attempt. He has never studied to push himself immaturely into the notice of the world, but waited the call of the public for all his productions ; and now, when he retires from the republic of letters into the vale of ease, I cannot help wishing success to Fingal in the last of his fields. ＊ ＊ ＊ ＊ Your influence to give Dr. Blair his last passport to the public will be very agreeable to the *literati* here, and will be a particular favour done to me. It will still farther enhance the obligation if you will write me such a letter as I can show him, *to quiet his fears.*"

Dr. Blair retired from the Professorship in 1788, in consequence of advanced age, and in a few years afterwards found himself also unable to discharge the duties of the pulpit. Such, however, was the vigour of his intellect, that in 1799, when past his eightieth year, he composed and preached one of the most effective sermons he ever delivered, in behalf of the Fund for the Benefit of the sons of the Clergy, the subject of which was—"The compassionate beneficence of the Deity."

In addition to his acquirements in theology and general literature, Dr. Blair was intimately acquainted with some of the sciences ; while it may be worthy of remark, he also indulged to a considerable extent in light reading. "The Arabian Nights' Entertainments," and "Don Quixote," were among his especial favourites. He was also an admirer of Mrs. Anne Radcliffe's talents for romance, and honoured Mr. Pratt's "Emma Corbett" with particular praise. In Church politics, although the Doctor took no active part, he was, like his intimate friend Principal Robertson, a decided Moderate, and was zealous to adopt any means of improving the worship of the Church of Scotland, where such could be done without an infringement of principle. With this view, during one of his visits to London, he procured singers from the Cathedral of York, by whose aid he originated an amendment in the conducting of the psalmody, which was at first looked upon as a daring innovation, but is now become pretty general throughout the Establishment.

There were some slight defects in the character of the Doctor, which have been admitted by his warmest friends—he was vain, and very susceptible of flattery. A gentleman one day met him on the street, and, in the course of conversation, mentioned that his friend Mr. Donald Smith, banker, was anxious to secure a seat in the High Church, that he might become one of the Doctor's congregation. "Indeed," continued this person, "my friend is quite anxious on this subject. He has tried many preachers, but he finds your sermons, Doctor, so superior in the graces of oratory, and so full of pointed observation of the world, that he cannot think of settling under any other than you."—"I am very glad to hear that I am to have Mr. Smith for a hearer," said the preacher with unconscious self-gratulation—" he is a very sensible man."

Dr. Blair's "taste and accuracy in dress," continues our authority, "were absolutely ridiculous. There was a correctness in his wig, for instance, amounting to a hair-breadth exactness. He was so careful about his coat, that not content with merely looking at himself in the mirror to see how it fitted in general, he would cause the tailor to lay the looking-glass on the floor, and then standing on tiptoe over it, he would peep athwart his shoulder *to see how the skirts hung.* It is also yet remembered in Edinburgh, with what a self-satisfied and finical air this great divine used to walk between his house and the church every Sunday morning, on his way to perform service. His wig frizzed and powdered so nicely—his gown so scrupulously arranged on his shoulders—his bands so pure and clean—and every thing about him in such exquisite taste and neatness."

Upon one occasion, while sitting for his portrait, he requested the painter to draw his face with a *pleasing smile.* The painter replied, "Well, then, you must *put on* a pleasing smile." The Doctor, in attempting to do this, made a most horrid *grin,* which, being immediately transferred to the canvas, gave his effigy the appearance of that of a downright idiot. This effect being pointed out to him by a friend, he immediately ordered the painting to be destroyed, and a new one forthwith commenced, the Doctor contenting himself with having it executed without the "pleasing smile."

During the latter part of his life almost all strangers of distinction who visited Edinburgh brought letters of introduction to Dr. Blair; and as he was quite at ease in point of worldly circumstances, and had then in a great measure ceased to study intensely, he in general entertained them frequently and well. On one of these occasions, when he had collected a considerable party at dinner to meet an English clergyman, a Scotsman present asked the stranger what was thought of the Doctor's sermons by his professional brethren in the south. To his horror, and to the mortification of Mrs. Blair, who sat near, and who looked upon her husband as a sort of divinity, the Englishman answered, "Why, they are not partial to them at all."—" How, sir," faltered out the querist—" how should that be?"—"Why," replied the southron, "because they are so much read, and so generally known, that our clergymen can't borrow from them." The whole company, hitherto in a state of considerable embarrassment, were quite delighted at this ingenious and well-turned compliment.

Dr. Blair died in the 83rd year of his age, on the 27th December,

1800. He was buried in the Greyfriars' Churchyard—the Westminster Abbey of Scotland—where a tablet to his memory, containing a highly elegant and classical Latin inscription, is affixed to the southern wall of the church. He married, in 1748, his cousin, Katherine Bannatyne, daughter of the Reverend James Bannatyne, one of the ministers of Edinburgh, by whom he had a son and daughter. The former died in infancy, and the latter when about twenty-one years of age. Mrs. Blair also died a few years previous to the demise of her husband. Dr. Blair's usual place of residence in summer was at Restalrig—in winter in Argyle Square.

THE HONOURABLE HENRY ERSKINE,

Dean of the Faculty of Advocates.

THE Hon. Henry Erskine was the third son of Henry David, tenth Earl of Buchan, by Agnes, daughter of Sir James Stewart of Goodtrees, and was born at Edinburgh on the 1st November, 1746. His patrimony was trifling, and had it not been for the exemplary kindness of his eldest brother, who took a paternal charge both of Henry and his younger brother Thomas, afterwards Lord Erskine, he would not have been able to defray the expenses attendant upon the course of study requisite to be followed in order to qualify him for the bar. In the year 1765, Mr. Erskine was admitted a member of the Faculty of Advocates. He had previously prepared himself for *extempore* speaking, by attending the Forum Debating Society established in Edinburgh, in which he gave promise of that eminence as a pleader which he afterwards attained.

The brilliant talents of Mr. Erskine soon placed him at the head of his profession. His legal services were as much at the command of the poor as of the wealthy, and he gratuitously devoted his abilities in behalf of any individual whom he believed to be ill-used, with greater zeal than if he had been amply remunerated for his exertions. So well was this benevolent trait in his character known, that it was said of him by a poor man, who lived in a remote district of Scotland, when a friend would have dissuaded him from entering into a certain lawsuit, "There's no a puir man in a' Scotland need to want a friend or fear an enemy, sae lang as Harry Erskine's to the fore."

During the Coalition Administration, Mr. Erskine held the office of Lord Advocate of Scotland. He succeeded Henry Dundas (afterwards Lord Melville). On the morning of the appointment, he had an interview with Dundas in the Outer House ; when, observing that the latter gentleman had already resumed the ordinary stuff-gown which advocates are in the custom of wearing, he said gaily, that he "must leave off talking, to go and order his silk-gown" (the official costume of the Lord Advocate and Solicitor-General). "It is hardly worth while," said Mr. Dundas, drily, "for the time you will want it ; you had better borrow mine." Erskine's reply was exceedingly happy —" From the readiness with which you make the offer, Mr. Dundas,

I have no doubt that the gown is a gown made to *fit any party;* but however short my time in office may be, it shall ne'er be said of Henry Erskine that he put on the *abandoned habits* of his predecessor." The prediction of Mr. Dundas proved true, however ; for Erskine held office only for a very short period, in consequence of a sudden change of Ministry. He was succeeded by Ilay Campbell, Esq., afterwards Lord President of the Court of Session, to whom he said upon resign-ing his gown, " My Lord, you must take nothing *off it*, for I'll soon need it again." To which Mr. Campbell replied, " It will be *bare enough*, Harry, before you get it." On the return of the Whigs to power in 1806, Mr. Erskine once more became Lord Advocate, and was at the same time returned member for the Dumfries District of Burghs. But this Administration being of short duration, he was again deprived of office.

After a long, laborious, and brilliant professional career, extending over a period of forty-four years, Mr. Erskine retired from public life to his villa of Amondell, in West Lothian, where he died on the 8th of October, 1817, in the seventy-first year of his age.

In person Mr. Erskine was above the middle size, and eminently handsome. His voice was powerful; his manner of delivery pecu-liarly graceful ; his enunciation accurate and distinct—qualities which greatly added to the effect of his oratory.

Mr. Erskine's first wife (Miss Fullarton) was a lady of somewhat eccentric habits—she not infrequently employed half of the night in examining the family wardrobe, to see that nothing was missing. On one of these occasions, she awoke her husband in the middle of the night, by putting to him the appalling interrogatory, " Harry, love, where's your white waistcoat?" The relater of this anecdote thus in-cidentally speaks of his reminiscences of Mr. Erskine, as he appeared in his retreat at Amondell :—" I recollect the very grey hat that he used to wear, with a bit of the rim torn, and the pepper-and-salt short coat, and the white neckcloth sprinkled with snuff."

While Mr. Erskine practised at the bar, it was his frequent custom to walk after the rising of the Court to the Meadows, and he was often accompanied by Lord Balmuto, one of the judges—a very good kind of man, but not particularly quick in the perception of the ludicrous. His lordship never could discover, at first, the point of Mr. Erskine's wit, and after walking a mile or two perhaps, and long after Mr. Erskine had forgotten the saying, he would suddenly cry out, " I have you now, Harry—I have you now, Harry !" stopping and bursting into an immoderate fit of laughter.

With all the liveliness of fancy, however, and with all these shining talents, Mr. Erskine's habits were domestic in an eminent degree. His wishes and desires are pleasingly depictured in the following lines by himself :—

> " Let sparks and topers o'er their bottles sit,
> Toss bumpers down, and fancy laughter wit ;
> Let cautious plodders, o'er their ledger pore,
> Note down each farthing gain'd, and wish it more ;
> Let lawyers dream of wigs, poets of fame,
> Scholars look learn'd, and senators declaim ;

Let soldiers stand, like targets in the fray,
Their lives just worth their thirteenpence a·day.
Give me a nook in some secluded spot,
Which business shuns, and din approaches not—
Some snug retreat, where I may never know
What Monarch reigns, what Ministers bestow—
A book—my slippers—and a field to stroll in—
My garden-seat—an elbow chair to loll in—
Sunshine, when wanted—shade, when shade invites,
With pleasant country laurels, smells, and sights,
And now and then a glass of generous wine,
Shared with a chatty friend of 'auld langsyne;'
And one companion more, for ever nigh,
To sympathise in all that passes by,
To journey with me in the path of life,
And share its pleasures and divide its strife.
These simple joys, Eugenius, let me find,
And I'll ne'er cast a lingering look behind."

Mr. Erskine was long a member of the Scottish Antiquarian Society. One of the members remarked to him that he was a very bad attender of their meetings, adding, at the same time, that he never gave any donations to the Society. A short time afterwards he wrote a letter to the Secretary apologising for not attending the meetings, and stating that he had "inclosed a donation, which, if you keep long enough, will be the greatest curiosity you have !" This was a guinea of George III.

He had an inveterate propensity for puns. A person once said to him that punning was the lowest species of wit, to which he replied, "Then it must be the best species, since it is the *foundation* of the whole."

Mr. Erskine meeting an old friend one morning returning from St. Bernard's Well, which he knew he was in the habit of daily visiting, exclaimed, "Oh, S——e ! I see you never weary in *well*-doing."

Being told that Knox, who had long derived his livelihood by keeping the door of the Parliament-House, had been killed by a shot from a small *cannon* on the King's birthday, he observed that "it was remarkable a man should *live* by the *civil*, and *die* by the *canon law.*"

Lord Kellie was once amusing his company with an account of a sermon he had heard in a church in Italy, in which the priest related the miracle of St. Anthony, when preaching on shipboard, attracting the fishes, which, in order to listen to his pious discourse, held their heads out of the water. "I can well believe the miracle," said Mr. Henry Erskine. "How so ? "—" When your lordship was at church, there was at least one fish out of the water."

Mr. Erskine of Alva, a Scotch advocate, afterwards one of the Senators of the College of Justice, and who assumed the title of Lord Barjarg, a man of diminutive stature, was retained as counsel in a very interesting cause, wherein the Hon. Henry Erskine appeared for the opposite party. The crowd in court being very great, in order to enable young *Alva* to be seen and heard more advantageously, a *chair* was brought him to *stand* upon. Mr. Erskine quaintly remarked, " That is one way of *rising* at the bar."

Mr. Erskine, holding an appointment from the Prince of Wales, generally presided at the anniversary meeting of his Royal Highness's household in Edinburgh. On one of these occasions, while a gentleman was singing after dinner, the Prince's tobacconist accompanied the song with his fingers upon the *wainscoting* of the room, in a very accurate manner. When the music finished, the chairman said, "He thought the Prince's tobacconist would make a capital *King's counsel*." On being asked "Why?" Harry replied, "Because I never heard a man make so much of a *pannel*."

An English nobleman, walking through the New town in company with Mr. Erskine, remarked how odd it was that St. Andrew's Church should so greatly *project*, whilst the Physicians' Hall, immediately opposite, equally *receded*. Mr. Erskine admitted that George Street would have been, without exception, the finest street in Europe, if the *forwardness* of the *clergy*, and the *backwardness* of the *physicians*, had not marred its *uniformity*.

One day Mr. Erskine was dining at the house of Mr. William Creech, bookseller, who was rather penurious, and entertained his guests on that occasion with a single bottle of *Cape wine*, though he boasted of some particularly fine *Madeira wine* he happened to possess. Mr. Erskine made various attempts to induce his host to produce a bottle of his vaunted Madeira, but to no purpose; at length he said, with an air of apparent disappointment, "Well, well, since we can't get to *Madeira*, we must just *double the Cape*."

In his latter years Mr. Erskine was very much annoyed at the idea that his witticisms might be collected together in a volume. Aware of this, a friend of his resolved to tease him, and having invited him to dinner, he, in the course of the evening, took up a goodly looking volume, and turning over the pages began to laugh heartily. "What is the cause of your merriment?" exclaimed the guest. "Oh, it's only one of your jokes, Harry."—"Where did you get it?"—"Oh, in the new work just published, entitled *The New Complete Jester, or every man his own Harry Erskine!*" Mr. Erskine felt very much amazed, as may be supposed, upon the announcement of the fictitious publication.

Mr. Erskine was twice married, and by his first marriage he had the present Earl of Buchan, Major Erskine, and two daughters: one married to the late Colonel Callender of Craigforth, and another to Dr. Smith. By his second wife, Miss Munro (who still survives), he had no issue.

JAMES BRUCE, ESQ.,

The Abyssinian Traveller.

JAMES BRUCE of Kinnaird, the Abyssinian traveller, was born on the 14th December, 1730, at Kinnaird, in the county of Stirling, and was eldest son of David Bruce of Kinnaird, by Marion, daughter of James Graham of Airth, Judge of the High Court of Admiralty in Scotland.

At the age of eight years, Bruce, who was then rather of a weakly
habit and gentle disposition, though afterwards remarkable for robust-
ness of body and boldness of mind, was sent to London to the care of
an uncle.   Here he remained until he had attained his twelfth year,
when he was removed to Harrow, where he won the esteem of his
instructors by his amiable temper and extraordinary aptitude for
learning.   In 1747 he returned to Kinnaird, with the reputation of a
first-rate scholar.   It having been determined he should prepare himself for the Bar, he, for that purpose, attended the usual classes in
the University of Edinburgh ; but finding legal pursuits not suited to
his disposition, it was resolved that he should proceed to India.   With
this intention he went to London in 1753 ; but while waiting for permission from the East India Company to settle there as a free trader,
he became acquainted with Adriana Allan, the daughter of a deceased
wine-merchant, whom he married, and abandoning the idea of India,
embarked in the excellent business left by his father-in-law.   The death
of his wife, however, which took place, soon after their marriage, at
Paris, whither he had taken her for the recovery of her health, again
altered Bruce's destiny.   Deeply affected by her loss, he first devolved
the cares of his business on his partner, and soon afterwards withdrew
from the concern altogether.

Some time subsequent to these occurrences, Bruce had become
acquainted with Lord Halifax, who suggested to him that his talents
might be successfully exerted in making discoveries in Africa ; and, to
give him every facility, his Lordship proposed to appoint him consul
at Algiers.   He repaired to his post in 1763, where he employed himself a year in the study of the Oriental languages ; and this appointment was the first step to the discovery of the source of the Nile.

As our readers must be familiar with the perilous adventures of this
traveller, as depicted by himself in one of the most entertaining works
in our language, it would be altogether idle to attempt any abridge-
ment of them.   After many hair-breadth escapes, and overcoming
many difficulties both by sea and land, Bruce returned in safety to
Marseilles in March, 1773, and was received with marked consideration
at the French court.

On his arrival in Great Britain he had an audience of George the
Third, to whom he presented drawings of Palmyra, Baalbec, and other
cities, with which he had promised to furnish his Majesty previous to
his departure.   It had been insinuated that Mr. Bruce was an indifferent draughtsman, and that the drawings which he had brought
home were not done by himself, but by the artist he had taken along
with him.   This charge was perfectly untrue, although it derived
some countenance from his declining to comply with a request of the
King, that he should draw Kew.   When he had submitted the above-
mentioned draughts, his Majesty said, " Very well, very well, Bruce ;
the colours are fine, very fine—you must make me one—yes ; you
must make me one of Kew ! "   Bruce evaded compliance by saying, " I
would with the greatest pleasure obey your Majesty, but here I cannot get such colours."

It was not until seventeen years after his return to Europe, that he
gave that work to the world which has perpetuated his name.   It

appeared in 1790, and consisted of four large quarto volumes, besides a volume of drawings, and was entitled, " Travels to Discover the Source of the Nile, in the years 1768-69-70-71-72-73. By James Bruce of Kinnaird, Esq., F.R.S."

The long interval that elapsed between the period of his return and the publication of his travels, had induced many people to pretend that he had nothing worth while communicating to the world. This malicious report was mentioned to him by a friend. He replied, " James, *let them say*, as my maternal grand-aunt said. You have," continued he, " no doubt seen that inscription upon Airth—are you acquainted with its origin ? "—" No," was the rejoinder. " Then," said he, " I'll tell you. My grand-uncle was amongst others a great sufferer during the Usurpation, and, owing to his adherence to the Stuarts, was obliged to fly to Sweden. His wife, by her judicious management, and by carrying on a small trade in the coal line, made a considerable fortune, and built the wing of the house at Airth, now standing. Some evil-minded persons chose to insinuate that she had acquired this fortune in a way not very creditable to her chastity. Treating this slander with the contempt it merited, she, with conscious innocence, caused the inscription of ' *Let them say*,' to be placed over the door."

The singular incidents detailed in these Travels—the habits of life there described, so totally unlike anything previously known in Europe —and the style of romantic adventure which characterised the work— led many persons to distrust its authenticity, and even to doubt whether its author ever had been in Abyssinia at all. Those doubts found their way into the critical journals of the day, but the proud spirit of Bruce disdained to make any reply. The amusing " Adventures of Baron Munchausen" were written purposely in ridicule of him, and were received by the public as a just satire on his work. To his daughter alone he opened his heart on this vexatious subject; and to her he often said, " The world is strangely mistaken in my character, by supposing that I would condescend to write a romance for its amusement. I shall not live to witness it; but you probably will see the truth of all I have written completely and decisively confirmed."

So it has happened. Recent travellers have established the authenticity of Bruce beyond cavil or dispute. Dr. Clark, in particular, states, in the sixth volume of his Travels, that he and some other men of science, when at Cairo, examined an ancient Abyssinian priest—who perfectly recollected Bruce at the court of Gondar—on various disputed passages of the work, which were confirmed even in the most minute particular; and he concludes this curious investigation by observing, that he scarcely believes any other book of travels could have stood such a test. Sir David Baird, while commanding the British troops embarked on the Red Sea, publicly declared that the safety of the army was mainly owing to the accuracy of Mr. Bruce's chart of that sea, which some of the critics of the day ventured to insinuate he had never visited. On this subject Bruce is strikingly corroborated by that well-known traveller, Lieutenant Burnes. In a letter written from the Red Sea, so lately as 1835, he says—" I cannot quit Bruce without mentioning a fact which I have gathered here, and which

ALEXANDER WOOD, Surgeon

[*To face page 90*]

JAMES BRUCE, Esq.   PETER WILLIAMSON

Vol. I., Plate X.]

ought to be known far and wide in justice to the memory of a great and injured man, whose deeds I admired when a boy, and whose book is a *true* romance. Lord Valentia calls Bruce's voyage to the Red Sea an episodical fiction, because he is wrong in the latitude of an island called 'Macowar,' which Bruce says he had visited. Now this sea has been surveyed for the first time, and there are two islands called 'Macowar;' the one in latitude 23° 50', *visited by Bruce*, and the other in latitude 20° 45', visited by Valentia! Only think of this vindication of Bruce's memory! Major Head knew it not when he wrote his *Life*, and it is worth a thousand pages of defence."

The following rather amusing anecdote is told of Bruce:—It is said that once, when on a visit to a relative in East-Lothian, a person present observed it was "*impossible*" that the natives of Abyssinia could eat raw meat. Bruce very quietly left the room, and shortly afterwards returned from the kitchen with a raw beef-steak, peppered and salted in the Abyssinian fashion. "You will be pleased to eat this," he said, "or fight me." The gentleman preferred the former alternative, and with no good grace contrived to swallow the proffered delicacy. When he had finished, Bruce calmly observed, " Now, sir, you will never again say it is *impossible*."

Bruce was a man of uncommonly large stature, six feet four inches, and latterly very corpulent. With a turban on his head, and a long staff in his hand, he usually travelled about his grounds; and his gigantic figure in these excursions is still remembered in the neighbourhood. On the 20th of May, 1776, he took as his second wife, Mary, daughter of Thomas Dundas of Fingask, by Lady Janet Maitland, daughter of Charles sixth Earl of Lauderdale.

On the 26th of April, 1794, after entertaining a large party to dinner, as he was hurrying to assist a lady to her carriage, his foot slipped, and he fell headlong from the sixth or seventh step of the large staircase to the lobby. He was taken up in a state of insensibility, though without any visible contusion, and died early next morning, in the sixty-fourth year of his age.

Thus he who had undergone such dangers, and was placed often in such imminent peril, lost his life by an accidental fall. He left, by his second marriage, a son and a daughter. His son succeeded him in his paternal estate, and died in 1810, leaving an only daughter, who married Charles Cumming of Roseilse, a younger son of the family of Altyre, who assumed the name of Bruce, and in 1837 was member of Parliament for the Inverness district of burghs. His daughter, who survived him many years, became the wife of John Jardine, Esq., advocate, sheriff of Ross and Cromarty.

Bruce took with him in his travels a telescope so large that it required six men to carry it. He assigned the following reason to a friend by whom the anecdote was communicated :—" That, exclusive of its utility, it inspired the nations through which he passed with great awe, as they thought he had some immediate connection with Heaven, and they paid more attention to it than they did to himself."

PETER WILLIAMSON,

Author and Publisher.

PETER WILLIAMSON was born of poor parents at Hirnley, in the parish of Aboyne, county of Aberdeen, North Britain. When still very young he was sent to reside with an aunt in Aberdeen, as he tells us in his autobiography, "where, at eight years of age, playing one day on the quay with others of my companions, I was taken notice of by two fellows belonging to a vessel in the harbour, employed, as the trade then was, by some of the worthy merchants of the town, in that villainous and execrable practice called kidnapping; that is, stealing young children from their parents, and selling them as slaves in the plantations abroad. (*Vide* ' French and Indian Cruelty, exemplified in the Life and various Vicissitudes of Fortune of Peter Williamson, &c., dedicated to the Right Hon. William Pitt, Esq. Written by himself. Third edition, with considerable improvements. Glasgow: Printed by J. Bryce and D. Paterson, for the benefit of the unfortunate Author, 1758.') Being marked out by these monsters as their prey, I was cajoled on board the ship by them, where I was no sooner got than they conducted me between the decks to some others they had kidnapped in the same manner."

Neither Williamson nor any of his fellow-captives were permitted again to get on deck, and in about a month afterwards the ship sailed for America. On arriving on the coast of that country she was assailed by a storm, and driven in the middle of the night on a sand-bank off Cape May, near the Cape of Delaware, and in a short time filled with water. The ruffian crew, hoisting out their boats, made their escape to land, leaving the poor boys to their fate in the vessel. Fortunately she held together till the following morning, when the Captain sent some of his men on board to bring the boys, and as much of the cargo as they could, on shore, where Williamson and his fellow-captives remained in a sort of camp for three weeks, when they were taken to Philadelphia, and there sold at about £16 per head. Williamson was separated from his companions, and from this time never heard any more of them. He was himself fortunate enough to fall into the hands of an excellent master, a humane and worthy man. This person was a countryman of his own of the name of Wilson, from Perth, who had himself been kidnapped in his youth. With this man Williamson lived very happily, and much at his ease, till the death of the former, which occurred a few years afterwards, when he was left by him, as a reward for his faithful services, the sum of £120 in money, his best horse, saddle, and all his wearing apparel.

Our hero, who was only in his seventeenth year, being now his own master, employed himself in such country work as offered for the succeeding seven years, when, thinking he had acquired sufficient means to enable him to settle respectably in life, he married the daughter of a substantial planter, and was presented by his father-in-law with a deed of gift of a tract of land, comprising about 200 acres, situated on the frontiers of the province of Pennsylvania.

On this property there was a good house, which he furnished; and having stocked his farm, he sat down with the prospect of leading a peaceable and happy life—but these prospects were soon destroyed. As Williamson was sitting up one night later than usual, expecting the return of his wife, who had gone on a visit to her relations, he was suddenly alarmed by hearing the well-known and fatal war-whoop of the Indians. These dreadful sounds proceeded from a party of savages, to the number of twelve, who had surrounded his house for the purpose of robbery and murder. On hearing the ominous cry, Williamson seized a loaded gun, and at first endeavoured to scare away his horrible assailants, who were now attempting to beat in the door, by threatening to fire on them. But heedless of his menaces, and in their turn threatening to set fire to his house and burn him alive if he did not instantly surrender, he at length yielded, and, on promise of having his life spared, came out as they desired. Having got the unfortunate man into their power, the savages bound him to a tree, near his own door, plundered his house, and then set it on fire, together with his outhouses, barns, and stables, consuming all his grain, cattle, horses, and sheep; and thus, almost instantaneously, reducing him from a state of independence and comfort to one of beggary and misery. Having completed their diabolical work, one of the savages, advancing with uplifted tomahawk, threatened him with instant death if he did not cheerfully and willingly accompany them. Having consented to what he could not resist, they untied him, and loading him with the plunder of his own house, set off on their march homeward.

At daybreak, after having travelled all night, the savages ordered Williamson to lay down his load, when they again tied him to a tree by the hands, and so tightly, that the small cord by which he was bound forced the blood from his finger-ends. The wretches then kindled a fire close by their victim, who had no doubt that it was intended to roast him alive, and began dancing around him with the most hideous yells and gestures. Having satisfied themselves with this pastime, they each snatched a stick from the fire, and began to apply their burning ends to various parts of his body, causing him the greatest torture. Of this cruelty they at length tired, and unbinding the wretched captive, gave him a portion of some victuals which they had hastily cooked. They then again fastened him to a tree, to which they kept him bound till night, when they resumed their march, loading him with their booty as before. The savages now proceeded towards the Blue Hills, where, having hid their plunder, they attacked the house of a settler named Snider, and, having found admission, they scalped himself, his wife, and five children, and finally set fire to their dwelling, having previously plundered it. The only individual spared was a young man, a servant in the house, whom they thought might be useful to them. Having perpetrated this atrocious deed, they loaded Williamson and the young man whose life they had spared with their booty, and again directed their steps towards the Blue Hills.

During the march, Williamson's companion in misfortune continuing, notwithstanding all the former could say to him, to bemoan his situation so loudly as to attract the notice of the savages, one of them came up to him, and struck the unhappy young man a blow on the head with his tomahawk, which instantly killed him. They then scalped him, and left him where he fell.

The savages next proceeded to the house of another settler named Adams, where they perpetrated similar atrocities, murdering his wife and four children, burning his house, corn, hay, and cattle. Adams himself, however, a feeble old man, they reserved for further cruelties. Having loaded him with the plunder of his own house, he was marched along with them, and on their arriving at the Great Swamp, where they remained for eight or nine days, was subjected to every species of torture which savage ingenuity could suggest. At one time they amused themselves by pulling the old man's beard out by the root; at another, by tying him to a tree, and flogging him with great severity; and again, scorching his face and legs with red-hot coals. While in this encampment, the savages with whom Williamson was captive were joined by another party, who brought along with them three prisoners and twenty scalps.

These unhappy men, who gave Williamson and his companion in misfortune, Adams, the most shocking accounts of the barbarities that had been practised by the party into whose hands they had fallen, having subsequently attempted to escape, were retaken, and put to the most cruel deaths.

From their present quarters the savages, still carrying Williamson along with them, proceeded two hundred miles farther into the interior, where their wigwams, wives, and children were. Here Williamson was detained for two months, suffering severely from cold and hunger, as the Indians paid no attention to his comforts, but left him to shift for himself as he best could, always taking care, however, that he should not escape them. At length another expedition against the whites having been determined on, the Indians, who, by various additions to their numbers, now amounted to about 150, began their march, taking Williamson along with them towards the back parts of the province of Pennsylvania.

On arriving at the Blue Hills, Williamson was left there with ten Indians, it not being deemed safe to take him nearer the plantations, to await the return of the main body. Here Williamson began to meditate an escape, and watching an opportunity one night when his guards were asleep, having previously assured himself that they were so, by gently touching their feet as they lay around the fire, he softly withdrew, after having vainly attempted to possess himself of one of their guns, which they always kept beneath their heads when they slept. Williamson's terror was so great lest he should be discovered, that he stopped as he was retreating every four or five paces, and looked fearfully towards the spot where his savage masters were lying; seeing, however, no motion amongst them, he gradually mended his pace, and had gained a considerable distance, when he suddenly heard the war-cry of the savages, who had missed their captive, and were now in pursuit of him.

The terror of Williamson, on hearing these appalling sounds, increased his speed. He rushed wildly on through woods and over rocks, falling and bruising himself severely, and cutting his feet and legs in a miserable manner; but he eventually succeeded in eluding the vigilance of his pursuers. Continuing his flight until daybreak, he then crept into the hollow of a tree, but was here again alarmed by hearing the voices of the savages in his immediate vicinity, loudly talking of how they should treat him if he again fell into their hands. They, however, did not discover him, and soon after left the spot.

Williamson remained in his concealment till nightfall, when he again set out on his perilous journey, hiding himself in trees by day, and prosecuting his march by night. On one occasion during his route, he unknowingly approached so near a bivouac of savages, that the rustling he made amongst the trees alarmed them, when, starting from the ground and seizing their arms, they began to search around for the cause of the noise they had heard. Fortunately for Williamson, who stood stock-still, petrified with fear, a herd of wild swine at this critical moment made their appearance near the spot, when the savages thinking that they had been the cause of their alarm, gave up their search and returned to their fire. On observing this, Williamson recommenced his journey, and finally arrived in safety at his father-in-law's, on the 4th January, 1755, where he learned that his wife had died two months before.

Soon after his arrival, Williamson was called before the State Assembly, then sitting at Philadelphia, discussing measures for checking the depredations of the savages, to communicate such intelligence regarding them as his experience had put him in possession of, and ultimately entered himself a volunteer in one of the regiments raised to serve against the French and Indians.

In this service, during which he was engaged in numerous skirmishes, he remained three years, having previously obtained the rank of Lieutenant, when he was taken prisoner by the French on the surrender of Oswego, marched to Quebec with other prisoners, and there embarked, according to stipulation, on board the La Renomme, a French packet-boat, for Plymouth, where he arrived on the 6th of November, 1756. In about five months after, Williamson, with a party who had been quartered with him at Kingsbridge, were ordered to Plymouth Dock to be drafted into other regiments, but on being inspected he was found unfit for service, in consequence of a wound he had received in one of his hands, and was discharged.

On receiving his discharge, Williamson, who was now entirely destitute of means, being possessed of no more than six shillings, which had been allowed by Government to carry him home, proceeded to York. He there submitted the manuscript of his adventures amongst the Indians to some benevolent persons, who recommended its publication, and having by this means raised a little money, he set out for Aberdeen, where he arrived in June, 1758. But although now in his native place, his misfortunes had not yet terminated.

The little volume of his adventures which he had published at York, contained some reflections on the characters of the merchants of Aberdeen, implicating them in the practice of kidnapping, of which Williamson had himself been a victim. He had no sooner offered the work for sale in the traduced city, than he was called before the magistrates to answer to a complaint of libel on the character and reputation of the merchants of Aberdeen ; and he was ordered to sign a recantation, of what they called his calumnies, on pain of imprisonment, and was appointed to find caution to stand trial on the complaint, at any time when called for, and to be confined in jail till performance.

To this judgment was added an order, that all his books should be forthwith lodged in the clerk's chamber. His books were accordingly seized, the offensive leaves cut out, and burned at the market-cross by the hands of the common hangman. Williamson was subsequently amerced in the sum of ten shillings, and finally banished the city as a vagrant.

By the advice and assistance of some friends, however, he afterwards raised a process of oppression and damages against the magistrates of Aberdeen before the Court of Session, and ultimately obtained damages to the amount of £100, with all the costs of process.

Previously to his obtaining this judgment, Williamson had settled in Edinburgh, where he first kept a tavern, then became a bookseller, printer, publisher, and projector. He appears some time before this to have published in York, " Some Considerations on the present State of Affairs ; wherein the defenceless situation of Great Britain is pointed out, and an easy, rational, and just scheme for its security at this dangerous crisis proposed in a Militia, formed on an equal plan, that can neither be oppressive to the poor nor offensive to the rich, as practised by some of his Majesty's colonies abroad, &c. York ; printed for the author, and sold by all the booksellers in town, 1758," 8vo. pp. 56.

In 1762, he addressed the following letter to the Printers of the *Edinburgh Evening Courant :—*

" As the scarcity of hands on account of the present war, and, of consequence, the great increase of the price of labour, have been for some time a most general complaint in this much depopulated country, that person must surely deserve well of the public who shall discover a method to supply the one, and reduce the other. Now the season is approaching which is appointed by Providence to crown the labours of the year, and in which the industrious farmer hopes to reap the fruits of his toil. This penury of hands, in a climate so variable as Scotland, may soon be felt in the severest manner. The high prices of grain, and the prospect of a plentiful crop, are certainly very urgent motives for embracing every means that may facilitate the cutting down of the corns with speed and safety. It is with a view to remedy, in a great measure, this universal complaint that I communicate, through the channel of your paper, my having, at a considerable expense, invented a machine, which I am able to demonstrate will, in the hands of a single man, do more execution in a field of oats in one day, and to better purpose, than it is in the power of six shearers to do. This machine is now completed, and is constructed in such a manner, that where the corn is tolerably thick, it will cut down near a sheaf at a stroke, and that without shaking the grain or disordering the straw, besides laying down the corn as regularly as the most expert shearer is capable to do. It is attended with another advantage, that the sun in a short time will so dry the grass and weeds, as well as win the straw and corn, that it may be fit either for putting into the stack or carrying into the barn. It is not from any principle of vanity or conceit that I have expatiated on the properties of this machine. My sole aim by this letter is, to intimate my invention to the honourable society for the encouragement of arts, sciences, &c., to any of whom I am ready to show the machine; and, if they should think proper, give them ocular demonstrations of its answering the purposes intended, by my own hands. At the same time, if they shall approve of it, and be of opinion that it may in a great degree contribute to remove the grievance complained of, I have reason to hope that the Society will not withhold a suitable encouragement for the invention. In that event, I propose, for a moderate premium, to instruct any overseer, or principal servant on a farm, how to handle the machine, so that he may with his own hands cut down several acres of corn in a day. I am, Gentlemen, yours, &c.

"*July*, 1762. "PETER WILLIAMSON,

"Author of a book entitled, 'French and Indian Cruelty, exemplified in the Life and various vicissitudes of Fortune of the said Peter Williamson, who was carried off from Aberdeen in his infancy, and sold as a Slave in Pennsylvania. Containing the History of the Author's Adventures in North America; his Captivity among the Indians, etc. To which is added an Account of the Proceedings of the Magistrates of Aberdeen against him, on his return to Scotland: a brief History of the Process against them before the Court of Session; and a short Dissertation on Kidnapping. Sold by the Author, at his Shop, in the Parliament House, and the other Booksellers in town and country, price 1s. 6d. sewed, and 2s. bound. This book is illustrated with a new and correct whole-sheet Map of America; likewise adorned with a fine copperplate Frontispiece, representing the Author in the habit of a Delaware Indian.' Commissions from the country will be punctually answered for this and all other sorts of books; as also stationery ware of all sorts. Where is likewise to be had, a 'General View of the whole World; containing the names of the principal Countries, Kingdoms, States, and Islands; their Length, Breadth, and Capital Cities, with the Longitude and Latitude; also the Produce, Revenue, Strength, and Religion of each Country, price 6d.'"

An engraving of this "machine" is given in one of the magazines of the day. It is now in use under the name of a basket-scythe.

The following advertisement by Peter (April 9, 1772) is amusing enough:—"This day was published, price one shilling the pack, and sold by Peter Williamson, printer, in the head of Forrester's Wynd, Edinburgh, the IMPENETRABLE SECRETS, which is called the PROVERB CARDS, containing excellent Sentiment, and are so composed that they discover the thoughts of one's mind in a very curious and extraordinary manner. The explanation of the Secret is given gratis with the pack: each set consists of twenty cards, and ten lines upon each card." He at the same time announces his "new invented portable printing presses," by which two folio pages may be printed with the greatest expedition and exactness. Next follow his stamps, and liquid for marking linen, books, etc., "which stands washing, boiling, and bleaching, and is more regular and beautiful than any needle." He concludes by intimating that he has a large and commodious tavern to let.

In the year 1776, Williamson engaged in a periodical work, after the manner of the *Tatler* and *Spectator*, called *The Scots Spy, or Critical Observer*, published every Friday. Complete copies of this curious production, which forms a volume of upwards of three hundred pages, are now very rare. It is chiefly valuable for local information, although some of the papers are by no means deficient in merit. It commences on the 8th of March, 1776, and terminates on the 30th August following. In 1777 (August 29), he began *The New Scots Spy, or Critical Observer*, which, having met with less patronage than its predecessor, was abandoned on the 14th November following. This latter volume is also very scarce. The late Mr. Archibald Constable, who thought all "his geese were swans," had both works, which he valued at five guineas!

In the month of November, 1777, he married Jean Wilson, daughter of John Wilson, bookseller in Edinburgh, a connection which, as will immediately be seen, turned out to be a very unfortunate one.

Williamson had the merit of establishing the first Penny Post in Edinburgh. He also published a Directory, "which he sold at his General Penny-Post Office, Luckenbooths." The copy before us, for 1788, is dedicated to the Lord Provost and Magistrates of Edinburgh; and the following dedicatory epistle is prefixed:—

"My LORDS AND GENTLEMEN,—At the earnest request of a respectable part of the inhabitants of Edinburgh, I have been induced once more to make an actual survey of the city and its much-extended suburbs, and to publish a Directory for the present year.

"The patronage I have always received from the Magistrates of Edinburgh I acknowledge with gratitude; and I flatter myself they will approve of the present publication.

"That the city may flourish to the remotest ages—that the noble efforts made by the present Chief Magistrate for its embellishment, the convenience of its inhabitants, and for the desirable object of making the port and harbour of Leith (so intimately connected with the city) more extensive and commodious for trade, may be crowned with success—is the sincere wish of,

"My Lords and Gentlemen,

"Your most obedient humble servant,

P. WILLIAMSON."

At this period his wife and daughter appear to have contributed their assistance to the maintenance of the family, as the following notice is printed on the cover of the Directory:—

"MRS. WILLIAMSON AND DAUGHTER,

at their House, first fore stair above the head of Byre's Close, Luckenbooths, Engraft Silk, Cotton, Thread, and Worsted Stockings, make Silk Gloves, and every article in the Engrafting branch, in the neatest manner, and on the most reasonable terms; likewise Silk Stockings washed in the most approved stile; also, Grave Cloaths made on the shortest notice.

"*N.B.*—Mantua-Making carried on in all its branches as formerly. Orders given in at P. Williamson's General Penny-Post Office, Luckenbooths, will be punctually attended to."

From a process of divorce which he instituted in the year 1789 against his wife, and in which he was successful, it appears that but for the gross misbehaviour of the former, he might have attained pretty easy circumstances.

The Procurator for the defender, in the case just alluded to, represents his Penny-post as being a very lucrative business, bringing him in ready money every hour of the day, and employing four men to distribute the letters at four shillings and sixpence weekly each.

In his replies, Williamson alleges that his income was but trifling; that his Directory paid him very poorly; and that his wife robbed him of three-fourths of the profit of the post. In corroboration of this state of his finances, he pursued the divorce, as a litigant, on the poor's roll.

It may be added that the opposing party hinted at Peter's having acquired tippling habits; but it is impossible to attach any credit to a statement evidently made for the purpose of creating a prejudice in the minds of the judges against him.

The following notice of his death occurs in a newspaper of the period, 19th January, 1799:—

"At Edinburgh, Mr. Peter Williamson, well known for his various adventures through life. He was kidnapped when a boy at Aberdeen, and sent to America, for which he afterwards recovered damages. He passed a considerable time among the Cherokees, and on his return to Edinburgh amused the public with a description of their manners and customs, and his adventures among them, assuming the dress of one of their chiefs, imitating the war-whoop, &c. He had the merit of first instituting a Penny-post in Edinburgh, for which, when it was assumed by Government, he received a pension. He also was the first who published a Directory, so essentially useful in a large city."

From the intimation that he received a pension from Government, we should hope the latter days of this very enterprising and singular person were not embittered by penury.

WILLIAM MARTIN,

Bookseller and Auctioneer.

MARTIN, or "Bibles" as he was commonly called, is supposed to have been born at or near Airdrie, about the year 1744; and like his contemporary, Lackington of London, was originally bred a shoemaker. He used to boast that he was in *arms* during the Rebellion 1745. For several years after he came to Edinburgh, Martin occupied a small shop in the High Street, near the head of the West Bow, where he combined the two very opposite professions of bookseller and cobbler. He also frequented the country towns around Edinburgh on fairs and other market-days, exposing his small stock of books for sale; and, by dint of great perseverance and industry, was soon able to withdraw his allegiance from Crispin altogether, and to devote the whole of his attention to the sale of books.

It is uncertain at what period Martin came to Edinburgh. His

burgess-ticket is dated 1786—but he must have been well established
in business many years previously. From a letter of condolence
written by him to the widow of his brother, who died in America, he
appears to have been in thriving circumstances so early as 1782. He
says, "The awfully sudden and unfortunate death of my brother—the
helpless situation in which you were left, and so many fatherless children—situate in a country surrounded with war and devastation, my
thoughts thereupon may be more easily conceived than described.
. . . My uneasiness has been much increased by the thoughts of
the boy coming to me, that I might receive him safely, and that he
might escape the dangers of so long a voyage. Indeed it has been
the will of Providence to take all my children from me, and my intention is to adopt him (his nephew) as my own son. My situation in
business I have no cause to complain of. I have a shop in the book-
selling way in the Lawnmarket of Edinburgh, to which occupation
I mean to put William, my namesake, and in which I hope he will do
very well. I will give him the best education, and he shall be as well
clothed as myself. . . . My wife has been very much indisposed
for some time bypast, and is not yet much better. She is most anxious
about William, and wishes much to see him, from which you may
conclude his arrival would make us both very happy." The letter
from which the foregoing extract is taken, is dated June 2, 1782, and
directed to "Mrs. Martin, relict of Captain Martin, to the care of Mr.
William Pagan, merchant, New York." The nephew, for whom he
expresses so much anxiety, arrived safe in Scotland, and continued
with him for several years, but returning to America, died not long
after. His wife also, whose bad health he mentions, did not long
survive.

Amid these severe domestic afflictions, Martin's business continued
to flourish. Finding his old place of business too small, he removed
to more commodious apartments in Gourlay's Land, Old Bank Close,
in one of the large rooms of which he held his auction-mart. Here
he seems to have been eminently successful. In 1789, he purchased
these premises from the trustee for the creditors of the well-known
William Brodie, cabinet-maker; and in 1792 the fame of his prosperity was so great as to attract the notice of a perpetrator of verses,
of the name of Galloway, by whom he is associated with "King
Lackington" of London, in the following *immortal* epistle. The
subject of this exquisite *effort of genius* will be sufficient apology for
its insertion. The author, GEORGE GALLOWAY, was born in Scotland
on the 11th of October, 1757. He was bred a mechanic—then turned
musician—next went to sea, and was taken prisoner by the Spaniards.
After a lapse of many years he returned to London, and there set
about courting the Muses, having been rendered unfit for mechanical
labour, owing to weakness of vision caused by long confinement
abroad. While living in the capital he produced material for the
volume from which the epistle is selected. In justice to George, we
must say that his address to "Lackington and brother Martin" is
the worst in the collection. He was the author of two plays, "*The
Admirable Chrichton; a tragedy in five acts. Edin.*, 1802, 12mo;"
and "*The Battle of Luncarty, or the Valiant Hays triumphant over*

the Danish Invaders; a drama in five acts. Edin., 1804, 12mo "—
the perusal of which will afford a treat to those who have any perception of the ludicrous. The last production from his pen that we have
seen is an "*Elegy on the Death of Henry, Duke of Buccleuch.*
Edin., 1812, 8vo;" which is stated "to be printed for and sold by
the Author":—

> "TO MESSRS. LACKINGTON AND MARTIN, BOOKSELLERS."
>
> "Honour and fame from no condition rise,
>   Act well thy part, there all thy honour lies."—POPE.

> "While booksellers jog in *Newmarket haste*,
> Racing with Crispins for the bankrupt list;
> Hail! then, King LACKINGTON, and brother MARTIN,
> Fate's doom'd thee to survive the wreck for certain.
> When you relinquished being *shoe-retailers*,
> You shunn'd the dangerous rocks of leather-dealers;
> Now, now, your BURNS, your MORRISSES, and PINDARS,
> The product of their brain to you surrenders.
> For which, *one* word, you've often sworn and said it,
> You utterly abhor what *fools give—credit!*
> Thus, you're the blades who can extract the honey,
> For all your creed's in *two* words, '*ready money.*'
> Now *eunuch-built* booksellers all conivell,
> And with thee tumbled headlong to the devil.
> Sell, brother Crispins, sell (and spurn their clamour),
> Quick as your *welt-eye*, or the auction hammer;
> While others write, till eyes drop from their sockets,
> Racking their brain for gold to line your pockets.
> Since Heav'n has cut and form'd thee out for gain,
> And fate has fixed thee in the *richest vein;*
> Led by Dame Fortune, that blind fickle b——h,
> Who's *smit* you with the whilie silver itch,
> Selling what hungry authors coin in heaps,
> Supporting printers' presses, and their types.
> Now since you've rais'd yourselves by your own *merit*,
> *Deil take them who envy what you inherit.*"

About 1793, Mr. Martin sold his premises in Gourlay's Land to the
Bank of Scotland, when he removed to 94 South Bridge, where he
continued for a number of years. Not long after this he bought the
Golf-House, at the east end of Bruntsfield Links, as a private residence, where he resided for several years. In 1806 Martin moved to
No. 2 Lothian Street, but in a year or two after retired altogether
from business, and died in the month of February, 1820, nearly eighty
years of age.

He was twice married, and by his first wife had several children;
but as he mentions himself, in the letter already alluded to, they died
in infancy. His second wife (to whom he was married in December,
1788) was a Miss Katherine Robertson, daughter of Mr. Robertson,
schoolmaster in Ayr. She had a brother many years surgeon in the
42nd Highlanders. Mrs. Martin survived her husband about seven
years; and at her death, his nephews in America received a sum equal
to the half of his estate, and her brother received the remainder.

While in his auction-room, Martin was full of anecdote and humour, but somewhat fond of laughing at his own jokes. "He is apt," says Mr. Kay, "to grin and laugh at his own jests, and the higher that prices are bid for his prints, the more he is observed to laugh and the wider to grin." Martin (nothing to his discredit, considering his humble origin), was somewhat illiterate—at least he was no classical scholar—and perhaps in the course of his business he frequently suffered by his ignorance of the dead languages. Owing to ignorance, he sold many valuable Greek and Latin books for mere trifles. Sometimes when at a loss to read the title of a Latin or French book, he would, if he could find a young student near him, thrust the book before him, saying, "Read that, my man; it's sae lang since I was at the College I hae forgotten a' my Latin." If the book he was about to sell happened to be Greek, his usual introduction was— "Here comes *crawtaes*, or whatever else you like to call it;" and on other occasions, if the volume happened to be in a more modern language, but the title of which he was as little able to read, he would say to the students, after a blundering attempt, "Gentlemen, I am rather rusty in my French, but were it *Hebrew, ye ken* I would be quite at hame!" Having one night made even a more blundering attempt than usual to unriddle the title of a French book, a young dandy, wishing to have another laugh at Martin's expense, desired him to read the title of the book again, as he did not know what it was about. "Why," said Martin, "it's something about manners, and that's what neither you nor me has owre muckle o'."

Martin, however, was certainly more "at hame" in some instances than he was either in French, Latin, Greek, or Hebrew. On one occasion, at the time *Manfredo* was performing in Edinburgh, Martin, in the course of his night's labour, came across the "Life of Robinson Crusoe." Holding up the volume, and pointing to the picture of Robinson's man, *Friday*, he exclaims, "Weel, gentlemen, what will ye gi'e me for my *Man-Fredo?*—worth a dizen o' the Italian land-louper." Manfredo, who happened to be present, became exceedingly wroth at this allusion to him. "Vad do you say about Manfredo? Call *me* de land-loupeur!" Nothing disconcerted by this unexpected attack, Martin again holding up the picture, replied—"I'll refer to the company if my *Man-Fredo* is no worth a dizen o' him! The Italian fumed and fretted, but, amidst the general laughter, was obliged to retire.

In these days "rockings" in the country, and parties in the town, were very frequent. On such occasions the auctioneer was wont to be extremely merry, and seldom failed to recite in his best style "The Edinburgh Buck," by Robert Fergusson. He used also to sing tolerably well the ballad of "Duncan Gray." This seldom failed to be forthcoming—more particularly when a tea-party surrounded his own fireside. In this there was perhaps a little touch of domestic pride— at least, the second Mrs. Martin always thought so. During courtship, some trifling misunderstanding had taken place—

> " Maggie coost her head fu' heigh,
> Look'd asklent an' unco skeigh,
> Gart poor Duncan stand abeigh."

But Martin, like the famed Duncan, cooled, and discontinued his visits for some time, till Katherine "grew sick as he grew hale," and at last condescended to let the bookseller know her surprise why he had discontinued his visits. Martin, who had been, like his favourite, " a lad o' grace "—

> " Couldna' think to be her death;
> Swelling pity smoor'd his wrath."

So he accordingly resumed his visits, and Katie became his wife, being "crouse an' canty baith;" but she never could endure the song of "Duncan Gray."

Of Mr. Martin's social habits, perhaps the best proof is the fact of his being a member of the "Cape Club." The Cape Club comprised, amongst its numerous members, many men of talents, and of private worth. Fergusson (who alludes to the Club in his poem of " Auld Reekie ") was a member; as were Mr. Thomas Summers, his friend and biographer; Wood, the Scottish Roscius, as he was called; and Runciman, the painter. The Club derived its name from the following circumstance:—" A person who lived in the suburbs of Calton was in the custom of spending an hour or two every evening with one or two city friends; and, being sometimes detained till after the regular period when the Netherbow Port was shut, it occasionally happened that he had either to remain in the city all night, or was under the necessity of bribing the porter who attended the gate. This difficult *pass*, partly on account of the rectangular corner which he turned, immediately on getting out of the Port, as he went homewards down Leith Wynd, and partly, perhaps (if the reader will pardon a very humble pun), because a *nautical* idea was most natural and appropriate on the occasion of being *half-seas over*, the Calton burgher facetiously called doubling the Cape; and it was customary with his friends, every evening when they assembled, to inquire " how he turned the Cape last night."

The Club, on the 22nd September, 1770 (the birth-day of the author of " The Seasons "), held a musical festival in honour of the poet, and resolved to have similar meetings every tenth year. Accordingly, in the years 1780, 1790, and 1800, under the superintendence of Mr. Wood, who composed and recited verses on the occasion, the entertainments were repeated with increased effect.

In 1780, when letters of marque were issued against the Dutch, the Knights of the Cape, at a very thin meeting of their Order, on the 26th December, subscribed two hundred and fifty guineas towards fitting out a privateer.

His diploma of knighthood is as follows:—" Be it known to all mortals whether clerical or laical, that we, Sir James Gray, Knight of Kew, the supereminent sovereign of the most capital knighthood of the Cape, having nothing more sincerely at heart than the glory and honour of this most noble Order, and the happiness and prosperity of the Knights-Companions: And being desirous of extending the benign and social influence of the Order to every region under the grand Cape of Heaven; being likewise well informed and fully satisfied with the abilities and qualifications of William Martin, Esq., with the advice and concurrence of our Council—We do create, admit, and receive him a Knight-Companion of the most social Order, by the name, style, and title of *Sir William Martin*, Knight of Roger, and of E. F. D.—Hereby giving and granting unto him all the powers, privileges, and pre-eminences that do, or may belong to this most social Order. And we give command to our Recorder to registrate this our patent in the Records of the Order, in testimony of the premises. We have subscribed this with our own proper *fist*, and have caused appended the Great Seal of the Order.—At Cape Hall, this 20th day of the month called October, in the year of grace 1792. (Signed)—BED, Deputy-Sovereign.—Entered into the Records of the Order by Sir CELLAR, Recorder.—L. Box, Secretary."

The "Great Seal of the Order," enclosed in a tin-box, has the letters "E. F. D.," surmounted by a coronet, enclosed with laurel, and the whole encircled with the words—" Sigillum communé Equitum de Cape—Concordiæ fratrum decus."

So much for the good-fellowship of the "grinning auctioneer." Besides being a burgess, he was a member of the Society of Booksellers, and of the Merchant Company of Edinburgh. He was also a member of the Kirk-Session of the Parish of St. Cuthbert's.

The late Mr. Archibald Constable prevailed on Martin to sit for an hour to Mr. Geddes, portrait painter; but the sketch was never finished, as he could not be induced to sit again. Although rough, it is a capital likeness, and was bought at Mr. Constable's sale by a friend of "the Knight of Roger."

WILLIAM MACPHERSON, ESQ.,

Writer to the Signet.

MR. WILLIAM MACPHERSON, whose father was sometime deacon of the masons in Edinburgh, was a Writer to the Signet, and, in many respects, a man of very eccentric habits. He lived in that famed quarter of the city, the West Bow, three stairs up, in a tenement which immediately joined the city wall, and looked towards the west, but which has been recently removed to make way for the improvements now in progress, and which have all but annihilated the Bow. Mr. Macpherson continued a bachelor through life, and seemed from many circumstances to have conceived a determined antipathy to the "honourable state of matrimony." He had two maiden sisters who kept house with him; but whether they entertained similar prejudices, or remained single from necessity, we do not pretend to know. The bachelor respected his sisters very much, although in his freaks he called the one *Sodom*, and the other *Gomorrah*.

Like most of his contemporary lords of the quill, Macpherson possessed many "social qualities;" but he quaffed so deeply and so long, that towards night he seldom found his way up the High Street in a state short of total inebriety. On arriving at the West Bow, and when he came to the bottom of the stair, he used to bellow to *Sodom* or *Gomorrah* to come down and help up their *drunken brother*, which they never failed to do ; and, for additional security in such cases, it is said he generally ascended the stair *backwards*.

Notwithstanding his potations, Macpherson maintained for some time a degree of respectability, at least, consistent with the laxity of the times. When associating with the more respectable *bon vivants* of these his better days, his favourite saying, before tossing off his glass of claret, of which he was very fond, used to be, " Here goes another peck of potatoes." A glass of claret was then equal in price to a peck of potatoes. The origin of this saying is attributed to Mr. Creech, bookseller, but afterwards became a standing remark with Macpherson. Macpherson at length became, we regret to say, a habitual drunkard. A loss of respectability in his profession was the consequence ; and from the practice which he followed of signing Signet letters for very small sums of money, and other low habits of business, inconsistent with the dignity of the Society, his professional brethren at last urged him to retire upon an annuity. This, however, his pride would never allow him to consent to ; and he continued a member of the Society of Writers to the Signet till the day of his death.

No case, however trifling—no client, however poor or disreputable, was latterly beneath the legal aid of Macpherson ; and no mode of payment, whether in goods or currency, was deemed unworthy of acceptance. As an instance of his practice, he was seen one day very tipsy, plodding his way up the West Bow from the Grassmarket, with an armful of " neeps" (turnips), which he had obtained from some green-stall keeper, in remuneration for legal services performed. Not being able to maintain a proper equilibrium, his occasional " bickers" at last unsettled his burthen ; one or two of the turnips, like Newton's apple, found the centre of gravity, and in attempting to recover these, nearly the whole of his armful trundled down the causeway. Macpherson, determined not to lose what might otherwise contribute much to a favourite dinner, coolly, and as steadily as possible, set about collecting the turnips, and actually succeeded, to the astonishment of every one, in accomplishing his object. On arriving with his load at the accustomed stair-foot, he shouted, as usual, for *Sodom* and *Gomorrah* to render assistance ; and by their aid he and his cargo eventually reached his apartments in safety.

There is another amusing anecdote told of this decayed, but still independent lawyer. The Governor of Edinburgh Castle had been in want of a respectable cook, and applied to Mr. Creech, the bookseller, to do what he could to procure one. Creech having found some difficulty in fulfilling the commission, felt considerably annoyed by the frequent messages from the Castle concerning the much-wanted cook. One day the Governor's black lackey came into the shop to make the usual inquiry. The Bailie observed Macpherson pass the door at the moment, and determined to get rid of his black tormentor by any means, directed Mungo's attention to the bacchanalian, who happened to be sober at the time, it being then early in the forenoon. The servant, assured that Macpherson was a cook in want of a situation, marched boldly after the lawyer, and giving him a gentle tap on the shoulder, said " The Governor wants to see you at the Castle."— " Just now ?" inquired Macpherson, his countenance brightening up with the anticipation of something to his advantage.—" Soon as possible," said Mungo.

Macpherson immediately returned to the West Bow, cropped his beard of three days' standing, and, assisted by *Sodom* and *Gomorrah*, prepared for the appointment. His sisters were equally on the tiptoe of expectation as to what the Governor could possibly be wanting in such haste. Macpherson made various conjectures, but in vain. Every suggestion appeared to him unlikely, save the commencement of some important process, which nothing but his superior talents could have pointed him out as the proper person to undertake. Brushed up, and bedecked in something like the style of his better days, the renovated Writer to the Signet hurried to the Castle, and was ushered into—the *lobby !* where, to his astonishment, he was desired to wait till the Governor came. This, to a W.S., was the reverse of courtesy; but he naturally supposed the apparent incivility arose from the ignorance of the lackey, and imagined the mistake would soon be rectified by the Governor himself. The Governor came. "Well, have you got a character?" was his first salutation. "A character!" said Macpherson, astonished beyond measure at such a question being put to a *lawyer.* "Why, what do you mean by a character?"—"Have you *not* got a character?" repeated the Governor. "To be sure I've got a character!" replied Macpherson, still more astonished. "Where is it, then—can't you show it?" "Show it!" reiterated the lawyer, his bluff cheeks colouring with a sense of insult, "there's not a gentleman in Edinburgh but knows me!" "That may be," said the Governor, "but no one should presume to ask a place without having a character in his pocket." "The d——l take the place—what place have I solicited?—why, I was sent for to speak with the Governor." "What are you?" said the latter, at last conceiving the possibility of a mistake. "I'm a Writer to the Signet," answered Macpherson, with corresponding dignity of manner. "Writer to the Signet! astonishing—this is all a mistake—*I wanted a Cook!*" "Confound you and your cook both!" vociferated the indignant W.S., turning on his heel and hurrying off to drown his mortification in a meridian libation. Nothing so easily irritated Macpherson in after times as any allusion to this unlucky incident.

There was one redeeming virtue in the character of Macpherson rarely to be found in professional men, and least of all in such a character as himself, which speaks more than language can do for the natural goodness of his heart. Rather than allow any person whom he had been employed to prosecute to be put in jail, he has been frequently known to advance the sum himself, even when he had not the most distant chance of repayment.

Mr. Macpherson died on the 9th of May, 1814. His sister, *Sodom*, died in Gillespie's Hospital in 1837.

ALEXANDER WOOD,

Surgeon.

THE pencil of Kay has done justice to the memory of this eminent surgeon and very excellent man, by the production of two striking portraits of him. The first possesses the real octogenarian demeanour of the "kind old Sandy Wood," who is represented as passing along the North Bridge with an umbrella under his arm, in allusion to the circumstance of his having been the first person in Edinburgh who made use of that very convenient article—now so common.

Mr. Wood's father was the youngest son of Mr. Wood of Warriston, in Midlothian—now the property of the Earl of Morton. He long possessed a house and grounds, situated immediately to the north of Queen Street, and rented from the Town of Edinburgh, where Mr. Wood was born in the year 1725.

Mr. Wood completed his medical education in Edinburgh; and having taken out his diploma, he established himself at Musselburgh, where he practised successfully for some time. He then removed to Edinburgh, became a fellow of the Royal College of Surgeons, and entered into a copartnership with Messrs. Rattray and Congalton, men of eminence in their day, and to whose practice he subsequently succeeded.

Being gifted with strong natural talents, great tact, and an activity of mind and person rarely surpassed; and possessing a perfect simplicity and openness of character, with a singularly benevolent disposition and peculiar tenderness of heart, Mr. Wood soon rose to high professional celebrity.

Not long after connecting himself with Messrs. Rattray and Congalton, he married Miss Veronica Chalmers, second daughter of George Chalmers, Esq., W.S., an individual of great worth and respectability. In reference to this connection a very pleasing anecdote is told. Mr. Wood, on obtaining the consent of the lady, having proposed himself to Mr. Chalmers as his son-in-law, that gentleman addressed him thus: —" Sandy, I have not the smallest objection to you; but I myself am not rich, and *should*, therefore, like to know how you are to support a wife and family?" Mr. Wood put his hand into his pocket, drew out his lancet-case, and said, "I have nothing but this, sir, and a determination to use my best endeavours to succeed in my profession." His future father-in-law was so struck with this straightforward and honest reply, that he immediately exclaimed, "Vera is yours!"

Notwithstanding a certain bluntness and decision of manner, which was liable to be occasionally misunderstood, and which gave rise to some curious scenes and incidents in the course of his professional practice, Mr. Wood's philanthropy and kindness were proverbial; and his unremitting attention to the distresses of the indigent sick, whom he continued to visit in their wretched dwellings, after he had given up general practice, was a noble trait in his character. What has been said of the illustrious Boerhaave may be equally applied to him— " that he considered the poor as his best patients, and that he never

neglected them." To his other qualities he added an enthusiastic
warmth and steadiness in his friendships, with a total freedom from
selfishness—and, in his social relations, that kind and playful manner,
which softened asperities, and rendered available all the best sympa-
thies and affections of which human is susceptible; and being of a
most convivial disposition, his company was courted by all ranks. In
fact, few men have ever been so universally beloved as Mr. Wood, and
proportionally numerous are the testimonies to his worth.

During the long course of his useful career, he enjoyed the unanimous good will and approbation of his brethren, who, without any
jealous feelings, allowed him the palm of superiority he deservedly
merited—a tribute due not only to the soundness of his practical knowledge, and the dexterity of his skill in operating (which tended much
to raise the reputation of the surgical department of the Royal Infirmary), but to his personal character.

In a fragment of a fifth Canto of "Childe Harold," which appeared
in *Blackwood's Magazine* for May, 1818, he is thus alluded to:—

"Oh ! for an hour of him who knew no feud—
The octogenarian chief, the kind old Sandy Wood ;"

and, in a note on this stanza, he is spoken of as "Sandy Wood—one
of the delightful reminiscences of Old Edinburgh—who was at least
eighty years of age, when in high repute as a medical man he could
yet divert himself in his walks with the "Hie Schuil laddies," or bestow the relics of his universal benevolence in feeding a goat or a raven.

He is also alluded to in a spirit of tenderness and affection by Sir
Walter Scott, in a prophecy put into the mouth of Meg Merrilees:
"A gathering together of the powerful shall be made amidst the caves
of the inhabitants of Dunedin. Sandy is at his rest. They shall beset
his goat; they shall profane his raven; they shall blacken the buildings of the Infirmary ; her secrets shall be examined ; a new goat shall
bleat, until they have measured out and run over fifty-four feet nine
inches and a half." And the late celebrated John Bell, who had been
a pupil of Mr. Wood, dedicates to him his first volume of "Anatomy,"
in a concise but elegant tribute to his skill, his disinterested conduct,
and public and private virtues.

Mr. Wood's character is further commemorated by the late Sir
Alexander Boswell of Auchinleck, in these lines—part of an epitaph
composed by him on Mr. Wood:—

"But cold the heart that feels no genial glow,
Pondering on him whose ashes sleep below:
Whose vivid mind, with grasping power, could reach
Truths that the plodding schools can never teach.
Who scorned, in honesty, the specious wiles
Of dull importance, or of fawning smiles:
Who scouted feelings frittered and refined,
But had an ample heart for all mankind."

The following anecdote is a proof of Mr. Wood's popularity with
the lower classes. During a riot in Edinburgh, some of the mob,
mistaking him at night (owing to a great resemblance in figure) for
Sir James Stirling, then the Lord Provost of the City, and at that

time far from being a favourite, seized Mr. Wood on the North Bridge, and were going to throw him over the parapet, when he cried out, " I'm lang Sandy Wood—tak' me to a lamp and ye'll see." Instead of executing their vengeance, he was cordially cheered and protected from farther outrage.

Sir James and Mr. Wood, although thus in such different esteem with the lower class of the inhabitants of Edinburgh, were intimate friends. It is told of them, that on one occasion the Provost—with his cocked hat, and long spare figure—meeting the Doctor in the High Street, he jocularly put a guinea into his hand, and giving a piteous account of his sufferings from indigestion, and the state of his stomach, asked his advice. The Doctor—with a figure almost equally spare, and the same head-dress—retreated from the Provost, who continued to follow him, reproaching him for pocketing the money without giving him any opinion on his case. At last, after this scene had lasted some considerable space, Mr. Wood replied to Sir James's remonstrances :—" You're quite wrong, Sir James; I have been giving you the best possible advice all this while. If you'll take hold of my coat-tail, and only follow me for a week as you've been doing for the last ten minutes, you'll have no more trouble with your stomach."

Although very confident in his own practice, and very decided, Mr. Wood never failed to call in the aid of his professional brethren when there appeared to be real danger. The celebrated Dr. Cullen and he were frequently in attendance together, and on the most friendly and intimate footing. Upon one occasion they were in the sick room of a young nobleman of high promise, who was afflicted with a severe fever—the Doctor on one side of the bed, in his usual formal and important manner, counting the patient's pulse, with his large stop-watch in his hand—Mr. Wood on the other, and the parents anxiously waiting the result. The Doctor abruptly broke the silence—"We are at the crisis; in order to save him, these pills must be taken instantly," producing some from his waistcoat pocket. Mr. Wood, who had a real affection for the young Lord, shook his head significantly, and said with a smile, " O Doctor, Doctor, nature has already done her work, and he is saved. As to your pills—you may just as well gie him some pease meal." The young Lord, now a most distinguished and venerable Earl, tells this anecdote of his old friend, and always adds, that he remembers the whole scene as well as if it had happened yesterday.

A second Print represents Mr. Wood in the full possession of all that activity and fire for which he was distinguished in the hey-day of middle age. The cane is thrown smartly over his shoulder, while the whole bearing of the portrait is admirably illustrative of the bold and original character of the man.

In addition to the foregoing reminiscences, there are a few other characteristic anecdotes of Mr. Wood, which may with propriety be given here. The following humorous one has been related to us by a citizen of Edinburgh, then in his eighty-third year. This gentleman was at the time an apprentice to Deacon Thomson, a glover and breeches-maker by profession. The Deacon was a guzzling hypochondriacal sort of a genius, and, like many others of similar habits, was subject to much imaginary misery. One night he took it into his head that he was dying. Impressed with this belief, he despatched a messenger for Mr. Wood; but, being very impatient, and terrified that the "grim king" should seize him before the Doctor could come to his rescue, and suspecting that the messenger might dally with his mission, the dying breeches-maker started from the couch of anticipated dissolution, and went himself to the house of Mr. Wood. He knocked violently at the door, and, in a state of great perturbation, told the servant to hurry his master to his house, "For," continued he, "Deacon Thomson is just dying!" Having thus delivered his doleful mission, away hobbled the epicurean hypochondriac, anxious, from certain unpleasant suggestions which instinctively occurred to him, to get again into bed before the Doctor should arrive. In this wise resolution he was however baulked: Mr. Wood, although half undressed when he received the summons, lost no time in hastening off, and pushed past the Deacon just as he was threading his way up his own turnpike. "Oh, Doctor, it is me," said the hypochondriac. "You!" exclaimed the justly-indignant Sandy Wood, at the same time applying the cane to the back of his patient with the utmost good-will. He then left him to ascend the remainder of the stair with the accelerated motion which the application of this wholesome regimen inspired, and so effectual proved the cure, that our informant has frequently heard the Deacon mention the circumstance in presence of the Doctor.

Another ridiculous story is told of Mr. Wood. The Honourable Mrs. —— had taken a fancy to sit upon hens' eggs, in order that she might hatch chickens. Her relations becoming alarmed for her health, went to consult the Doctor on the subject, who, promising a perfect cure, desired them to make his compliments to their friend (with whom he was well acquainted), and tell her that he meant to have the pleasure of drinking tea with her that evening. The lady, resolving to do honour to her guest, ordered her servant to place her best set of china on the table, and to wheel it up opposite her nest. Mr. Wood made his appearance at the appointed hour, and having, with all due gravity, partaken of a dish of tea, he suddenly laid hold of a portion of the favourite tea-equipage, rushed towards the window, which he opened, and seemed about to throw the whole into the street. Mrs. ——, alarmed at the insane-like proceeding of her guest, flew to save the valuable china, when Mr. Wood, seizing the opportunity, *herried* the nest, and broke all the eggs. By this stratagem the whim of his patient was effectually put to flight.

Mr. Wood was an enthusiastic admirer of the great Mrs. Siddons. At her first visit to Edinburgh, many were the fainting and hysterical fits among the fairer portion of the audience. Indeed, they were so common that to be supposed to have escaped might almost have argued a want of proper feeling. One night, when the house had been thrown into confusion by repeated scenes of this kind, and when Mr. Wood was most reluctantly getting from the pit (the favourite resort of all the theatrical critics of that day) to attend some fashionable female, a friend said to him in passing, "This is glorious acting, Sandy," alluding to Mrs. Siddons; to which Mr. Wood answered, "Yes, and a d——d deal o't too," looking round at the fainting and screaming ladies in the boxes.

When routs were first introduced in Edinburgh, they were very formal affairs, being in no way congenial to the manners or temper of the people. At one of the first that had been given, by a person of distinction, the guests were painfully wearing away the time, stiffly ranged in rows along the sides of the room, and looking at each other, the very pictures of dulness and ennui, when Mr. Wood was announced, who, casting his eyes round him, proceeded up the empty space in the middle of the drawing-room, and then addressed the lady of the house, saying, " Well, my lady, will ye just tell me what we are all brought here to do?"—an inquiry which every one felt to be so perfectly appropriate that it was followed by a hearty laugh, which had the effect of breaking up the formality of the party, and producing general hilarity and cheerfulness for the rest of the evening.

If Mr. Wood's kindness of disposition widely diffused itself towards his fellow-creatures, young and old, he was almost equally remarkable for his love of animals. His pets were numerous, and of all kinds. Not to mention dogs and cats, there were two others that *individually* were better known to the citizens of Edinburgh—a sheep and a raven, the latter of which is alluded to by Sir Walter Scott, in the quotation which has been given from Guy Mannering. Willy, the sheep, pastured in the ground adjoining to the Excise Office, now the Royal Bank, and might be daily seen standing at the railings, watching Mr. Wood's passing to or from his house in York Place, when Willy used to poke his head into his coat-pocket, which was always filled with supplies for his favourite, and would then trot along after him through the town, and sometimes might be found in the houses of the Doctor's patients. The raven was domesticated at an ale and porter-shop in North Castle Street, which is still, or very lately was, marked by a tree growing from the area against the wall. It also kept upon the watch for Mr. Wood, and would recognize him even as he passed at some distance along George Street, and taking a low flight towards him, was frequently his companion during some part of his forenoon walks—for Mr. Wood never entered his carriage when he could possibly avoid it, declaring that unless a vehicle could be found that would carry him down the closes and up the turnpike stairs, they produced nothing but trouble and inconvenience.

It may be superfluous to state that the subject of these brief sketches was rarely spoken of as *Mr.* Wood, but as *Sandy* Wood. This general use of the Christian name, instead of the ordinary title, proceeded from a feeling the very opposite of disrespect. It was the result of that affection for his person with which his universal and inexhaustible benevolence and amiable character inspired all who knew him.

Mr. Wood continued to maintain that professional eminence which had been so early conceded to him, and was considered the unrivalled head of the surgical practice in his native city, till within a few years of his death, when increasing infirmities obliged him to retire. He died on the 12th of May, 1807, at the advanced age of eighty-two.

LORD BRAXFIELD,

Of the Court of Session.

THIS eminent lawyer and judge of the last century was born in 1722. His father, John M'Queen, Esq., of Braxfield, in the county of Lanark, was educated as a lawyer, and practised for some time; but he gave up business on being appointed Sheriff-Substitute of the Upper Ward of Lanarkshire. He was by no means wealthy, and, having a large family, no extravagant views of future advancement seem to have been entertained respecting his children. Robert, who was his eldest son, received the early part of his education at the grammar-school of the county town, and thereafter attended a course at the University of Edinburgh, with the view of becoming a writer to the signet.

In accordance with this resolution, young M'Queen was apprenticed to Mr. Thomas Gouldie, an eminent practitioner, and, during the latter period of his service, he had an opportunity of superintending the management of processes before the Supreme Court. Those faculties of mind which subsequently distinguished him both as a lawyer and a judge, were thus called into active operation; and feeling conscious of intellectual strength, he resolved to try his fortune at the bar. This new-kindled ambition by no means disturbed his arrangement with Mr. Gouldie, with whom he continued until the expiry of his indenture. In the meantime, however, he set about the study of the civil and feudal law, and very soon became deeply conversant in the principles of both, especially of the latter.

In 1744, after the usual trials, he became a member of the Faculty of Advocates. In the course of a few years afterwards, a number of questions arising out of the Rebellion in 1745, respecting the forfeited estates, came to be decided, in all of which M'Queen had the good fortune to be appointed counsel for the crown. Nothing could be more opportunely favourable for demonstrating the young advocate's talents than this fortuitous circumstance. The extent of knowledge which he displayed as a feudal lawyer, in the management of these cases—some of them of the greatest importance—obtained for him a degree of reputation which soon became for him substantially apparent in the rapid increase of his general practice. The easy unaffected manners of Mr. M'Queen also tended much to promote success. At those meetings called consultations, which, for many years after his admission to the bar, were generally held in taverns, he "peculiarly shone," both in legal and social qualifications. Ultimately his practice became so great, especially before the Lord Ordinary, that he has been repeatedly known to plead from fifteen to twenty causes in one day. Some idea of the influence and high character to which he had attained as an advocate, may be gathered from the couplet in the "Court of Session Garland," by Boswell:—

> " However of our cause not being ashamed,
> Unto the whole Lords we straightway reclaimed ;
> And our petition was appointed to be seen,
> *Because it was drawn by Robbie Macqueen.*"

THE GOOD SHALL MEET A BROTHER — ALL A FRIEND

SIR WILLIAM FORBES

[To face page 170

J. Kay del. & sculp: 178?

LORD BRAXFIELD

On the death of Lord Coalston, in 1766, Mr. M'Queen was elevated to the bench by the title of Lord Braxfield—an appointment, it is said, he accepted with considerable reluctance, being in receipt of a much larger professional income. He was prevailed upon, however, to accept the gown by the repeated entreaties of Lord President Dundas, and the Lord Advocate, afterwards Lord Melville. In 1780, he was appointed a Lord Commissioner of Justiciary; and, in 1787, was still more highly honoured by being promoted to the important office of Lord Justice-Clerk of Scotland. " Mr. M'Queen had contracted an intimacy with Mr. Dundas, afterwards Lord President of the Court of Session, and his brother, Lord Melville, at a very early period of life. The Lord President, when at the bar, married the heiress of Bonnington, an estate, situated within a mile of Braxfield. During the recesses of the Court, these eminent men used to meet at their country seats, and read and study law together. This intimacy, so honourable and advantageous to both, continued through life."

Lord Braxfield was equally distinguished on the bench as he had been at the bar. He attended to his duties with the utmost regularity, daily making his appearance in court, even during winter, by nine o'clock in the morning; and it seemed in him a prominent and honourable principle of action to mitigate the evils of the " law's delay," by a despatch of decision, which will appear the more extraordinary considering the number of causes brought before him while he sat as Judge Ordinary of the Outer House.

As Lord Justice-Clerk, he presided at the trials of Muir, Palmer, Skirving, Margarot, Gerrald, etc., in 1793-4. At a period so critical and so alarming to all settled governments, the situation of Lord Justice-Clerk was one of peculiar responsibility, and indeed of such a nature as to preclude the possibility of giving entire satisfaction. During this eventful period Lord Braxfield discharged what he conceived to be his duty with firmness, and in accordance to the letter and spirit of the law, if not always with that leniency and moderation which in the present day would have been esteemed essential.

The conduct of Lord Braxfield, during these memorable trials, has indeed been freely censured in recent times as having been distinguished by great and unnecessary severity ; but the truth is, he was extremely well fitted for the crises in which he was called on to perform so conspicuous a part ; for, by the bold and fearless front he assumed, at a time when almost every other person in authority quailed beneath the gathering storm, he contributed not a little to curb the lawless spirit that was abroad, and which threatened a repetition of that reign of terror and anarchy which so fearfully devastated a neighbouring country. But if the conduct of his lordship in those trying times was thus distinguished by high moral courage, that of the prisoners implicated in these transactions, it cannot be denied, was marked by equal firmness. During the trial of Skirving, this person conceiving Braxfield was endeavouring by his gestures to intimidate him, boldly addressed him thus : " It is altogether unavailing for your lordship to menace me ; for I have long learned to fear not the face of man."

As an instance of his great nerve, it may be mentioned that Lord Braxfield, after the trials were over, which was generally about mid-

night, always walked home to his house in George Square alone and
unprotected. He was in the habit, too, of speaking his mind on the
conduct of the Radicals of those days in the most open and fearless
manner, when almost every other person was afraid to open their lips,
and used frequently to say, in his own blunt manner, "They would a'
be muckle the better o' being *hanged!*"

When his lordship paid his addresses to his second wife, the courtship was carried on in the following characteristic manner. Instead
of going about the bush, his lordship, without any preliminary over-
tures, deliberately called upon the lady, "and popped the question"
in words to this effect :—"Lizzy, I am looking out for a wife, and I
thought you just the person that would suit me. Let me have your
answer, aff or on, the morn, and nae mair about it!" The lady, who
understood his humour, returned a favourable answer next day, and
the marriage was solemnized without loss of time.

Lord Braxfield was a person of robust frame—of a warm or rather
hasty temper—and, to "ears polite," might not have been considered
very courteous in his manner. "Notwithstanding, he possessed a
benevolence of heart," says a contemporary, "which made him highly
susceptible of friendship, and the company was always lively and
happy of which he was a member."

His lordship was among the last of our judges who rigidly adhered
to the *broad* Scotch dialect. "Hae ye ony counsel, man?" said he
to Maurice Margarot, when placed at the bar. "No." "Do you
want to hae ony appointit?" continued the judge. "No," replied
Margarot, "I only want an interpreter to make me understand what
your lordship says!"

Of Lord Braxfield and his contemporaries there are innumerable
anecdotes. When that well-known bacchanalian, Lord Newton, was
an advocate, he happened one morning to be pleading before Braxfield, after a night of hard drinking. It so occurred that the opposing
counsel, although a more refined devotee of the jolly god, was in no
better condition. Lord Braxfield observing how matters stood on
both sides of the question, addressed the counsel in his usual uncere-
monious manner—"Gentlemen," said he, "ye may just pack up your
papers and gang hame; the tane o' ye's rifting punch, and the ither's
belching claret—and there'll be nae gude got out o' ye the day!"

Being one day at an entertainment given by Lord Douglas to a few
of his neighbours in the old Castle of Douglas, port was the only description of wine produced after dinner. The Lord Justice-Clerk, with
his usual frankness, demanded of his host if "there was nae claret in
the Castle?" "I believe there is," said Lord Douglas, "but my
butler tells me it is not good." "Let's pree't," said Braxfield, in his
favourite dialect. A bottle of the claret having been instantly produced and circulated, all present were unanimous in pronouncing it
excellent. "I propose," said the facetious old judge, addressing himself to Dr. M'Cubbin, the parish clergyman, who was present, "as a
fama clamosa has gone forth against this wine, that you *absolve* it."
"I know," replied the Doctor, at once perceiving the allusion to
Church-court phraseology, "that you are a very good judge in cases
of civil and criminal law; but I see you do not understand the laws of

the Church. We never absolve *till after three several appearances!*" Nobody could relish better than Lord Braxfield the wit or the condition of absolution.

After a laborious and very useful life, Lord Braxfield died on the 30th of May, 1799, in the 78th year of his age. He was twice married. By his first lady, Miss Mary Agnew, niece of the late Sir Andrew Agnew, he had two sons and two daughters. By his second lady, Miss Elizabeth Ord, daughter of the late Lord Chief Baron Ord, he had no children.

His eldest son, Robert Dundas M'Queen, inherited the estate of Braxfield, and married Lady Lilias Montgomery, daughter of the late Earl of Eglintoun. The second entered the army, and was latterly a Captain in the 18th regiment of foot. The eldest daughter, Mary, was married to William Honeyman, Esq. of Graemsay, afterwards elevated to the bench by the title of Lord Annandale, and created a Baronet in 1804. The second, Catherine, was married to John Macdonald, Esq. of Clanronald.

THE REV. JOHN ERSKINE, D.D.,
Of Old Greyfriar's Church.

DR. ERSKINE, born on the 2nd of June, 1721, was the eldest son of John Erskine, Esq. of Carnock, Professor of Scots Law in the University of Edinburgh, and well known as the author of the Institutes of the Law of Scotland. The early education of young Erskine was conducted with a view to the legal profession, of which his father was so much an ornament; and although he had almost from infancy discovered a more than common seriousness of temper, and, as he advanced in years, manifested a strong predilection in favour of the pulpit, he repressed his aspirations so far as to submit to the usual course of discipline formerly prescribed in Scotland for those who intended to become advocates.

He entered the University of Edinburgh towards the end of the year 1734, where he acquired a thorough classical knowledge, and became acquainted with the principles of philosophy and law. Among other youths of great promise at that time at the college, was the late Principal Robertson, with whom young Erskine formed an intimate friendship, which, notwithstanding the shades of opinion in matters of church polity, and even in some doctrinal points, mutually entertained by them in after life, continued to be cherished, amid their public contests, with unabated sincerity. While in the ardent pursuit of his classical acquirements, however, Dr. Erskine by no means neglected the study of theology; on the contrary, his predilections in favour of the pulpit had increased, and so strong was his conviction of the duty of devoting his talents to the service of religion, that he resolved to acquaint his parents with his determination, and to endure their utmost opposition. The comparatively *poor* Presbyterian Church of Scotland had never been an object of aristocratical ambition;

besides this pecuniary objection, the friends of young Erskine conceived that the profession of the law, while it presented a wider field,
was more adapted for the display of his talents, and were therefore
entirely hostile to his views. Their opposition, however, could not
shake his resolution—he persevered in his theological studies, and
was, in 1742, licensed to preach by the Presbytery of Dunblane.

The future progress of the young divine, till his settlement in the
metropolis, is easily told :—" In May, 1744, he was ordained minister
of Kirkintilloch, in the Presbytery of Glasgow, where he remained till
1754, when he was presented to the parish of Culross, in the Presbytery of Dunfermline. In June, 1758, he was translated to the New
Greyfriar's, one of the churches of Edinburgh. In November, 1766,
the University of Glasgow conferred on him the honorary degree
of doctor of divinity; and, in July, 1767, he was promoted to the
collegiate charge of the Old Greyfriar's, where he had for his colleague
his early friend Dr. Robertson."

In these various movements towards that field of honour and usefulness, in which his talents ultimately placed him, Dr. Erskine
carried along with him the universal respect of his parishioners.
They had been delighted and improved by his public instructions—
and were proud of having had a clergyman amongst them, at once
combining the rare qualifications of rank, piety, and learning. He
was most exemplary in his official character; ever ready to assist and
counsel his parishioners, he "grudged no time, and declined no
labour, spent in their service."

Dr. Erskine was not only zealous for the interests of religion at
home, but equally so for its diffusion abroad; and in order to obtain
the earliest and most authentic intelligence of the state of the Gospel
in the Colonies of North America, where a remarkable concern for
religion had manifested itself about the time he obtained his license,
he commenced a correspondence with those chiefly interested in
bringing about that interesting event. He also, some time after,
opened a communication with many distinguished divines on the
Continent of Europe—a correspondence which he unweariedly cultivated during the remainder of his life. This practice added much to
his labour, not only by an increased and voluminous epistolary intercourse, but in "being called upon, by the friends of deceased divines,
to correct and superintend the publication of posthumous works."

In his continental correspondence, the Doctor had seriously felt the
want of a knowledge of the Dutch and German languages; and, at an
advanced period of life, actually set about overcoming this difficulty,
which he successfully accomplished in a remarkably short space of
time. A rich field, in the literature of Germany, being thus thrown
open to him, the result of his industry was soon manifested by the
publication of "Sketches and Hints of Church History and Theological Controversy, chiefly translated and abridged from modern foreign
writers," the first volume of which appeared in 1790, and the second
in 1798.

As might have been expected from the Doctor's enthusiastic character, he took an active interest in the Society for Propagating
Christian Knowledge. So long as his strength continued, he was one

of its most zealous members; and when the infirmities of age would no longer permit him to attend personally at their meetings, he was frequently consulted on matters of importance to the Society at his own house.

Dr. Erskine had never been in possession of much corporeal strength; and his weakly constitution began the sooner to feel the effects of approaching old age. Indeed, it is much to be wondered that his slender frame so long endured such an excess of mental, and even bodily labour, as distinguished his whole life. For several winters previous to his death he had not been able to preach regularly; and, for the last thirteen months, was compelled to leave it off altogether, his voice having become so weak as to be incapable of making himself heard. His mind, however, survived unimpaired amid the gradual decay of his bodily powers. His judgment was as clear, and his memory as good as in his younger years; and almost to the last minute of existence he maintained the pursuit of those labours which had constituted the business and the pleasure of his existence. On the 19th of January, the day previous to his demise, he was occupied in his study till a late hour. About four o'clock on the morning of the 20th (1803) he was suddenly taken ill; and although the alarm was immediately given, he expired, seemingly without a struggle, before his family could be collected around him.

His body was interred in the Greyfriar's Churchyard. The funeral was attended by a vast train of mourners, and an immense concourse of spectators assembled to witness the last obsequies to the remains of their venerable and much respected pastor. At the request of his widow, the Reverend Dr. Davidson, who was an esteemed friend of the deceased, preached a funeral sermon in the Old Greyfriar's Church, on the following Sunday, to a numerous and affected audience.

Dr. Erskine was married to the Honourable Miss M'Kay, daughter of Lord Reay, by whom he had a family of fourteen children, but only four survived—David Erskine, Esq. of Carnock, and three daughters, one of whom was the mother of James Stuart, Esq. of Dunearn.

Of Dr. Erskine's voluminous writings we cannot here even attempt a bare enumeration. They are, however, extensively known throughout the country. His first work, "On the Necessity of Revelation," written in his twenty-first year, and in which he had occasion to advocate some of the opinions maintained in Dr. Warburton's "Divine Legation of Moses," procured him the approbation and friendship of that distinguished prelate. His detached sermons, published while a country clergyman, were remarkable for a propriety and correctness of taste; while his Theological Dissertations, which appeared so early as 1765, were full of masterly disquisition on some of the most interesting points of divinity; and, in short, his whole works are distinguished for "precision of thought and originality of sentiment."

Dr. Erskine's opinions in matters of Church polity are at once known from the prominent position which he maintained for many years as leader of the popular party in the General Assembly, in opposition to his old schoolfellow, Dr. Robertson. In state politics he was equally bold and independent in his views. In 1769, on the breach with America, he published a discourse entitled " Shall I go to war with my American brethren?" which is said to have given great offence to some of those in high quarters at the time, and was considered as treasonable by many. It is even said the Doctor could get no bookseller to run the risk of publication, which seems to be corroborated by the fact that the sermon was actually published in London without any publisher's imprint being attached to it. The discourse, however, was reprinted at Edinburgh, in 1776, with the author's name, and the addition of a preface and appendix, even more in opposition to the views of Government than the discourse itself. On the subject of the American war he was strongly opposed to the sentiments of Mr. Wesley, who was a warm defender of the somewhat questionable policy pursued by the ministers of that ruinous period. He was opposed also to the constitution afterwards given to Canada, conceiving that the Roman Catholic religion had been too much favoured; and, in 1778, he was equally opposed to the attempt then made to repeal certain enactments against the Catholics of Great Britain, on which subject he entered into a correspondence with Mr. Burke, which was published. Without reference to their merits, the political sentiments of Dr. Erskine were at least entitled to respect, from the conscientiousness with which they were entertained, and the independence with which they were asserted.

As a man, Dr. Erskine was remarkable for the simplicity of his manner, and his conduct exhibited a genuine example of that humility and charitableness so prominent in the character of Christianity. He was ardent and benevolent in his disposition, and his affections were lasting and sincere. In proof of this, his continued friendship for his opponent, Dr. Robertson, is instanced as a noble example. The moderate, and perhaps somewhat *liberal*, views of the latter gentleman respecting the repeal of the penal statutes against the Catholics in Scotland, had so highly incensed the mob of Edinburgh in 1778, that a furious party had actually assembled in the College-yard for the purpose of demolishing the house of the Principal, which they would in all probability have done, in defiance of the military, had they not been quieted and dispersed by the interference and exhortation of Dr. Erskine. The funeral sermon preached by the reverend gentleman on the death of the historian, is another noble example of the triumph of mind over the frailties of humanity.

Of Dr. Erskine's pulpit oratory, perhaps a more correct idea cannot be given than is furnished in the description of the great novelist, Sir Walter Scott. "Something there was of an antiquated turn of argument and metaphor, but it only served to give zest and peculiarity to the style of elocution. The sermon was not read—a scrap of paper, containing the heads of the discourse, was occasionally referred to; and the enunciation, which at first seemed imperfect and embarrassed, became, as the preacher warmed in his progress, animated and distinct; and, although the discourse could not be quoted as a correct specimen of pulpit eloquence, yet Mannering had seldom heard so much learning, metaphysical acuteness, and energy of argument, brought into the service of Christianity."

An "Account of the Life and Writings of Dr. Erskine," by the Rev. Sir Henry Moncrieff Wellwood, was published in 1818, 8vo, which presents much interesting and valuable information in regard to the ecclesiastical state of Scotland during the last century.

In a second full length sketch of Dr. Erskine, Kay has been equally felicitous as in the former. He is here depicted to the very life. The Doctor had rather an odd custom of carrying his left glove in a manner suspended by the tops of two of his fingers, which the artist has not omitted.

Dr. Erskine was frequently very absent. In the course of his wandering one day in the Links of Edinburgh, he stumbled against a cow. With his usual politeness, he took off his hat, made a low bow and a thousand apologies, and then walked on. A friend, who witnessed what had happened, accosted him, and inquired why he had taken off his hat; he replied, that he had accidentally jostled a stranger, and was apologising for his rudeness. His amazement may be conceived, when he was informed that he had been offering his excuses to a cow! On another occasion, he met his wife in the Meadows; she stopped, he did so too; he bowed, hoped she was well, and bowed again, and went on his way. Upon his return home, Mrs. Erskine asked him where he had been; he answered in the Meadows, and that he had met a lady, but he could not for the world imagine who she was!

It may not be here out of place to remark that Dr. Erskine was by no means so morose or so studious as to be insensible to the lighter enjoyments of society. The following anecdote of him and his friend, Dr. Webster, shows that he could both *practise* as well as entertain a good joke. The well-known convivial propensities of the latter, the universal respect in which he was held, and the great excellence of his conversational powers, frequently led to social sittings, not altogether in accordance with his clerical character. Like most other *gudewives*, Mrs. Webster did not silently succumb to his repeated infringements of domestic regularity; and, in answer to her close-questioning on these occasions, the minister used frequently to excuse himself by saying, that he had "just been down calling for Dr. Erskine, and the Doctor had insisted on him staying to supper." Dr. Erskine, at length coming to understand in what manner his good name was made the excuse of his friend's derelictions, resolved in a good humoured way to put a stop to the deception. "One night, therefore, when Dr. Webster was actually in his house, in an accidental way, he made an excuse to retire, and leaving Webster to sup with Mrs. Erskine, went up to the Castlehill to call for Mrs. Webster. Dropping in as if nothing unusual was in the wind, he consented to remain with Mrs. Webster to supper; and thus the two clergymen supped with each other's wives, and in each other's houses, neither of the said wives being aware of the fact, and Webster equally ignorant of the plot laid against his character for verity. Long before Webster's usual hour for retiring, Dr. Erskine took leave of Mrs. Webster, and returned to his own house, where he found his friend as yet only, as it were, pushing off from the shore of sobriety. When his time was come, Webster went home, and being interrogated as usual, 'Why,' answered he, now at least speaking the truth, 'I've just been down at Dr. Erskine's.' The reader may conceive the torrent of indignant reproof which, after having been restrained on a thousand occasions when it was deserved, burst forth upon the head of the unfortunate and for once innocent Doctor. When it had at length subsided, the Doctor discovered the hoax which had been played off upon him; and the whole affair was explained satisfactorily to both parties the next day by Dr. Erskine's confession. But Mrs. Webster declared that, from that time forth, for the security of both parties from such deceptions, she conceived it would be as well, when Dr. Webster happened to be supping with Dr. Erskine, that he should bring home with him a written affidavit, under the hand of his host, testifying the fact."

Another anecdote, highly characteristic of his unbounded charity and extreme simplicity of manner, is told of the worthy and unostentatious old clergyman. For several Sabbaths Dr. Erskine had returned from church *minus* his pocket-handkerchief, and could not account for the loss. The circumstance attracted the particular notice of Mrs. Erskine, who had for some time past observed an elderly-looking poor woman constantly occupy a seat on the stair leading to the pulpit. Suspicion could scarcely attach itself to so demure a looking Christian; but Mrs. Erskine resolved to unriddle the mysterious affair, by sewing a handkerchief to the pocket of Mr. Erskine's Sunday coat. Next Sabbath, the old gentleman thus "armed against the spell," was proceeding in his usual manner towards the pulpit, when, on passing the suspected, demure-looking carling, he felt a gentle "nibble" from behind. The Doctor's displeasure could not be roused however; he turned gently round, and "clapping detected guilt" on the head, merely remarked, "No the day, honest woman, no the day!"

SIR WILLIAM FORBES OF PITSLIGO,

Banker in Edinburgh.

THE words of the engraving, "The good shall mourn a brother—all a friend," were never more appropriately applied than in allusion to the character of Sir William Forbes. In the language of the Rev. Mr. Alison, there was no person of the age "who so fully united in himself the same assemblage of the most estimable qualities of our nature; the same firmness of piety, with the same tenderness of charity; the same ardour of public spirit, with the same disdain of individual interest; the same activity in business, with the same generosity in its conduct; the same independence towards the powerful, and the same humanity towards the lowly; the same dignity in public life, with the same gentleness in private society."

SIR WILLIAM FORBES was born at Edinburgh on the 5th of April, 1739. He was descended (both paternally and maternally) from the ancient family of Monymusk, and by his paternal grandmother from the Lords Pitsligo. His father, who was bred to the bar, died when Sir William was only four years of age. His mother, thus left with two infant sons, and very slender means of support, retired among her friends in Aberdeenshire. His younger brother did not long survive.

Though nurtured in rather straitened circumstances, Sir William by no means lacked an excellent education, which he received under the superintendence of his guardians—Lord Forbes, his uncle; Lord Pitsligo, his maternal uncle; Mr. Morrison of Bogny; and Mr. Urquhart of Meldrum, among whom he was trained to the habits and ideas of good society; but it was principally to the sedulous care of his widowed mother, who instilled into his young mind the sentiments of rectitude and virtue, that, as he frequently in after life declared, he "owed everything." Both his parents belonged to the Scottish Episcopal Church, to which communion Sir William remained during his life a steady and liberal adherent.

In 1753 Lady Forbes returned to Edinburgh, with the view of choosing some profession for her son, who had now attained his fourteenth year. Fortunately, through the influence of a friend, Mr. Farquharson of Haughton, he was taken into the banking-house of Messrs. Coutts, and bound apprentice to the business the following year.

Sir William's term of servitude lasted for seven years, on the expiry of which he acted for two years more in the capacity of a clerk in the establishment. During this time he continued to reside with his mother, and felt much satisfaction in being enabled, from the gradual increase of his salary, to contribute to her comforts. By his undeviating rectitude, steady application, and the display of very superior qualifications for the profession, he had early attracted the notice of Messrs. Coutts, with whom he was, in 1761, admitted into partnership, with only a small share in the profits. Owing to the death of one of these gentlemen, and the retirement of the other, on account of bad health (the other two brothers being settled in London), a new company was formed in 1763, consisting of Sir William Forbes, Mr. James Hunter (afterwards Sir James Hunter Blair), and Sir Robert Herries. Although neither of the Messrs. Coutts had any share in the new concern, the firm continued under the old name until 1773, when, on the withdrawal of Sir Robert Herries, who formed a separate establishment in London, the name of the firm was changed to that of Forbes, Hunter, & Co. Sir William was at the head of the concern, over which he ever after continued to preside, and the uncommon success which attended its operations is in no small degree attributable to his peculiar sagacity and prudence. In 1783 the Company commenced to issue notes, which obtained an extent of credit almost without parallel.

Sir William married, in 1770, the eldest daughter of Dr. (afterwards Sir James) Hay, which event obliged him to separate from the "venerated guide of his infant years," who lived to a good old age, happy in the growing prosperity and kind attention of her son.

Sir William had now fairly commenced that career of usefulness which so much distinguished his long life. Naturally of a benevolent disposition, his attention was early directed to the charitable institutions of the city, many of which, previous to his taking an interest in them, were in a languishing state. The Charity Workhouse, of which he became a Manager in 1771, felt, in an especial manner, the effects of his persevering solicitude. In 1777 he published a pamphlet on the improvement of this institution, which was characterized as "full of practical knowledge and enlightened benevolence; and he continued through life to take an active interest in its welfare. Of the Orphan Hospital, too, he was a Manager for many years, and always, from 1774, one of its most zealous and efficient directors.

The erection of the late High School, in which Sir Walter Scott and other eminent men were educated, is another proof of Sir William's public spirit as a citizen, and his active perseverance and power of overcoming difficulties. He was a zealous Manager of the Royal Infirmary, to which, at his death, he left £200. The Lunatic and Blind Asylums owed much to his exertions; and, in short, no improvements were contemplated, and no benevolent work projected, which did not find in Sir William ready and efficient support.

In accordance with a long-cherished desire of restoring his family, which had been reduced by attainder, to its former dignity and fortune, Sir William embraced a favourable opportunity of purchasing seventy acres of the upper barony of Pitsligo, including the old mansion-house, at that time roofless and deserted. By the death of Mr. Forbes, 1781, Sir William succeeded as heir to the lower barony also, and thus had his early dreams almost realized. The property he had acquired was extensive, but, from the misfortunes of the family, sadly out of condition. Sir William immediately set about its improvement: He established numbers of poor cottars on the most uncultivated portions of the estate, erected the village of New Pitsligo, and, by the utmost liberality as a landlord, induced settlers to come from a distance. In the course of a short space of time he had the satisfaction of seeing a thriving population, and "several thousand acres smiling with cultivation, which were formerly the abode only of the moor-fowl or the curlew." He also established a spinning-school at New Pitsligo, introduced the linen manufacture, and erected a bleachfield; he built a school-house, a chapel of ease connected with the Established Church, and a chapel for those of the Episcopal persuasion. To the estate of Pitsligo, Sir William soon after added, by purchase, those of Pittoulie and Pittindrum, which were contiguous, and from their proximity to the sea-shore, afforded excellent facilities of improvement.

In 1774 Sir William became a member of the Merchant Company, and was elected Master in 1786, a situation which he was frequently afterwards called upon to fill. He was a warm promoter of the plan adopted by that body for rendering annuities to widows a matter of right, instead of a gift of charity, as formerly. But his attention was by no means confined to local matters: He was one of the committee of merchants appointed to confer with Sir James Montgomery, then Lord Advocate, " on the new Bankrupt Act introduced in 1772, and many of its most valuable clauses were suggested by his experience ;" again, in 1783, on the expiry of the new Act, he was Convener of the Mercantile Committee in Edinburgh, when further improvements were effected in the Bankrupt laws.

As we have already mentioned, Sir William was by descent attached to the Episcopal communion. Under his fostering management the Cowgate chapel was built, " afterwards known as the most popular place of worship in Edinburgh ;" and, in 1800, he was chiefly instrumental in bringing the Rev. Mr. Alison to that chapel, then settled in a remote rectory in Shropshire.

Sir William was a gentleman of the most polished and dignified manners; and although much of his time must necessarily have been occupied in the prosecution of those manifold pursuits which conferred so much benefit on his native city and the country in general, he still found leisure to indulge in a taste for literature, and to make himself acquainted with the progress of science. He was one of the original members of the Antiquarian Society, instituted chiefly by the exertions of the Earl of Buchan; and so early as 1768 he had spent nearly twelve months in London, in the family of Sir Robert Herries, where he became a member of the London Literary Club, and formed an acquaintance with the principal literary characters of that period, among whom was Sir Joshua Reynolds, who executed two admirable portraits of Sir William, and received a considerable portion of his esteem.

By such an extended circle of acquaintance, Sir William was led into an interesting and extensive correspondence, for which he evidently had a high relish, although almost the only relic of his talents in composition is an "Account of the Life and Writings of James Beattie, LL.D.," author of the "Essay on Truth" (in answer to some of the Essays of David Hume, the celebrated philosopher and historian) —"The Minstrel," &c. This work was published in 1806, and has passed through three or four editions. It includes many original letters of his early and esteemed friend, and is an excellent specimen of what might have been expected from Sir William's pen, had not perhaps higher and more important duties engrossed the greater portion of his time.

Sir William's circle of friends, however, was by no means confined to men of professional literary talents, or to those who might benefit by his patronage: he was intimately acquainted with Lord Melville and with Mr. Pitt, who had frequent interviews with Sir William on subjects of finance. In short, his house in Edinburgh was the resort of all ranks; and few foreigners of distinction visited Scotland without having letters of introduction to him. He was frequently offered a seat in Parliament, both for the city of Edinburgh and the county of Aberdeen, but he uniformly declined the honour; in doing so he sacrificed the gratification of a laudable ambition to a sense of duty, which he conceived to be limited to the sphere in which he had already been the promoter of so many benefits. From similar praiseworthy motives, he also declined the honour of an Irish Peerage, proposed to him by Mr. Pitt in 1799.

The health of Sir William began to decline in 1791, at which period he had a severe illness, and in 1802 Lady Forbes died, a circumstance which sensibly affected his spirits. On his return from London in 1806, whither he had been summoned as a witness on Lord Melville's trial, he began to feel symptoms of decay; and after having been confined to the house from the 28th June, he expired on the 12th November, 1806, surrounded by his friends, and inspired by every hope which a virtuous and useful life is so capable of affording. Sir William had a large family; besides his eldest son and successor, he left Lord Medwyn, Mr. George Forbes, and five daughters, four of whom are now married—Lady Wood, Mrs. M'Donnell of Glengarry, Mrs. M'Kenzie of Portmore, and Mrs. Skene of Rubislaw. His successor, Sir William, was cut off in the middle of his years and usefulness, leaving three sons. The eldest, Sir John Stuart Forbes, who succeeded him in the title and estates, married a daughter of the late Marquis of Lothian; the second, Charles, is a banker in the firm of Sir William Forbes & Co.; and the third, James, is at present Professor of Natural Philosophy in the University of Edinburgh.

The scene represented in the background of the Print is referable to the charity almost daily bestowed by Sir William on a number of "pensioners," who were in the habit of frequenting the Parliament Square at stated periods, where they were certain of meeting their benefactor as he entered or retired from the banking-house. The same practice is still continued by several of the partners of that respectable firm.

THE MARQUIS OF HUNTLY,

Afterwards Duke of Gordon.

THIS Print represents the MARQUIS of HUNTLY, when about the age of twenty-one. He was born at Edinburgh on the 1st of February, 1770. His first entry on public life was by adopting the profession of arms, and in being appointed Captain of an independent company of Highlanders raised by himself in 1790, and with which he joined the 42nd regiment, or Royal Highlanders, the following year. Shortly afterwards, the regiment remained nearly a twelvemonth in Edinburgh Castle, during which period Kay embraced the opportunity of etching the "Highland Chieftain." The daring exploit—a race on horseback, from the Abbey Strand, at the foot of the Canongate, to the Castle-gate—betwixt the Marquis and another sporting nobleman, still alive, which occurred about this period, will be remembered by many of the inhabitants of Edinburgh.

In 1792, he entered the 3rd regiment of Foot Guards as Captain-Lieutenant. In 1793, when orders were issued by his Majesty to embody seven regiments of Scottish Fencibles, the Duke of Gordon not only raised the Gordon Fencibles, but the Marquis made an offer to furnish a regiment for more extended service. Early in 1794, he accordingly received authority for this purpose, and so much did the family enter into the spirit of constitutional loyalty, that besides the Marquis, both the Duke and Duchess of Gordon "recruited in their own person." The result of such canvassing was soon manifest; in the course of three months the requisite numbers were completed, and the corps embodied at Aberdeen on the 24th June. As a matter of course the Marquis was appointed Lieutenant-Colonel Commandant.

The first movement of the "Gordon Highlanders" was to England, where they joined the camp at Nettley Common, in Southamptonshire, and were entered in the list of regular troops as the 100th regiment. They were soon afterwards despatched for the Mediterranean,

JAMES, THIRD EARL of HOPETOUN

[To face page 133]

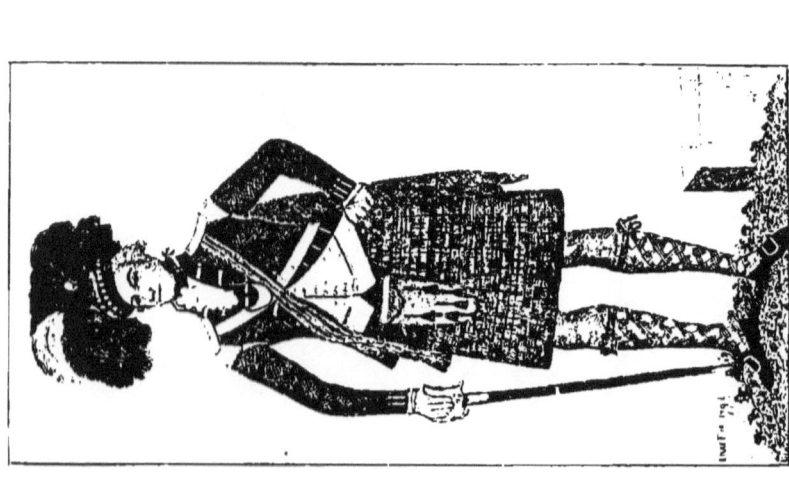

A HIGHLAND CHIEFTAIN

THE MARQUIS of HUNTLY

Vol. I., Plate XII.]

where the Marquis accompanied them, and where they remained for several years. Leaving his regiment at Gibraltar, his lordship embarked on board a packet at Corunna, on his passage home; but, after having been three days at sea, the vessel was taken by a French privateer, and the Marquis was plundered of every thing valuable: he was then placed on board a Swedish ship, in which he arrived at Falmouth in September, 1796.

The "Gordon Highlanders" returned to Britain in 1798, but in consequence of the disturbances then breaking out in Ireland, they were immediately hurried off there. The Marquis directly followed, resumed the command, and was actively employed with the regiment until tranquillity was restored. Notwithstanding the irksome and disagreeable nature of a soldier's duty connected with civil commotion, the conduct of the "Gordon Highlanders" in Ireland was highly exemplary; so much so, that on leaving the county of Wexford, in which district they had been principally employed, an address was presented by the magistrates and inhabitants to the Marquis, in which, after paying a marked compliment to the orderly conduct of the men, they stated that "peace and order were established, rapine had disappeared, confidence in the Government was restored, and the happiest cordiality subsisted since his regiment came among them."

In the expedition to the Helder in 1799, the "Gordon Highlanders," whose number a short time previously had been changed to the 92nd, with the Marquis at their head, formed part of General Moore's brigade, and although not engaged in repelling the first attack of the enemy, bore a distinguished part in the great action at Bergen on the 2nd October, in which the Marquis was severely wounded. So entirely did the conduct of the regiment on this occasion give satisfaction to General Moore, "that when he was made a Knight of the Bath, and obtained a grant of supporters for his armorial bearings, he took a soldier of the Gordon Highlanders, in full uniform, as one of these supporters, and a lion as the other."

The Marquis had obtained the rank of Colonel in the Army in 1796—that of Major-General in 1801, and was placed on the North British Staff as such from 1803 till 1806, when he was appointed Colonel of the 42nd, or Royal Highland Regiment. At the general election of that year he was chosen Member of Parliament for Eye, in Suffolk; but he only remained a short time in the Commons, having been, on the change of Ministry which soon followed, summoned by writ to the House of Peers, by the title of Baron Gordon of Huntly, in the county of Gloucester. In 1808, he was raised to the rank of Lieutenant-General in the Army; and the same year, on the resignation of his father the Duke of Gordon, the Marquis was appointed Lord-Lieutenant of the county of Aberdeen.

In the unfortunate "Walcheren Expedition," undertaken in 1809, under the late Earl of Chatham, the Marquis commanded the fourth division. The object of this armament, which had been fitted out on a very extensive scale, was the destruction of the fleet and arsenal at Antwerp, but except in the bombardment of Flushing, the expedition entirely failed of success.

With the Walcheren expedition closed the foreign military career

of the Marquis of Huntly. His subsequent life was distinguished by
a patriotic and active zeal in whatever tended to the honour or advantage of his native country. He was long a member, and frequently
President of the Highland Society, an association which has done so
much to improve the agriculture and condition of the peasantry of
Scotland. As a mark of distinction, in 1813, the Marquis was appointed General of the ancient body denominated the Royal Archers
of Scotland, or King's Body Guard. Of the Celtic Society, he was
also an equally honoured member; and, in short, in all patriotic or
national associations, he was found to yield enthusiastic co-operation.

On the death of his lordship's father in 1827, he succeeded to the
dukedom of Gordon in Scotland, and the earldom of Norwich in England; and in the still more extended sphere of influence thus opened
to him, the spirit which had animated the Marquis continued to be
manifested in the Duke. The great improvements which he effected
on his extensive estates—the exquisite taste displayed in laying out
the grounds and ornamenting the lawns around the princely Castle of
Gordon—together with his successful exertions in improving the breed
of Highland cattle, and promoting agriculture, are well-known instances of the Duke's untiring zeal and perseverance.

He married, in 1813, Elizabeth, daughter of the late Alexander
Brodie, Esq., of Arn-hall, but had no issue. His Grace died at London
in June 1836, and with him the dukedom of Gordon and earldom of
Norwich became extinct. The title of Marquis of Huntly, and some
of the inferior dignities, devolved to his Grace's "heir-male whatso-
ever," the Earl of Aboyne. The estates passed by virtue of an entail
to his nephew, the Duke of Richmond.

In the foregoing sketch, the character of the late Duke of Gordon
has been drawn chiefly from the events of his public career. His
conduct in the social relations of domestic life will be best estimated
by those—and there are many—who had an opportunity of personal
intercourse. Although not present on the memorable event of the
King's Visit to Scotland in 1822, his name was not forgotten by the
Scottish muse on that occasion. In the "Highland Chieftains'
Welcome," the Marquis is thus eulogised:—

> "And Huntly, at once the delight and the glory,
> The boast and the pride of the clans of the north;
> Renowned, not more in warrior's story,
> Than in home's happy circle, for true manly worth."

In the second part of "Carle now the King's come," by the late Sir
Walter Scott, he is also familiarly alluded to:—

> "Cock o' the North, my Huntly bra',
> Where are you with my Forty-twa?
> Oh! waes my heart that ye're awa'—
> Carle now the King's come!"

The Marquis obtained the distinctive appellation of the "Cock o' the
North," in allusion to his spirited conduct, as well as to the circumstance of his being the representative of an ancient and powerful
family. Amid the occasional frolics of youth and the allurements of
high life, however, the native goodness of his heart continued uncor-

rupted : he was an especial friend to the poor, and kind and affable to all.   In reference to this feature in his character, the following pleasing anecdote is told :—A certain gentleman, " clothed with a little brief authority," was allowed by the Duke (the Marquis's father) a handsome sum annually for incidental charities.   It was, however, strongly suspected that not one farthing of the money was expended among the poor.   The rumour having reached Huntly's ears, he resolved upon an expedient to ascertain whether the general suspicions were well-founded.   Having attired himself in the lowly guise of a beggar, he repaired to the house of the little great personage, and there assuming the " trembling steps " of three-score-and-ten, he knocked at the door and solicited alms.   One of the menials ordered him to be gone, as no beggar was allowed access to the house.   In well-feigned accents the mendicant pleaded his absolute necessity, and expressed his confidence that the master himself would not use him so.   The master at length appeared with a stern countenance, and in spite of the beggar's tale of deep distress, threatened, if he did not instantly depart, to " hound the dogs at him."   Thus thoroughly convinced that the charges were not without foundation, the Marquis took care to be present at the next annual settlement, when the usual debit—" to incidental charities "— appearing as formerly, he drew his pen through the entry, at the same time reminding the pretended almoner of his conduct to the beggar, and declaring that he would in future manage these charities himself.

It is said that the Marquis was such an adept in the art of counterfeiting characters, that even his most intimate associates were occasionally made the dupes of his deceptions.   Some of his exploits happening to become the topic of conversation on one occasion, a gentleman present took a bet with his lordship, that he for one would be proof against his art, let him assume whatever disguise he might. The wager was instantly accepted ; and, in the course of a few days afterwards, the Marquis had himself rigged out in all the ragged paraphernalia of a veteran gaberlunzie—with budgets and wallets arranged in such a manner that even *Edie Ochiltree* might not have been ashamed of the personification.   Thus equipped, he proceeded to the mansion of his friend, and having on his journey avoided neither " dub nor mire," he seemed the very picture of one of those sturdy mendicants of whom the country was prolific during last century.   He met the lord of the manor in the avenue leading to the house, to whom he gave the obeisance due from a person of his assumed calling ; and after gratifying his curiosity by answering a few inquiries, he was ordered by the gentleman to the hall, and there to " see what he could find fitting for a keen appetite."   Huntly accordingly stalked into the hall, where he was served with an ample plate of cold meat and abundance of bread and beer ; but he partook very sparingly, and in short enacted this part of his assumed character so indifferently as to call forth a remark from the housekeeper, that " to be a rachel-looking carle he had a very gentle stomach."   Having thus far succeeded without discovery, Huntly resolved to make a still bolder attempt on his friend's boasted discrimination.   Quitting the house, he studiously crossed the path of the gentleman, and again made his obeisance. " Well, old boy," said the latter, with his wonted good humour, "how

did you fare at the hall?" "Very so so, indeed," replied Huntly;
"nothing but cold beef, sour bread, and stale beer." "You must
truly be a saucy scoundrel!" exclaimed the gentleman, nettled by the
arrogant reply. "Not exactly that," continued Huntly, "but I have
never been accustomed to such low fare." Irritated beyond endurance
by the provokingly cool impudence of the supposed mendicant, the
gentleman threatened to have him *caged*, and actually called some of
the domestics to lay hands upon him, when, like the *Gudeman o' Bal-
langeich* (in one of his nocturnal adventures) he doffed his

> "Duddie clouts—his meally bags an' a',"

and stood forward in his own proper person, to the utter amazement
of the bystanders, and the conviction of his defeated friend, whose
wrath was quickly changed to merriment.

SIR JAMES MONTGOMERY OF STANHOPE,

Lord Chief Baron of Exchequer.

LORD CHIEF BARON MONTGOMERY was the second and youngest son of
William Montgomery, Esq., of Macbiehill, Tweeddale, and was born
in 1721. This gentleman was a devoted agriculturist at a period when
that useful branch of knowledge was too little attended to in this country. He had the merit of introducing an early species of pease and of
oats, which were named after his estate of Macbiehill; but the latter
has for these last forty years been more generally known as the "red
oat." So early as 1745, he cultivated potatoes to the extent of several
acres annually; but the land so cultivated was uniformly sown down
with bere and artificial grasses. He sold his potatoes by the Tweeddale oat-firlot streaked, at 16s. per boll—an amazingly high sum at
that period.

Sir James, being educated for the law, became a member of the
Faculty of Advocates soon after he had attained his majority. His
talents were by no means of the highest order; yet, by judicious mental cultivation—by throwing aside all ingenious subtleties, and boldly
grasping at the solid practical view of every question, he in time
acquired the character of a sound lawyer.

In 1748, when the Scottish heritable jurisdictions were finally abolished Sir James was one of the first sheriffs appointed by the Crown.
He obtained the sheriffdom of Tweeddale, his native county; and it
may be noticed that he was the last survivor of all those appointed at
the same period. His conduct as a judge in his situation—the more
irksome from its being the first of a new order of things—proved so
highly satisfactory, that in 1764, he was promoted to the office of
Solicitor-General for Scotland, and elected to represent his native
county in the British Parliament. A few years after, he was still
farther honoured by the appointment of Lord Advocate; and in 1777,
on the death of Lord Chief Baron Ord, he was appointed Lord Chief

Baron of his Majesty's Court of Exchequer. He was the first Scotsman who held this office since the establishment of the Court in 1707. This situation he held until 1801, when he found it necessary to retire from public business. The title of Baronet was then conferred upon him (July 16, 1801), as a mark of royal esteem for his long and faithful services.

Sir James, like his father, had early formed a just estimate of the importance of agriculture as a study; and, even amid the laborious duties of his official appointments, was enthusiastic in its pursuits. On his farm of Wester-Deans, in the parish of Newlands, he had turnips in drills, dressed by a regular process of horse-hoeing, so early as 1757; and he was amongst the first, if not the very first, in Scotland who introduced the light horse-plough, instead of the old cumbrous machine, which, on the most favourable soil, required four horses and a driver to manage them.

For the purpose of enlarging his practical knowledge, Sir James travelled over the most fertile counties of England, and embraced every opportunity which could possibly tend to aid him in promoting his patriotic design of improving the agriculture of his native country. The means of reclaiming waste lands in particular occupied a large share of his attention. His first purchase was a portion of land, remarkable for its unimproveable appearance, lying upon the upper extremities of the parishes of Newlands and Eddlestone. This small estate, selected apparently for the purpose of demonstrating the practicability of a favourite theory, obtained the designation of the "*Whim*," a name which it has since retained. He also rented, under a long lease, a considerable range of contiguous ground from Lord Portmore. Upon these rude lands, which consisted chiefly of a deep moss soil, Sir James set to work, and speedily proved what could be accomplished by capital, ingenuity, and industry. In a few years the "*Whim*" became one of the most fertile spots in that part of the country.

His next purchase was the extensive estate of Stanhope, lying in the parishes of Stobo, Drummellier, and Tweedsmuir, and consisting principally of mountainous sheep walks. Here, too, he effected great improvements, by erecting enclosures, where serviceable—planting numerous belts of young trees—and building comfortable tenements, and other premises, for his tenantry, to whom he afforded every inducement to lay out capital, by granting long leases, and otherwise securing to them the prospect of reaping the reward of their industry. To such management as this the extraordinary agricultural advancement of Scotland, during the last half-century, is mainly owing—an advancement which the present tenant-at-will system (extensively prevalent in certain districts of the country) threatens seriously to impede, if not thoroughly to counteract. Sir James also possessed the estate of Killeen in Stirlingshire, which he obtained by marriage.

On attaining the dignity of Chief Baron, Sir James found himself in possession of more leisure than he could previously command; but this relaxation from official duties only tended to increase his labours in the cause of public improvement. He was one of the most useful members of the Board of Trustees for the encouragement of arts,

manufactures and commerce in Scotland; and it may be observed
with truth that a great portion of the business of the Board latterly
devolved upon him. His extreme kindliness of disposition, readiness
of access, and the universal estimation in which he was held, led him
into a multiplicity of gratuitous, but not the less salutary or important
labour. In the arrangement of private affairs among his neighbours,
and in becoming the honoured arbiter in matters of dispute, he was so
frequently engaged as materially to interfere with his own convenience; but whether to persons of his own rank, or to the poor, his
opinions were equally and always open.

Sir James died in April 1803. He married Margaret, daughter and
heiress of Robert Scott of Killeen, county Stirling, who survived him,
and lived till the 17th of February 1806. His eldest son, Colonel
William Montgomery, died a few years before him. His second son,
Sir James, inherited the title and estates, and was some time Lord
Advocate and Member for the county of Tweeddale. His third son,
Archibald, went to the East Indies; and his fourth son, Robert, was
an English barrister. His eldest daughter was married to Robert
Nutter, Esquire, of Kailzie—the youngest, to Major Hart of the East
India Service. The second daughter remained unmarried.

" Sir James," says a biographical notice written immediately after
his death, " was in stature a little taller than the middle size, of a
remarkably slender make; his air, though not undignified, had more
in it of winning grace than of overawing command. His appearance
in his old age was particularly interesting; his complexion clear and
cloudless; his manner serene and cheerful. Two pictures of him are
preserved, for which he sat when above eighty years old; one at
Stobbs House, the other at Kailzie.   Sir James at one time lived in
the third part of the Bishop's land, formerly occupied by Lord
President Dundas. He subsequently removed to Queensberry House,
situated near the foot of the Canongate, the use of which he gratuitously obtained from Duke William.

THE REV. GREVILLE EWING.

THE subject of this sketch was a native of Edinburgh, where he was
born in 1767. Being originally designed for a secular profession, he
was, at the usual age, bound apprentice to an engraver. A strong
desire, however, to be engaged in the work of the ministry, induced
him, at the close of his apprenticeship, to relinquish his intended profession, and devote himself to study. He accordingly entered the
University of Edinburgh, where he passed through the usual curricu-
lum of preparatory discipline; and in the year 1792 he was licensed
to preach, in connection with the National Church, by the Presbytery
of Hamilton. A few months after this he was ordained as colleague
with Dr. Jones, to the office of minister of Lady Glenorchy's Chapel,
Edinburgh.

A deep interest in the cause of missions seems, at an early period of

Mr. Ewing's ministry, to have occupied his mind. At that time, such enterprises were, to a great degree, novelties in this country; and even by many who wished them well, great doubts were entertained of their ultimate success. By his exertions and writings, he contributed much to excite a strong feeling in regard to them in Edinburgh; nor did he content himself with this, but, fired with a spirit of true disinterested zeal, he determined to devote himself to the work of preaching the gospel to the heathen. For this purpose he united with a party of friends, like-minded with himself, who had formed a plan of going out to India, and settling themselves there as teachers of Christianity to the native population. The individuals principally engaged in this undertaking, besides Mr. Ewing, were the Rev. David Bogue, D.D., of Gosport; the Rev. William Innes, then one of the ministers of Stirling, now of Edinburgh; and Robert Haldane, Esq., of Airthrey, near Stirling—by the latter of whom the expenses of the mission were to be defrayed. Of these gentlemen, the two latter still survive. The peremptory refusal of the East India Company, after repeated applications and memorials on the subject, to permit their going out, caused the ultimate abandonment of this scheme. Mr. Ewing, however, and his associates, feeling themselves pledged to the missionary cause, and seeing no opening for going abroad, began to exert themselves for the promotion of religion at home. A periodical, under the title of *The Missionary Magazine*, was started in Edinburgh, of which Mr. Ewing undertook the editorship; the duties of which office he discharged in the most efficient manner for the first three years of its existence. This periodical has continued till the present day, under the successive titles of *The Missionary Magazine*, *The Christian Herald*, and *The Scottish Congregational Magazine*. It has, for the last forty years, been the recognised organ of the Congregational churches of Scotland. Exertions of a missionary kind were also made in different parts of Scotland, where a necessity for such appeared.

Out of these efforts ultimately arose the secession of Messrs. Ewing and Innes from the National Church; for feeling themselves hampered in their efforts among their countrymen by the restrictions which an Establishment necessarily imposes, they were led—from this, as well as from other considerations of a conscientious kind—to resign their respective charges, and occupy themselves in preaching the gospel without being connected with any religious denomination whatever. They very soon, however, adopted the principles of Independency, or Congregationalism; after which Mr. Ewing removed to Glasgow, where he remained till the close of his life as the pastor of a large and influential Congregational church.

In connection with his pastoral duties, Mr. Ewing for many years sustained the office of Divinity Professor to the denomination with which he was connected. In this office he was associated with Dr. Wardlaw, the well-known author of "Lectures on the Socinian Controversy," and other valuable theological works. The department of study presided over by Mr. Ewing was that of Biblical Criticism and Church History.

Mr. Ewing was three times married. His first wife was the sister of his friend, Mr. Innes; but neither she nor his second wife, whose maiden name was Jamieson, were long spared after their marriage. His last wife, who was a daughter of the late Sir John Maxwell, of Pollock, Bart., died in the year 1828, in consequence of a melancholy accident experienced by the overturning of their carriage, while she, with her husband and a party of friends, were visiting the scenery on the banks of the Clyde, near Lanark.

After the distressing event above referred to, the health of Mr. Ewing began gradually to decline. He continued, however, to officiate both as a minister and a tutor for several years afterwards, until his growing infirmities compelled him to resign the latter office, and only occasionally to engage in the duties of the former. His death occurred on the morning of the 2nd of August, 1841, terminating a life of singular activity and usefulness in a decease no less singular for gentleness and peace. He had one child—a daughter—by his second marriage, who is now the wife of the Rev. Dr. Matheson of London.

Mr. Ewing appeared frequently before the public as an author. His principal works are:—" Essays to the Jews," London, 1809; " An Essay on Baptism," 2nd edit., Glasgow, 1824; " A Greek Grammar, and Greek and English Lexicon," published first in 1801, again in 1812, and again in a very enlarged form, in 1827. These, and all his other writings, are marked by extensive and accurate learning, ingenuity of argument, and, where the subject is such as to admit of it, by great vigour and eloquence of composition. They have proved of eminent service to the cause of sound and literate theology.

In private life, Mr. Ewing was distinguished by that pervading courteousness and cheerfulness which form such important ingredients in the character of the perfect gentleman, as his public career was marked by all that can add dignity and influence to the Christian minister. In his younger days, his countenance is said to have been very handsome; and even in his later years it was highly prepossessing. Kay's portrait was taken while he was minister of Lady Glenorchy's Chapel.

JAMES, THIRD EARL OF HOPETOUN.

THE immediate ancestor of the Earls of Hopetoun was Henry Hope, a merchant of considerable extent in Edinburgh, who married Jacquiline de Tott, a French lady, by whom he had two sons. The eldest, Thomas, was bred a lawyer, and, by his eminent talents, obtained great practice, and amassed a considerable fortune, with which he made extensive landed purchases. He was appointed Lord Advocate by James VI., and created a Baronet in 1628. His grandson Charles was the first Earl of Hopetoun. Henry, the second son, went to Amsterdam, and was the ancestor of that opulent branch of the family long settled there.

James, third Earl, the subject of this sketch, was born in 1741. He entered the army when very young, and held an ensign's commission in the 3rd Regiment of Foot Guards. He was with the troops in Germany, and, when only eighteen years of age, was engaged at the memorable battle of Minden in 1759, where the British infantry signally distinguished themselves. He continued in the same regiment till 1764, when he retired from the army, in consequence of the ill-health of his elder brother, Lord Hope, with whom he travelled some time on the Continent, but without producing any beneficial change in the state of his health, and who died in 1766. On the death of his father in 1781, he succeeded to the earldom, and was chosen one of the sixteen representative Peers of Scotland at the General Election in 1784. The Earl took an active part in all political questions, and continued to sit in the House of Lords during a great many succeeding years.

On the death of his grand-uncle, the third Marquis of Annandale, in 1792, Lord Hopetoun succeeded to the large estates of that nobleman, on which occasion he added the surname of Johnstone to his own. On the breaking out of the French War in 1793, when seven regiments of Fencibles were directed by his Majesty to be raised in Scotland, the Earl, who was firmly and sincerely attached to the British Constitution, stood forward in defence of his country, and embodied a corps called the Southern or Hopetoun Fencibles, of which he was appointed Colonel. The officers belonging to this regiment were men of the first rank and respectability : Lord Napier was Lieutenant-Colonel ; the veteran Clarkson, Major ; the Earl of Home, Captain of Grenadiers ; Mr. Baillie of Mellerstain, and Mr. M'Lean of Ardgower, Captains, etc. The Earl assiduously attended to his military duties, and soon brought the discipline of the corps to great perfection.

While the regiment was stationed at Dalkeith, several attempts were made by some of the more desperate members of the British Convention, to seduce the soldiers from their allegiance, or at all events to sow the seeds of discontent among them ; but without effect.

At Dumfries, where the corps was quartered in 1794, the following curious circumstance occurred :—"One of the Hopetoun Fencibles, now quartered in that town," says a newspaper of the day, " was discovered to be a *woman*, after having been upwards of eighteen months in the service. The discovery was made by the tailor, when he was trying on the new clothes. It is remarkable that she has concealed her sex so long, considering she always slept with a comrade, and sometimes with two. She went by the name of John Nicolson, but her real name was Jean Clark. Previous to her assuming the character of a soldier, it seems she had accustomed herself to the dress and habits of a man : having been bred to the business of a weaver at Closeburn, and employed as a man-servant at Ecclefechan."

The services of the Hopetoun Fencibles were at first limited to Scotland, but were afterwards extended to England. They remained embodied till 1798, when they were disbanded, after the regular militia had been organized.

His lordship afterwards, as Lord Lieutenant of the county of Linlithgow, embodied a yeomanry corps and a regiment of volunteer infantry, both of which were among the first that tendered their services to Government. These he commanded as Colonel, and took a deep interest and a very active part in training them, and rendering them efficient for the public service. During those times of alarm, when the country was threatened by foreign invasion, his influence, his fortune, and his personal exertions were steadily devoted to the public safety; and so much were his services appreciated by the Executive, that he was created a Baron of the United Kingdom in 1809, by the name, style, and title of Baron Hopetoun of Hopetoun.

The Earl died at Hopetoun-House, on the 29th May 1816, at the advanced age of 75. He married, in 1756, Elizabeth, daughter of the Earl of Northesk, by whom he had six daughters. They all died prior to himself, except Lady Anne, upon whom the Annandale estates devolved, and who married Admiral Sir William Johnstone.

Inheriting from his ancestors high rank and ample fortune, Lord Hopetoun maintained the dignity and noble bearing of the ancient Scotch baron, with the humility of a Christian, esteeming the religious character of his family to be its highest distinction; and he was not more eminent for the regularity of his attendance on all the ordinances of religion, than for the sincerity and reverence with which he engaged in them. He was an indulgent landlord, a most munificent benefactor to the poor, and a friend of all who lived within the limits of his extensive domains.

The following lines, written at the period of his death, describe his estimable character in glowing and forcible language :

" For worth revered, lo ! full of years,
    Does Hopetoun to the tomb descend,
Amid the sorrowing people's tears,
    Who mourn their constant, kindest friend.

Oft have I heard, as o'er his land
    I wandered in my youthful days,
The farmer bless his fostering hand,
    And ploughman's ruder note of praise.

Oft, too, in Humbie's fairy vale—
    Romantic vale ! so sweetly wild—
Of Hopetoun have I heard the tale
    Of sorrow soothed or want beguiled.

The mausoleum may arise,
    Displaying well the sculptor's art ;
But far superior are the sighs
    That rise from many a wounded heart.

The historic record shall survive,
    And unimpaired its meed bestow ;
The legendary tribute live
    When time has laid the structure low.

In early life to warfare trained,
    He gained the glory arms can yield ;
When Gallia had her lilies stained
    On Minden's memorable field.

Hence wreathed, the titled path he trod—
    A path (how few pursue his plan !)
Bright, marked with piety to God
    And warm benevolence to man.

The niche he leaves a brother fills,
Whose prowess fame has blazoned wide ;
Long, long o'er Scotia's vales and hills
Shall Niddry's deeds be told with pride !"

Having no male issue, the Earl of Hopetoun was succeeded by his half-brother John, fourth Earl, G.C.B., and General in the Army, who had distinguished himself so much by his gallantry and abilities in the West Indies in 1794; in Holland in 1799 ; and at the battles of Corunna, Bayonne, Bourdeaux, and Toulouse. For these services he was created a British Peer in 1814, by the title of Baron Niddry. He died at Paris on the 27th August, 1823. A handsome equestrian statue has lately been erected to his memory in St. Andrew Square, in front of the Royal Bank, by the citizens of Edinburgh.

Earl John was twice married,—first, in 1798, to Elizabeth, youngest daughter of Charles Hope Vere of Craighill, who died without issue in 1801 ; secondly, in 1803, to Louisa Dorothea, third daughter of Sir John Wedderburn of Ballendean, by whom he had twelve children, of whom seven sons and one daughter still survive. It will be recollected, that when George IV. visited Scotland in 1822, his Majesty embarked at Port-Edgar, having previously partaken of a repast at Hopetoun-House with the Earl, his family, and a select company assembled for the occasion. While at breakfast, one of the earl's sons, a lively boy about twelve years of age, came into the room and sat beside his mother. The King asked the Countess how many children she had ? On being answered by her ladyship that she had ten sons and an infant daughter, his Majesty, either struck by the number of male children, or by the beautiful and youthful appearance of the mother, exclaimed, " Good God ! is it possible ? " After breakfast Lady Alicia, then an infant, was presented to his Majesty, by whom she was affectionately kissed. Thomas and Adrian, the two youngest sons, were next led into the dining-room, and presented by the Earl to his royal guest. The King graciously received the little boys ; and raising Adrian's frock, took hold of his leg, saying, " What a stout little fellow !" The child, thinking the King was admiring his frock, held it up with both his hands, and cried, " See, see !" His Majesty was amused with the notion of the child, and said, " Is that a new frock, my little man ? " The other sons of Lord Hopetoun were presented to the King in the drawing-room. During his Majesty's short visit at Hopetoun-House, the honour of knighthood was conferred on Captain Adam Ferguson, and Mr Henry Raeburn, the celebrated painter. Notwithstanding the unfavourable state of the weather, the lawns around the princely mansion presented a scene of the most animating description. Great preparations had been made for the reception of his Majesty, and an immense concourse of all ranks, including a body of his lordship's tenantry on horseback, were assembled to greet their sovereign. The band of Royal Archers, who acted as the King's body guard, were in attendance, under the command of the Earl of Elgin. The Earl of Hopetoun was the commander-general of this ancient body, and acted as such on the day of his Majesty's arrival at Holyrood-House. As a memorial of that event, they entreated the Earl to sit for his picture in the dress which he wore on the occasion. The painting was executed by Mr John Watson, and has been hung up in the Archers' Hall.

John, the eldest, succeeded to the titles, and married, in 1826, Louisa Bosville, eldest daughter of the late Lord Macdonald, by whom he has issue one son. His lordship's remaining six brothers and one sister are all unmarried. Charles, the third son, is at present Member of Parliament for the county of Linlithgow. The Countess-Dowager died at Leamington in 1836.

LORD NEWTON,

Of the Court of Session.

CHARLES HAY, son of James Hay, Esq. of Cocklaw, Writer to the Signet, was born in 1747. He is said to have been descended from the Hays of Rannes, an ancient branch of the family of Hay. After the usual preparatory course of education, he passed advocate in 1768, having just attained the years of majority; but, unlike most young practitioners, Hay had so thoroughly studied the principles of the law, "that he has been frequently heard to declare he was as good a lawyer at that time as he ever was at any after period." He soon became distinguished by his strong natural abilities, as well as by his extensive knowledge of the profession, which embraced alike the minutest forms of the daily practice of the Court and the highest and most subtle points of jurisprudence. As a pleader he was very effective. His pleadings were never ornamental, but entirely free of "those little arts by which a speaker often tries to turn the attention of his auditors on himself;" at the same time they were acute, argumentative, and to the purpose. Mr Hay was, during the whole course of his life, a staunch Whig of the old school. In 1806, on the death of David Smythe, Lord Methven, he was promoted by the Fox administration to the bench, when he assumed the title of Lord Newton. This appointment was the only one which took place in the Court of Session during what was termed the reign of "the talents,"— a circumstance on which it is said he always professed to set a high value.

Whilst at the Bar, the opinions of his lordship were probably never surpassed for their acuteness, discrimination and solidity; and as a judge, he now showed that all this was the result of such a rapid and easy application of the principles of law, as appeared more like the effect of intuition than of study and laborious exertion.

Perhaps in none of his predecessors or contemporaries were so happily blended those masculine energies of mind, so requisite to constitute the profound lawyer, with that good nature and unpresuming simplicity so endearing in private life. "Those who saw him only on the bench were naturally led to think that his whole time and thoughts had for all his life been devoted to the laborious study of the law. Those, on the other hand, who knew him in the circle of his friends, when form and austerity were laid aside, could not easily

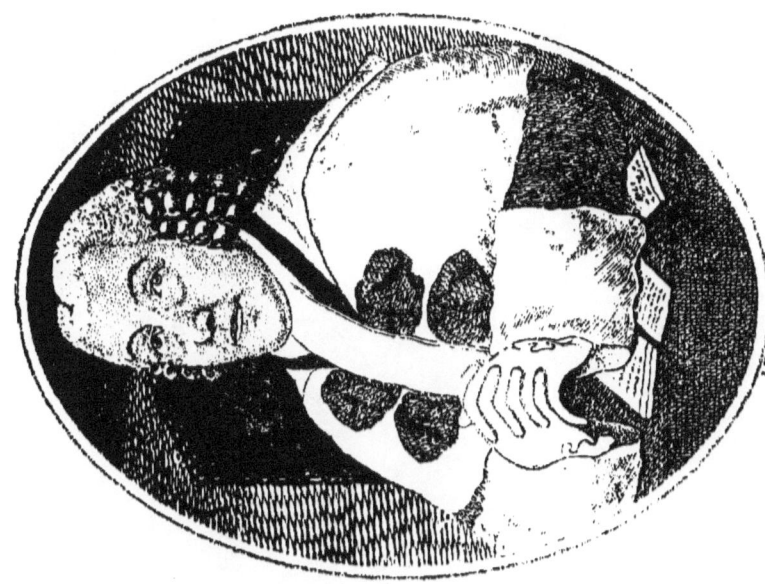

[To face page 144.

LORD DUNSINNAN

I KAY. 1779

LORD NEWTON

Vol. I., Plate XIII.]

I KAY. 1814

conceive that he had not passed his life in the intercourse of society." He possessed an extraordinary fund of good-humour, amounting almost to playfulness, and entirely devoid of vanity or affectation. There was, perhaps, a strong dash of eccentricity in his character; but his peculiarities appeared in the company of so many estimable qualities, that they only tended to render him more interesting to his friends. His lordship was of a manly and firm mind, having almost no fear of personal danger. He possessed great bodily strength and activity till the latter years of his life, when he became excessively corpulent.

Lord Newton's extraordinary judicial talents and social eccentricities are the subjects of numerous anecdotes. On the bench he frequently indulged in a degree of lethargy not altogether in keeping with the dignity of the long-robe, and which, to individuals unacquainted with his habits, might well seem to interfere with the proper discharge of his duties. On one occasion, while a very zealous but inexperienced counsel was pleading before him, his lordship had been dozing, as usual, for some time—till at last the young man, supposing him asleep, and confident of a favourable judgment in his case, stopped short in his pleading, and addressing the other lords on the bench, said—"My lords, it is unnecessary that I should go on, as Lord Newton is fast asleep." "Ay, ay," cried Newton, whose faculties were not in the least affected by the leaden god, "you will have proof of that by and by," when, to the astonishment of the young advocate, after a most luminous review of the case, he gave a very decided and elaborate judgment against him.

Lord Newton participated deeply in the bacchanalian propensities so prevalent among lawyers of every degree, during the last and beginning of the present century. He has been described as one of the "profoundest drinkers" of his day. A friend informs us that, when dining alone, his lordship was very abstemious; but, when in the company of his friends, he has frequently been known to put three "lang-craigs" under his belt, with scarcely the appearance of being affected by it. On one of these occasions, he dictated to his clerk a law-paper of sixty pages, which has been considered one of the ablest his lordship had ever been known to produce. The manuscript was sent to press without being read, and the proof sheets were corrected at the bar of the Inner House in the morning.

It has been stated that Lord Newton often spent the night in all manner of convivial indulgences—drove home about seven o'clock in the morning—slept two hours, and mounting the bench at the usual time, showed himself perfectly well qualified to perform his duty. Simond, the French traveller, relates that "he was quite surprised, on stepping one morning into the Parliament House, to find in the dignified capacity, and exhibiting all the dignified bearing of a judge, the very gentleman with whom he had just spent a night of debauch, and parted only an hour before, when both were excessively intoxicated. His lordship was also exceedingly fond of card-playing; so much so, that it was humorously remarked, "Cards were his profession, and the law only his amusement."

During the sitting of the Session, Lord Newton, when an advocate, constantly attended a club once a week, called "The *Crochallan* Fencibles," which met in Daniel Douglas's Tavern, Anchor Close, and consisted of a considerable number of literary men and wits of the very *first water*. The club assumed the name of *Crochallan* from the burthen of a Gaelic song, which the landlord used sometimes to entertain the members with; and they chose to name their association *Fencibles*, because several military volunteer corps in Edinburgh then bore that appellation. In this club all the members held some pretended military rank or title. On the introduction of new members, it was the custom to treat them at first with much apparent rudeness, as a species of initiation, or trial of their tempers and humours; and when this was done with prudence, Lord Newton was much delighted with the joke, and he was frequently engaged in drilling the recruits in this way. His lordship held the appointments of Major and Muster-Master General to the corps. The late Mr Smellie introduced the poet Burns to this corps in January 1787, when Lord Newton and he were appointed to drill the bard, and they accordingly gave him a most severe castigation. Burns showed his good-humour by retaliating in an extemporaneous effusion, descriptive of Mr Smellie, who held at that time the honourable office of *hangman* to the corps.

The eccentricities of Lord Newton were frequently a source of merriment amongst his friends. He had an unconquerable antipathy to punning, and in order to excite the uneasiness he invariably exhibited at all attempts of that nature, they studiously practised this novel species of punishment in his company.

His lordship had two estates (Newton and Faichfield,) and was fond of agricultural improvements; although, like most other lawyers who cultivate their own lands, he did not know much about farming. One day, when shown a field of remarkably large turnips, he observed that, in comparison, those in his own grounds were only like "gouf ba's,"—an expression which his waggish friend frequently afterwards turned to his annoyance, by asking him how his "gouf ba's" were looking.

We have already mentioned that Lord Newton was an uncompromising Whig. From his independent avowal of principles, and occasional vehement declamation against measures which he conceived to be wrong, he was dubbed by his opponents the "Mighty Goth." This, however, was only in the way of good-natured banter; no man, perhaps, passed through life with fewer enemies, even among those who were his political opponents. All bore testimony to his upright conduct as a judge—to his talents as a lawyer—and to his honesty as a man.

Lord Newton died at Powrie, in Forfarshire, on the 19th of October 1811. His lordship, who is understood not to have relished female society, was never married; and the large fortune which he left was inherited by his only sister, Mrs Hay Mudie, for whom he always entertained the greatest affection.

Lord Newton, when an advocate, continued to wear the gown of Lockhart, "Lord Covington," till it was in tatters, and at last had a new one made with a fragment of the neck of the original sewed into it, whereby he could still make it his boast that he wore "Covington's gown." Lord Covington died in 1782, in the eighty-second year of his age. He practised for upwards of half a century at the bar previous to his elevation to the bench in 1775. He and his friend, Ferguson of Pitfour, rendered themselves conspicuous by becoming voluntary counsel for the unfortunate prisoners tried at Carlisle in 1746, for their concern in the Rebellion, and especially by the ingenious means they devised to shake the wholesale accusations against them.

WILLIAM SMELLIE,

Author and Printer.

THE late Mr. William Smellie, Printer, author of "The Philosophy o Natural History," and translator of the works of Buffon, is by no means one of Kay's happiest efforts, as instead of the vacant expression delineated, the prevailing cast of Mr. Smellie's features was grave and thoughtful; but this defect may have arisen in consequence of the figure being originally that of a Mr. Gavin, and afterwards changed to Mr. Smellie. He was born in the Pleasance of Edinburgh, in 1740. Both his father and grandfather were architects, and were possessed of considerable property at St. Leonards, in the neighbourhood of Edinburgh. He married, in March, 1763, Miss Jane Robertson, daughter of an eminent army-agent in London. This lady was full cousin to the present Mrs. Oswald of Dunnikier, their mothers having been sisters. Mr. Smellie's only brother, named John, married Miss Agnes Ferrier, sister of the late James Ferrier, Esq., Principal Clerk of Session.

Independently of his professional eminence—being the most learned printer of his day—Mr. Smellie's talents procured him the constant society and friendship of nearly all the eminent literary characters who flourished towards the latter end of the last century. For his great convivial qualities and brilliant wit, we have the testimony of many kindred spirits; among whom may be mentioned the poet Burns, who, in a letter to a venerable old gentleman, lately deceased, Mr. Peter Hill, bookseller, thus describes him:—"There in my eye is our friend Smellie, a man positively of the first abilities and greatest strength of mind, as well as one of the best hearts and keenest wits that I have ever met with," etc.—*Burns' Works*, Letter 56.

Mr. Smellie was one of the principal writers in the *Edinburgh Magazine and Review*—a work which commenced in 1773, and was conducted for some years with great spirit, and much display of talent. It would assuredly have succeeded, had its management been committed entirely to the calm, judicious, and conciliatory control of Mr. Smellie; but owing to the harsh irritability of temper, and the severe and almost indiscriminate satire in which Dr. Gilbert Stewart, the principal editor, indulged, several of the reviews which appeared in that periodical gave great offence to many leading characters of the day; the consequence of which was such a diminution in the sale of the work as to render it necessary to discontinue it altogether. This took place in August, 1776, after the publication of forty-seven numbers, forming five octavo volumes. Had the work been only conducted upon the principles developed in the prospectus, it would have had few rivals and fewer superiors.

Mr. Smellie was likewise editor of the first edition of the "Encyclopedia Britannica," three volumes, quarto, 1771. The whole plan was arranged, and all the principal articles were written or compiled by him. He also wrote a great number of pamphlets on various subjects, among which may be particularised his "Address on the Nature, Powers, and Privileges of Juries," published in 1784. It is an admirable treatise, and ought to be carefully studied by every true friend to the Constitution, especially by such as have occasion to act as jurymen. It may be remarked, that this pamphlet inculcated those doctrines which have since been recognised as English law, in Mr. Fox's celebrated Bill on the subject of libels. The late Honourable Thomas Erskine (afterwards Lord Chancellor), in his defence of the Dean of St. Asaph for a libel, paid Mr. Smellie a very high compliment for this defence of the rights of juries.

Such was the high character of Mr. Smellie as an author, that when the first volume of his "Philosophy of Natural History" was announced as preparing for the press, the late Mr. C. Elliot made him an offer of one thousand guineas for the copyright, and fifty guineas for every subsequent edition, besides the employment of printing it. This was the largest sum ever previously given—at least, in Edinburgh—for the literary property of a single quarto volume of similar extent, and evinced both the liberality of the bookseller, and the high estimation in which the fame and talents of the author were held. It was, besides, an odd volume, being the first of the work. It is remarkable, that this bargain was finally concluded before a *single page* of the book was written.

In his translation of Buffon (9 vols. 8vo), Mr. Smellie introduced many original notes, observations, and illustrations of great importance, pointing out particular passages and opinions in which he differed from his author, and furnishing many new facts and reasonings. The Count de Buffon, as appears from his own letters to Mr. Smellie on the occasion, was highly pleased with this translation, of which a considerable number of editions was published. In these nine volumes he comprehended all that was contained in the original, which consisted of sixteen large quarto volumes. The method he pursued of rendering it into the English language was somewhat unusual. Instead of translating literally, paragraph by paragraph, and sentence by sentence, he deliberately read over six or eight pages at a time, making himself perfectly master of their substance, and then wrote down the whole in English, in his own words and arrangement. The greater part of this task he performed in a small correcting-room connected with his printing-office, amidst the continued interruption arising from the introduction of proof-sheets of other works for his professional revisal, and the almost perpetual calls of customers, authors, and idle acquaintances. Yet such was his self-possession, that as usual with almost everything he wrote, he gave it out to his compositors page by page, as fast as it was written, and hardly ever found it necessary to alter a single word, after the types were set up from his first uncorrected manuscript.

In August, 1871, Mr. Smellie drew up the first regular plan for procuring a statistical account of the parishes of Scotland. This plan was printed and distributed by order of the Society of Antiquaries; and, although no other result followed at the time than a statistical report, by the Earl of Buchan, of the parish of Uphall, in which his lordship then resided, along with three or four others, which were printed in the Society's Transactions, yet it is proper to mention the circumstance, as it was the precursor of the scheme which the late Sir John Sinclair afterwards brought to maturity.

On the death of Dr. Ramsay in 1775, Mr. Smellie became a candidate for the Chair of Natural History in the University of Edinburgh. The patronage being in the gift of the Crown, his friends made strong and ardent applications in his favour to Lord Suffolk; but, from the superior political influence of his opponent, Dr. Walker, these exertions were unsuccessful.

Mr. Smellie was one of the original founders of the Society of Antiquaries. In 1781 he was appointed Superintendent of its Museum of Natural History; and in 1793 he was elected Secretary. It is not intended here to give a history of that Society; yet, as a considerable portion of the strange and inexplicable opposition which that association encountered in their application for a Royal Charter from two highly respectable public bodies, originated out of circumstances intimately connected with Mr. Smellie's history, a short account of these transactions may be given. Mr. Smellie having announced his intention of giving a course of lectures, at the request of the Society, on the " Philosophy of Natural History," to be delivered in their hall, this proposal gave great dissatisfaction to Dr. Walker, the recently elected Professor of Natural History, already mentioned; although every attempt was made by the Earl of Buchan to satisfy him that Mr. Smellie's lectures would not interfere with those of the University, and although Dr. Walker had not even given a single lecture for nearly seven years after his appointment. Nothing, however, would satisfy him; and his answer to the Earl's pacific endeavours was—" In the professorship I am soon to undertake I have foreseen many difficulties, which I yet hope to surmount; but the lectures of Mr. Smellie, under the auspices of the Antiquarian Society, is a new discouragement which I did not expect." This discontent was communicated to the Senatus Academicus, and through that respectable body an unexpected opposition arose when the Society of Antiquaries transmitted a petition to the King praying for a charter. The Curators of the Advocates' Library likewise objected to the grant, under the idea that the institution of the Society might prove injurious to their magnificent Library, by intercepting ancient manuscripts and monuments illustrative of Scottish history and antiquities, which would be more useful if collected into one repository. All this opposition, however, proved of no avail. Much to the honour of the late Lord Melville—who was at that time Lord Advocate for Scotland—his lordship signified, by a note to the

Secretary of the Society, that he saw no reason for refusing the prayer of the petition, and at the same time transmitted the draft of such a charter as he considered was proper to be granted. In consequence, therefore, of his lordship's favourable interposition, the royal warrant, in which his Majesty was pleased voluntarily to declare himself patron of the Society, passed the Privy Seal next day. As soon as it was received in Edinburgh, a charter was extended under the Great Seal. The gentlemen of this public office, sensible of the many advantages likely to accrue from the establishment of the Society, generously refused to accept their accustomed fees, and the royal charter, which is dated the 29th March, was finally ratified, by passing through all the customary forms, on the 5th and 6th of May, 1783.

During the time Mr. Smellie attended the class of Botany in the University, the Professor, Dr. Hope, having met with an accident which confined him to the house for a long time, requested Mr. Smellie —of whose knowledge and abilities he was highly sensible—to carry on his lectures during his necessary absence. This was done by Mr. Smellie for a considerable time—(his widow has stated, during six weeks)—to the entire satisfaction of his fellow-students.

Mr. Smellie was about the middle size, and had been in his youth well-looking and active; but when rather past the middle of life he acquired a sort of lounging gait, and had become careless and somewhat slovenly in his dress and appearance. These peculiarities are well described in the following lines, produced by Burns at the meeting of the *Crochallan* Club, alluded to in our notice of Lord Newton :—

> ———"To Crochallan came,
> The old cocked hat, the brown surtout the same;
> His bristling beard just rising in its might,
> ('Twas four long nights and days to shaving-night);
> His uncombed grisly locks, wild-staring, thatched—
> A head for thought profound, and clear unmatched:
> And, though his caustic wit was biting rude,
> His heart was warm, benevolent and good."

In grave and philosophical discourse, Mr. Smellie was clear, candid, and communicative, as well as thoroughly informed. He never withheld his judgments and opinions from a narrow-minded feeling, nor obtruded them unnecessarily, or at unseasonable times, from vanity or affectation. His manners were uncommonly mild, gentle, and inoffensive, insomuch that none, even of his own family, ever remember to have seen him out of temper. In his last and long illness he was never in the smallest degree peevish, fretful, or melancholy. He died on the 24th June, 1795.

LORD DUNSINNAN,
Of the Court of Session.

THIS gentleman was the son of Sir William Nairne, the second baronet of Dunsinnan. Not being the oldest son, and having only a distant prospect of succeeding to the estate, he was educated for the profession of the law, and admitted an advocate in 1755. He was, in 1758, appointed Commissary-Clerk of Edinburgh, conjunctly with Alexander Nairne, a relative of his own. SIR WILLIAM (then Mr. Nairne), continued to practise at the bar upwards of thirty years; and, if he did not acquire the fame of a great orator or a profound lawyer, he was at least respectable in both capacities, and his virtues gained him what was perhaps better—the esteem of all who knew him.

On the death of Lord Kennet, in 1786, Sir William was promoted to the bench, and took his seat as Lord Dunsinnan—a circumstance which called forth the following complimentary *pun* from the late Duchess of Gordon. A short time after his elevation, her grace, happening to meet the newly appointed judge, inquired what title he had assumed—*Dunsinnan* was of course the reply. "I am astonished at that, my lord," said the Duchess, "for I never knew that you had *begun sinning.*"

In 1790 Sir William succeeded to the baronetcy, on the death of his nephew, and thus became the fifth in succession who bore the title. He, at the same time, bought the estate of Dunsinnan from another nephew, for the sum of £16,000; and having almost no funds remaining, he was under the necessity of adopting the utmost economy in order to clear off the purchase money. With this view he continued to live a bachelor, keeping almost no company; and so strictly did he abide by the rules he had laid down in this respect, that he was accused by many of being actuated by very narrow and parsimonious feelings. It is told of him, as illustrative of his peculiar economy, that he had only *one bed* at Dunsinnan, besides those occupied by his servants, thus to preclude the possibility of being put to the expense of entertaining visitors. It so occurred that the late George Dempster of Dunnichen, one of the most intimate of the very few friends with whom his lordship associated, paid him a visit at Dunsinnan on one occasion; and having tarried a little later than usual, a violent storm arose, which induced Mr. Dempster to think of remaining all night. Dunsinnan, unwilling to declare the inhospitable arrangement of his mansion, evaded the proposition by every means possible, in hopes that the storm might abate. At last, finding no likelihood of this, he sallied forth to the stable to order his friend's coach to the door, as the only effectual *hint* to his guest; but Dempster's coachman was not to be so caught: he positively refused to harness the horses in such a night, especially as the roads were so bad and dangerous, preferring rather to lie in the stable, if he could get no other accommodation, till daylight. Lord Dunsinnan, thus driven to extremities, returned to his guest, and made known the dilemma in which they were placed. "George," said he, "if you stay, you will go to bed at ten and rise at three; and then I shall get the bed after you."

The property of Dunsinnan, which included nearly the entire parish of Collace, was far from being in a state of improvement when it came into his hands; a great part of the lands consisted of what is termed "outfield," and the farms were made up of detached portions, many of these at considerable distances. No sooner had Sir William obtained possession of the estate than he set about dividing the lands into compact and regular farms, which he enclosed, and gave to each a certain portion of outfield; at the same time he built comfortable dwellings for many of his tenants, and, by proper encouragement, induced others to do so for themselves. He thus, with no niggardly hand, promoted alike the prosperity of the tenant, and ensured the rapid improvement of the soil.

Sir William was appointed a Lord of Justiciary, in 1792, on the death of Lord Stonefield; and continued to attend the duties of the circuit until 1808, when he resigned, and the following year retired from the Court of Session altogether. He died, at a very advanced age, at Dunsinnan House, on the 25th March, 1811. The title became extinct in his person, and a nephew (his sister's son) succeeded to the estate and assumed the name of Nairne.

His lordship's residence in Edinburgh was Minto House, Argyle Square. Previous to his removal thither, he occupied a tenement at the head of the Parliament Stairs, lately a printing-office; but now removed to make way for the new Justiciary Court-Room.

Before concluding this sketch, it may be noticed that Lord Dunsinnan was uncle to the famous Catherine Nairne or Ogilvie, whose trial, in 1765, for the crimes of murder and incest, excited such general interest. She married, in that year, Thomas Ogilvie, Esq. of Eastmiln, Forfarshire—a gentleman, as was stated at the trial, of forty years of age and of a sickly constitution—the lady's own age being only nineteen. Shortly before the marriage, a younger brother of this gentleman, named Patrick, and a lieutenant in the 89th foot, had returned, on account of bad health, from India, and had taken up his residence as a visitor at his brother's house. The marriage took place three or four days after Patrick's return; and, in less than a week, the intercourse betwixt him and his brother's wife, which led to such tragical consequences, was stated to have commenced. Four months afterwards, in pursuance of a diabolical plot betwixt Mrs. Ogilvie and her seducer, the former effected the death of her husband by means of arsenic. She and her accomplice were accordingly brought to trial, when both were found guilty, and condemned to be hanged. Sentence was executed upon Patrick Ogilvie, in the Grassmarket of Edinburgh; but Catherine Nairne, whose sentence had been delayed in consequence of pregnancy, made her escape from the tolbooth soon after her accouchement. She effected this by assuming the garb and demeanour of the midwife, Mrs. Shiells, who had, for several days previously, attended on her patient with her head muffled up, under pretence of a violent attack of toothache.

There is every reason to believe that the stratagem was matured under the connivance of her uncle Sir William, then Mr. Nairne; and, at least, some of the prison guards were not ignorant of what was to take place. There have been various conjectures as to the precise time Catherine Nairn quitted the city—some asserting that she remained concealed in Edinburgh for some days prior to her flight to the continent. It appears almost certain, however, that she left the city the same night (Saturday the 15th March, 1766) on which she escaped from the jail;—a carriage was in waiting at the foot of the Horse Wynd, in which was Mr. Nairne's clerk—the late Mr. James

Bremner, afterwards solicitor of Stamps—who accompanied Mrs. Ogilvie as far as Dover, on her way to France.

Notwithstanding her very critical situation, Mr. Bremner was in momentary dread all the way of a discovery, in consequence of her extreme frivolity of behaviour, as she was continually putting her head out of the window and laughing immoderately. She was, as previously noticed, very young, and had only been married in January 1765; and the crime for which she was tried was completed, by the death of her husband, in the month of June following. She was described, in the proclamation issued for her apprehension by the magistrates of Edinburgh, as attired in "an officer's habit, with a hat slouched in the cocks, and a cockade in it;" and "about twenty-two years of age, middle-sized, and strong made; has a high nose, black eyebrows, and a pale complexion." Two rewards were offered for her apprehension,—one by Government, and another by the city of Edinburgh, of one hundred pounds each. It is said she was afterwards very fortunate, having been married to a Dutch gentleman, by whom she had a numerous family. Rumour also represents her as having ultimately retired to a convent and taken the veil; and adds, that she survived the French Revolution, and died in England in the present century.

THE LEVELLING OF THE HIGH STREET,

Edinburgh.

THE idea of levelling the High Street was entertained so far back as 1785; and the "contest" which ensued is a matter of some notoriety in the civic history of the Scottish capital. The projected improvement was one of considerable importance, as it contemplated the reduction of a very inconvenient and somewhat dangerous rise in the centre of the street, which greatly incommoded the communication by the north and south approaches. Under the patronage of Sir James Hunter Blair, then Lord Provost, the undertaking was acceded to by a majority of the Town Council, and an advertisement issued in consequence, stating that a contractor was wanted "to level the High Street, and to dig and carry away from it about 6000 cubic yards of earth." This advertisement was generally understood to mean simply the reduction of the "crown o' the causey" to a level with the sides; but, when the operation commenced, it was discovered that the plan was much more extensive, and that, in following it out, some parts of the street would require to be lowered more than five feet. The proprietors of houses and shops became alarmed. Meetings were called, and a serious and formidable opposition to the measure was organised. A bill of suspension and interdict (somewhat analogous to an injunction in England) was presented; and subsequently, on the 8th October, an interlocutor was pronounced, appointing a condescendence (or specification of facts) to be given in, showing in what manner the adjacent houses, vaults, &c., would be affected by the proposed alterations. Reports were then lodged by Messrs. Brown and Kay, on the part of the Town Council; and by Messrs. Young and Salisbury, on that of the proprietors. The bill of suspension was passed.

This municipal squabble was of course too good a subject for the genius of Kay to overlook; accordingly we are presented with a group of the persons most zealous and interested in this bone of contention.

Mr. ORLANDO HART, who carried on business as a shoemaker in the High Street, opposite the Old City Guard-House, and was considered one of the most fortunate of the city politicians. For a series of twenty or twenty-five years he was almost constantly a member of the Town Council, or a Deacon, or a Trades Councillor—having been first elected Deacon of the Cordiners in 1766, and thereafter Convener of the Trades in 1771. He possessed a happy knack of suiting himself to circumstances, and was peculiarly sagacious in keeping steady by the leading men in the magistracy; the consequence of which was, in addition to extensive patronage in the way of his calling, the enjoyment of the pretty lucrative situation of Keeper of the Town's Water Works, &c. He was of course favourable to the Lord Provost's plan of levelling the street.

The popularity of Mr. Hart among the jolly sons of St. Crispin appears to have been of very early growth. In 1757, he was the victorious candidate for the honour of *monarchy*, in the spectacle of King Crispin, in opposition to Deacon Malcolm, whose party, determining not to be thrown into the shade, crowned him king also; so that, what was perhaps unprecedented in the annals of Christendom, two rival kings and their subjects actually walked in the same procession, without producing a single "broken bane or bluidy head."

Mr. Hart, though never famed among his friends for the depth of his understanding, appears, nevertheless, to have had a pretty good opinion of himself. On one occasion Mr. (afterwards Provost) Creech happened to put the question to Daft Davie Erskine—"Who is the wisest man in the city?" He received for reply, "Mr. Hart." The next time Mr. Creech met the Deacon, he told him the story; upon which the latter modestly replied, "Davie is no sic a fool as ye tak' him for."

The Deacon and Provost Dalrymple resembled each other extremely in personal appearance; so much so, that a gentleman, meeting the Provost one day, challenged him for not sending home his boots. The Provost, comprehending the mistake, which doubtless had occurred on other occasions, good-humouredly replied, "I will attend to it to-morrow."

Mr. Hart built the centre house on the north side of Charlotte Square, which, we have been informed, cost about £10,000. He died on the 9th September, 1791; and was followed to the grave, in seven days afterwards, by his widow. His son, Macduff Hart, whom he had assumed as a partner, under the firm of Orlando Hart and Son, continued to carry on the business, and was elected Deacon of the craft in 1782. He was particularly celebrated for his vocal powers.

Mr. WILLIAM JAMIESON, mason and architect, whose father, Mr. Patrick Jamieson, built the Royal Exchange, which was begun in 1753. The parties in the agreement for erecting this building were—

the Right Honourable William Alexander, Lord Provost; David Inglis, John Carmichael, Andrew Simpson, and John Walker, Bailies; David Inglis, Dean of Guild; Adam Fairholm, Treasurer, &c., on the part of the City—and Patrick Jamieson, mason; Alexander Peter, George Stevenson, and John Moubray, wrights; John Fergus, architect—all burgesses, freemen, members of Mary's Chapel of Edinburgh—undertakers. In the contract, the sum to be laid out in purchasing houses and grounds whereon to erect the Exchange is stated at £11,749 6s. 8d., and the cost of erection at £19,707 16s. 4d.—amounting, in all, to £31,457 3s. sterling. The first stone was laid in 1753, by George Drummond, Esq., at that time Grand Master of the Freemasons. A triumphal arch, and theatres for the Magistrates, and galleries for the spectators, were erected on the occasion. The work, however, was not fully entered upon till the year following, and was finished in 1761. He was elected one of the Deacons of Mary's Chapel in 1767; and, like his friend Mr. Orlando Hart, was very successful in avoiding those political quicksands which, in the good old days of corporate omnipotence, were so dangerous to individual prosperity. As a reward for his steadily having "shoulder kept to shoulder," he possessed for many years the sinecure office of Engraver to the Mint in Scotland, with a salary of £50 a-year—in which appointment he succeeded Convener Simpson. This sinecure is now abolished; and no wonder, when the duties of the office could be sufficiently performed by a stone-mason.

The most memorable public performance of Mr. Jamieson was the renovation of the Tron Kirk, which he accomplished much to the satisfaction of the public. The steeple was built principally of wood, and existed until the great fire in November, 1824, when some of the embers from the burning houses having lodged in it, and the wind blowing hard, the steeple was set on fire and destroyed, along with the bell, which had been hung in 1673, and cost 1490 merks. The steeple was rebuilt in 1828, and the bell re-cast and placed in its old situation, where it now again performs its usual functions.

Mr. Jamieson was also contractor for making the public drains of the city, at an estimate of no less than £100,000—the rubbish from the excavations of which was to be carted to Portobello, without being subject to the dues leviable at the toll of Jock's Lodge, the bar being partly under the management of the Town Council. The toll-keeper, however, having taken it into his head that he ought to be paid the regular dues, on one occasion closed the gate against the carts of the contractor. The circumstance being made known to Mr. Jamieson, "Weel, weel," said he to the carters, "just coup the carts at the toll-bar;" which was accordingly done, to the grievous annoyance of the toll-keeper, who never afterwards refused the right of egress and ingress.

The greatest part of Portobello was the Deacon's property at one period, and feued out by him. He himself latterly resided there, although, when Kay's Print was done, his house was in Turk's Close.

Mr. Jamieson married, about the year 1759, Miss Christian Nicholson, sister of the late Sir William Nicholson of Jarvieswood, by whom he had six sons and six daughters. The eldest daughter married

James Cargyll, Esq., W.S., and died only a few years ago; the next was married to a Mr. Stoddart, who had realised a fortune abroad; the third to James Marshall, Esq., present Secretary to the Provincial Bank of Ireland in London; and the youngest, who also survives, to the late Reverend Dr. Robertson of South Leith. The rest mostly died when young. The only son who reached manhood was the late William Jamieson, W.S., who died in 1826. This gentleman attained a temporary celebrity by his attacks on the Judges of the Court of Session; for which, however, he smarted pretty severely—perhaps more so than the case required. His widow and family still reside at Portobello.

Mr. ARCHIBALD M'DOWALL, clothier, North Bridge, for many years a leading member of the Town Council. He is represented as holding in his hand a plan of the improvement proposed by the Magistrates.

Mr. M'Dowall was a cadet of the ancient family of M'Dowall of Logan. His father, James M'Dowall of Canonmills, was nearly related to the late Andrew M'Dowall, Lord Bankton. In the entail of the estate of Bankton, in East-Lothian, and certain other property, executed in 1756, he is a *nomination* substitute, and is therein stated to be his lordship's cousin. The present Mrs. Gilmour of Craigmillar is the great-grandchild of this James M'Dowall, and was consequently grand-niece of Mr. Archibald M'Dowall. Being the descendant of his eldest brother, she succeeded to the property of Canonmills, on the death of her father, while in minority. It may not be out of place to mention, that Mr. Patrick M'Dowall, the father of James M'Dowall of Canonmills, was the first private banker who discounted bills in Edinburgh. He carried on business before the erection of the Bank of Scotland, under the Act of Parliament in 1695, and for a considerable time afterwards.

Mr. M'Dowall was born in 1748, and married in early life a near relation of the late Dr. John Macfarlan, minister of the Canongate Church (who married his sister), and father of John Macfarlan of Kirkton, Esq., advocate, and also of the present Dr. Patrick Macfarlan of Greenock. He commenced the first cloth manufactory in Scotland, similar to those carried on so extensively at Leeds, and brought a number of workmen from England for that purpose. In order to encourage Mr. M'Dowall's manufactory, the Earl of Buchan proposed that such gentlemen of the Antiquarian Society as intended to be present at the first anniversary meeting of the Society, on the 30th November 1781, should be dressed entirely in "home-made" articles. Accordingly, they all appeared with clothes of M'Dowall's manufacture, worsted hose, &c. Lord Buchan, being the last who made his appearance, on looking round, immediately exclaimed, "Gentlemen, there is not one of you dressed according to agreement, myself excepted; your buckles and buttons are entirely English, whereas mine are made from jasper taken from Arthur's seat." And very beautiful they were. The bed of jasper is now exhausted. This establishment was at Paul's Work, at the South Back of Canongate, now called M'Dowall Street, from which he afterwards removed to Brunstain Mill, near Portobello. Being, however, unable to compete with the English manufactories, the speculation proved unsuccessful.

Dr. Wm. CULLEN

[To face page 156.

Orlando Hart .   Wm. Jamieson .   Arch. M'Dowall .

THE LEVELLING OF THE HIGH STREET

Vol. I., Plate XIV.]

Mr. M'Dowall entered the Town Council in 1775, and in politics took the same side as his friend Sir James Hunter Blair. He was several times in the magistracy; and, before his retirement, was offered the Provost's chair, which he prudently declined, in consequence of the depressed state of his manufactory. He was a very public-spirited man, and devoted much of his time to the improvement of the city.

Mr. M'Dowall died December, 1816, leaving six sons. The oldest, after being unsuccessful as a merchant, settled in Van Dieman's Land, where he obtained a grant of land, which he has denominated, after that of his ancestor, the estate of Logan. For two of his sons Mr. M'Dowall obtained appointments in the East India Company's Service. One of them (Colonel Robert) was nearly thirty years in India, during which time he distinguished himself at the siege of Seringapatam, and on various other occasions—particularly in the surprise and complete dispersion of above 3000 Pindaries—for which he received the thanks of the Governor-General in Council, and of the Court of Directors. He afterwards was at the capture of Tavoy and Mergui, of which he was appointed Governor; but was unfortunately killed, in command of two brigades of native infantry, at the conclusion of the Burmese war. The other son who went to India (Mr. William), after being about twenty years in the Madras Medical Establishment, has returned, and now resides at Bellevue Crescent. Two other sons of Mr. M'Dowall entered the mercantile profession; and his youngest son (Mr. Charles) is a Writer to the Signet.

In the back ground the Lord Provost (Sir James Hunter Blair), is represented as busily employed in digging and shovelling out the earth; while Mr Hay, Deacon of the Surgeons, and a most violent anti-leveller, is as eagerly engaged in shovelling it back again. Mr Hay was a leader of the opposition in the Council.

This civic squabble gave birth to various local effusions; and among others, to a satirical poem in Latin doggerel, entitled, "*Streetum Edinense, carmen Macaronicum,*"—in which Mr Hay is made to sustain a prominent part. This mock-heroic poem was the joint-production of the late Mr. Smellie, printer, and of Mr Little of Liberton. It will be found in "Kerr's Memoirs of Smellie." After alluding to the zeal displayed in the matter by Sir James Hunter Blair, and just at that moment that assent has been given to the measure by the Councillors present, the Deacon is represented as bursting into the Council Chamber, backed by a posse of anti-levellers, and in a harangue of most uncouth hexameters, declaims against the project, and dares his brethren to carry it into effect.

THOMAS NEIL,

Wright and Precentor.

IT is now forty-two years since this "son of song" departed to the "world of spirits;" yet he is well remembered by many of the old inhabitants of Edinburgh. He was forty years a precentor in the Old

Church; and, it is believed, the last time he officiated was at the re-opening of that place of worship, at the close of last century, after it had undergone some extensive repairs.

Perhaps no man in Edinburgh of his time possessed greater local notoriety than "Tam Neil." He was a universal favourite, and seemed formed for the very purpose of "smoothing the wrinkled brow of care;" and although his wit may not have been of the most brilliant description, yet there was in the manner of the humourist an inimitable archness, which irresistibly compelled even the most serious of his auditors to "hold their sides" for a time.

As we have already said, Tam was a precentor. The clear, strong, musical voice with which he was endowed peculiarly adapted him for the desk, and no derogatory tongue has yet dared to say that he did not perform his duties regularly and with propriety; but there was a solemnity in the walls, and a dulness in the long faces of a church, which by no means comported with his own mirth-creating features. It was in the tavern that Tam was glorious! There, in giving due effect to some humorous Scottish ditty, his whole powers of music and mimicry found ample scope. He could also sing, with great pathos, many of our most pathetic national melodies; but Tam had not a heart for sadness.

"He possesses the knack of setting off his songs with so much drollery," is the remark of Kay in his notes, "and such a singular peculiarity of manner, that in all probability he will never have an equal or successor. He has the art of adapting not only his voice, but his very features so much to the subject of the song—especially where it will admit of mimicry—that a stranger, who may have seen him in the 'Old Man's Wish' in one company, would not know him half-an-hour after as the 'Old Wife' in another—so very different a turn does he give to his voice, features, and action."

The latter of these songs, in the character of which he is represented in the print, was one of his particular favourites. With a handkerchief wrapped over his head, his lips compressed, and his long chin set prominently forward, his imitations of the querulous voice of age, were quite inimitable.

There was another production (a catch), familiar to the vocalists of the present day, called "The Merry Christ's Church Bells," in which Neil displayed, with wonderful effect, the compass and harmony of his voice; and so peculiar was the volubility of his tongue, that his audience would almost fancy they heard the very chiming of the merry bells. "In short," observes his limner, "he may justly be considered the Momus of modern times, and the catch clubs of Edinburgh will only have to regret that he is not immortal."

Upon the late James Livingstone of Glasgow, who died there only in 1836, may be said to have descended the inspiring mantle of Thomas Neil; and our readers of the West, from their recollections of the one, will be the better able to form a proper estimate of the other. There was a *difference*, however, in the characters of the two. Perhaps Livingstone surpassed his predecessor, not in the more genuine, but in the more varied version of the national comic song; while the other possessed in a higher degree, the power and harmony of voice necessary

to constitute a superior glee and catch-singer. Livingstone, in private
company, was the most simple and unaffected creature imaginable—
temperate and recluse. Not so with his witty Bacchanalian precursor,
who, in the words of the song was

——"a canty chiel,
And dearly lo'ed the whisky."

Tam's facetious talents furnished him with a ready passport to all
classes of society. He was frequently a solicited guest at the table of
the great, and always a welcome visitor to many a well-known "howff"
in the city. With the magistracy he sat cheek-for-jowl at all civic
feasts; and occasionally enlivened the club meetings of the Caledonian
Hunt with his presence, his wit, and his songs. In company, a very
frequent salutation was—" Come, now, Tam, gie's your *thrifty* sang "
—a request with which he immediately complied, by chanting, in his
own inimitable manner, the following stanzas, well known to our
" auld forbears," but now almost obsolete :—

" Sweet sir, for your courtesie, when you come by the Bass, then,
For the love ye bear to me, buy me a keeking-glass then."

" Keek into the draw-well, Janet, Janet ;
And there ye'll see your bonnie sel', my jo, Janet."

" Keeking in the draw-well clear, what if I should fa' in, then,
Syne a' my kin will say an' swear I drown'd mysel' for sin, then."

" Haud the better by the brae, Janet, Janet ;
Haud the better by the brae, my jo, Janet."

" Good sir, for your courtesie, coming through Aberdeen, then,
For the love you bear to me, buy me a pair o' shoon, then."

" Clout the auld, the new are dear, Janet, Janet ;
A'e pair may sair ye ha'f a year, my jo, Janet."

" But what, if dancing on the green, and skipping like a mankin,
If they should see my clouted shoon of me they will be tankin'."

" Dance aye laigh, and late at e'en, Janet, Janet ;
Syne a' your faults will no be seen, my jo, Janet."

" Kind sir, for your courtesie, when ye gae to the cross, then,
For the love ye bear to me buy me a pacing horse, then."

" Pace upon your spinnin' wheel, Janet, Janet ;
Pace upon your spinnin' wheel, my jo, Janet."

Unlike modern professional gentlemen, it was no part of Tam's economy to charm his friends out of their money; it will not, therefore,
be surprising that his talents proved in some measure destructive of
his industry. He frequently felt the " pinging " gnawings of an
empty pocket; yet " poor but hearty " continued to be his motto—and

" A cog o' gude swats, an' an auld Scottish sang,"

together with the approbation of his friends, were sufficient to set poverty and care at defiance. Tam worked for many a day as a journeyman wright, even after he became precentor. He at length set up in a small way for himself, and might have succeeded well; but his customers were neglected, and his trade gradually dwindled down by a species of consumption not uncommon in such cases. Coffins were a staple commodity of Tam's manufacture, although he could not properly be considered an undertaker; and, in this line, notwithstanding his tippling propensities, and when almost every other species of employment had left him, he continued to receive a degree of patronage. Even on this grave subject the precentor's drollery could not be restrained. When any of his cronies (and many a one of them he screwed down in their last narrow house) were complaining, he used to rally them with a very professional observation—" Hech, man, but ye smell sair o' fir."

Tam was employed on one occasion to make a coffin for a youth who had died at Easter Duddingston, and in the evening he and his apprentice went to take the article home. The coffin was enclosed in a bag, that it might be the more easily carried. On arriving at the village of Duddingston, it being a cold moonlight night in November, Tam felt an irresistible desire to fortify himself with a glass. He and his apprentice accordingly entered the first public-house, and having drank a "gill of the best," the landlady was called in, and Tam began to explore his unfathomable pockets for the odd sixpence upon which he had speculated, but not a bodle was there. Tam looked astonished, apologised for the awkward circumstance, and promised to "look in" as he came past. But "Na!"—the prudent hostess "didna get her drink for naething, and couldna let it gang that gait." Tam promised, flattered, and threatened; but all would not do. " Weel, weel," said he, " since ye're sae doubtfu' o' my honesty, as I'm gaun to play at a bit dance oot by at Easter Duddingston the nicht, I'll e'en leave the case o' my bass fiddle till I come back." This seemed to satisfy the landlady; and Tam, with the aid of his apprentice, soon unbagged the coffin! Inspired with that feeling of awe, if not of terror, which that emblem of mortality, under such circumstances, was calculated to produce, the landlady exclaimed, with unfeigned perturbation, " Awa', ye gallows-looking blackguard; gin that be the case o' yir bass fiddle, neither you nor it shall stay in my house." Her request, as may be well imagined, was very readily complied with.

Tam was questioned one day by a lady, at whose house he was employed in making some repairs, as to the reason why people of his profession were so extravagant in their charges for coffins. Tam looked very mysterious, and agreed to inform her of *the secret* for the matter of a good glass of " Athole brose;" which moderate stipulation being immediately implemented, he told her, " It's juist because they are ne'er brought back to be mended." As we have already hinted, the precentor's wit consisted more in the *method* than the matter; and hence the reason, although he never failed to " set the table in a roar," that there are few of his sayings which do not lose materially by being written down. There are still one or two anecdotes not altogether unworthy of notice. Tam was one night engaged in a tavern with a party of select friends, among whom was the late Mr. Home Drummond, a gentleman then young, and who, it is said, could relish a night's diversion well, provided he did not "buy his joys o'er dear." During the evening, Tam delighted the company with his very best songs, and, in return, was plied at every interval with an excess of liquor. Mr. Drummond, in particular, perhaps with the view of making him tipsy, pressed the songster without mercy, frequently adding, that if he did not drink off his glass he should have *Keltic's mends*—(*i.e.*, fill the glass and make him drink it over again.) When the debauch was finished, and the parties came to the street, one of those present, who was by no means sober, feeling an increase of thirst from the excess of his libations, put his head to the mouth of the well in the High Street, and commenced drinking most vigorously. "Out wi't," cried the songster, chuckling over his imagined victory—"out wi't; or, by my sang, ye shall hae *Keltic's mends*."

Tam and a drouthy crony accidentally met in the Potterrow (*Scottice*, Patterraw) one forenoon, after a night of heavy drinking. They both stood much in need of a drop to brace their nerves, but not a stiver was betwixt them. In vain they looked round for some kindly invitation—in vain some dernier howff was suggested. The precentor's *licht* was now on the wane; yet he "couldna think of parting dry-mouth'd." "Como," said Tam, a fancy having struck him; "let's see what chance will provide." They accordingly dived into the house of an old acquaintance whom they had not seen for some time. A gill was called, and the landlady desired to sit down and tak' "the poison aff the glass;" which she readily did, to oblige "sae auld a friend as the precentor." The whisky went round, and a conversation ensued upon the common topics of the day—the American war, the dearth of provisions, &c.; and Tam took care not to overlook the modern alterations going on in the city. "What wi' levelling streets, and bigging brigs, they'll no leave ae stane o' the auld town aboon anither," said the landlady.—"It's a confounded shame," rejoined Tam; "and sic an *auncient* city, too! I'm tauld the Apostle Paul ance visited this very district we're sitting in the noo." "Nonsense!" exclaimed his crony. "Ye're gyte now," said the landlady; "I'm sure I've read the Testament mony a time, an' I ne'er saw sic a thing in't."—"What'll ye bet, then?" quoth the wily precentor. "It's no for the like o' me to be betting," said she; "but in a case like this, I'll haud ye the gill on the table there's no a word about the Patterraw." The Testament was produced—Tam turned over the leaves with affected difficulty—till at last he hit upon the passage, Acts xxi. 5,—"And we came with a straight course into Coos, and the day following into Rhodes, and from thence into P-a-t-a-r-a." Against such conclusive evidence the simple hostess could urge no appeal; and was so highly pleased with the discovery, that, like Eve, she wished the "gudeman" to be made as wise as herself, even at the expense of another gill. John, who had been engaged in the cellar, very opportunely made his appearance, and, being told of the astonishing fact, was as incredulous as his rib had been. John was better acquainted with the process of reducing bead twenty-two to thirty than he was with the contents of the New Testament; nevertheless, he could with great security " wager ony man half-a-mutchkin that the Patterraw, nor ony ither *raw* in a' Edinburgh, was nae sae muckle as mentioned between the twa buirds o' the Bible." The half-mutchkin stoup, instead of the small tantalizing measure which had hitherto occupied the table, was accordingly filled by the gudewife, who was secretly gratified that John's wisdom, so immaculate in his own estimation, was about to be found somewhat faulty. We need scarcely add, that the " P-a-t-a-r-a " of the text at once decided who should " pay the piper; " and Tam, thus plentifully supplied, was spared the alternative he had dreaded of parting with a dry mouth.

Like most others whose talents become so much an object of social gratification, Tam, who at first drank for the sake of good company, latterly drank for the sake of good liquor. He knew and felt this, and by no means attempted either to deceive himself or others on the subject. Mr. Nisbet of Dirleton (himself an excellent musician, and contemporary of the musical Earl of Kelly) happened to meet the jovial precentor pretty early one forenoon, in the High Street, rather more than half-seas-over. Dirleton challenged Tam for being " so groggy before meridian." "Why," said he, "don't you let your debauch stand till night?" Tam acknowledged the justice of his censure—"Vera true, sir, vera true; but as I maun aye be this way ance a day, I maun just tak' it when I can get it."

Tam continued to be *that way* very frequently for a great length of time—his constitution apparently experiencing little or no bad effects from the practice. He lived to a good old age, and died within a few days of the close of last century. His death is thus recorded in the *Edinburgh Magazine* for 1800:—" Died, December 7, Thomas Neil, wright, and precentor in the Old Church of Edinburgh, aged about 70 years. In the profession of a precentor he has held the incumbency for full forty years. He excelled in singing old humorous Scots songs, and that certainly was his forte."

MAJOR CAMPBELL,

Of the Thirty-fifth Regiment.

CAMPBELL was a native of the " East-neuk of Fife," where his father possessed an estate which yielded, some eighty years ago, a very comfortable income of nearly £500 per annum; but the wholesale hospitality maintained by the *laird*, and an extravagant indulgence in the luxury of foreign wines, which were then landed without molestation at all the little bays on the east coast of Scotland, at last brought the "mailing" to the hammer. Claret could then be had for £15 a hhd.

Mr. Campbell entered the army, and shared in all the harassing campaigns of the first American war, in which he had been frequently and severely wounded. While on service there, it is said he received an injury which totally altered the original form of the most prominent feature in his countenance, having received a blow in the face with a musket from a soldier of his own regiment, whom he had been reprimanding. According to Kay's MS., the man was immediately tried by a court-martial, and condemned to be shot; but the Major stayed the execution of the sentence, and subsequently applied for and obtained a free pardon for the offender.

Although this anecdote is by no means inconsistent with the amiable character of Major Campbell, it is rendered somewhat apocryphal by the fact that he was too much beloved by the soldiers of his company, who rejoiced in his eccentricities, to be injured by any of them.

Major Campbell was a gentleman of very peculiar manners. His speech, like the Baron of Bradwardine's, was usually interlarded with scraps of Latin. He had studied at St Andrews,—a circumstance which he delighted to refer to. A very slight and casual allusion instantly furnished him with an opportunity for introducing his favourite remark—" at the College of St Andrews, where I was taught languages, sciences, and various *sorts of particulars*, my dear." *My dear* he used indiscriminately in addressing persons of whatever rank—whether General O'Hara, the stern governor, or a drum-boy.

At Gibraltar, on one occasion, the General ordered a regiment, which had newly arrived to replace another about to embark on different service, to be inspected by several of the field-officers—each private to step six paces in front of the line for that purpose. The corps thus to be scrutinized was a battalion of the Scots Brigade, which had been raised in Edinburgh in 1794, by the late Lieut.-General Ferrier, and of such a diminutive size were the men, that they were called " the Garvies " by the inhabitants. Major Campbell was one of the inspectors, and he patiently endured the tedious process of overhauling this very indifferent sample of his countrymen, till at length one peculiarly coarse-visaged, short, cross-made, elderly little fellow stepped out his six paces. Unable longer to contain himself, and running up to the soldier, he stooped to the level of the ill-favoured " militaire," then grinning, or rather *girning* in his face, he bawled out—" Well, doubly d——n me ! (his usual exclamation), but you are an ugly b—— ! my dear." Then turning to a fellow-officer (Lieut.-General Ainslie) who stood by—" He seems conglomerated, my dear; from *con* and *glomeo*, as we used to say at St Andrews, my dear."

Major Campbell remained with his regiment until a very old man, and so worn out that he could not poise his sword without the assistance of both his hands.

He married Miss Macalister, sister to Lieut.-Colonel Macalister, 35th regiment, by whom he had one son, Henry Fletcher.

Our hero, died more than forty years since. His son was an officer in the same regiment, and having retired, married a sister of Sir Charles Turner, of Abberley, near Witherley, in Yorkshire, by whom he obtained a handsome fortune. He died some thirty years ago.

THE ROYAL EDINBURGH VOLUNTEERS.

The Edinburgh (or, as they were afterwards called, the Royal) Volunteers, were embodied in 1794. The plan of instituting the corps was first contemplated in the month of June of that year; and, on the third of July following, a general meeting of the proposed members was held in the Sheriff Court-Rooms, when certain leading articles of regulation were established, and a committee of management appointed. The Volunteers were to bear all their own expenses of clothing and other necessaries; and half-a-guinea of entry-money was exacted from each member, towards defraying contingencies. Subsequently, however, on application to Government, the usual pay was obtained for an adjutant; pay and clothing for a sergeant-major and twenty sergeants; and also for twelve drummers and twelve fifers. The entire scheme of embodying the citizens as volunteers, it is said, was solely projected by the late James Laing, Deputy City Clerk. By one of the articles, the uniform is described to consist of a blue coat, with a red cape and cuff, white lining turned up in the skirts, two gold epauletes, and a button bearing the name of the corps and arms of the city; white cassimere vest and breeches, and white cotton stockings; short gaiters of black cloth; a round hat, with two black feathers and one white; and black cross-belts. The belts of the Edinburgh Volunteers were painted white, which soon gave the corps an awkward appearance on account of the paint scaling off, and leaving portions of white and black alternately. They were accordingly soon laid aside, and the common buff belt substituted. The uniform underwent many other changes. The two grenadier companies had a bear-skin and a grenade on the hat, and grenades at the joining of the skirts of the coat; while the officers of the corps were only distinguished by their swords.

The regiment, being assembled in Heriot's Green on the 26th September, 1794, was presented with a stand of colours by the Lord Provost (Sir James Stirling), attended by the two senior Magistrates, the Principal of the University, and the whole Members of the Town Council, in their robes. The colours were very handsome: the one elegantly embroidered with a crown, and the letters G. R.; and the other with the City Arms. A vast crowd of spectators attended to to witness the presentation.

The original officers of the corps were: *Lieutenant-Colonels*—Thos. Elder, Old Provost; William Maxwell, Colonel in the Army (now General Sir William Maxwell). *Majors*—Roger Aytoun, Lieutenant-Colonel in the Army; Archibald Erskine, late Major of 22nd Foot. *Captains*—Patrick Crichton, a Captain in the Army; Charles Kerr, late Captain 43rd Foot; Andrew Houston, late Lieutenant of the Carbineers; John Anstruther, late Lieutenant 17th Foot; Robert Hamilton, late Lieutenant 82nd Foot; William West, Captain in the Army; Robert Arbuthnot, Lieutenant in the Army; Thomas Armstrong, late Lieutenant 80th Foot; Captain-Lieutenant George Abercromby. *Lieutenants*—Baine Whyt, W.S.; William Coulter; Malcolm Wright; John Clark; David Reid; John Pringle; Thomas Hewen, late Captain in

4th Dragoons; Archibald Campbell, late Lieutenant in the Army; David Hume, late Lieutenant of Marines; Henry Jardine (now Sir H. Jardine), W.S.; Robert Dundas (the late Sir Robert Dundas. Baronet, of Dunira); Robert Hodgson Cay, Advocate. *Ensigns*— John Dundas, John Menzies, John Wood, Lachlan Mactavish, James Brown, James Dickson, Charles Phin, Morris West. *Chaplain*— Rev. G. Baird. *Adjutant*—Patrick Crichton. *Quartermaster*—David Hunter. *Treasurer*—Hugh Robertson. *Secretary*—Henry Jardine. *Surgeon*—Thomas Hay. *Assistant-Surgeons*—John Rae and James Law.

In a pamphlet, entitled "View of the Establishment of the Royal Edinburgh Volunteers," published in June, 1795, an alphabetical list of all the members is given, amounting to 785; which, but for its extreme length, might have been worth transcribing. At that period, no less than 55 members of the celebrated "Cape Club" were enrolled in the corps. Five old sovereigns of the Cape were doing duty in one company, and seven knights were officers of the Volunteers.

The Lord Provost, by virtue of his office, was Colonel of the regiment; and all the other commissions were conferred by the King on the recommendation of the Volunteers themselves. The privates of each company were permitted to name individuals of their number to be their officers; and it is related as a curious fact, that several of these officers owed their elevation solely to their being unfit to march, or keep their places in the ranks properly, having been selected by the privates in order that they might get rid of the annoyance of an awkward comrade.

The first review of the Volunteers took place at Bruntsfield Links, on the 22nd November, 1794, when they were inspected by the Duke of Buccleuch, Lord Lieutenant of the County. On this occasion the spectators were very numerous, and highly respectable. Among the nobility and gentry present were—the Duchess of Buccleuch and family, the Earl of Morton, Lord Ancrum, the Lord President, the Lord Advocate, and many of the Lords of Session. On the 6th of July, 1795, they had another "grand field-day" at the Links, when the Right Honourable Mr. Secretary Dundas was received as a volunteer into the corps. The same day he gave an elegant entertainment in Fortune's Tavern to the Lord Provost, Magistrates, and Council, and to several other gentlemen. As a mark of respect, Mr. Dundas was immediately afterwards requested by the Lord Provost, in name of the corps, to accept the station of Captain-Lieutenant, which he declined, but gratefully acknowledged the honour in a highly complimentary letter.

The patriotic example of arming in defence of their country, which had been shown by the gentlemen of Edinburgh, was speedily followed throughout Scotland. Every district had its band of armed citizens—the discontented became silent, and loyalty was the order of the day—

"We'll give them a welcome, we'll give them a grave,"

was the prevailing sentiment, should the enemy dare to set a foot on Scottish ground. Burns, in his impassioned song of "The Dumfries

Volunteers," seems to have thoroughly embodied in it the spirit of the times—

> " Does haughty Gaul invasion threat?
> Then, let the loons beware, sir :
> There's wooden walls upon our seas,
> And volunteers on shore, sir.
> The Nith shall rin to Corsincon,
> And Criffel sink in Solway,
> Ere we permit a foreign foe
> On British ground to rally !"
>
>   *   *   *   *   *
>
> " The kettle o' the Kirk an' State,
> Perhaps a clout may fail in't ;
> But deil a foreign tinkler loon
> Shall ever ca' a nail in't."
> Our fathers' bluid the kettle bought
> And wha wad dare to spoil it ?
> By heaven ! the sacrilegious dog
> Shall fuel be to boil it."

In consequence of the alliance of Spain with France, a meeting of the Lieutenants of the city, and the officers of the Edinburgh Volunteers, was held on 14th September, 1796, when they resolved,—"that as this apparent increase of strength, on the part of our enemies, must give them additional confidence, it is highly necessary to show them that this country is capable of increasing its exertions in proportion to the force brought against it." Accordingly, an augmentation of their corps being deemed necessary, another battalion was speedily organized, called the Second Regiment of Edinburgh Volunteers.

In 1797, when the French were every day expected to attempt a landing in Ireland, the First Regiment tendered their services to perform the duty of the Castle, in order to allow the withdrawal of the regular troops; and, in 1801, when the danger seemed more immediately to menace our own shores, the former offer of service was followed up with characteristic spirit.

The Lieutenant-Colonel commanding, the Right Hon. Charles Hope (afterwards Lord President and Privy Councillor), in his letter to General Vyse, at this alarming crisis, says—"In the event of an enemy appearing on our coast, we trust that you will be able to provide for the temporary security of Edinburgh Castle by means of its own invalids, and the recruits and convalescents of the numerous corps and detachments in and about Edinburgh; and that, as we have more to lose than the brave fellows of the other volunteer regiments who have extended their services, we trust you will allow us to be the first to share in the danger, as well as in the glory which we are confident his Majesty's troops will acquire under your command, if opposed to an invading army."

On the cessation of hostilities in 1802, the Volunteers were disbanded, after eight years of military parade; during which period they had "many a time and oft" marched to and from the camp at Musselburgh, and, on the sands of Leith, maintained the well-contested bloodless fight. They closed their first period of service on the 6th of May, 1802. Early in the afternoon of that day they assembled in Heriot's Green, where they first obtained their colours; and, having formed a hollow square, the Lieutenant-Colonel read Lord Hobart's circular letter, conveying his Majesty's thanks, and also the thanks of the two Houses of Parliament. He likewise read a resolution of the Town Council of Edinburgh, conveying, in the strongest and most handsome terms, the thanks of the community to the whole Volunteers of the city; and a very flattering letter from his excellency Lieut.-General Vyse. The regiment was afterwards marched to the Parliament Square, where, being formed, the colours were delivered to the Magistrates, who lodged them in the Council Chamber, and the corps was dismissed.

Such is a sketch of the first era of the Royal Edinburgh Volunteers. They were not, however, allowed to remain long unembodied. The peace, which had been proclaimed with great ceremony at the Cross of Edinburgh, on the 4th of May 1802, lasted something less than a year, when the threatening aspect of affairs again roused the scarcely tranquil feelings of the country. The preparations made by the Emperor Napoleon to invade this country, were met by a correspond-ing effort on the part of the British Government, which was supported by the united energies of the whole people. In few places was the spirit of the country more signally displayed than in Edin-burgh. Upwards of four thousand volunteers were enrolled; and notwithstanding the great sacrifice of time which the proper training to arms required, all men seemed actuated with one spirit, and cheerfully and without complaint submitted to the tedious process of military instruction, aware of the importance of order and disci-pline against an enemy whose bravery was unquestioned, and who had given so many proofs of great military skill and enterprise. On the 30th September, 1803, the Royal Edinburgh Volunteers resumed their warlike banners. On this occasion the regiment was augmented to a thousand rank and file; and in conformity with the general orders previously issued, their dress was changed to scarlet with blue facings.

Notwithstanding the "mighty note of preparation," the military operations which followed this new enrolment were happily not of a more sanguinary nature than those of the former. With the exception of forming guard occasionally when a fire occurred in the city, the duties of the Volunteers were confined to the usual rou-tine of drills, field-days, and reviews—and these they continued to perform year after year with unabating zeal. In 1806, when new regulations were issued limiting the allowance to volunteer corps, the First Regiment stood unaffected by them. The circumstance seemed rather to stimulate their patriotism. "I wish to remind you," said their Lieut.-Colonel, addressing them one day while on parade, "that we did not take up arms to please any minister, or set of ministers, but to defend our land from foreign and domestic enemies."

One of their great field-days occurred on his Majesty's birth-day, 1807, when the Lieutenant-Colonel, the Right Honourable Charles Hope (then Lord Justice-Clerk), was presented with a valuable sabre, of superb and exquisite workmanship, in testimony of their regard for him as an officer and a gentleman. The sword was presented by Thomas Martin, Esq., sergeant of grenadiers, in name of the non-commissioned officers and privates.

In the year 1820, during the disturbances of the West, the Edinburgh Volunteers garrisoned the Castle, to enable the regular troops stationed there to proceed to Glasgow. The corps volunteered, if necessary, to leave Edinburgh, and co-operate with the regular troops, and one night remained actually under marching orders. It was then. as many professional gentlemen were enrolled as privates, no infrequent occurrence to find barristers pleading in the Parliament House. attired in warlike guise, with their gowns hastily thrown over their red coats. A short time afterwards the corps was somewhat unceremoniously disbanded.

GEORGE PATON,

Bibliographer and Antiquary.

Mr. GEORGE PATON was a keen bibliographer and antiquary. His father, Mr. John Paton, a respectable bookseller in the Old Parliament Square, was one of the committee of philanthropic citizens. who, in conjunction with the worthy Provost Drummond, originated that invaluable institution the Royal Infirmary. The facts and circumstances in the history of Mr. Paton, the younger, are scanty. He received a liberal education, but without any professional design, having been bred by his father to his own business. This, however, he relinquished, on obtaining a clerkship in the Custom-House, at a salary for many years of only £60. In this humble situation, the emoluments of which were subsequently augmented to £80, he continued during the remainder of his long life, apparently without the smallest desire of attaining either to higher honour or greater wealth.

The chief aim of his ambition seemed to be the acquisition of such monuments of antiquity as might tend to elucidate the literature, history, and topography of his native country. His father had been an antiquary of some research, and at his death left a valuable collection, which the subject of our sketch took care, by every means within the compass of his narrow income, to augment. As illustrative of the strong bibliomania both in father and son, it is told of them, that whenever they happened to meet with any curious publication, instead of exposing it in the shop for sale, they immediately placed it in their private library. By singular regularity in the arrangement of his time, and strict frugality, Mr. Paton not only discharged his duties in the Custom-House with fidelity, but found leisure to acquire a degree of antiquarian lore, and was enabled to increase his curious collections to an extent seldom attained by a single individual.

He was well known to almost all the literary characters of his own country, and to many English antiquaries and men of letters. Apparently unambitious of figuring in the world as an author himself, Mr. Paton was by no means chary of assisting others. His services—his knowledge—his time—as well as his library, were at the command of all his friends. It is said the late Archibald Constable derived much of his knowledge of the rarity of books from his acquaintance with Mr. Paton. These ultimately became a sort of common, where our antiquarian writers of last century were wont to luxuriate, and whence they would return, like bees, each to his own peculiar locality, laden with the spoil obtained from the stores of this singularly obliging and single-hearted individual.

Mr. Paton was thus led into a very extended circle of literary acquaintance, with whom he maintained a constant and very voluminous correspondence. Amongst others, we may instance Lord Hailes, Dr. Robertson, Gough, Percy, Ritson, Pennant, George Chalmers (author of Caledonia), Captain Grose, Callander of Craigforth, Riddel of Glenriddel, Law (author of the "Fauna Orcadensis"), Herd (the Collector of Scottish Ballads), &c.

Of the "Paton Correspondence," preserved in the Advocates' Library, two small volumes have been published; the one in 1829, the other in 1830. The former is entitled "Letters from Joseph Ritson, Esq., to George Paton;" the latter, "Letters from Thomas Percy, D.D. (afterwards Bishop of Dromore), John Callander of Craigforth, David Herd, and others, to George Paton." These volumes, not generally known, from the limited impression thrown off, are enriched by many interesting editorial notes, and are highly entertaining and curious. They also bear unquestionable testimony to the status in which Mr. Paton was held as a literary antiquary, and to the alacrity with which he laboured to supply the desiderata of his friends.

It is a curious fact, however, that, with the exception of Gough, few or none of those who were so materially indebted to him for information and assistance had the candour to acknowledge the source from whence they were aided; and many of them afterwards seemed desirous of suppressing all knowledge of the fact. The correspondence between Gough and Paton at once show the extent and importance of the information furnished by the latter; and, indeed, this is acknowledged in handsome terms by Gough, in the preface to his *new* edition of the *British Topography*. Alluding to the article upon Scottish topography, he says—"by the indefatigable attention of his very ingenious and communicative friend, Mr. George Paton, of the Custom-House, Edinburgh," he had been enabled nearly to double the space which the article occupied in the first volume.

In the collection and arrangement of his ancient "Scottish Ballads," David Herd received material assistance from Mr. Paton; and there are even strong reasons for believing that he "partly, if not wholly, edited the first edition."

Mr. Paton remained all his life a bachelor; but, although naturally of a retiring disposition—solitary in his domestic habits—and by no means voluble in general conversation, he was neither selfish in his disposition, nor unsocial in the circle of those friends with whom kindred pursuits and sentiments brought him into association. The best proof of this is the fact of his having regularly frequented "Johnie Dowie's tavern"—the well-known rendezvous of the Scottish literati during the latter part of the last century. In a humorous description of this "howff," ascribed to the muse of Mr. Hunter of Blackness, the subject of this sketch is alluded to in one of the verses:—

> " O, Geordie Robertson, dreigh loun,
>   And antiquarian Paton soun',
>   Wi' mony ithers i' the toun,
>   What will come o'er ye,
>   Gif Johnie Dowie should stap doun
>   To the grave before ye?"

A farther illustration of the social habits, as well as a glimpse of the peculiar domestic economy of "antiquarian Paton," is given in a pleasant editorial note affixed to one of David Herd's Letters to Mr. Paton, which letter is dated "*Johnie Dowie's, Tuesday Evening*," 23rd *December*, 1788.—" For many years of his life our friend (the antiquary) invariably adjourned to take his bottle of ale and gude 'buff'd herring,' or 'roasted skate and ingans,' to this far-famed tavern, which was divided into cells, each sufficient, with good packing, to hold six persons; and there, with Herd, Cumming of the Lyon Office, and other friends of the same kidney, the evenings pleasantly passed away. These meetings were not infrequently enlivened by the presence, at one period, of Fergusson the poet, and more recently of Burns. Let it not be supposed that honest George indulged in habits of intemperance. Such was not his custom; one bottle of ale would suffice for him, certainly not more; and when his usual privation is considered, it is surprising how moderate his desires were. He rose early in the morning, and went to the Custom-House without tasting anything. Between four and five (afternoon) he uniformly called at the shop of a well known bibliopolist of those times (Bailie Creech), from whom he was in the habit of picking up rarities, and refreshed himself with a drink of cold water. He would then say, 'Well, I'll go home and take breakfast.' This breakfast consisted of one cup of coffee and a slice of bread. Between seven and eight he adjourned to the place of meeting; and some of the dainties enumerated in the poem (already alluded to), and a bottle of 'strong ale,' formed the remaining refreshment of the day. The moment eleven 'chappit' on St. Giles, he rose and retreated to his domicile in Lady Stair's Close. His signal for admittance was the sound of his cane upon the pavement as he descended. In this way this primitive and excellent person spent the best part of his days. Upon a salary of £80 per annum he lived contented, happy, and universally respected."

No man within the walls of Edinburgh, it has been said, ever passed a more inoffensive life than did "honest George Paton;" yet, by the literary services which he rendered to others, he did not escape the displeasure of one or two individuals, whom his critical strictures had offended. The article formerly mentioned—on Scottish topography—gave mighty offence to Martyn John Armstrong, who, in company with his son, had published, in 1774-5, surveys of several counties in Scotland. Armstrong addressed two very ill-natured letters—one to Paton and the other to Gough—on the subject. This philippic appears to have roused the temper of the antiquary. In writing to Gough, ignorant of the counterpart which that gentleman had received, he thus gives vent to his indignation :—" While writing this, the enclosed impertinent, ignorant, scurrilous rhapsody was brought before me ; forgive my transmitting it for perusal, which be kind enough to return at pleasure. I am diffident of resolution whether such a blundering blockhead of an impostor shall have any answer made him ; horse-whipping would serve him better than a reply. . . . . He is below notice, and despise him, as he is generally so here. The joint tricks of father and son being so well known in this place, they could remain no longer with us." From this specimen of " hard words," it may be inferred, that however quiet and inoffensive he might be, " honest George " by no means lacked spirit to resent injury or insult. From a similar cause he also incurred the displeasure of his irritable countryman and fellow-antiquary, John Pinkerton, from whom he had the honour of a very violent epistle. These petty ebullitions of offended authorship, however, which threatened to disturb the wonted quiet current of the antiquary's life, evaporated without mischief.

The personal appearance of Mr. Paton was somewhat peculiar. His dress was plain and neat ; and he always wore a black wig.

The death of Mr. Paton occurred on the 5th of March, 1807, having attained the great age of eighty-seven.

His valuable library was sold by auction in 1809 ; and his manuscripts, prints, coins, etc., were disposed of in a similar manner in 1811. The first sale occupied a month ; the latter about ten days.

THE LAST LORD PITSLIGO.

In our notice of Sir William Forbes, we stated that he was maternally descended from the Lords of Pitsligo. His grandson, the present Sir John Stuart Forbes, is the heir of the family—the Master of Pitsligo having died without issue. Alexander, the last Lord Pitsligo, was attainted in 1745. He had been out with Mar in 1715, and for several years afterwards took refuge in France. Although an old man (being sixty-seven years of age) when Prince Charles raised his standard in 1745, Lord Pitsligo again took the field, at the head of a party of Aberdeenshire gentlemen, forming a body of well-equipped cavalry, about 100 strong, and with whom he joined the Pretender in Edinburgh, after the battle of Preston. He shared in all the subsequent movements of the Jacobite army ; and, after the final overthrow at Culloden, instead of flying abroad, he found shelter in his native country, and among his own peasantry. His preservation was very extraordinary, and can only be attributed to the excellence of his character, and the esteem in which he was held by all who knew him. The place of his concealment was for some time a cave, constructed under the arch of a bridge, at a remote part of the moors of Pitsligo, and the disguise which he assumed was that of a mendicant. This disguise, though it did not deceive his friends and tenants, saved them from the danger of receiving him in his own person, and served as a protection against soldiers and officers of justice, who were desirous to apprehend him for the sake of the price set upon his head. On one occasion he was seized with asthma just as a patrol of soldiers were coming up behind him. Having no other expedient, he sat down by the road-side, and, anxiously waiting their approach, begged alms of the party, and actually received them from a good-natured fellow, who condoled with him at the same time on the severity of his asthma.

In this way the romantic adventures and narrow escapes of the old Lord Pitsligo were numerous and interesting. At length, in 1748, the estate having been confiscated and seized upon by Government, the search became less rigorous. His only son, the Master of Pitsligo, had married the daughter of James Ogilvy, of Auchiries, and the house of Auchiries received the proscribed nobleman occasionally under the name of Mr. Brown. The search, however, was frequently renewed; and on the last occasion his escape was so very singular, that it "made a deep impression at the time, and was long narrated by some of the actors in it with those feelings of awe which the notion of an approach even to the supernatural never fails to produce.

" In March, 1756, and, of course, long after all apprehension of a search had ceased, information having been given to the then commanding officer at Fraserburgh, that Lord Pitsligo was at that moment in the house of Auchiries, it was acted upon with so much promptness and secresy, that the search must have proved successful, but for a very singular occurrence. Mrs. Sophia Donaldson, a lady who lived much with the family, repeatedly dreamed on that particular night that the house was surrounded by soldiers. Her mind became so haunted with the idea, that she got out of bed, and was walking through the room in hopes of giving a different current to her thoughts before she lay down again. When day beginning to dawn, she accidentally looked out at the window as she passed it in traversing the room, and was astonished at actually observing the figures of soldiers among some trees near the house. So completely had all idea of a search been by that time laid asleep, that she supposed they had come to steal poultry, Jacobite poultry-yards affording a safe object of pillage for the English soldiers in those days. Under this impression, Mrs. Sophia was proceeding to rouse the servants, when her sister, having awaked, and inquiring what was the matter; and being told of soldiers near the house, exclaimed in great alarm, that she feared they wanted something more than hens! She begged Mrs. Sophia to look out at a window on the other side of the house, when not only soldiers were seen in that direction, but also an officer giving instructions by signals, and frequently putting his fingers on his lips, as if in enjoining silence. There was now no time to be lost in rousing the family; and all the haste that could be made was scarcely sufficient to hurry the venerable man from his bed into a small recess behind the wainscot of an adjoining room, which was concealed by a bed, in which a lady, Miss Gordon of Towie, who was there on a visit, lay, before the soldiers obtained admission. A most minute search took place. The room in which Lord Pitsligo was concealed did not escape. Miss Gordon's bed was carefully examined; and she was obliged to suffer the scrutiny of one of the party, by feeling her chin, to ascertain that it was not a man in a lady's night-dress. Before the soldiers had finished their examination in this room, the confinement and anxiety increased Lord Pitsligo's asthma so much, and his breathing became so loud, that it cost Miss Gordon, lying in bed, much and violent coughing, which she counterfeited, in order to prevent the high breathings behind the wainscot being heard. It may easily be conceived what agony she would suffer, lest by overdoing her part, she should increase suspicion, and in fact lead to a discovery. The *ruse* was fortunately successful. On the search through the house being given over, Lord Pitsligo was hastily taken from his confined situation, and again replaced in bed; and, as soon as he was able to speak, his accustomed kindness of heart made him say to his servant, 'James, go and see that these poor fellows get some breakfast, and a drink of warm ale, for this is a cold morning; they are only doing their duty, and cannot bear me any ill-will.' When the family were felicitating each other on his escape, he pleasantly observed, 'A poor prize had they obtained it—an old dying man!'"

By degrees the heat of civil rancour ceased, and Lord Pitsligo, like others in his situation, was permitted to steal back into the circle of his friends unpersecuted and unnoticed. The venerable old nobleman was thus suffered to remain at his son's residence of Auchiries unmolested during the last years of an existence protracted to the extreme verge of human life. He died on the 21st December, 1762, in the 85th year of his age.

The character of Lord Pitsligo was of the most amiable description, and he embarked in the cause of the exiled Stuarts from national feelings alone. He was a Protestant, of the Episcopal Church, and sincerely attached to his religion. He was of a literary turn of mind; and left behind him several manuscript essays, which were published shortly after his death. To one of these—entitled " Thoughts Concerning Man's Condition and Duties in this Life, and his Hopes in the World to Come "—an interesting memoir of his life is prefixed.

DR. WILLIAM CULLEN,

Professor of Chemistry.

DR. WILLIAM CULLEN was born in the parish of Hamilton, county of Lanark, in the year 1710. He received the first part of his education under Mr. Brisbane, at the grammar-school of Hamilton; and, having chosen medicine as a profession, he was apprenticed to a surgeon-apothecary in the city of Glasgow. It does not appear that he went through a regular course of education at the University, so that the chief means of improvement he possessed at this time were derived from observing his master's practice, and perusing such medical works as fell in his way. It is not known at what age he went to Glasgow, nor how long he continued there; but in very early life he engaged as a surgeon to a vessel that traded between London and the West Indies, and performed several voyages in that capacity. Disliking a sea-faring life, he attempted to get into medical practice in his native country, and first settled in the parish of Shotts. He remained there only for a short time, and then removed to Hamilton, where he was chosen one of the magistrates of that burgh. The Duke of Hamilton happening to be taken suddenly ill, Dr. Cullen was called in ; and his mode of treatment was much approved by Dr. David Clark, who had been brought from Edinburgh. This accidental circumstance added much to his medical reputation in that quarter.

During his residence at Hamilton, Dr. Cullen became acquainted with Mr. William Hunter. These two celebrated characters, who were destined to do so much, each in his own line, for the advancement of medical science, had very early entered into habits of the strictest intimacy. Dr. Hunter had been originally intended for the Church ; and with that view had attended some of the classes at the University of Glasgow. Cullen's conversation, however, gave a different direction to his studies, and he resolved to study medicine.

In consequence of the extension of his practice, Cullen resolved to apply to the University of Glasgow for a medical degree, and this he accordingly obtained upon the 14th September, 1740. On the 13th November, 1741, he married Ann Johnston, the daughter of a neighbouring clergyman, by whom he had a numerous family. His eldest son, Robert, was a Lord of Session and Justiciary.

During the residence of Dr. Cullen in Hamilton, Archibald Earl of Islay, afterwards Duke of Argyle, being in that part of the country, required some chemical apparatus. It was suggested to him that Dr. Cullen was more likely to have what his lordship wanted than any other person. He was accordingly invited to dinner by his lordship, and fortunately made himself very agreeable. This interview was one of the chief causes of his future rise in life. He had secured the patronage of the Prime Minister of Scotland, the future Duke of Argyle, besides the countenance of the Duke of Hamilton. In 1746, the lectureship on chemistry, in the University of Glasgow, which is in the gift of the College, became vacant. Cullen offered himself as a candidate, and was accordingly elected. He commenced his lectures in the month of October of the same year. In 1751, the professorship of medicine (in the gift of the Crown) becoming vacant, the interest of Argyle procured it for him. He appears to have taught both classes. In 1755, he transmitted a paper to the Physical and Literary Society of Edinburgh, "On the cold produced by Evaporating Fluids, and of some other means of producing cold,"—the only chemical essay he ever published.

In 1756, he was unanimously elected Professor of Chemistry in the University of Edinburgh, where the medical school was already formed ; and he had much greater incitements to exertion than he had in Glasgow. Dr. Whytt, who taught the institutes of medicine, died in 1766, and Dr. Cullen obtained the vacant chair. Dr. John Gregory, a short time before, had succeeded to the chair of the practice of physic ; and these two Professors continued each to teach his own class for three sessions. At the conclusion of the session, 12th April, 1769, Dr. Cullen proposed to the patrons that Dr. Gregory and he should alternately teach the institutes and the practice. This was complied with ; and it was declared that the survivor should have in his option which professorship he preferred. Upon the lamented death of Dr. Gregory,

10th February, 1773, Dr. Cullen chose the practice; and upon the 17th of the same month he was duly installed into the office.

When Dr. Cullen taught the " Institutes," he published " Heads of Lectures for the use of Students in the University of Edinburgh," but he proceeded no farther than physiology. In 1772, appeared, in two volumes octavo, " Synopsis Nosologiæ Methodicæ," which was written in Latin. The merit of this performance is universally admitted. He criticised impartially the works of those who had gone before him in this department of medical science, and candidly pointed out in what respects his own arrangement might be objected to. This seems to have been particularly designed, in order to prepare the public for his great work, which he was then composing, and which was looked for with general impatience: it, however, did not appear till 1776. It was entitled " First Lines of the Practice of Physic." Its circulation through Europe was both rapid and extensive. It became exceedingly popular, and not only raised his reputation very high, but enriched him considerably, as it is said to have produced upwards of three thousand pounds sterling. About a year before his death, he published "A Treatise on the Materia Medica," in two volumes quarto.

The high respect in which the genius and character of the venerable Professor were held by the patrons, professors, and students of the University of Edinburgh, as also by societies in Ireland and America, will appear from the following addresses and resolutions:—

" On the 8th January, 1790, the Lord Provost, Magistrates, and Council of Edinburgh voted a piece of plate, of fifty guineas value, to Dr. Cullen, as a testimony of their respect for his distinguished merits and abilities, and his eminent services to the University, during the period of thirty-four years in which he has held an academical chair. On the plate was engraved an inscription expressive of the high sense the Magistrates, as patrons of the University, had of the merit of the Professor, and of their esteem and regard."

" A meeting of the Pupils of Dr. Cullen was held on the 12th, in the Medical Hall, when an address to the Doctor was agreed upon, and ordered to be presented by the following gentlemen:—Dr. Jackman, Mr. Gagahan, and Mr. Gray, annual presidents of the Medical Society; Dr. Black, Dr. Gregory, Dr. Duncan, Mr. Alexander Wood, Mr. Benjamin Bell, Dr. James Hamilton, and Dr. Charles Stuart. A motion was also made, and unanimously agreed to, that a statue, or some durable monument of the Doctor, should be erected in a proper place, to perpetuate the fame of the illustrious Professor. The execution of this, and of all necessary measures for the purpose, was also committed to the above gentlemen."

" The Royal Physical Society presented an address to Dr. Cullen. The gentlemen of the deputation were very politely received by the Doctor's sons, Robert (afterwards Lord Cullen) and Dr. Henry Cullen, (Dr. Cullen himself being much indisposed), and a suitable answer returned."

Similar addresses were presented by the Hibernian Medical Society, and by the American Physical Society of Edinburgh.

The following resolution was agreed to by the Senatus Academicus of the University of Edinburgh :—

" Edinburgh College, January 27.—The Principal and the Professors of the University of Edinburgh being this day convened in the Senatus Academicus, Dr. Gregory informed them, that, at a meeting of the Royal Medical Society, and of the other gentlemen, the former and present pupils of Dr. Cullen, it had been resolved to erect some durable monument of grateful respect for their venerable instructor ; and the committee appointed for carrying this determination into execution, thinking a conspicuous place in the new College would be most proper for that purpose, he was empowered to request, in their name, the consent of the Senatus Academicus.

" The members of the Senatus Academicus, thoroughly acquainted with the eminent and various talents of their illustrious colleague, and sensible how much they have contributed towards increasing the reputation of the school of medicine in the University, unanimously expressed the warmest approbation of this resolution ; and they have no doubt their venerable patrons, who, with their usual attention to the welfare of the University, have already given a public and honourable testimony of the estimation in which they hold the genius and merit of Dr. Cullen, will readily concur with them in granting what is desired. And the Senatus Academicus desired their secretary to furnish Dr. Gregory with an extract of this minute, to be by him communicated to the Royal Medical Society, and the other gentlemen concerned.

(Signed) " WM. ROBERTSON, Principal.
" ANDW. DALZIEL, Secretary."

Dr. Cullen, now far advanced in years, had thus the satisfaction of anticipating, from these flattering testimonials of respect, in what estimation his character was likely to be held by posterity. He died, at his house in the Mint Close, on the 5th of February, 1790, aged eighty-one.

WILLIAM BRODIE:

Tried for Breaking into the Excise Office.

THE trial of this individual for breaking into the Excise Office (then in Chessels's Court, Canongate), on the 5th March, 1788, created an unprecedented excitement in Edinburgh, arising not only from the extent and aggravated nature of the burglary, but from the respectable sphere of life in which the criminal previously moved.

His father, Convener Francis Brodie, carried on an extensive trade as a wright and cabinet-maker in the Lawnmarket, and was for many years a member of the Town Council. On his death, in 1780, his only son, William, succeeded to his business ; and he was, in 1781, chosen one of the ordinary Deacon Councillors of the City.

Unfortunately for the prosperity of the young deacon, he had at an early period imbibed a taste for gambling, and acquired considerable expertness in turning this degrading vice to account as a source of revenue ; and it appears, from an action raised against him by one

SIR JAMES GRANT

[To face page 176.

GEORGE SMITH.   WILLIAM BRODIE.

Vol. I., Plate XV.]

Hamilton, a chimney-sweeper, that he did not scruple to have recourse to the usual tricks resorted to by professed gamblers. In this action he is accused of having used loaded or false dice, by which Hamilton lost upwards of six guineas. In the gratification of this ruling passion, he was in the habit of meeting, almost nightly, a club of gamblers at a house of a most disreputable description, kept by a person of the name of Clark, in the Fleshmarket Close. Notwithstanding his profligate habits, Brodie had the address to prevent them from becoming public; and he contrived to maintain a fair character among his fellow-citizens. So successful was he in blinding the world, that he continued a member of the Council until within a short period of the time he committed the crime for which he afterwards suffered; and it is a singular fact, that little more than a month previously, he sat as a juryman in a criminal cause in that very court where he himself soon afterwards received sentence of death!

Although Brodie had for many years been licentious and dissipated, it is believed that it was not until 1786 that he commenced that career of crime which he ultimately expiated on the scaffold. About that time he became acquainted with his fellow-culprit, George Smith; and shortly afterwards, at the gambling haunt, with Ainslie and Brown —men of the lowest grade and most abandoned principles. The motives that induced Brodie to league himself with these desperate men are not very obvious. In comfortable circumstances, and holding situations of trust among his fellow-citizens, it is not easy to guess what could impel him to a line of conduct so very unaccountable. Let his motives have been what they might, however, Brodie, from his professional knowledge and his station in Society, had great facilities for furthering his contemplated depredations, and he became the leader of these miscreants, who acted by his orders, and were guided by his information.

About the latter end of 1787, a series of robberies were committed in and around Edinburgh, and no clue could be had of the perpetrators. Shops were opened, and goods disappeared as if by magic. The whole city at last became alarmed. An old lady mentions that a female friend of her's, who, from indisposition, was unable to go one Sunday to church, was, during divine worship, and in the absence of her servant, surprised by the entrance of a man, with a crape over his face, into the room where she was sitting. He very coolly took up the keys which were lying on the table before her, opened her bureau, and took out a considerable sum of money that had been placed there. He meddled with nothing else, but immediately re-locked the bureau, replaced the keys on the table, and, making a low bow, retired. The lady was panic-struck the whole time. Upon the exit of her mysterious visitor, she exclaimed, "Surely that was Deacon Brodie!" But the improbability of a person of his opulence turning a housebreaker, induced her to preserve silence at the time. Subsequent events, however, soon proved the truth of her surmises. In the most of these Brodie was either actively or passively concerned; but it was not until the last "fatal affair"—the robbery of the Excise Office—that he was discovered, and the whole machinery laid open.

This undertaking, it appears, was wholly suggested and planned by

Brodie. A friend of his, a Mr. Corbett from Stirling, had occasion to visit the Excise Office for the purpose of drawing money. Brodie accompanied him; and, while in the cashier's room, the idea first occurred to him. He immediately acquainted his colleagues with the design, and frequently made calls at the office, under the pretence of asking for Mr. Corbett, but with the sole purpose of becoming better acquainted with the premises. On one of those visits, in company with Smith, he observed the key of the outer door hanging on a nail, from which he took an impression of the wards with putty; and on the night of the 30th November, with the key formed from this model, they opened the outer door by way of experiment, but proceeded no farther.

It was not till the 5th of March following that the final attempt was made; on which occasion all hands were engaged. Their plan of procedure was previously well-concerted, and their tools prepared. They were to meet in the house of Smith about seven o'clock; but Brodie did not appear till eight, when he came dressed in an old-fashioned suit of black, and armed with a brace of pistols. He seemed in high spirits for the adventure, and was chanting the well-known ditty from the "Beggars' Opera"—

> " Let us take the road,
> Hark! I hear the sound of coaches!
> The hour of attack approaches;
> To your arms, brave boys, and load.
> See the ball I hold;
> Let the chemists toil like asses—
> Our fire their fire surpasses,
> And turns our lead to gold."

Brodie also brought with him some small keys and a double picklock. Particular duties were assigned to each. Ainslie was to keep watch in the courtyard; Brodie inside the outer door; while Smith and Brown were to enter the cashier's room. The mode of giving alarm was by means of a whistle, bought by Brodie the day before, with which Ainslie was to call once, if only one person approached—if two or more, he was to call thrice, and then proceed himself to the back of the building to assist Brown and Smith in escaping by the windows. All of them, save Ainslie, were armed with pistols. Brown and Smith had pieces of crape over their faces. They chose the hour of attack from the circumstance of the office being generally shut at eight, and no watchman being stationed till ten.

The party accordingly advanced to the scene of action. Ainslie and Brodie took up their respective positions, while Brown and Smith proceeded to the more arduous task of breaking into the cashier's room. Smith opened the first door with a pair of curling-irons; but in forcing the second or inner door, they had to use both the iron crow and the coulter of a plough, which they had previously stolen for the purpose. Having with them a dark lantern, they searched the whole apartment, opening every desk and press in it. While thus engaged a discovery had nearly taken place, the Deputy-Solicitor, Mr. James Bonnar, having occasion to return to the office about half-past eight. The outer door he found shut, and on opening it a man in black (Brodie) hurriedly passed by him, a circumstance to which, not having the slightest suspicion, he paid no attention. He went to his room up stairs, where he remained only a few minutes, and then returned, shutting the outer door hastily behind him. Perceiving this, Ainslie became alarmed, gave the signal, and retreated. Smith and Brown did not observe the call, but thinking themselves in danger, when they heard Mr. Bonnar coming down stairs, they cocked their pistols, determined not to be taken. After remaining about half-an-hour, they got off with their booty, which, much to their disappointment, amounted only to £16 odds, while they expected to have found as many hundreds. In their search they had overlooked a concealed drawer in one of the desks, where, at the very time, there were £600 deposited. On coming out, they were surprised not to find either Brodie or Ainslie; but, after returning to their former rendezvous, the latter soon joined them. In order to prevent suspicion, Brown and Ainslie immediately went to one Fraser's, who kept a tavern in the New Town, where, in company with some others, they supped and spent the night. Brodie, it appears, had hurried home, where he changed his dress, and then proceeded to the house of Jean Watt (who had several children to him), in Libberton's Wynd, where he remained all night. The parties met on the Friday evening following, and divided the booty in equal portions.

The robbery having been discovered about ten o'clock the same night it was committed, the town was in consternation, and the police on the alert in all directions. Brown (alias Humphry Moore), who appears to have been the greatest villain of the whole, was at the time under sentence of transportation for a crime committed in England; and having seen an advertisement from the Secretary of State's Office, offering a reward and a pardon to any person who should discover the robbery of Inglis and Horner's shop, he resolved on turning King's evidence, foreseeing that the public prosecutor would be under the necessity of obtaining pardon for his previous offence, before he could be admitted as a witness. Accordingly, on Friday evening, immediately after securing his dividend at Smith's, he proceeded to the Procurator-Fiscal's, and gave information, but without at the time mentioning Brodie's name as connected with the transaction. The reason of this appears to have been an intention to procure money from Brodie for secrecy, as, on ascertaining that he had fled, he no longer kept silence. He likewise conducted the officers of justice to Salisbury Craigs, where they found a number of keys concealed under a large stone, which he said were intended for future operations. In consequence of this, Ainslie, Smith, and his wife, and servant-maid, were all apprehended; and, after a precognition, lodged in prison.

Brodie, suspecting he stood on ticklish ground, fled on Sunday morning; and, from the masterly manner in which he accomplished his escape, baffled all pursuit for a time. On the Wednesday following, Mr. Williamson, King's messenger for Scotland, was despatched in search of him. He traced Brodie to Dunbar and Newcastle, and afterwards to London: from thence Williamson went to Margate, Deal, and Dover, but lost sight of him altogether; and, after eighteen days' fruitless search, returned to Edinburgh. But for Brodie's own imprudence, impelled apparently by a sort of fatuity frequently evinced by persons similarly situated, there was every chance of his finally escaping. He remained in London, it appears, until the 23rd March, when he took out his passage, in the name of John Dixon, on board one of the smacks bound for Leith, called the *Endeavour*. After the vessel had gone down the river Thames, Brodie came on board in a small boat, about twelve o'clock at night, disguised as an old gentleman in bad health. He was accompanied by two of the owners, who stopped on board for a short time. On going out to sea, as it no doubt had been previously arranged, the *Endeavour* steered for Flushing instead of Leith, where Brodie was put ashore, and immediately after took a Dutch skiff for Ostend.

So far so well: but, unfortunately for Brodie, there had been a Mr. Geddes, tobacconist in Mid-Calder, and his wife, fellow-passengers, with whom he frequently entered into conversation. On parting, he had given Geddes three letters to deliver in Edinburgh—one addressed to his brother-in-law, Matthew Sherriff, upholsterer; another to Michael Henderson, Grassmarket; and the third to Ann Grant, Cant's Close, Brodie's favourite mistress. She had three children to him. These letters, as he might well have expected, were the means of his discovery. On landing at Leith, Geddes became acquainted with the circumstances of the robbery, and immediately suspecting that Mr. John Dixon was no other than Deacon Brodie, he opened the letters, and became doubly strengthened in his opinion; but not having made up his mind how to proceed, Mr. Geddes did not deliver the letters to the authorities till near the end of May. Even, then, however, they were the means of Brodie's apprehension, and were afterwards put in evidence against him. Information of the circumstances was instantly despatched to Sir John Potter, British Consul at Ostend, in consequence of which Brodie was traced to Amsterdam, where, on application to Sir James Harris, then Consul, he was apprehended in an alehouse, through the instrumentality of one Daly, an Irishman, on the eve of his departure to America, and lodged in the Stadthouse. A Mr. Groves, messenger, was despatched from London, on the 1st of July, for the prisoner, by whom he was brought to London; and from thence to Edinburgh by Mr. Williamson, who was specially sent up to take charge of him. On the journey from London Brodie was in excellent spirits, and told many anecdotes of his sojourn in Holland.

The trial took place in the High Court of Justiciary, on the 27th August, 1788, before Lords Hailes, Eskgrove, Stonefield, and Swinton. The Court, from the great excitement in the public mind, was crowded to excess at an early hour. Smith and Brodie only were indicted, the other two having become "king's evidence." The trial commenced at nine o'clock in the morning of Wednesday, and the jury were enclosed till six o'clock in the morning of the following day. All the facts we have previously narrated were fully borne out by the evidence, as well as by the declarations of Smith while in prison. An attempt was made to prove an *alibi* on the part of Brodie, by means of Jean Watt and her maid; but the jury, "all in one voice," returned a verdict finding both panels "guilty." They were sentenced, therefore, to be executed at the west end of the Luckenbooths, on Wednesday, the 1st October, 1788. When the sentence had been pronounced by the Lord Justice-Clerk, Brodie manifested a desire to address the Court, but was restrained by his counsel. "His behaviour during the whole trial was perfectly collected. He was respectful to the Court; and when anything ludicrous occurred in the evidence, smiled as if he had been an indifferent spectator. His conduct on receiving sentence was equally cool and determined. Smith was much affected."

The counsel for the Prosecutor were—Ilay Campbell, Esq., Lord Advocate (afterwards Lord President); Robert Dundas, Esq., Solicitor-General (afterwards Lord Chief Baron); William Tait, Esq., and James Wolfe Murray, Esq. (afterwards Lord Cringletie), Depute-Advocates; and Mr. Robert Dundas, Clerk to the Signet.

For William Brodie—The Hon. Henry Erskine, Dean of Faculty; Alexander Wight, Esq., Charles Hay, Esq. (afterwards Lord Newton); Agents, Mr. Robert Donaldson and Mr. Alexander Paterson, Writers to the Signet.

For George Smith—John Clerk, Esq. (afterwards Lord Eldin); Robert Hamilton, Esq.; Mr. Æneas Morrison, agent.

The jurymen were—Robert Forrester, banker; Robert Allan, banker; Henry Jamieson, banker; John Hay, banker; William Creech, bookseller; George Kinnear, banker; William Fettes (afterwards Sir Wm.), merchant; James Carfrae, merchant; John Milne, founder; Dunbar Pringle, tanner; Thomas Campbell, merchant; Francis Sharp, merchant; James Donaldson, printer; John Hutton, stationer; Thomas Cleghorn, coachmaker.

During the whole period of Brodie's confinement, his self-possession and firmness never forsook him. He even at times assumed a Macheath-like boldness; and, with an air of levity, spoke of his death as a "leap in the dark." On the Friday before his execution, he was visited by his daughter, Cecill, about ten years of age; and here "nature and the feelings of a father were superior to every other consideration; and the falling tear, which he endeavoured to suppress, gave proof of his feeling. He embraced her with emotion, and blessed her with the warmest affection." Brodie's manner of living in prison was very abstemious; yet his firmness and resolution seemed to increase as the fatal hour approached—the night previous to which he slept soundly for five or six hours. On the morning he suffered, he conversed familiarly with a select number of his friends, and wrote a letter to the Lord Provost, requesting, as a last favour, "that as his friends, from a point of delicacy, declined witnessing his dissolution, certain gentlemen [whom he named] might be permitted to attend, and his body allowed to be carried out of prison immediately upon being taken down"—which request was readily granted.

The following account of the execution we give from one of the periodicals of the day:—"About a quarter-past two, the criminals appeared on the platform, preceded by two of the magistrates in their robes, with white staves, and attended by the Rev. Mr. Hardy, one of the ministers of Edinburgh—the Rev. Mr. Cleeve, of the Episcopal persuasion, in their gowns, and the Rev. Mr. Hall, of the Burghers. When Mr. Brodie came to the scaffold, he bowed politely to the magistrates and the people. He had on a full suit of black—his hair dressed and powdered. Smith was dressed in white linen, trimmed with black. Having spent some time in prayer, with seeming fervency, with the clergymen, Mr. Brodie then prayed a short time by himself.

"Having put on white nightcaps, Brodie pointed to Smith to ascend the steps that led to the drop, and, in an easy manner, clapping him on the shoulder, said, 'George Smith, you are first in hand.' Upon this Smith, whose behaviour was highly penitent and resigned, slowly ascended the steps, and was immediately followed by Brodie, who mounted with briskness and agility, and examined the dreadful apparatus with attention, and particularly the halter designed for himself. The ropes being too short tied, Brodie stepped down to the platform, and entered into conversation with his friends. He then sprang up again, but the rope was still too short; and he once more descended to the platform, showing some impatience. During this dreadful interval Smith remained on the drop with great composure and placidness. Brodie having ascended a third time, and the rope being at last properly adjusted, he deliberately untied his neckcloth, buttoned up his waistcoat and coat, and helped the executioner to fix the rope. He then took a friend (who stood close by him) by the hand, bade him farewell, and requested that he would acquaint the world that he was still the same, and that he died like a man. He then pulled the nightcap over his face, and placed himself in an attitude expressive of firmness and resolution. Smith, who, during all this time had been in fervent devotion, let fall a handkerchief as a signal, and a few minutes before three they were launched into eternity. Brodie on the scaffold neither confessed nor denied his being guilty. Smith, with great fervency, confessed in prayer his being guilty, and the justice of his sentence, and showed in all his conduct the proper expressions of penitence, humility, and faith. This execution was conducted with more than usual solemnity; and the great bell tolled during the ceremony, which had an awful and solemn effect. The crowd of spectators was immense."

In explanation of the wonderful degree of firmness, if not levity, displayed in the conduct of Brodie, a curious and somewhat ridiculous story became current. It was stated that he had been visited in prison by a French quack, of the name of Degravers, who undertook to restore him to life after he had hung the usual time; that, on the day previous to the execution, he had marked the temples and arms of Brodie with a pencil, in order the more readily to know where to apply the lancet; and, that with this view, the hangman had been bargained with for a short fall. "The excess of caution, however," observes our worthy informant, who was himself a witness of the scene, "exercised by the executioner, in the first instance, in shortening the rope, proved fatal by his inadvertency in making it latterly too long. After he was cut down," continues our friend, "his body was immediately given to two of his own workmen, who, by order of the guard, placed it in a cart, and drove at a furious rate round the back of the Castle." The object of this order was probably an idea that the jolting motion of the cart might be the means of resuscitation, as had once actually happened in the case of the celebrated "half-hangit Maggie Dickson." This woman had been executed for child-murder, and her body delivered to her relatives for interment, who put it in a cart to transport it a few miles out of town. Strange to say, half the journey was not accomplished, when, to the consternation of those present, the poor woman revived. She lived afterwards several years, and bore two children to her husband. The body was afterwards conveyed to one of Brodie's own workshops in the Lawnmarket, where Degravers was in attendance. He attempted bleeding, &c., but all would not do ; Brodie "was fairly gone."

Before closing our memoir of Deacon Brodie, it may not be uninteresting to give one or two extracts from those letters which proved the means of his discovery. In one addressed to his relative, Mr. Sherriff, he says—"My stock is seven guineas, but by the time I reach Ostend it will be reduced to six. My wardrobe is all on my back, excepting two check shirts, and two white ones. My coat out at the arms and elbows." In another addressed to Henderson, dated April 10, he writes—"I arrived in London on the 13th March, where I remained till the 23rd, snug and safe in the house of an old female friend, within five hundred yards of Bow Street. I did not keep the house all this time, but so altered, excepting the scar under my eye, I think you could not have *rapt* (swore) to me. I saw Mr. Williamson twice ; but although countrymen usually shake hands when they meet from home, yet I did not choose to make so free with him, *notwithstanding he brought a letter to me.* My female gave me great uneasiness by introducing a flash man to me, but she assured me he was a true man ; and he proved himself so, notwithstanding the great reward, and was useful to me. I saw my picture [his description in the newspapers] six hours before, exhibited to public view ; and my intelligence of what was doing at Bow Street Office was as good as ever I had in Edinburgh. I make no doubt but that designing villain Brown is in high favour with Mr. Cockburn [the Sheriff], for I can see some strokes of his pencil in my portrait. Write me how the main went—how you came on in it—if my black cock fought and gained," &c. He was passionately fond of cock-fighting. Here we have the mind of Brodie strongly imbued with his ruling passion for gambling. Immediately the recollection of his unhappy situation conjures up matter of serious reflection. He feelingly alludes to his children —"They will miss me more," says he, "than any other in Scotland. May God in his infinite goodness stir up some friendly aid for their support, for it is not in my power at present to give them any assistance. Yet I think they will not absolutely starve in a Christian land, where their father once had friends, and who was always liberal to the distressed." He then states his intention of proceeding to some part of North America, probably to Philadelphia or New York, and desires that his working tools might be purchased for him, and forwarded to either of those places, adding, that although it is hard to begin labour at my years, yet I hope, by industry and attention, to gain a livelihood. He was anxious to know what became of Brown, Smith, and Ainslie. And, in allusion to them, says—"I shall ever repent keeping such company ; and whatever they may allege, I had no direct concern in any of their depredations, except the last fatal one, by which I lost ten pounds in cash ; but I doubt not all will be laid to my charge, and some I never heard of."

GEORGE SMITH,

Accomplice of Deacon Brodie.

GEORGE SMITH was a native of Berkshire, in England. He and his wife were hawkers, and travelled the country with a horse and cart. He came to Scotland about the middle of the year 1786 ; and, on arriving in Edinburgh, put up at Michael Henderson's, a house at that period much frequented by the lower order of travellers. In consequence of bad health, he was under the necessity of parting with all his goods, and, latterly, with his horse, in order to support himself and his wife. While thus confined in Henderson's, the "first interview" took place, on which occasion Brodie suggested the possibility of "something being done to advantage, provided a due degree of caution were exercised." There is every reason to suppose that the *doing of something* was nothing new to Smith, who appears to have embraced very cordially and readily the propositions of Brodie. He soon became a visitor of the gambling-house of Clark, at the head of the Fleshmarket Close, where he formed acquaintance with Ainslie and Brown.

In his declarations, Smith confessed to the robbery of the College—of Tapp's dwelling-house—of a shop in Leith—and also of the shop of Inglis and Horner. The latter individual was father of Francis Horner, Esq., M.P., and Mr. Leonard Horner, sometime Warden of London University. He also disclosed the extensive robbery committed on the shop of John and Andrew Bruce. In describing this affair we will quote in part the language of the declaration, which is graphically illustrative of the career of Brodie, who had actually been a participator in almost all the forementioned depredations :—

"That Brodie told the declarant that the shop at the head of Bridge Street, belonging to Messrs. Bruce, would be a proper shop for breaking into, as it contained valuable goods; and he knew the lock would be easily opened, as it was a plain lock, his men having lately altered that shop door, at the lowering of the street: that the plan of breaking into the shop was accordingly concerted betwixt them; and they agreed to meet on the evening of the 24th of December, 1786, being a Saturday, at the house of James Clark, vintner, where they generally met with company to gamble: that, having met there, they played at the game of hazard, till the declarant lost all his money; but at this time Brodie was in luck, and gaining money: that the declarant often asked Brodie to go with him on their own business; but Brodie, as he was gaining money, declined going, and desired the declarant to stay a little and he would go with him." Smith, however, becoming impatient, as it was near four in the morning, went himself to the Messrs. Bruce's shop, from which he took a number of watches, and a variety of jewellery articles, amounting in all to the value of £350. Brodie called upon Smith next day, when the latter told him he could not expect a full share, "but that there were the goods, and he might choose for himself." Brodie accordingly took a gold seal, a gold watch-key set with garnet stones, and two gold rings. As the safest method, it was agreed that Smith should go to England and dispose of the goods—Brodie giving him five guineas and a-half to defray his expenses. The goods were accordingly sold in Chesterfield, to one John Tasker *alias* Murray, who had been previously banished from Scotland. Smith repaid the money advanced by Brodie, besides giving him three ten-pound notes more to keep for him, in case of suspicion, which he afterwards got in sums as he wanted it.

While in prison, a desperate attempt to escape was made by Smith and Ainslie—the latter of whom occupied a room on the highest floor. It occurred in the night between the 4th and 5th of May, by converting the iron handle of the jack (or bucket) into a pick-lock, and one of the iron hoops into a saw. Smith took one door off the hinges, and opened the other which led to Ainslie's apartment. Both prisoners setting then to work, they cut a hole in the ceiling, together with another in the roof of the prison, and had prepared about sixteen fathoms of rope, manufactured out of the sheets of their beds. The falling of the slates on the street, however, attracted the notice of the sentinel, who, giving the alarm, they were immediately secured. After this failure, Smith seems to have given up all hope. He at one time intended to plead guilty, and prepared a speech in writing for the purpose; but was afterwards prevailed upon to take his chance of a trial. He also, with his own hand, drew up a list of robberies—some of them of great magnitude—intended for future commission.

During Smith's stay in Edinburgh, he kept a kind of grocery shop in the Cowgate; and he affirmed that his wife knew nothing of his criminal mode of life. Her evidence was not taken in Court.

Of the history of the other accomplices nothing seems to have been known, even by their companions. In the list of witnesses, the designation of the one is, John Brown *alias* Humphry Moore, sometime residing in Edinburgh; of the other, Andrew Ainslie, sometime shoemaker in Edinburgh.

JOHN WRIGHT,
Lecturer on Law.

MR. WRIGHT was the son of a poor cottar in Argyleshire, who, by smuggling between that coast and the Isle of Man, was enabled to maintain his family for many years in comparative comfort; but, finding his "occupation gone," in consequence of the strict prohibitory measures enforced by Government, a short time prior to the transfer of the sovereignty of that island in 1765, he left the Highlands and settled in Greenock. Here the future "lecturer on law," who had been bred to the humble occupation of a shoemaker, manifested an uncommon desire for knowledge. Whilst employed at his laborious avocation, his mind was generally engaged in study. It is told of him, that to aid his memory in acquiring a knowledge of the Latin language, and not having the command of writing materials, he used to conjugate the verbs on the wall of his work-room with the point of his awl.

Having mastered the rudiments of the Latin tongue, he removed to Glasgow, where, with no other assistance than the proceeds of his labour, he entered a student at the University; and, notwithstanding the manifest disadvantages under which he laboured, made rapid progress in his studies. Indeed, so decided was his success, that he soon found himself almost wholly relieved from the drudgery of shoe-making, by giving private lessons to his less assiduous class-fellows—many of whom, being the sons of noblemen and wealthy commoners, remunerated him liberally for his instructions. The views of our scholastic aspirant being directed towards the Church, he was in due course of time licensed to preach; but finding himself destitute of patronage—and perhaps aware, from a deficiency in oratorical powers, that he might never become popular in the pulpit—he yielded to the advice of several of the Professors, whose friendship his talents had secured, and set about attaining a more thorough knowledge of the higher branches of mathematics, which at that period were not con-sidered so essential as they now are to the student of divinity.

After having attained, if not the reality, but what was in his case much better, the reputation of knowledge in this new study, Mr. Wright removed to Edinburgh, where he commenced teaching mathe-matics and the science of military architecture. This proved a very lucrative speculation, a great number of young men about Edinburgh being at the time preparing to go out to India.

With the view of ultimately pushing himself forward to the bar, Mr. Wright now directed his attention to the Roman law; and, after a short time spent in preparatory study, commenced giving lectures on the subject. He subsequently gave lectures on Scots law. Both sets of lectures were well attended.

In 1781, having qualified himself in the usual manner, he applied o be admitted a member of the Faculty of Advocates. The following information as to the opposition offered by the faculty to his entry, is recorded in the minutes of the 8th December, 1781:—

"The vice-dean (John Swinton, afterwards Lord Swinton) informed the faculty that Mr. John Wright, who for many years had exercised the profession of a private teacher of the civil and municipal law and mathematics, had called upon him, and acquainted him that he had presented a petition to the Court of Session, praying a remit to the Dean and Faculty of Advocates to take him on his trial. Upon this Mr. Swinton observed, that he wished this step postponed—a proposi-tion which was assented to by Mr. Wright—till he had had an oppor-tunity of mentioning the intention to the faculty. He added—'that so far as ever he could learn, Mr. Wright bore a fair and irreproachable character, and he did not mean the slightest reflection against him; but that the circumstances which appeared peculiar in his case were, that at his advanced time of life, it might be presumed he did not mean to take himself entirely to the profession and practice of the law, but only wished to add the character of advocate to his present employment.'

"The Hon. Henry Erskine acquainted the faculty that Mr. Wright had conversed with him upon this subject, and had authorised him to assure the faculty, that in case of his being admitted advocate, he

truly intended to follow the profession of the bar, and to lay aside
private teaching of mathematics, or any other science, except law;
and even to confine that teaching to private lectures to such as chose
to attend them in his own house."

A considerable difference of opinion appears to have been entertained, but the good sense of the majority ultimately settled that the
Faculty should not interfere; and Mr. Wright was admitted an
advocate upon the 25th January, 1783.

It has been said that the real cause of the opposition of Mr.
Swinton, and his party, originated in their objections to Mr. Wright's
humble birth; and that the Hon. Henry Erskine bantered them so
much, that they at last gave way. After listening to the observations
of the opposition—"Well, well," said Mr. Erskine, "they say I am
the *son* of the *Earl of Buchan*—and you (pointing to ————) are
the *son* of the Laird of ————;" and thus going over the whole
opposition in a strain of inimitable and biting sarcasm, he wound up
the enumeration in his usual forcible manner—"Therefore no thanks
to us for being here; because the learning we have got has been
hammered into our brains!—whereas, all Mr. Wright's has been
acquired by himself; therefore he has more merit than us all. However, if any of you can put a question to Mr. Wright that he cannot
answer, I will hold that to be a good objection. But, otherwise, it
would be disgraceful to our character as Scotsmen were such an act of
exclusion recorded in the books of this society. Were he the son of a
beggar—did his talents entitle him—he has a right to the highest
distinction in the land."

Mr. Wright never attained to great eminence as a pleader. He
spoke so very slow that his pleadings were far from being effective.
On one occasion he was engaged in conducting a case before Lord
Hailes. Mr. ————, the opposing counsel, who first addressed the
bench, spoke so thick, fast, and indistinct, that his lordship was under
the necessity of requesting him to speak slower, that he might understand him; but the judge found himself in the adverse predicament
with Mr. Wright. "Get on a little faster," said his lordship, addressing the advocate, "for I am tired following you." "If it were
possible," observed Erskine, *sotto voce*, "to card the two together,
something good might be made of them both."

Mr. Wright was unquestionably more fitted for a lecturer than an
advocate; and to his success in the former avocation he was chiefly
indebted for a livelihood. He also derived no inconsiderable income
from his literary labours. For many years he wrote all the Latin
theses. One work on mathematics brought him a very considerable
sum. ("Elements of Trigonometry, Plane and Spherical; with the
Principles of Perspective and Projection of the Sphere." In 8vo.
Edinburgh, 1772.) This he entered in Stationers' Hall; but as the
law then only secured copyrights for seven years, at the end of that
period he had the mortification to find his treatise inserted in the
Encyclopædia Britannica, without permission sought or obtained.
Mr. Wright was so much offended at this appropriation of his pro-
perty that he seriously contemplated bringing the case before the
Court of Session; but he was dissuaded from this step by his friend

Mr. Erskine, who, in his usual strain of pleasantry, told him "just to wait the expiry of other seven years, and then to retaliate, by printing the whole of the Encyclopædia along with his own work!"

A short time prior to his demise, Mr. Wright became so much re-duced in his circumstances as to be compelled to apply for relief to the Faculty of Advocates, from whom he obtained an annuity of £50 per annum. He died in 1813. He resided, about the year 1787, in Gavinloch's Land; and subsequently removed to the New Assembly Close, now called the Commercial Bank Close. His lecture-room was at the head of the Old Assembly Close. The late Sheriff Anstruther met Henry Erskine the day after Wright's demise—"Well, Harry, poor Johnny Wright is dead." "Is he!" answered Henry. "He died very poor. They say he has left no effects." "That is not surprising," was the rejoinder; "as he had no *causes*, he could have no *effects*."

JAMES MARSHALL, ESQ.,
Writer to the Signet.

THIS is a striking etching of a somewhat eccentric yet active man of business—one of the few specimens of the old school who survived the close of last century. The smart gait—the quick eye—aquiline nose—compressed lips—the silver spectacles, carelessly thrown up-wards—the cocked hat firmly crowning the old black wig—and the robust appearance of the whole figure, at once bespeak the strong nerve and decisive character of the original.

Almost every sexagenarian in Edinburgh must recollect Mr. JAMES MARSHALL, Writer to the Signet. He was a native of Strathaven, in Lanarkshire, and made his *debut* upon the stage of life in the year 1731. From his having become a writer to the signet at a period when that society was more select than it is at present, we may fairly presume that his parents were respectable, and possessed of at least some portion of the good things of this world.

Mr. Marshall was both an arduous and acute man of business; but he possessed one *accomplishment* that might have been dispensed with, for he was one of the most profound swearers of his day; so much so, that few could possibly compete with him. Every sentence he uttered had its characteristic oath; and, if there was any degree of wit at all in the numerous jokes which his exuberance of animal spirits suggested, it certainly lay in the peculiar magniloquent manner in which he displayed his "flowers of eloquence." As true chroniclers, however, we must not omit recording a circumstance which, notwith-standing this most reprehensible habit, does considerable credit to the heart of the *heathen* lawyer. One day the poor washerwoman whom he employed appeared at his office in Milne's Square, with her head attired in a mourning coif, and her countenance unusually rueful. "What—what is the matter, Janet?" said the writer, in his usual quick manner. Janet replied, in faltering accents, that she had lost her *gudeman*. "Lost your man!" said Marshall; at the same time throwing up his spectacles, as if to understand the matter more thoroughly, "How the d—— did that happen?" Janet then stated the melancholy occurrence by which she had been bereaved. It seems that at that time extensive buildings were going on about the head of Leith Walk; and, from the nature of the ground, the foundations of many of them were exceedingly deep. Janet's husband had fallen, in the dark, into one of the excavations—which had been either imperfectly railed in, or left unguarded—and, from the injuries sustained, he died almost immediately. Marshall patiently listened to the tale, rendered doubly long by the agitated feelings of the narrator; and, as the last syllable faltered on her tongue, out burst the usual exclamation, but with more than wonted emphasis—"The b——s, I'll make them pay for your gudeman!"

No sooner said than done : away he hurried to the scene of the accident—inspected the state of the excavation—and, having satisfied himself as to all the circumstances of the case, and the liability of the contractors, he instantly wrote to them, demanding two hundred pounds as an indemnity to the bereaved widow. No attention having been paid to his letter, he immediately raised an action before the Supreme Court, concluding for heavy damages; and, from the active and determined manner in which he went about it, soon convinced his opponents that he was in earnest. The defenders became alarmed at the consequences, and were induced to wait upon Mr. Marshall with the view of compounding the matter, by paying the original demand of two hundred pounds. "Na, na, ye b——s!" was the lawyer's reply; "that sum would have been taken had ye come forward at first, like gentlemen, and settled wi' the puir body; but now (adding another oath) three times the sum 'll no stop the proceedings." Finding Marshall inexorable, another, and yet another hundred was offered—not even five hundred would satisfy the lawyer. Ultimately the parties were glad to accede to his own terms; and it is said he obtained, in this way, upwards of *seven hundred pounds* as a solatium for the "lost gudeman"—all of which he handed over to his client, who was thus probably made more comfortable by the death of her husband than she had ever been during his life.

In the winter season, Mr. Marshall resided in Milne's Square, but in summer he retired to Greenside House (his own property), situated in the Lover's Lane, near Leith Walk, where he kept a capital saddle horse; but for what purpose it was impossible to divine, no man ever having seen him on horseback (indeed, it was generally supposed he could not ride), and he would allow no one else, not even the stable-boy, to mount the animal. From this it may be inferred that the horse was in high favour with its master. Well fed, and well attended to, the only danger likely to have occurred from this luxurious mode of life arose from the want of exercise. To obviate this, the discipline adopted was truly worthy of the eccentric lawyer. Almost daily he had the horse brought out to the field behind the house, where, letting him loose, he would whip him off at full gallop; and then, to increase the animal's speed and insure exercise enough, his dog (for he always kept a favourite dog) was usually despatched in pursuit. Thus would Marshall enjoy, with manifest pride and satisfaction, for nearly an hour at a time, the gambols of the two animals.

Having no near relatives to whom he cared bequeathing his property, Mr. Marshall had selected, as the favoured individual, one of the judges of the Court of Session; but an incident occurred about two years prior to his death, which entirely changed his views on the subject. In politics he had been, if anything, an adherent of Henry Dundas, afterwards Lord Viscount Melville, and felt very deeply the injustice of the charges latterly preferred against that distinguished nobleman. While the impeachment against him was going on in London, Mr. Marshall, although then in his seventy-fourth year, daily repaired to the Parliament House, where the news of the day were generally discussed. The all-engrossing topic was of course "the impeachment;" and the innocence or guilt of Melville decided upon according to the political bias of the disputants. Having one day paid his accustomed visit, old Marshall was astonished to find the sentiments of his intended heir decidedly adverse to the fallen minister. This appeared the more intolerable to Marshall, knowing, as he did, that this individual entirely owed his elevation to the very person whom he now villified. "O the ungrateful scoundrel!" exclaimed the old man; and working himself up into a towering passion, he strode up and down the floor of the court-house, cursing with more than usual vehemence—then grumbling through his teeth as he left the court—"He shall never finger a farthing of my money"—he hurried directly home, ere his accumulated wrath should be expended, and committed the "will" to the flames.

Mr. Marshall died at Greenside House on the 23rd May, 1807, in the seventy-sixth year of his age. He married a Miss Janet Spens, who died in 1788.

SIR JAMES GRANT, BART.,
Of Grant.

AT a period when many of the extensive Highland proprietors, actuated by a violent frenzy for improvement, were driving whole districts of people from the abodes of their forefathers, and compelling them to seek for that shelter in a foreign land which was denied them in their own—when absenteeism, and the vices of courtly intrigue and fashionable dissipation, had sapped the morality of too many of our landholders, SIR JAMES GRANT escaped the contagion; and, during a long life, was distinguished for the possession of those virtues which are the surest bulwarks of the peace, happiness, and strength of a country. Possessed of extensive estates, and surrounded by a numerous tenantry, his exertions seemed to be equally devoted to the progressive improvement of the one, and the present comfort and enjoyment of the other.

Sir James was born in 1738, and succeeded to the family estates and title on the death of his father, Ludovic, in 1773. He represented the county of Moray in Parliament so early as 1761, and for several years afterwards. He was also some time member for Banff; and, although he made no attempt to figure in the political arena, or to become an intriguing partizan of either party, his zeal for constitutional liberty, in the hour of danger, was neither less prompt nor less efficient than that of some blustering persons, misnamed patriots, who attempted to make their local influence the pedestal of future elevation.

On the declaration of war in 1793, Sir James was among the first, if not the very first, to step forward in the service of the country with a regiment of fencibles, raised almost exclusively among his own tenantry, and with such alacrity, that in less than two months even more than the complement of men were assembled at Forres, the headquarters of the regiment. Almost immediately after the fencibles were embodied, Sir James raised another corps, called the 97th, or Strathspey Regiment, for more extended service, which consisted of eighteen hundred men. This regiment was embodied in 1794, and immediately marched into England. Of both these regiments Sir James was, of course, appointed Colonel. Next year, the 97th were drafted into other corps—the two flank companies being incorporated with the 42nd, then preparing for the West Indies.

The fencibles continued embodied till 1799, and did duty in various parts of Scotland. While stationed at Linlithgow, proposals were made for extending the services of the regiment to England and Ireland ; but, from some misunderstanding on the subject among the men, they would not agree. This attempt on the part of the officers, who acted without duly consulting the soldiers in a matter which concerned them so materially, gave rise to much discontent and distrust in the ranks ; but confidence was soon restored by the presence of Sir James, who hurried to join the regiment as soon as he was aware of the circumstances.

In 1795, the Strathspey Fencibles were quartered at Dumfries, where a trifling affair happened, which, as it constitutes the only *warlike* affray that occurred in Scotland during the whole volunteer and fencible era, is perhaps worth recording. " On the evening of the 9t June, the civil magistrates of Dumfries applied to the commanding officer of the 1st Fencibles for a party to aid in apprehending some Irish tinkers, who were in a house about a mile and a half distant from the town. On the party's approaching the house, and requiring admittance, the tinkers fired on them, and wounded Sergeant Beaton very severely in the head and groin; John Grant, a grenadier, in both legs ; and one Fraser, of the light company, in the arm : the two last were very much hurt, the tinkers' arms being loaded with rugged slugs and small bullets. The party pushed on to the house ; and, though they had suffered so severely, abstained from bayoneting them when they called for mercy. One man, and two women in men's clothes, were brought in prisoners. Two men, in the darkness of the night, made their escape ; but one of them was apprehended and brought in next morning, and a party went out, upon information, to apprehend the other. Fraser's arm received the whole charge, which, it is believed, saved his heart. Beaton, it is expected, will soon recover." So says the chronicle of this event. One of the soldiers, however, afterwards died of his wounds. The leader of the tinkers, named John O'Neill, was brought to Edinburgh for trial. He was a Roman Catholic; and at that time a number of genteel Catholic families being resident in Dumfries, they resolved to be at the expense of defending O'Neill, on the ground that he was justifiable in resisting any attempt to enter his own house. With this view, they prevailed on the late Mrs. Riddell of Woodley Park to go to Edinburgh and procure counsel. Mrs. Riddell was a great beauty, and a poetess of no inconsiderable note. She wrote a critique on the poems of Burns, and materially assisted Dr. Currie in writing the life of the poet. She found no difficulty in obtaining the services of Henry Erskine, without fee or reward; but, notwithstanding, O'Neill was found guilty, and condemned to be hanged. The good offices of Mrs. Riddell, however, did not terminate here. She applied to Charles Fox; and, through him, obtained a commutation of his sentence.

A still more unpleasant affair occurred in the regiment, while at Dumfries, only a few days after the encounter with the tinkers. One of the men being confined for some trifling instance of improper conduct, an attempt was made by a few of his comrades to effect a rescue; but they failed in the endeavour, and the ringleader was taken prisoner. A court-martial having been immediately held, the prisoners were remanded back to the guard-room; but on the way the escort was attacked by fifty or sixty of the soldiers, with fixed bayonets, and the prisoners rescued. By great exertions on the part of the lieutenant-colonel and officers, most of the parties were afterwards secured, when they expressed deep regret for their improper conduct, and peaceably submitted to their fate. Sir James was not with the regiment at this period, and arrived too late to interfere with propriety and effect. At a general court-martial, held at Mussel-burgh soon after, five of the mutineers were found guilty—four were adjudged to suffer death, and one to receive corporeal punishment. The melancholy spectacle of a military execution took place in consequence at the Links of Gullen, on the 19th July, 1795, in presence of all the regular and volunteer troops in the neighbourhood. When the prisoners had been marched to the scene, the sentence was restricted to two individuals, who suffered accordingly. The Strathspey Fencibles, along with most of the other similar regiments, was disbanded in 1799.

Sir James was one of the original office-bearers of the Highland Society of Edinburgh, instituted in 1784; and continued to be one of the most zealous members of that society. In 1794 he was appointed Lord-Lieutenant of the County of Inverness—which office he filled till he was compelled to resign, in consequence of ill-health, in 1809, when his son was nominated his successor. In 1795 he was preferred as Cashier to the Excise, when his seat in Parliament became vacuated, in consequence of which Mr. M'Dougal Grant succeeded him in the representation of Banffshire.

After a lingering illness, Sir James died at Castle Grant on the 18th February, 1811, deeply regretted. He married, in 1763, Jane, only child of Alexander Duff of Hatton, Esq., by whom he had seven sons and six daughters. The eldest, Lewis Alexander Grant, succeeded to the estates and earldom of Seafield on the death of his cousin James,

Earl of Findlater and Seafield, in 1811. The second son, Colonel the Hon. Francis-William Grant, the present Earl, succeeded his brother in 1840.

DR. ALEXANDER MONRO, SECUNDUS,

Professor of Anatomy.

THE father of this celebrated anatomist was the first efficient professor of the science in the University of Edinburgh, and may be considered as the founder of the medical school for which it has been subsequently so justly famed. He was a descendant of the Munros of Milntoun, and grandson of Sir Alexander Monro of Beerscroft—a strenuous opponent of Oliver Cromwell.

MONRO, *secundus*, was born in this city in 1732; and, although the youngest son, his father early designed that he should be his successor, and no exertion was spared to initiate him in the practice as well as the theory of his profession. That his whole time and attention might be devoted to the science, his father—presuming on the strength of thirty years' devotion to the medical chair, and emboldened by the fame which the seminary had acquired under his professorship—ventured to memorialise the Town Council on the subject of appointing his son assistant and successor. Among other motives which urged the professor to this step, it is stated in the memorial, that the acquisition of so much knowledge of an extensive science as a teacher ought to have, cannot be obtained without some neglect of the other branches; and, therefore, a prospect of suitable advantage from that one branch must be given, to induce any person to bestow more time and pains on it than on others.

The memorial thus proceeds:—" That the professor's youngest son has appeared to his father, for some years past, to have the qualifications necessary for a teacher; and this winter he has given proof, not only dissecting all the course of his father, but prelecting in most of it. That he is already equal to the office; for testimony of which, it is entreated that inquiry may be made at the numerous students who were present at his lectures and demonstrations." It was farther stated, that if " the patrons agreed to the proposition, the education of the young professor should be directed, with a view to that business, under the best masters in Europe. He should have all his father's papers, books, instruments, and preparations, with all the assistance his father can give in teaching, while he is fit for labour."

This document throws great light upon the history of the young anatomist, and of the profitable manner in which he had spent his time. It contains also a plain but sensible statement of his father's sentiments concerning his proficiency. There was likewise produced to the patrons certificates from the different Professors of Latin and Greek, of Philosophy and Mathematics, and of the Professors of Medicine in the University of Edinburgh, under whom he had studied; together with attestations from a great number of the students who had attended his demonstrations and lectures. Evidence was also produced that he was above twenty-one years of age. These papers were laid before the patrons in June, 1754, and the prayer of the petition was granted.

Mr. Monro did not immediately repair to the Continent, but remained in Scotland for a year. The reason of this was probably a wish that he might graduate at the University of Edinburgh. This he accordingly did upon the 20th October, 1755. He chose as the subject of his thesis "De Testibus et Semine in variis Animalibus." He could hardly have selected one more difficult to discuss. It is fully twice the size of ordinary theses, and is accompanied with plates, in order to explain the situation of the parts, their functions, and his reasoning concerning them. It is long since it became very scarce. Such as have examined it, uniformly concur in opinion that it possesses great merit, and affords an excellent specimen of what was to be expected from him as a professor of anatomy.

When he went abroad, it was with the view principally of studying anatomy under the best masters in Europe. At Berlin he attended Professor Meckel's lectures, whose reputation as an anatomist stood very high. He now and then referred to him in his own lectures, and spoke of his old master in very high terms. He was for some time at Leyden; but whether he ever visited Paris we are not informed. Upon his return to Scotland, he was admitted a licentiate of the Edinburgh Royal College of Physicians on the 2nd of May, 1758, and elected a fellow on the 1st May, 1759.

His character as a lecturer on anatomy stood very high during the long period that he discharged its duties. As an anatomist he was well known, not only throughout the British dominions and in America, but over the whole Continent of Europe; and he contributed most essentially to spread the fame of the University of Edinburgh as a medical school. He was not only a skilful anatomist, but an enthusiast in the study of it; and was constantly employed in exercising his mechanical genius in inventing and improving surgical instruments. Neither he nor his father read any of their lectures. His elocution was distinct—slow, but somewhat formal—and he generally detained the students more than an hour at lecture. The following notice of his death occurs in the *Scots Magazine*:—

"Oct. 22 [1817]. At Edinburgh, in the eighty-fifth year of his age, Alexander Monro of Craiglockhart, Esq., M.D., Professor of Medicine, Anatomy, and Surgery, in the University of Edinburgh. This distinguished physician was admitted joint Professor with his father, 12th July, 1754; and, during more than half a century, shone as one of the brightest ornaments of that much and justly celebrated seminary; his elegant and scientific lectures attracting students from all quarters of the globe."

He was succeeded by his son, the present and *third* Dr. Alexander Monro in lineal succession, who have reputably held the professorship upwards of a hundred years.

The print of Dr. Monro was executed in 1790, and is said to be extremely faithful; indeed, the present Professor thinks it one of the best representations ever given of any individual.

REV. JOHN KEMP, D.D.,

Of the Tolbooth Church.

`THE subject of this etching, born in 1745, was the son of the Rev. David Kemp, minister of Gask, in Perthshire, a man of piety and worth. By his father he was at an early period designed for the clerical profession, and passed through his academical studies at the University of St. Andrews with considerable credit. Having undergone the usual formula, and being licensed as a probationer by the Presbytery of Auchterarder, he was, on the 4th April, 1770, ordained minister of Trinity Gask—to which he was presented by the Earl of Kinnoull.

In 1776, he was called by the Town Council to the New Greyfriar's Church of Edinburgh; and from thence translated, on the death of Mr. Plenderleith, in 1779, to the Tolbooth Church, where he became the colleague of Dr. Webster, and subsequently of Dr. Davidson.

DR. KEMP was a clergyman of acknowledged acquirements and ability, and was distinguished by an active business disposition. He was for a great many years secretary to the Society for Propagating Christian knowledge—in which office he succeeded the Rev. Dr. John M'Farlane. The duties of the Secretaryship he discharged with great zeal and fidelity; and, by his intelligent and judicious management, tended materially to promote the highly useful and patriotic objects of the Society.

In his official capacity Dr. Kemp frequently visited the Highland districts of the country, to the improvement of which the missions of the Society were principally directed. In the summer of 1791, in particular, he undertook an extensive tour to the Highlands and Hebrides; and, that he might prosecute his journey with the greater facility, on application by the Society to the Board of Customs, the *Prince of Wales* brig, Captain John Campbell, was ordered to be in readiness at Oban for his use. In this vessel Dr. Kemp navigated with safety the dangerous creeks and sounds of the Western Isles—went round the point of Ardnamurchan, which stretches far into the Western Ocean, and is constantly beat by a turbulent sea—and visited all the islands of the Hebrides.

This extensive tour he accomplished in three months; and, on his return, presented a very excellent Report to the Society, not only as to the state of the schools and missions in general, but as to the cause of the destitution experienced in many of the districts, and the means by which it might be alleviated. The views entertained on the various topics embraced by the Report, and the remedial measures which it pressed on the attention of the Society, were at once liberal and enlightened, and displayed a thorough acquaintance with the capacities of the people and the resources of the country.

Dr. Kemp possessed very conciliatory and engaging manners. Wherever he went during his Highland tours he was exceedingly well received, and obtained the ready co-operation of all whose influence could possibly be of service. Even in those remote islands, where the Reformation had never penetrated, and where Roman Catholicism maintained undisputed sway, the secretary had the singular address to procure the aid and friendship of the clergy of that persuasion. While visiting the peasantry, it was no uncommon thing for him to be accompanied by the priest of the district, whose influence was highly necessary in breaking down the common prejudice against sending children to the schools of a Protestant association.

Dr. Kemp was three times married. First to a Miss Simpson, by whom he had a son and daughter; secondly, to Lady Mary Ann Carnegie (who died in 1798), daughter of the sixth Earl of Northesk; and, thirdly, to Lady Elizabeth Hope, daughter of John, second Earl of Hopetoun.

His son (who was a manufacturer) married a daughter of Sir James Colquhoun of Luss, Sheriff-Depute of Dumbartonshire—a connection which unhappily gave rise to proceedings of a rather singular nature. In the "Town Eclogue," the author (a clergyman), speaking of this marriage and Dr. Kemp's alleged familiarity with Lady Colquhoun, says—

> "To a weaver's arms consigns the high born Miss ;
> Then greets the mother with a holy kiss."

The remainder of the attack is so scurrilous that we refrain from inserting it.

Old Sir James, becoming jealous of his own lady and Dr. Kemp, actually raised an action of divorce against her, which, of course, equally affected the character of the Doctor; and, if successful, would have subjected him to heavy damages. While this novel case of litigation was pending in Court, death very suddenly stepped in to give it the quietus, by removing the two principal actors in the drama within a few days of each other. The deaths of Sir James and the Doctor are thus recorded in the newspaper obituaries for 1805 :— "April 18. At Weirbank House, near Melrose, of a stroke of palsy, aged sixty, the Rev. John Kemp, D.D., one of the ministers of the Tolbooth Church, Edinburgh, and secretary to the Society in Scotland for Propagating Christian Knowledge ;"—and on the 23rd, "At Edinburgh, Sir James Colquhoun of Luss, Bart., Sheriff-Depute of Dumbartonshire." Perhaps few local matters ever excited greater interest in Edinburgh than the probable issue of this unhappy law-suit. Dr. Kemp was characterised as a second Dr. Cantwell by one party, and as the most injured man breathing by the other. Even the reality of his death became matter of dispute; for it was affirmed and believed by not a few of his adversaries that his demise was a fiction, got up for the purpose of stifling investigation ; and it was positively asserted that, more than a year afterwards, he had been seen in Holland in the very best health and spirits. That this rumour was unfounded, may be presumed from the fact, which was well-known, of his having been struck with palsy some time prior to his death. Even admitting his demise to be a fiction, and that he was seen in Holland in the *best health and spirits*, it falls to be shown by what means such a miraculous recovery had been effected. The point, we think, is set at rest by the direct testimony of the late Mr. Charles Watson, undertaker (father of Dr. Watson, of Burntisland), who declared that he assisted in putting Dr. Kemp's body into the coffin, and in screwing down the lid. Mr. Watson was one of Dr. Kemp's elders, and a person of the utmost credit.

Dr. Kemp resided for several years in Ramsay Garden, Castle Hill. He subsequently occupied a house connected with the hall of the Society to which he was secretary (formerly Baron Maule's residence), at the Nether Bow, and which is now used by the Messrs. Craig as a hat manufactory.

THE EARL OF BUCHAN.

THE EARL OF BUCHAN was born in 1742, and succeeded to the title and estates of the family in 1767. His course of education being completed at the University of Glasgow, he soon after entered the army, in which he rose to the rank of lieutenant; but, disliking the profession of arms, he did not continue long in the service. In 1766 he was appointed Secretary to the British Embassy in Spain; but, on the death of his father the year following, he returned to his native land, resolved to prosecute pursuits more congenial to his strong literary bias.

The first instance of the Earl's activity was the formation of the Society of Scottish Antiquaries in 1780. The want of such a Society had long been felt; yet it is strange his lordship experienced illiberal opposition from parties, who afterwards, with much inconsistency, established another, having similar objects in view, called the Royal Society of Edinburgh. In 1792 the first volume of their transactions was published; and the following discourses by the Earl appear in it: —"Memoirs of the Life of Sir James Stuart Denham"—"Account of the Parish of Uphall"—"Account of the Island of Icolmkiln"—and "A Life of Mr. James Short, Optician." Besides various fugitive pieces, in prose and verse, he printed, in conjunction with Dr. Walter Minto, "An Account of the Life, Writings, and Inventions of Napier of Merchiston." 1787, 4to.

In addition to the other objects of this Society, it was resolved to establish a museum of natural history, for the better cultivation of that science, and of which museum Mr. Smellie was appointed curator. He was likewise permitted to deliver the projected course of lectures on the philosophy of natural history in the hall of the museum. The Society at the time having applied for a Royal Charter of incorporation, an unexpected opposition arose (already alluded to in our notice of Mr. Smellie) from Dr. Walker, Professor of Natural History in the University, and also from the Senatus Academicus as a body, who memorialised the Lord Advocate (Mr. Henry Dundas, afterwards Lord Viscount Melville) against the proposed grant of a charter, alleging that the Society would intercept the communication of many specimens and objects of natural history which would otherwise find their way to the College Museum, as well as documents tending to illustrate the history, antiquities, and laws of Scotland,

which ought to be deposited in the Advocates' Library. They likewise noticed that the possession of a museum of natural history might
induce the Society to institute a lectureship on that science, in opposition to the professorship in the University. The Faculty of Advocates
and other public bodies also joined in this opposition; but, after an
elaborate reply on the part of the Antiquaries, the Lord Advocate
signified his approval of their request; and, on the very next day, the
Royal warrant passed the Privy Seal, in which his Majesty voluntarily
declared himself patron of the Society.

Although engaged in literary and antiquarian research, the Earl of
Buchan was far from being an indifferent spectator of passing events.
He did not enter the political arena; but when invasion threatened
common ruin, he not only with his pen endeavoured to create union
among his countrymen, but, buckling on his sword, essayed to rouse
them by example.

The Earl, however, was no adherent of the powers that were; and
when the interference of the Court had completely set aside all sem-
blance of freedom in the election of the Scottish peers, he stood forward in defence of his order; and, although he long fought singly, he
at last succeeded in asserting its independence.

The residence of Lord Buchan had for many years been in Edinburgh; but, in 1787, he retired on account of his health to Dryburgh
Abbey—a property he acquired by purchase. Here he instituted an
annual festive commemoration of the author of "The Seasons," the
first meeting of which was held at Ednam Hill, on the 22nd September 1791—on which occasion he crowned a copy of the *first collected
edition* of the *Seasons* with a wreath of bays. The following may be
taken as a sample of the eulogium of the noble Lord on the occasion:
"And the immortal Prussian, standing like a herald in the procession
of ages, to mark the beginning of that order of men who are to banish
from the earth the delusions of priestcraft, and the monstrous prero-
gatives of despotic authority!" His lordship also took that opportunity
of attacking the great English lexicographer, "by whose rude hands
the memory of Thomson has been profanely touched." Burns wrote
his beautiful lines to the shade of the bard of Ednam for the occasion;
and only five years afterwards, at the usual anniversary in 1796, Lord
Buchan had the melancholy pleasure of placing an urn of Parian
marble beside the bust of Thomson, in memory of the bard of Ayrshire. The copy of the *Seasons* alluded to, enclosed in a beautifully
ornamented case, and enriched with some original autographs of the
Poet, was subsequently presented by his lordship to the University of
Edinburgh.

The political sentiments of the Earl of Buchan were generally
known; but, in a work published in 1792, entitled "Essays on the
Lives and Writings of Fletcher of Saltoun, and the Poet Thomson,
Biographical and Political," he embraced the opportunity of enforcing
his favourite doctrines.

In the same year, his lordship presented the President of the United
States with an elegantly mounted snuff-box, made from the tree which
sheltered Wallace. "This magnificent and truly characteristic present," says a Philadelphia Journal, of January 2, "is from the Earl of

Buchan, by the hands of Mr. Archibald Robertson, a Scots gentleman, and portrait painter, who arrived in America some months ago." The box had been presented to Lord Buchan by the goldsmiths of Edinburgh in 1782, from whom he obtained leave to transfer it to "the only man in the world to whom he thought it justly due." The box was made by Mr. Robert Hay, wright, afterwards in the Edinburgh Vendue.

In prompting this compliment to the American General, vanity had probably no inconsiderable influence; for, perhaps, there never lived an individual who thought so much of himself, or one who, in what he said or did, had his own glorification more in view. Some amusing anecdotes respecting him have recently appeared in *Fraser's Magazine;* and in the *Town Eclogue* the reverend author has thus satirised the foibles of the Earl :—

> " His brain with ill-assorted fancies stor'd,
>   Like shreds and patches on a tailor's board ;
>   Women, and Whigs, and poetry, and pelf,
>   And ev'ry corner stuff'd with mighty self—
>   With scraps and puffs, and comments without end,
>   On prince and patriot, parasite and friend;
>   Vaunting his worth—how all the great caress'd ;
>   How Hamilton dined, and how the Duchess dress'd;
>   And Ariosto sang the BUCHAN crest."

Amongst other extraordinary exhibitions got up by his lordship, was a sort of assembly, upon Mount Parnassus, of Apollo and the nine Muses. The scene of action was his lordship's drawing-room, where he presided over the smoking tea-urn, crowned with a garland of bays—nine young ladies of the first rank in Edinburgh enacted the Muses. To complete the tableaux, the noble Lord thought that the presence of Cupid was indispensable; and the astonishment of the Muses and the company present may be conceived, when the door opened, and a blooming boy of ten or twelve years of age entered as the god of love, with his bow and quiver—but in *puris naturalibus ! !*

After all, vain as his lordship undoubtedly was, and mean as many of his actions may be characterised, still, as the Editor of the *Percy Letters* remarks, "he is entitled to more credit than is usually allowed him. By his laudable economy he retrieved the fortunes of the ancient family he represented—an example which it would not be unwise for many of our noblemen to follow ; he paid off every farthing of debt left by his predecessor—a step equally worthy of imitation ; he begrudged no labour which might advance the interests of science and literature, and he spared no pains to promote the success of those whom he deemed worthy of his patronage. With these merits his personal vanity may be overlooked, and even his parsimony be forgiven, for we all know how difficult it is to eradicate early habits—habits, too, engendered at a period when these acquisitions were a merit rather than a demerit; for never let it be forgotten, that besides gradually paying off debts for which he was not legally responsible, he for years submitted to the severest privation, to enable him suitably to maintain and bring up his brothers, Henry and Thomas."

Lord Buchan contributed largely to the periodical works of his time

—particularly to the "Gentleman's Magazine," the "Scots Magazine," and still more particularly to the "Bee." In 1812, he collected these stray productions, of which he published one volume at Edinburgh, entitled "The Anonymous and Fugitive Pieces of the Earl of Buchan." The preface announced the succession of other volumes, but no more ever appeared. To Grose's "Antiquities of Scotland," his lordship furnished the "Description of Dryburgh."

Besides the voluminous correspondence which he almost constantly maintained with men of literature of all nations, and the incessant exertions into which his active mind betrayed him, the Earl was not insensible to the softer wooings of the muses, to whom his leisure moments were sometimes devoted. Only a very few of these productions, however, have been given to the public; but we have been informed that he excelled in a "light, elegant, extemporaneous style of poetry."

The Earl of Buchan married, on the 15th October, 1771, Margaret, eldest daughter of William Fraser, Esq. of Fraserfield, but had no issue. His lordship died in 1829, and was succeeded by his nephew, Henry David, eldest son of his brother, the Hon. Henry Erskine.

There are numerous portraits and busts of his lordship. An excellent painting (from Sir Joshua Reynolds') adorns the hall of the Scottish Antiquaries. Another, by Alexander Runciman, is in the museum of the Perth Antiquarian Society. He also presented to the Faculty of Advocates a portrait in crayons, with an inscription written by himself, and highly complimentary to the donor.

CAPTAIN M'KENZIE,

Of Red Castle.

THE small estate bearing this name is situated in the neighbourhood of Montrose. The old castle, now in ruins, on the banks of the Lunan, is supposed to have been built by William the Lion.

This gentleman was an officer in Seaforth's regiment of Highlanders at the time of their revolt in 1778. The regiment had for some time been quartered in the Castle of Edinburgh; but, contrary to expectation, they were at length ordered to embark for Guernsey. Previous to this, a difference existed between the officers and men—the latter declaring that neither their bounty nor the arrears of their pay had been fully paid up, and that they had otherwise been ill-used. On the day appointed for embarkation (Tuesday, the 22nd September), the regiment marched for Leith; but farther than the Links the soldiers refused to move a single step. A scene of great confusion ensued; the officers endeavoured to soothe the men by promising to rectify every abuse. About five hundred were prevailed on to embark, but as many more were deaf to all entreaty; and, being in possession of powder and ball, any attempt to force them would have proved both ineffectual and dangerous. The mutineers then moved back to

Arthur Seat, where they took up a position, and in which they continued encamped more than ten days. They were supplied plentifully with provisions by the inhabitants of Edinburgh, and were daily visited by crowds of people of all ranks. In the meantime, troops were brought into the city with the view of compelling the mutineers to submission, but no intimidation had any effect. General Skene (then second in command in Scotland), together with the Earl of Dunmore, and other noblemen and gentlemen, visited the mutineers; and at last, after a great many messages had passed between the parties, a compromise was effected. The terms were—a pardon for past offences; all bye money and arrears to be paid before embarkation, and a special understanding that they should not be sent to the East Indies—a report having prevailed among the soldiers that they had been sold to the East India Company. So cautious were the mutineers, a bond had to be given confirming the agreement, signed by the Duke of Buccleuch, the Earl of Dunmore, Sir Adolphus Oughton, K.B., Commander-in-Chief, and General Skene, second in command in Scotland. After this arrangement, the Highlanders cheerfully proceeded to Leith and embarked.

Kay relates an anecdote of Captain M'Kenzie, which occurred during the prevalence of the mutiny, highly characteristic of his fortitude and determined disposition. One day while he was in command over the Canongate Jail, where a few of the mutineers were confined, a party from Arthur Seat came to demand their liberation. The Captain sternly refused—the soldiers threatened to take his life, and pointed their bayonets at him; but he bared his breast, and telling them to strike, at the same time declared that not a single man should be liberated. The effect of this resolute conduct was instantaneous—the men recovered arms, and retired to their encampment.

Captain M'Kenzie afterwards incurred an unfortunate celebrity from a circumstance which reflected less credit upon him than the above act of heroism; and for which abuse of power he was tried at the Old Bailey, London, on the 11th December, 1784.

He had been sent out in 1782, as captain of an independent company, to act against the Dutch on the coast of Africa; and was there appointed to the command of a small fortification, called Fort Morea. Among the prisoners of the fort was a person of the name of Murray Kenneth M'Kenzie *alias* Jefferson, who had been confined for desertion. Jefferson, possessing more than common address, prevailed on the sentry to let him escape; upon learning which, Captain M'Kenzie was in a violent passion. He caused the sentinel to be punished with more than fifteen hundred lashes, and immediately despatched a party of soldiers in search of the runaway. The men returned, however, without success; upon which he ordered the guns to be charged and directed against a small village in the neighbourhood, named Black Town, where he supposed the prisoner had taken refuge, and he gave notice that, if Jefferson was not instantly delivered up, he would blow the town to atoms. A shot or two soon had the desired effect. About three thousand of the natives were seen approaching towards the fort, with Jefferson in the centre. No sooner had the prisoner been brought into the court than the Captain gave him to understand that he had not a moment to live. Then ordering one of the cannons to be prepared, had him instantly lashed to the muzzle of the piece. The prisoner bade one of his comrades beg for one half hour to say his prayers; but the answer the Captain returned was— "No, you rascal; if any man speaks a word in his favour I will blow out his brains;" at the same time brandishing the pistol which he held in his hand. A portion of the burial-service being read to the prisoner, the Captain ordered the prayer-book to be pulled out of his hands. Jefferson then hastily took leave of his comrades; and, after upbraiding the tyrant, as he called the Captain, gave the signal. In a moment the match was applied, and the next the prisoner was blown over the wall. His remains were afterwards picked up by the men and interred.

In defence of such an extraordinary and savage stretch of power, Captain M'Kenzie endeavoured to prove that his company were mutinous—that Jefferson had been a ringleader, and had been repeatedly heard to threaten the life of the Captain. The evidence was by no means conclusive as to this allegation; and the implicit obedience displayed by the men in the execution of an illegal and shocking sentence does not strengthen his assertion. It appeared, however, from unquestionable authority, that he had a very worthless set of characters under his command—the garrison being mostly composed of convicts; and, besides, he had not the means of forming a court-martial for the trial of the prisoner. The unfortunate Murray M'Kenzie *alias* Jefferson had been a drummer in the 3rd Regiment of Foot Guards; but, unluckily, about twelve years previous to his death, he fell in with a gang of shop-lifters. He had been ten times tried, and four times sentenced to be hanged; but always found friends to obtain a mitigation of his sentence.

The jury found M'Kenzie guilty of wilful murder; but, in consideration of the "desperate crew he had to command," they recommended him to mercy. During the trial and passing of sentence, the Captain behaved with the utmost composure. His execution was first stayed for a week—then he was respited—and ultimately pardoned.

After obtaining his liberty, the Captain returned to his native country; and, during his stay in Edinburgh, afforded Kay an opportunity of taking his likeness as one of "The Bucks." On observing the print in the booksellers' windows, the Captain was offended at being classed, as he said, "with fiddlers and madmen." He called on the artist, and offered a guinea to have it altered; but, finding his entreaty vain, he insisted on leaving half-a-guinea, for which he soon after got a miniature painting of himself.

Although M'Kenzie had incapacitated himself for the British service, yet being still "intent on war," he resolved to try his hand against the Turks. With this view, he entered the ranks of the Russian army, and served in the war against the Turks. He was at last killed in a duel with a fellow-officer not far from Constantinople.

THE REV. ANDREW HUNTER, D.D.,

Professor of Divinity.

DR. ANDREW HUNTER was the eldest son of Andrew Hunter, Esq., of Park, Writer to the Signet (descended from a branch of the family of Hunter of Hunterstone in Ayrshire). His mother, Grisel Maxwell, was a daughter of General Maxwell of Cardoness, in the stewartry of Kirkcudbright—a gentleman alike distinguished for his bravery and his piety. He was a zealous supporter of the Protestant interest; and, at the Revolution of 1688, was one of those who accompanied the Prince of Orange from Holland.

Dr. Hunter was born in Edinburgh in 1743, and, at an early period, gave evidence of that mildness of temper and goodness of disposition which so much endeared him in after life to all who had the pleasure of his acquaintance. He was educated at the school taught by Mr. Mundell, one of the most distinguished teachers in Edinburgh at that period. Nearly fifty years afterwards, out of respect to him, a club was formed, consisting of those who had been his scholars—among whom we may enumerate the Earl of Buchan, Lord Hermand, Lord Polkemmet, Lord Balmuto, and other distinguished individuals, including Dr. Hunter. The members were in the habit of dining together at stated periods in honour of his memory. At these social meetings the parties lived their boyish days over again; and each was addressed in the familiar manner, and by the juvenile *soubriquet* which he bore when one of the "schule laddies." Any deviation from these rules was punished by a fine.

After passing through his academical studies at the University of Edinburgh, Dr. Hunter spent a year at Utrecht, which he chiefly devoted to the study of theology—such a course being at that time considered highly necessary to perfect the student of divinity. Thus prepared for the Church, Dr. Hunter was licensed as a probationer by the Presbytery of Edinburgh in 1767; but he refused to accept of any charge till after the death of his venerable father, towards whom he manifested the utmost degree of filial affection, cheering the evening of his days by his kind attention and solicitude.

While attending the University, Dr. Hunter became intimate with several young gentlemen, afterwards distinguished in their various walks of life: among others, Sir Robert Liston (for many years ambassador to the Ottoman Court), Dr. Alexander Adam (rector of the High School), Dr. Sommerville (minister of Jedburgh, the historian), and Dr. Samuel Charteris (minister of Wilton). He was also connected with several literary and theological societies formed among his fellow-students; and was a member of the Newtonian Society, instituted in 1760, which for several years continued to meet weekly in one of the rooms of the College, and which may be said to have been the precursor of the present Royal Society of Edinburgh.

An anecdote is told of Dr. Hunter in connection with this Society. He was at the time very young, and not sufficiently practised in the art of literary *condensation*. When it came to his turn to produce an

essay for the evening, he had entered so sincerely and fully upon the
subject, that he appeared at the forum with an immense bundle of
papers under his arm; and commenced by stating that his discourse
consisted of *twelve* different parts! This announcement alarmed the
preses for the night so much, that he interrupted him by declaring
that he had *twelve* distinct objections to the production of such a mass
of manuscripts. The preses accordingly stated his twelve reasons,
and was followed on the same side by six other members, who pre-
faced their observations by a similar declaration. During this opposition the temper of the young theologian remained unruffled; and it
was not till the last speaker had finished his oration, that he took up
his papers, and, without deigning to reply, walked out of the room.

In 1770, Dr. Hunter was presented to the New Church of Dumfries;
and, soon afterwards, became the purchaser of the estate of Barjarg
in that county, which had previously belonged to James Erskine of
Barjarg and Alva—one of the Senators of the College of Justice. He
remained at Dumfries for nine years, and was much esteemed by all
classes of the community.

In 1779, he was presented to the New Greyfriars' Church, Edinburgh; and, whilst there, was appointed the colleague of Dr. Hamilton
(father to the late eminent physician) in the Divinity Professorship of
the University; and, until the death of that gentleman, continued to
teach his class without any remuneration.

In 1786, he was translated by the Magistrates to the Tron Church,
where he became associated with Dr. Drysdale—a clergyman much
esteemed for his talents and amiable character. Although differing
on some points of Church polity, the two incumbents lived on terms
of the closest intimacy during the short period of their connection;
and the kind attentions of Dr. Hunter contributed much to promote
the comfort of his venerable friend in the declining years of his long
and useful life.

The lectures of Dr. Hunter, as Professor of Divinity, were distinguished by a plain, clear, and accurate statement of the evidences
and doctrine of Christianity; and it was his uniform and earnest
endeavour to promote practical piety and ministerial usefulness among
his students. For this purpose he cultivated an acquaintance with
them in private; and, to such as he found most worthy and most in
want of assistance, he not only made presents of books, but frequently
aided them with sums of money, which he conveyed in such a way as
to insure the gratitude without injuring the feelings of the receiver;
while, for those who were distinguished by piety and talents, he endeavoured to procure situations of usefulness and respectability. He
also, from his own funds, gave a prize yearly for the best theological
essay on a prescribed subject; and he was remarkable for the candour
and impartiality which he observed in adjudging the reward.

In the pulpit, Dr. Hunter had an earnest and affectionate manner
of delivery; and his discourses were sound in their doctrine and
practical in their tendency. Several of his sermons, on particular
occasions, have been published: one, in 1792, is entitled "The Duties
of Subjects," which seems to have been written with a view to
counteract the Republican mania, which the French Revolution had

introduced into the country. The discourse is characterised by a comprehensive view of the relative duties of those who govern and of the governed. The arguments are judicious and forcible, and the language moderate and conciliatory. We find another published sermon by Dr. Hunter, entitled "Christ's Drawing all Men unto Him," preached before the Edinburgh Missionary Society, in Lady Glenorchy's Chapel, on Thursday, the 20th of July, 1797; and in the " Scottish Preacher "—a publication of very considerable excellence— two other discourses will be found.

In discharging the private duties of his profession, no individual could be more zealous than Dr. Hunter. The great aim of his life seemed to be in every possible way to extend the knowledge and practice of true religion. To all the religious and charitable institutions of Edinburgh he contributed largely from his own substance; and wide and judicious was the range of his private beneficence. Both in his pastoral conduct, and in the discharge of his duties as a Professor of Theology, no individual could be more completely divested of bigotry or party spirit. He judged of others by himself; and uniformly gave credit to those who were opposed to him on minor points of religious opinion, or as to questions of church polity, for the same integrity and purity of intention by which his own conduct was governed. By his brethren he was much respected; and his well-known candour procured every attention to his opinions in the church courts. He was appointed Moderator of the General Assembly in 1792.

In the following quotation, the character of Dr. Hunter has been drawn by one who knew him intimately, and whose judgment may well be considered no slight authority :—" But shall I not mention the known integrity and purity of his mind—the candour and sincerity which so eminently distinguished him through life, and which ever commanded the confidence of those who differed from him most in judgment—the fair, and open, and generous spirit which he invariably discovered, when he judged of other men, or acted with them—the scorn with which he ever contemplated an unfair, an interested, a disingenuous proceeding—the mildness of his temper, of which, by the grace of God he had acquired the entire command; and (what can certainly be said of few amongst us all), which was scarcely ever known to have been roused into passion, either in public or domestic life—the earnestness and godly sincerity with which he followed every good work, and co-operated with other men whom he believed to be sincerely disposed to be useful; with no shade of worldly selfishness to pervert his conduct; without ostentation; superior to envy, and superior to pride; gentle and forbearing with all men; but firm and immoveable where he saw his duty before him; fervent in spirit, serving the Lord." In the private relations of life few men could be more estimable. He was one of the kindest of husbands—an affectionate parent—and the most attached of friends.

At a period of life, when actively employed in discharging the duties of his profession, and in the full enjoyment of health, on returning from the sacramental services at Leith, he was suddenly seized with inflammation, and died, after a few days' illness, on the 21st of April, 1809. The closing scene of his life was as exemplary and instructive as his whole previous conduct had been; and he looked upon his approaching dissolution with all the calmness, resignation, and hope, which a well-spent life can inspire. Funeral sermons were preached on the occasion by his colleague the Rev. Dr. Simpson, and the Rev. Sir Henry Moncrieff Wellwood, Bart.; and most gratifying tributes of respect were paid to his memory by almost all the clergy of the city.

Dr. Hunter married, in 1779, Marion Shaw, eldest daughter of William sixth Lord Napier, by whom he had four children. His eldest son, a member of the faculty of advocates (who afterwards took the name of Arundel, in compliance with the wishes of his wife, who was a relative of Lord Arundel of Wardour), succeeded to the estate, and died a few years since, leaving several children. His youngest son, the Rev. John Hunter, is one of the ministers of the Tron Church —which charge he has held since October, 1832, in conjunction with Dr. Brunton, Professor of Hebrew in the University.

LORD CRAIG,

Of the Court of Session.

THE father of his lordship, Dr. William Craig, was one of the ministers of Glasgow, author of "An Essay on the Life of Christ," and two volumes of excellent sermons. WILLIAM—the subject of Kay's Print— was born in 1745. He studied at the College of Glasgow, where he was distinguished for his classical acquirements. In 1768, he was admitted to the bar, and became intimate with several young persons, chiefly of the same profession, who met once a-week for the improvement of their professional knowledge.

As an advocate Mr. Craig was not so successful as might have been anticipated from his talents. His tastes and habits were perhaps too literary to lead him to legal eminence. He nevertheless had a fair share of business; and, in 1784, when Sir Ilay Campbell became Lord Advocate, he and his intimate friends, Blair and Abercromby, were appointed Advocate-deputes. In 1787, he became Sheriff-depute of Ayrshire; and, on the death of Lord Hailes in 1792, took his seat on the bench as Lord Craig. In 1795, he succeeded Lord Henderland as a Commissioner of Justiciary. This situation he held till 1812, when he resigned it on account of declining health; but retained his seat in the Civil Court until his death.

Lord Craig was more distinguished on the bench than he had been at the bar. His conduct was upright and honourable; and to excellent professional talents, and a profound knowledge of law, he joined the most persevering exertion. There were few of his colleagues who despatched more business, or with greater accuracy, than his lordship. His judgments, formed after careful and anxious consideration, were generally clear and well-founded.

The fame, however, of Lord Craig does not rest solely on his character either as a lawyer or a judge. His well known attainments, and

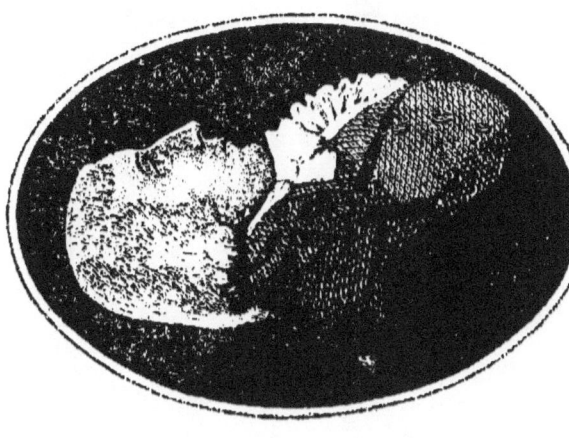

Illustrious Martyr in the glorious cause
Of truth, of freedom, and of equal laws.

THOMAS MUIR, Es.

[To face page 206.

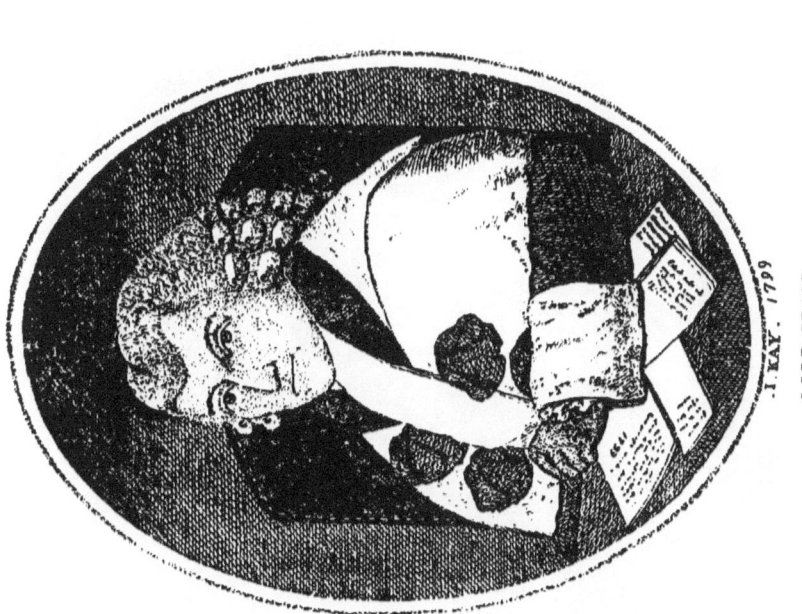

.J. KAY . 1799

LORD CRAIG

Vol. I., Plate XVII.]

especially his connection with "The Mirror" and "The Lounger," have raised his name to an honourable place among the literary characters of his native land. Most of our readers are aware that the *Mirror* and *Lounger* were the joint productions of a club of gentlemen —of whom Henry Mackenzie, author of the "Man of Feeling," was the only individual whose name was made public at the time.

Besides Mackenzie and Lord Craig, the gentlemen connected with the club were—Mr. Alex. Abercromby, afterwards Lord Abercromby (uncle of Lord Dunfermline); Mr. Robert Cullen, afterwards Lord Cullen; Mr. Macleod Bannatyne, afterwards Lord Bannatyne; Mr. George Home [by a strange mistake, in the new edition of *Scott's Works* this gentleman has been seated on the bench as Lord Wedderburn], afterwards a Principal Clerk of Session; Mr. William Gordon of Newhall; and Mr. George Ogilvie. The association was at first termed the *Tabernacle;* but when the resolution of publishing was adopted, it assumed the name of the *Mirror Club.* To the ninth edition of the *Mirror,* published in 1792, and the sixth of the *Lounger,* in 1794, are prefixed the names of the authors. Among the correspondents were—Lord Hailes, Mr. Baron Hume, Mr. Tytler and his Son (Lord Woodhouselee), Professor Richardson, Dr. Beattie, Dr. Henry, and other eminent literary persons.

The origin and progress of the club is related in the concluding number of the *Mirror.* The object at first contemplated by the contributors was simply that of relaxation from severe studies; and, by committing their thoughts to writing, to improve and extend their tastes on various subjects connected with the *belles lettres.* Their essays were read at weekly meetings held for the purpose; and for some time no farther extent of publicity was given to the transactions of this club, which generally met in a tavern. The club met sometimes in *Clerihugh's,* Writers' Court; sometimes in *Somers',* opposite the Guard House in the High Street; sometimes in *Stewart's* oyster house, Old Fishmarket Close; and fully as often, perhaps, in *Lucky Dunbar's*—a moderate and obscure house, situated in an alley leading betwixt Forrester's and Libberton's Wynd.

Lord Craig (then an advocate) was one of the most zealous members; and with him originated the idea of publishing the essays. Next to those of Mackenzie, the contributions of his lordship were the most numerous; and are distinguished for a chaste and elegant style of composition.

The *Mirror* commenced in January, 1779, and terminated in May, 1780. It was published weekly; and each number formed a small folio sheet, which was sold at three-half-pence. The thirty-sixth number of this work, written by Lord Craig, "contributed," says Dr. Anderson (*Lives of the Poets,* vol. ii. p. 273), "in no inconsiderable degree to rescue from oblivion the name and writings of the ingenious and amiable young poet, Michael Bruce." The *Lounger,* to which Lord Craig also contributed largely, was commenced several years afterwards by the same club of gentlemen; and both periodical works have passed through numerous editions, and become standard British classics. In one of the numbers of this periodical work appeared a short review of the first (or Kilmarnock) edition of the poems of Burns.

The notice was written by Henry Mackenzie; and, it may be said with some truth, that this production of the "Man of Feeling" proved the means of deciding the fate, and probably the fame, of the bard. He was an unknown wight, and on the eve of bidding farewell to his native country, when the *Lounger*, and the kind exertions of Dr. Blacklock, the poet, happily brought him into notice, and procured for him the patronage of the learned and fashionable circles of Edinburgh.

In private life, Lord Craig was much esteemed for his gentle and courteous manners, and the benevolence and hospitality of his disposition. In person he might be reckoned handsome, and was rather above the middle size. A fine portrait of him, in his latter years, by Sir Henry Raeburn, is in the possession of Robert Sym, Esq., George's Square.

Lord Craig never possessed a robust constitution, and fell into bad health several years before his death, which happened at Edinburgh on the 8th July, 1813, in the sixty-eighth year of his age. He resided for many years in George's Square; but latterly removed to York Place. While Sheriff-Depute of Ayrshire, he chiefly occupied a house called Strathaird, on the banks of the Water-of-Ayr.

MUNGO WATSON,

Beadle of Lady Yester's Church.

MUNGO was a living chronicle of the Presbyterian Church, or rather of the passing events in what he called the religious world. He was keeper of the hall for the meetings of the Society for the Propagation of Christian Knowledge, beadle of Lady Yester's Church, and one of the door-keepers during the sittings of the General Assembly.

Such a variety of official employments gave him every opportunity of acquiring early notice of what was going on, and enabled him to fill up the rest of his time profitably—for Mungo never lost sight of profit—as the following anecdote proves:—Mr. Black, the minister of Lady Yester's Church, was perhaps the most popular preacher of his day; and strangers visiting the church generally gave a trifle to the beadle to procure a seat. A gentleman had conformed to this practice in the forenoon, and returned to resume his seat in the afternoon, but was prevented by Mungo. The gentleman reminded him he had paid him in the forenoon. "O but," said Mungo, "I let my seats twice a-day."

During the sittings of the General Assembly, he contrived, in his capacity of door-keeper, to make the most of the situation, and pocketed as much of "the needful" as he possibly could exact by an embargo upon visitors. He was highly esteemed by a large circle of old ladies of the middle ranks, who eagerly listened to the gossip he contrived to pick up in the course of the day. He could inform them of the proceedings of the Edinburgh Presbytery—what had been done at the last, and what was forthcoming at the next General Assembly

—whose turn it was to preach at Haddo's Hole on the Tuesday or Friday following—whether the minister would preach himself, or by proxy—whether John Bailie would be at the plate, or his son Tam in the precentor's desk—with various other scraps of local news equally edifying and instructive to his auditors.

It has been rumoured that he made a regular charge for his visits; and hence the inscription on Kay's Print of " Prayers at all Prices." By way of improvement in the art of ghostly admonition, the beadle sometimes ascended the pulpit of Lady Yester's Church, and held forth to the vacant benches. On one of these occasions, it is said Dr. Davidson happened to come upon him unawares—" Come down, Mungo," said the Doctor, " toom (empty) barrels make most sound," in allusion to the rotundity of his person, and his somewhat large paunch.

The gravity of his manner was well calculated to make an impression on the ignorant or the weak; and those who could appreciate his merits were greatly edified by his prayers and ghostly exhortations. There was a peculiar degree of solemnity about his features. The ponderous weight of his nether jaw gave a hollow tone, not only to his words, but even when closing on the tea and toast, a dram, or a glass of wine, it was excellently adapted to produce the effect—*solemn.*

Watson was married, and had a son and daughter. He died in December, 1809. His widow died in the Trinity Hospital about the year 1834.

THOMAS MUIR, ESQ.,
Younger of Huntershill.

MR. THOMAS MUIR, whose father was a wealthy merchant in Glasgow, and proprietor of the small estate of Huntershill, in the parish of Calder, was born in 1765. He studied at the University of his native city, where, it is said, he was distinguished not less for talent than gentleness of disposition. He chose the law as a profession; and was admitted to the bar, where he practised, with every appearance of ultimate success, for a few years, till the well known events in France gave a new impulse to the democratic spirit of this, as well as of almost every other country in Europe. Muir, whose principles had always been of a liberal cast, now stepped publicly forward; and, ranging himself among " The Friends of the People," at once embarked in the cause with all the characteristic zeal of youth.

The conduct of Muir having rendered him obnoxious to the existing authorities, was apprehended in the beginning of January, 1793, while on his way to Edinburgh, to be present at the trial of Mr. James Tytler. On alighting from the coach at Holytoun, he was taken prisoner by Mr. Williamson, king's messenger, in whose custody he finished the remainder of the journey. About an hour after his arrival in Edinburgh, he was brought before Mr. Sheriff Pringle and Mr. Honyman (afterwards Lord Armadale), Sheriff of Lanarkshire. These gentlemen were proceeding to interrogate him in the usual manner, but Muir declared that in *that place* he would not answer any question whatever. " He considered such examinations as utterly inconsistent with the rights of British subjects—instruments of oppression, and pregnant with mischief." Mr. Muir was liberated on finding bail to appear in February following.

Immediately after this occurrence he proceeded to London; and from thence to Paris, commissioned, as reported at the time, to intercede in behalf of the French king. Be that as it may, he was detained in France beyond the possibility of returning in time to stand his trial, and was in consequence outlawed on the 25th February. The enemies of Muir represented his absence as an intentional flight from justice, arising from consciousness of guilt; but he accounted for the circumstance by the menacing attitude then assumed by the two countries, and the consequent difficulty of obtaining a conveyance home. He at last found a passage in a vessel cleared out for America, but which in reality was bound for Ireland. After a short detention in Dublin, where he became a member of the "Society of United Irishmen," and was warmly received by the Reformers of that city, he sailed for Scotland in the month of July, professedly with the intention of standing trial. In this intention, however, he was anticipated; for, on his arrival in Stranraer, he was recognised by an under officer of the customs, upon whose information he was arrested, and had all his papers taken from him. From the prison of Stranraer he was once more conducted to Edinburgh, under the charge of Williamson, where he was brought to trial on the 30th August.

The Court was opened by the Lord Justice-Clerk (M'Queen of Braxfield) and four Lords Commissioners of Justiciary—Lord Henderland, Lord Swinton, Lord Dunsinnan, and Lord Abercromby.

The gentlemen of the jury were—Sir James Foulis of Collington, Bart.; Captain John Inglis of Auchindinny; John Wauchop of Edmonstone; John Balfour, younger, of Pilrig; Andrew Wauchop of Niddry, Marischal; John Trotter of Mortonhall; Gilbert Innes of Stow; James Rocheid of Inverleith; John Alves of Dalkeith; William Dalrymple, merchant, Edinburgh; James Dickson, bookseller, Edinburgh; George Kinnear, banker, Edinburgh; Andrew Forbes, merchant, Edinburgh; John Horner, merchant, Edinburgh; Donald Smith, banker, Edinburgh.

In the indictment Muir was charged with creating disaffection by means of seditious speeches and harangues—of exhorting persons to purchase seditious publications—and, more particularly, of having been the principal means of convening a meeting of Reformers at Kirkintulloch on the 3rd November, 1792; also, of convening another meeting during the same month at Milltown, parish of Campsie: and, farther, " the said Thomas Muir did, in the course of the months of September, October, or November aforesaid, distribute, circulate, or cause to be distributed and circulated, in the town of Glasgow, Kirkintulloch, Milltown aforesaid, and at Lennoxtown, in the said parish of Campsie, and county of Stirling, or elsewhere, a number of seditious and inflammatory writings or pamphlets, particularly a book or pamphlet entitled ' The Works of Thomas Paine, Esq.,' &c." He was likewise charged with having been present at a meeting of the "Convention of Delegates of the Associated Friends of the People," held in Lawrie's Room, in James's Court, Edinburgh, at which he read "An Address from the Society of United Irishmen in Dublin to the Delegates for Promoting a Reform in Parliament," and proposed that the same should lie on the table, or a vote of thanks, or some acknowledgment be made to those from whom the address had been transmitted.

The witnesses brought forward established the various charges against the prisoner, but they almost unanimously bore testimony to the constitutional mode by which he recommended the people to proceed in their demands for a redress of grievances. Indeed, at this distance of time, and considered apart from that dread of everything approaching, even in name, to a Republic, which the horrors of the French Revolution had inspired, it is not easy to discover, from the evidence, the precise degree of guilt which could possibly be attached to the prisoner.

Muir had no counsel. He conducted the defence himself. His appearance at the bar has been variously represented. By those of opposite politics (and there are several gentlemen yet alive who witnessed his trial) he has been described as "a most silly creature, and a pitiful speaker." The records of the proceedings by no means support this assertion. Without deigning to descend to mere legal quibbling, his conduct of the case does not seem to have been deficient in tact, nor his appeals to the Bench and to the jury devoid of eloquence or power. "This is no time for compromise," said Muir, in his concluding address to the jury. "Why did the Lord Advocate not at once allow that I stand at this bar because I have been the strenuous supporter of Parliamentary reform? Had this been done, and this alone been laid to my charge, I should at once have pleaded guilty—there would have been no occasion for a trial; and their lordships and you would have been spared the lassitude of so long an attendance. But what sort of guilt would it have been? I have been doing that which has been done by the first characters in the nation. I appeal to the venerable name of Locke, and of the great oracle of the English law, Judge Blackstone. But why need I refer to writers who are now no more? The Prime Minister of the country, Mr. Pitt himself—the Commander-in-Chief of the Army, the Duke of Richmond—have once been the strenuous advocates of reform; and yet they have been admitted into the King's counsel. Are they then criminal as I am? But it is needless, gentlemen, to carry you beyond the walls of this house. The Lord Advocate (Robert Dundas, Esq.) himself has been a Reformer, and sat as a delegate from one of the counties for the purpose of extending the elective franchise." The concluding words of Muir were—"I may be confined within the walls of a prison—I may even have to mount the scaffold—but never can I be deprived or be ashamed of the records of my past life."

A verdict of guilty was returned by the jury, and sentence followed, transporting the prisoner beyond seas for the period of fourteen years.

Mr. Muir was detained in prison till the 15th of October, when he was conveyed on board the *Royal George* excise yacht, Capt. Ogilvie, lying in Leith Roads, for London. In the same vessel were sent the following convicts:—John Grant, convicted of forgery at Inverness;

John Stirling, concerned in robbing Nellfield House; —— Bauchope, for stealing watches; and James Mackay, who had been condemned to death for street robbery. The feeling of degradation which Muir must have experienced in being thus classed with thieves and robbers was in some degree alleviated by the presence of the Rev. Thomas Fyshe Palmer, who had been tried on the 12th September previous, for publishing a political address written by George Mealmaker.

Immediately on the arrival of the prisoners in the Thames, they were put on board the hulks, where they were detained so long that Skirving and Margarot were in time to be shipped in the same transport for New South Wales.

The following lines, written by the author on board the transport that was about to carry him into exile, independent of their poetical merit, are rendered interesting from the circumstances under which they were penned:—

> "*Surprise Transport, Portsmouth,*
> "*March 12, 1794.*

"TO MR. MOFFAT, WITH A GOLD WATCH AND CHAIN FROM MR. MUIR.

> " This gift, this little gift, with heart sincere,
>   An exile, wafted from his native land,
> To friendship tried, bequeaths with many a tear,
>   Whilst the dire bark still lingers on the strand.

> " These sorrows stream from no ignoble cause;
>   I weep not o'er my own peculiar wrong,—
> Say, when approving conscience yields applause,
>   Should private sorrow claim the votive song?

> " But, ah! I mark the rolling cloud from far,
>   Collect the dark'ning horrors of the storm;
> And, lo! I see the frantic fiend of war,
>   With civil blood, the civil field deform.

> " Roll on, ye years of grief, your fated course!
>   Roll on, ye years of agony and blood!
> But, ah! of civil rage, when dried the source,
>   From partial evil spring up general good.

> " Alas! my Moffat, from the dismal shore
>   Of cheerless exile, when I slow return,
> What solemn ruins must I then deplore?
>   What awful desolation shall I mourn?

> " Paternal mansion! mouldering in decay,
>   Thy close-barred gate may give no welcome kind;
> Another lord, as lingering in delay,
>   May harshly cry—another mansion find.

> " And, oh! my Moffat! whither shall I roam?
>   Flow, flow, ye tears! perhaps the funeral bier;
> No—flourish Hope— from thee I ask a home,—
>   Thy gentle hand shall wipe an exile's tear.

> " Yes, we shall weep o'er each lamented grave
>   Of those who join'd us in stern Freedom's cause;
> And, as the moisten'd turf our tears shall lave,
>   These tears shall Freedom honour with applause.

" I soon shall join the dim ærial band,—
  This stream of life has little time to flow.
  Oh ! if my dying eyes thy soothing hand
  Should close—enough—'tis all I ask below.

" This little relic, Moffat, I bequeath
  While life remains, of friendship, just and pure,—
  This little pledge of love, surviving death,
  Friendship immortal, and re-union sure.

                               "THOMAS MUIR."

Mr. William Moffat, to whom this flattering mark of esteem is
addressed, still lives in Edinburgh. He was admitted a solicitor in
1791, and was the legal agent of Mr. Muir. His son, Mr. Thomas
Muir Moffat, is named after the Reformer.

At Sydney they were treated by Governor Hunter (a Scotsman)
with all the humanity in his power. Here Muir purchased a piece of
land, and busied himself in its improvement; while in the society of
his exiled companions, he enjoyed as much happiness as the peculiarity
of his situation would permit. After remaining in the "distant land
of exile" nearly two years, he found means to escape in an American
vessel (the *Otter*), which had been fitted out at New York by some
individuals for the purpose of aiding him in his escape, and which
had anchored at Sydney for the ostensible purpose of taking in wood
and water. With the *Otter* he sailed for the United States; but,
unfortunately, having occasion to touch at Nootka Sound, he found
that a British sloop of war had unexpectedly arrived a short time
before; and as this vessel had only left Sydney a day or two previous
to the *Otter*, Muir deemed it prudent to go on shore—preferring to
travel over the whole American continent to the risk of detection.

After many hardships, he at length found a passage on board a
Spanish frigate bound for Cadiz; but Spain being then leagued with
the Republic of France, on arriving off the port of Cadiz, the frigate
was attacked by a British man-of-war. A desperate engagement
ensued, in which Muir is said to have fought with great bravery, and
was severely wounded. On the surrender of the frigate, he was concealed on board for six days, and then sent on shore with the other
wounded prisoners. In a letter from Cadiz, dated 14th August, 1797,
he thus describes his situation :—" Contrary to my expectation, I am
at last nearly cured of my numerous wounds. The Directory have
shown me great kindness. Their solicitude for an unfortunate being,
who has been so cruelly oppressed, is a balm of consolation which
revives my drooping spirits. The Spaniards detain me as a prisoner,
because I am a Scotsman : but I have no doubt that the intervention
of the Directory of the great Republic will obtain my liberty. Remember me most affectionately to all my friends, who are the friends
of liberty and of mankind."

Muir was not disappointed in the sincerity of the French Directory,
at whose request he was delivered up by the Spanish authorities. On
entering France he was warmly hailed by the people; and in Paris he
received every mark of respect from the government. He did not,
however, live long to enjoy the liberty which it had cost him such

peril to obtain. The seeds of a decline had been sown in his constitution before his departure from Scotland; and the many fatigues which he had subsequently undergone, together with the wounds he had received in the action, proved too complicated and powerful to be resisted. He died at Chantilly, near Paris, on the 27th September, 1798, where he was interred, with every mark of respect, by the public authorities.

— ——

SIR ARCHIBALD HOPE, BART.,
Of Pinkie.

THIS gentleman, who has been dubbed by the artist a " Knight of the Turf," was the ninth baronet of Craighall—the original designation of the family. He was grandson to Sir Thomas, a distinguished member of the College of Justice, and one of the early promoters of agricultural improvements in Scotland. By his skill in this latter department, the Meadows, now one of the pleasantest and most frequented walks about Edinburgh, was converted from its original marshy and waste condition into a state of high cultivation. In commemoration of this circumstance, it obtained the name of "Hope-Park;" but it is still generally known as "the Meadows."

The Hopes of Craighall are the stem from which has sprung the noble family of Hopetoun, noticed in a preceding part of this work. The designation of Craighall was laid aside by Lord Rankeillor, son of the second baronet, who had been knighted by the title of Sir Archibald Hope of that Ilk.

Sir Archibald, who succeeded to the title on the death of his grandfather in 1771, does not appear to have been ambitious of obtaining distinction either at the bar or in the senate; and the only public situation which he ever held was that of Secretary to the Board of Police, to which he had been appointed for life; and, on its abolition, received a compensation in lieu of the office.

On his own estate, and throughout the neighbourhood, he supported the character of a country gentleman, more intent on improving his lands than desirous of engaging in those political and party animosities, which so much distract the harmony of society, and retard the progress of substantial national improvement. On his property he established extensive salt and coal works, from which he derived very considerable emolument, and which still continue the source of much wealth; and, by his judicious management, he otherwise greatly enhanced the value of his estate.

Sir Archibald took an active hand in superintending his numerous colliers and salters. They were a rough, uncultivated set of people; and, like most workmen in similar employments, not very deeply impressed with proper notions of subordination. He had his own system of management, however; and, although not strictly in accordance with the principles of constitutional government, it proved not less efficacious than it was summary in its application. He

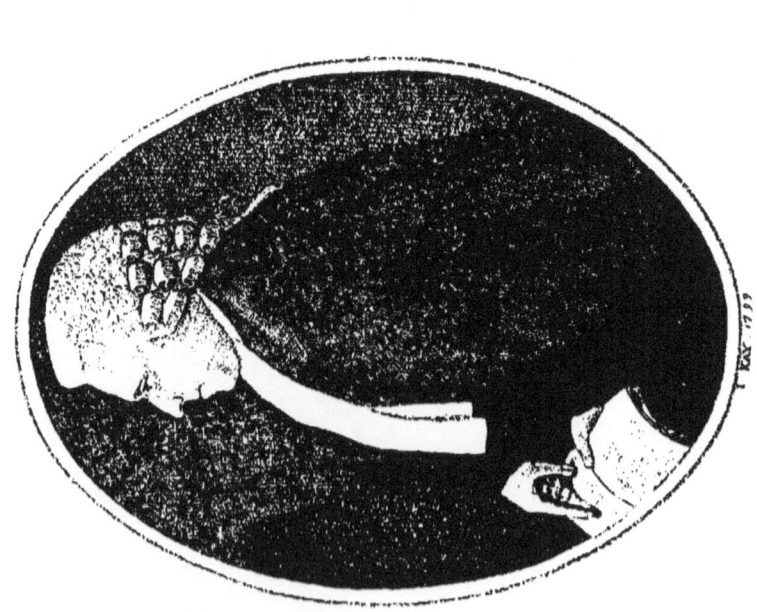

The Evening Walk

CAPTAIN JAMES JUSTICE

[*To face page 215.*]

LORD ROBERT BLAIR

Vol. I, Plate XVIII.

required no sheriff or justice courts to settle matters of dispute. Armed
with his jockey-whip, Sir Archibald united in his own person all the
functionaries of justice; and, wherever his presence was required, he
was instantly on the spot. On several occasions, when, by the
example and advice of neighbouring works, his men were in mutiny,
he has been known to go down to the pits, and, with whip in hand,
lay about him, right and left, until order was restored. The work
would then go on as formerly—the men as cheerful and compliant as
if nothing untoward had occurred. Upon the whole, his people were
happy and contented; and although the means which he took to
enforce obedience were somewhat arbitrary, his subjects felt little
inclination to object to them.

Although much of his time was thus devoted to his own affairs,
public matters of local interest received a due share of his attention;
and, on every occasion of a patriotic or charitable nature, he stepped
nobly forward with his counsel and assistance.

Sir Archibald resided chiefly at Pinkie House, where he maintained
the genuine hospitality of the olden times, and kept such an establishment of "neighing steeds" and "deep-mouthed hounds" as at once
declared the owner to be, in sentiment, one of those doughty "squires
of old," whose masculine ideas of enjoyment were widely at variance
with the effeminacy attributed to the luxurious landholders of more
modern times.

As might be anticipated from his character, Sir Archibald was a
member of the Caledonian Hunt—a body of Scottish gentlemen well
known to be somewhat exclusive in the admission of members. Of
this honourable club he held the high distinction of President in 1789,
at which period the etching of the "Knight of the Turf" was executed.

Sir Archibald married, in 1758, Elizabeth, daughter of William
M'Dowall, Esq., of Castle Semple, by whom he had two sons and five
daughters. On the death of this lady in 1778, he married (the year
following) Elizabeth, daughter of John Patoun, Esq.,—a gentleman
whose name was originally Paton; but who, having gone abroad in
his youth, and amassed a large fortune, on his return to his native
country, changed the spelling of it to *Patoun.* The issue of this second
marriage were three sons and one daughter.

Sir Archibald died at Pinkie House on the 1st of June, 1794. He
was succeeded by his second son of the first marriage; on whose death
in 1801, without issue, John, eldest son of the second marriage, became the eleventh baronet.

LORD ROBERT BLAIR,

President of the Court of Session.

AMONGST the many eminent persons who have attained celebrity as
senators of the College of Justice, the LORD PRESIDENT BLAIR occu-
pies a distinguished place. His father was the Rev. Robert Blair,
minister of Athelstaneford, in East-Lothian, author of "The Grave,"

and male representative of the ancient family of Blair, in Ayrshire. He married Isabella Law, daughter of William Law, Esq. of Elvingston, East-Lothian. The third son—the subject of our sketch—was born in 1741. His elder brothers were destined to mercantile pursuits, but Robert was educated for the legal profession.

He commenced his studies at the High School of Edinburgh, and from thence was transferred to the University, where he formed friendships which subsequently materially aided him in his progress through life. In particular he commenced an intimacy with Henry Dundas, afterwards Lord Melville, which only terminated with their lives. Mr. Blair was a year younger than his friend Lord Melville. The latter was admitted a member of the Faculty of Advocates in 1763, and the former the following year.

This adoption of a profession, in which so many fail of success, was considered at least a bold, if not an inconsiderate choice, by a young man without fortune; but the extended practice, which his talents almost instantaneously commanded, dispelled the apprehensions of his friends. Blair rapidly rose to eminence as a lawyer; and in most cases of importance was retained as a leading counsel. The celebrated Henry Erskine and he were generally pitted against each other, as the two most eloquent as well as able members of the bar. However much Erskine might surpass his opponent in witty observation, or ingenious remark, Blair was infinitely his superior as a clear reasoner and sound lawyer.

Mr. Blair was for several years one of the Assessors of the city of Edinburgh, and an Advocate-depute. In 1789, he was appointed Solicitor-General for Scotland; and, in 1801, was unanimously elected Dean of the Faculty of Advocates. His election of Dean was without a single dissentient voice, save that of Mr. Wilde, who cried out—"Harry Erskine for ever!" When the intelligence was communicated to Mr. Blair, his own words were—"Nothing gives me more pleasure than the fact, that those opposed to me in politics were the first to vote in my favour."

On the change of Ministry which took place in 1806, Mr. Blair was removed from the solicitorship; on which event he received a polite apology from the new minister, stating the necessity he was under of promoting his own party. This communication—no doubt dictated by good feeling—was perfectly unnecessary, in so far as the feelings of the ex-solicitor were concerned. Then, as now, a change in the Crown officers invariably succeeded a change in the Cabinet. The friends of either party were therefore prepared to rise or fall as the scale preponderated. Far from being out of temper with this turn of the political wheel, Mr. Blair showed his magnanimity, by proffering to his successor—John Clerk, afterwards Lord Eldin—the use of his gown, until the latter should get one prepared for himself.

On the return of his friends to power next year, Mr. Blair was offered the restoration of his former honour; but he declined not only this, but also the higher office of Lord Advocate. In 1808, on the resignation of Sir Ilay Campbell, he was raised to the Presidency of the College of Justice—a choice which gave satisfaction to all parties.

During the short period that his lordship discharged the duties of this high trust, his conduct as a judge realised the expectations formed from a knowledge of his abilities at the bar. In his character were not only blended those native qualities of mind, which, aided by the acquirements of study, combine to constitute superior talent, but he brought with him to the bench that " innate love of justice and abhor-rence of iniquity, without which, as he himself emphatically declared, when he took the chair of the Court, all other qualities avail nothing, or rather are worse than nothing."

In *Peter's Letters to his Kinsfolk* the character of the Lord Presi-dent is thus sketched :—" It would appear as if the whole of his clear and commanding intellect had been framed and tempered in such a way as to qualify him peculiarly and expressly for being, what the Stagyrite has finely called, ' a living equity '—one of the happiest, and perhaps one of the rarest, of all the combinations of mental powers. By all men of all parties the merits of this great man also were alike acknowledged; and his memory is at this moment alike held in reverence by them all. Even the keenest of his now surviving political opponents [the late Lord Eldin]—himself one of the greatest lawyers that Scotland ever has produced—is said to have contem-plated the superior intellect of Blair with a feeling of respectfulness not much akin to the common cast of his disposition. After hearing the President overturn, without an effort, in the course of a few clear and short sentences, a whole mass of ingenious sophistry, which it had cost himself much labour to erect, and which appeared to be regarded as insurmountable by all the rest of his audience, this great barrister is said to have sat for a few seconds ruminating with much bitterness on the discomfiture of his cause, and then to have muttered between his teeth—' My man ! *God Almighty spared nae pains when He made your brains!*' Those that have seen Mr. Clerk, and know his peculiarities, appreciate the value of this compliment, and do not think the less of it because of its coarseness."

The Lord President did not long enjoy that dignity which he gave such promise of rendering equally honourable to himself and beneficial to his country. He died suddenly on the 20th May, 1811, aged sixty-eight ; and it is not a little remarkable that the very same week terminated the life of his early and steady friend Lord Melville, who, as has been elsewhere mentioned, had come to Edinburgh to the President's funeral. The death of those two very eminent men, as it were by one blow, was looked upon as a national calamity. Their early friendship—their dying almost at the same period—and the high and important stations which they had occupied as public men, naturally created a more than ordinary interest on the occasion of their demise. Their houses being next to one another, with only a single wall between the bedrooms where the dead bodies of each were lying at the same time, made a deep impression on their friends. In a *Monody*, by an anonymous author, who has drawn the characters of Lord Melville and President Blair with tolerable ability, their friend-ship and death are thus alluded to :—

> " Two mighty oaks that, side by side,
> For ages towered, the forest's pride,
>   And nourished in their shade,

> Sapling and tree, and waving wood ;
> On whose broad breast October's flood,
> And winter's war, and whirlwind rude,
>   Their baffled might essayed.
>
> " Their musty boughs, compact on high,
> Seasons with all their storms defy—
> While some scant brook that oozes by,
>   Unheeded and unknown,
> Slow on each hidden fibre preys—
> Loosens amain the earth-fast base ;
> And far the forest wonder lays,
>   A thundering ruin prone !
>
> " Thus, thus, lamented chiefs ! ye fell
> From glory's loftiest pinnacle,
>   By destiny severe :
> Ere, tranced in sorrow, we had paid
> Due rites to Blair's illustrious shade,
> With heart-struck woe we hung dismay'd
>   O'er Melville's honoured bier."

The volume from which the above lines are taken, published in 4to at 4s., is entitled " Monody on the Death of the Right Hon. Henry Lord Viscount Melville, and of the Right Hon. Robert Blair of Avontoun, Lord President of the College of Justice." Edinburgh, 1811.

As a memorial of respect to his high talents, and to mark the estimation in which he was held, a statue of the Lord President Blair, by Chantry, is placed in the First Division of the Inner House of the Court of Session.

Mr. Blair married Isabella Cornelia Halkett, youngest daughter of Colonel Charles Craigie Halkett of Lawhill, Fifeshire, who still survives. He left one son and three daughters—one of whom is the wife of Alexander Maconochie, Lord Meadowbank, one of the Senators of the College of Justice, and a Lord of Justiciary.

About twenty years previous to his lordship's death, he purchased the small estate of Avontoun, near Linlithgow, beautifully situated, and which continued always to be his favourite residence. He took great pleasure in agricultural improvements, and brought it to the highest state of cultivation. The town residence of the family was, in 1773, that house upon the north side of the passage between Brown's and Argyle Square. The house was purchased by Mr. Blair from the Dutch ladies, the Miss Crawfurds.

CAPTAIN JAMES JUSTICE

Of Justice Hall.

SIR JAMES JUSTICE, descended from a family of that name in England, came to Scotland about the end of the seventeenth century, and held the office of Clerk to the Scottish Parliament. He acquired the estate of Crichton, with the celebrated castle, in the county of Edinburgh, which he left to his son, James Justice, Esq., who was one of the principal Clerks of the Court of Session. This gentleman was very fond of horticulture; and was the author of a book, published in 1755, entitled "The Scots Gardener's Director"—a work which, as the result of practical experience, with reference to the soil and climate of Scotland, was formerly in great repute, and is still worthy of consultation. The author was so great an enthusiast in this favourite pursuit, that he spent large sums in importing foreign seeds, roots, and trees. The collecting of tulips, being one of the fancies of his day, Mr. Justice was so deeply affected with the mania, that he has been known not to hesitate giving £50, or sometimes more, for a single rare tulip root. The rage for tulips was, for a long series of years, peculiar to the Dutch, who used to give very large prices for single roots of a rare description. For a short period it was very prevalent in Britain, where a gentleman is reported to have given a thousand pounds for a *black* tulip—he being at the time the owner of another root of the same description. Upon making the purchase, he put the root below his heel and destroyed it, observing that *now* he was the possessor of the *only* black tulip in the world!!! The extravagance of this propensity, with other causes, rendered it necessary for him to part with his estate of Crichton; and about the year 1735, it became the property of Mark Pringle, Esq. This gentleman killed William Scott of Raeburn, great grand-uncle of Sir Walter, in a duel. They fought with swords, as was the fashion of the time, in a field near Selkirk, called, from the catastrophe, the Raeburn Meadow. Mr. Pringle fled to Spain, and was long a captive and slave in Barbary.— *Lockhart's Life of Scott,* p. 4. vol. i. With the residue of the price of this large property, Mr. Justice purchased some lands in the vicinity of the village of Ugston, or Oxton, in the parish of Channelkirk, and county of Berwick, where he built a mansion-house, which he called Justice Hall—a name which it still retains. Justice Hall is now the property of Sir James Spittal.

By his second marriage, Mr. Justice left an only son, (the subject of the Print), who was born about the year 1755; but at what period he succeeded his father is not exactly known. He entered the army, as an officer, in the marine service; served abroad during the American war, and attained the rank of Captain. He was above six feet in height, and well proportioned. His address was peculiarly agreeable and fascinating; and, both in appearance and manner, he bore no slight resemblance to George IV.

The Captain inherited little of his father's enthusiasm for horticulture, being more enamoured with the "flowers of literature." He was exceedingly fond of the drama, and was one of the best performers at the private theatricals at Marrionville, (alluded to in our notice of Captain Macrae). His genius in this line was rather imitative than original, and his delineations of Cook, Kemble, and other eminent actors of his time, were very successful. Had his talents for the stage been cultivated, with the advantage of his fine personal appearance, it is possible he might have made a distinguished figure, and perhaps retrieved the fortunes of his family. Besides indulging his friends with declamations from Shakspeare, and other popular dramatic poets, he occasionally contributed to their amusement by writing plays; and we are assured that his compositions possessed some merit. One of these was entitled "Hell upon Earth, or the Miseries of Matrimony," and is said to have contained many scenes indicative of the Captain's personal experience on the subject.

The Captain's love for the drama continued long to hold undiminished ascendancy in his bosom, and was the occasion of his not infrequently patronising the humblest as well as the highest in the profession. While in Edinburgh, he was regular in his attendance at the Theatre; and no worn-out son of Thespis ever visited Justice Hall without experiencing the hospitality of the owner. A gentleman of our acquaintance, happening to call on the Captain one forenoon, was astonished to find him in his parlour, surrounded by a company of strolling players, who, on one of their migratory excursions, had called at Justice Hall, in the certainty of obtaining—what they probably had not known for some time before—an hour or two of comfortable entertainment. The wine was in free circulation; and the players, in merry tune, were repaying their host with speech and mimicry, in every variety of imitation, from the majestic Cato to the versatile Sylvester Daggerwood.

The Captain was at this period perhaps less choice than formerly in the selection of his amusements, and of the means which might contribute to them. He had been married to a Miss Campbell, by whom he had one child—a daughter; but the union proved unhappy, and a separation was the consequence. When disputes of this nature occur, it is a generally received maxim that there must be faults on both sides; and, in this instance, we are not prepared to assert the contrary. The Captain was undoubtedly one of the most kind-hearted mortals in existence; but it is possible he might lack other qualities necessary to the growth of domestic happiness. There was at least a degree of eccentricity in his character not exactly suited for matrimonial felicity.

Shortly after this unfortunate separation, a friend of his, accompanied by an acquaintance, went to visit him at Justice Hall. They found the Captain just returned from a solitary stroll in the fields, and a little in dishabille. He apologised for his appearance; and, on the stranger being introduced to him, "O," said he, in his usual voluble manner, "know your father well—not at all like him; no doubt of your mother—but—pshaw!—never mind. Welcome to Bachelor's Hall: 'tis Bachelor's Hall now, you know—Mrs. Justice has left me—no matter—she was a good sort of person for all that—a little hot tempered—only three days after marriage, a leg of mutton made to fly at my head; never mind—plenty of wine, eggs, at Bachelor's Hall—we can make ourselves merry." The lady and her daughter survived the unfortunate Laird of Justice Hall. The former, we believe, died in 1837; the latter was respectably married. She some years ago (through her mother) fell heir to a considerable fortune.

When Captain Justice's father, as already stated, sold the estate of Crichton to Mr. Pringle, a clause had been inserted in the deed of conveyance, by which the seller guaranteed (or, according to Scotch law phraseology, warranted) the purchaser and his successors against all augmentations of stipend which the clergyman of the parish might

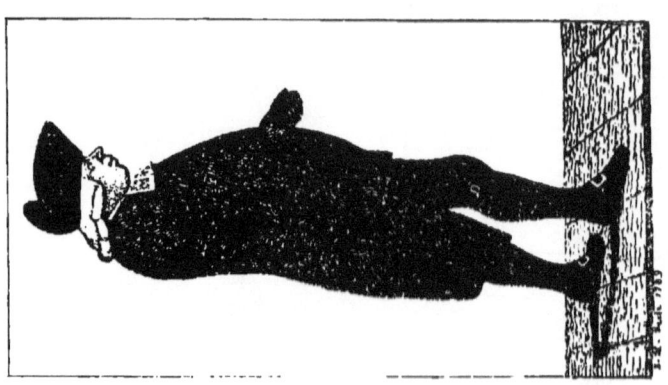

The Rev. ANDREW HUNTER, D.D.

[To face page 197.

The MARQUIS of GRAHAM and The EARL of BUCHAN

Vol. I., Plate XVI.

obtain subsequent to the date of the sale ; probably not anticipating that the practice of granting augmentation to the stipends of the clergy would be extended as it has been done. In process of time, various augmentations of stipend were obtained by the incumbents of the parish of Crichton. The proprietors of the estate of Crichton called upon Captain Justice, as representing the granter of the disposition or deed of conveyance, to relieve them from the share of increased stipend thus allocated upon them. This gave rise to a long and expensive law suit, in which Captain Justice argued that the warrandice which his father had given was not perpetual, but limited to the endurance of certain leases of tiends originally granted by Mr. Hepburn of Humbie, which had long since expired ; and the Court of Session decided the cause in favour of Captain Justice. An appeal, however, was taken to the House of Lords, and the judgment was reversed, by which a liability of upwards of £9000 was created against Captain Justice and his estate.

The Captain, who had borne with great fortitude the vexations of this protracted litigation, submitted to the fatal effect of it on his means and estate with astonishing resignation. The estate, in fulfilment of the decree of the House of Lords, was adjudged for payment of this debt, and was sold in lots to different purchasers. The unfortunate owner, unable to dwell longer even in the frugal manner in which he had done in the house of his father, rather than remove to some other part of the country, which his friends advised him to do, resolved to end his days, if not *in*, at least *within* sight of his old "dear home ;" and he accordingly took up his abode in a cottage in the adjoining village of Ugston, where he lived a season or two, and died about the year 1822.

The "fair one" in whose company the artist has thought proper to place Captain Justice, in " The Evening Walk," was at one time well known in the *beau monde* of Princes Street. The lady, we understand, is still alive ; and may be remembered by those who recollect the sympathy pretty generally excited by the fate of her accomplished daughter, who fell a victim to the arts of one whom a sense of gratitude and honour should have induced to have acted otherwise.

ANDREW DALZEL, F.R.S.,
Professor of Greek.

THE title of the "Successful Candidate" given to the Portraiture of this gentleman has reference to the memorable struggle for the office of Clerk to the General Assembly, which occurred in 1789. His opponent, Dr. Carlyle of Inveresk (who has already been noticed in a preceding part of this work), was supported by the moderate or Government party, and Mr. Dalzel by the popular, or, as they were then called, "the Wild Party."

After a keen discussion—on an amendment proposed by Henry Erskine (then Dean of Faculty), that the election should proceed under the proviso of a retrospective scrutiny of the votes, which was carried in the affirmative—the two candidates were then put in nomination, viz., "Dr. Carlyle, proposed by Dr. Gerard of Aberdeen and the Solicitor-General; and Professor Dalzel, proposed by Dr. Bryce of Johnston and the Dean of Faculty; and the vote having been put, it carried by 145 to 142 (being a majority of three) in favour of Dr. Carlyle. The Moderator (Dr. George Hill) being desired to declare in what manner he would give his casting vote, if, upon a scrutiny, there should appear an equality of votes, declared that he gave his vote for Dr. Carlyle.

"The Dean of Faculty then moved for a committee of scrutiny in behalf of Professor Dalzel; and Principal Davidson made the same demand on the part of Dr. Carlyle. A committee was accordingly named, consisting of ten members on each side, together with the Moderator; after which the roll of the Assembly, marked agreeably to the amendment, was sealed up upon the motion of the Dean of Faculty.

"Dr. Carlyle took his place and the oath as Clerk, and addressed the Assembly in a short speech, thanking them for the honour they had conferred upon him; and declaring that he reckoned it the chief glory of his life to have always stood forward in defence of the Church of Scotland against *fanaticism*.

"No less than 287 members voted on this occasion. The Assembly consists in all of 864; and, it is said, the greatest number ever known to have voted before this time was 221."

Such is a brief account of the election; but, when the scrutiny had been entered into, the precaution of the Dean of Faculty was found to have been highly judicious. On finding himself in a minority, Dr. Carlyle wisely withdrew his claim before the report of the committee was presented. Professor Dalzel was thereupon declared the "successful candidate."

PROFESSOR ANDREW DALZEL was the son of respectable, although not wealthy, parents. His father was a wright, or carpenter, at the village of Kirkliston, in Linlithgowshire. He was born in 1742, and educated at the school of the village. Dr. Drysdale was at that time minister of Kirkliston; and, fortunately, for the young scholar, took much interest in his progress, by assisting and directing him in his studies.

In course of time young Dalzel entered the University of Edinburgh; where, with a view to the ministry, he studied with much success, and acquired a classical as well as theological education. In the Divinity Hall he is known to have delivered the prescribed course of lectures to the satisfaction of Professor Hamilton; but it does not appear that he ever was licensed. About this time he was appointed tutor to Lord Maitland (the present Earl of Lauderdale), with whom he travelled to Paris, and pleased his pupil's father so much that, shortly after his return from France, the Earl resolved to use his influence with the Town Council of Edinburgh to procure his election to the Greek Chair, then vacant by the death of Professor Robert Hunter. Among other obstacles in the way of his preferment, some of the Council favoured another candidate, Mr. Duke Gordon, afterwards well known for many years as under-librarian of the College. The interest of the Earl of Lauderdale, however, prevailed, and Dalzel was appointed to the Greek Chair in 1773.

Mr. Duke Gordon was the son of a linen manufacturer, and born in the Potterrow, Edinburgh. His father was a native of Huntly—a Jacobite—and a thorough clansman. Hence, in testimony of his respect to the head of the clan, his son was called *Duke* Gordon. Duke (who abhorred the name) was educated at a school kept in the Cowgate by Mr. Andrew Waddell—a nonjurant—who had "been out in the forty-five," and was of course patronised by all his Jacobitical friends. Duke Gordon made great progress under Mr. Waddell; and, although compelled to follow his father's profession for several years, had imbibed such a desire for languages, that he contrived to prose-cute his studies; and, on the death of the old man, abandoned the manufacture of linen altogether, and devoted himself entirely to literature. He had views to the ministry; but some peculiar notions which he entertained on theology shut the church doors upon him. In 1768 he was appointed assistant-librarian of the College Library— a situation for which he was peculiarly well qualified by his extensive learning and general literary acquirements. The emoluments of the office being limited, he taught classes at his own house, by which he added considerably to his income. He never was married; and, such was his frugality, he died in 1802 worth a great deal of money. To three of his particular friends—Professor Dalzel, the Rev. Andrew Johnston, minister of Salton, and Mr. William White, writer in Edin-burgh—he conveyed, by his will, all his effects, burdened with a life annuity to his only sister, the wife of a respectable shoemaker, to-gether with several other private legacies. His public bequests were —£500 to the Royal Infirmary of Edinburgh; the reversion of a tenement of houses, of nearly the same value, to the poor of the parish of St. Cuthbert's; and such of his books to the Library of the University of Edinburgh as the librarian should think proper to be added to that collection.

The enthusiastic manner in which Prof. Dalzel immediately set about discharging the duties of the Greek Chair justified the choice which had been made. In the University of Edinburgh the taste for Grecian literature had been gradually giving way. Besides, the great fame of Professor Moor, of the Glasgow College, together with the excellent editions of the Greek classics, then issuing from the press of the Foulises, had well-nigh annihilated the reputation of the capital alto-gether. The enthusiasm and ability of Professor Dalzel, however, imparted new life to the study of classical learning; and the various improvements which he introduced in his system of tuition tended in an eminent degree to restore the character of the University, and to draw around him students from the most distant quarters. The ele-mentary class-books he compiled were so well adapted to the object for which they were designed, that they soon found their way into many of the chief schools of England; and, with certain modifications and improvements, are still very generally in use.

Professor Dalzel was in the habit of delivering a series of lectures to his students on Grecian history, antiquities, literature, philosophy, and the fine arts. These discourses were always well attended, and were deeply interesting even to the youngest of his auditors. "There was a witchery in his address which could prevail alike over sloth and over levity," and never failed to rivet the attention of his hearers.

When the Royal Society of Edinburgh was instituted in 1783, Mr. Dalzel was prevailed on to undertake the duties of Secretary to its literary class; and to his labours, while acting in this capacity, the Society is indebted for several able essays, and other interesting communications.

On the death of Dr. James Robertson, Professor of Oriental Languages, in 1795, Mr. Dalzel, who had been associated with him as conjunct Secretary and Librarian, was appointed Keeper of the College Library, having as his assistant Mr. Duke Gordon, with whom he lived on terms of great intimacy; and, on whose death in 1802, he did ample justice to his memory, in an exceedingly well written and very interesting memoir of his life, which he communicated to the editor of the *Scots Magazine*.

After a lingering illness, Mr. Dalzel died on the 8th December, 1806. He was married to a daughter of Dr. Drysdale, his early friend and benefactor—a lady of distinguished accomplishments and sweetness of temper, by whom he had several children.

The personal appearance of Professor Dalzel was prepossessing. In stature he was among the tallest of the middle size; his complexion was fair; his aspect mild and interesting; his eyes were blue, and full of vigorous expression; and his features plump, without heaviness or grossness. His address was graceful and impressive. He took little exercise; but when he did walk, his favourite resort was the King's Park. The attitude in which he is pourtrayed in the print represents him in one of his rural excursions. During the latter period of his life Mr. Dalzel resided within the College, in the house which had been long occupied by Principal Robertson.

DR. ALEXANDER HAMILTON,

Professor of Midwifery.

THE Medical School of Edinburgh had been established for a very considerable period of time, before it was found necessary to institute a Professorship to teach the principles and practice of Midwifery. So early as 1726, Mr. Joseph Gibson had been appointed by the Town Council to give instructions in the art of midwifery; but he appears to have confined his teaching to females only. The truth is, that in those days the practice of midwifery was almost solely confined to that sex, as it was only in difficult cases that the assistance of male practitioners was called in; and hence it very frequently happened that the labour was found to be too far advanced to admit of their aid being of material service, and thus, from want of skill, the lives of many mothers and children were lost. The public owe it to the strenuous exertions of Dr. Young (the first Professor of Midwifery in the College of Edinburgh), and of the subject of this memoir, that so few fatal cases occur in this way, in the metropolitan districts of Scotland. Both of these gentlemen were indefatigable in their efforts to impress upon the public the necessity and advantages of all who practised midwifery, both male and female, being regularly instructed in the art. In their days, they had very formidable prejudices to encounter. They had not only to contend with the gross ignorance of those who were in established practice, and whose interests were so nearly related to the continuance of the system; but such was the state of public feeling, that there were many who pretended to the name of philosophers, who encouraged the prejudice. The principal argument upon which they insisted, which happens not to be fact in all cases, was, that nature is the proper midwife. This, combined with certain fastidious notions of delicacy, had the effect of confining the obstetrical art to females. But such has been the gradual improvement of the age in which we live, that we have the highest authority (even that of the present excellent Professor in the University of Edinburgh) for affirming that the public conviction of the utility of the art is so great, that there is now hardly a parish of Scotland, the midwife of which has not been regularly taught; and it may with truth be added, that the propriety and advantage of males practising as accoucheurs is now so generally admitted, as to make it very probable that the employment of females in midwifery may in time be entirely superseded. In three of the four Universities of Scotland there are Professors of Midwifery, viz., in Glasgow, Marischal College, and in Edinburgh, in which city there was established, in 1791, a Lying-in Hospital, under the more immediate patronage of the magistrates, the Lord Provost being President, and the Professor of Midwifery Ordinary Physician.

The Plate contains a striking likeness of the late DR. ALEXANDER HAMILTON. This gentleman was born, in 1739, at Fordoun, near Montrose, where his father, who had been a surgeon in the army during Queen Anne's wars, was established as a medical practitioner. He came to Edinburgh about the year 1758, as assistant to Mr. John Straiton, a surgeon then in extensive practice; and on that gentleman's death, in 1762, he was urged by a number of respectable families to settle in Edinburgh. He accordingly, on application, was admitted a member of the College of Surgeons in that city, for the Royal College was not incorporated until 1778. Of an active and bustling disposition, it was not long before he was elected Deacon of the Incorporation, and consequently became a member of the Town Council. He was at the same time chosen Convener of the Trades.

Intent on the practice of midwifery, he found it necessary to obtain a medical degree as a physician before he could be admitted a Fellow of the Royal College of Physicians. This he accordingly obtained, having probably applied to the University of St. Andrews. The Royal College was founded in 1681, and according to the charter, every graduate of any of the Scottish Universities has a right to be admitted, upon paying the fees. He was first admitted a licentiate, and at a suitable interval chosen a fellow of the College.

In 1775, Dr. Hamilton published his " Elements of Midwifery," which has gone through several editions, under the title of " Outlines of Midwifery;" and in 1780, he published also a " Treatise on the Management of Female Complaints," adapted to the use of families, which continues to be a popular work. In the same year he was conjoined in the Professorship of Midwifery in the College of Edinburgh with Dr. Thomas Young ; and on the death of that gentleman, in 1783, he was appointed sole Professor.

Dr. Young and Dr. Hamilton gave alternately three courses of instructions annually to male and female pupils, till the death of the former, when the whole duty devolved upon the latter gentleman. Being now at liberty to adopt any improvement in teaching the class he might judge proper, he set about enlarging the plan of his lectures. His predecessors, though undoubtedly men of abilities, felt themselves narrowed in the sphere of their exertions, and cramped in their endeavours to perform their academical duty to their own satisfaction, in consequence of the strong prejudices that prevailed against the system of tuition. In his own time, these prepossessions were beginning to give way; but he completely effected what was obviously wanting in the scheme of medical education at the University of Edinburgh, by giving a connected view of the diseases peculiar to women and children. Still, however, the midwifery class was not in the list of those necessary to be attended before procuring the degree of Doctor of Medicine. His son has succeeded in accomplishing this object, after encountering a great deal of opposition.

Upon the 29th March, 1797, the Magistrates of Edinburgh, who are the patrons, had resolved that it should not be in the power of any Professor to appoint another to teach in his room, without their consent; but, upon application, Dr. Hamilton was allowed, on the 25th December, 1798, to employ his son as his assistant, and this office he discharged for two years. The doctor resigned his professorship upon the 26th of March, 1800, and on the 9th of April, his son, the late Professor, was unanimously elected to the chair.

Dr. Hamilton married Miss Reid of Gorgie, by whom he had a numerous family. He died upon the 23rd of May, 1802, in the sixty-fourth year of his age.

— —   — —

JAMES GREGORY, M.D.,

Author of " The History of the Western Highlands and Islands of Scotland."

DR. JAMES GREGORY, the son of Dr. John Gregory, sometime Professor of Medicine in King's College, Aberdeen, and afterwards in the University of Edinburgh, was born in the former city, in 1753, and received the earlier part of his education at the grammar school instituted by Dr. Patrick Dun. In consequence of his father's removal to Edinburgh in 1765, he subsequently studied at the University there, and took his degree of Doctor of Medicine in 1774. He then repaired

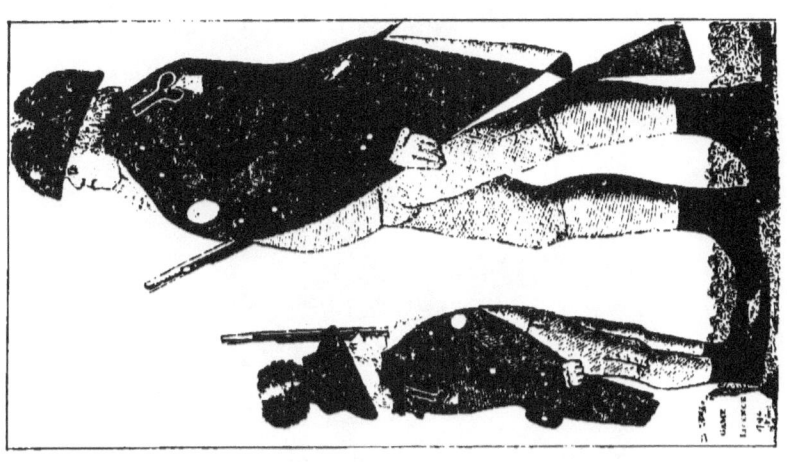

FRANCIS RONALDSON.   ALEXANDER OSBORNE

[To face page 226

JAMES GREGORY, M.D.

.

to Leyden, where he attended the lectures of the celebrated Gobius—the favourite student and the immediate successor of the great Boerhaave.

Dr. John Gregory died in 1773, before the education of his son had been completed; and, according to a previous arrangement, Dr. Cullen succeeded to the Practice of Physic. From this period the Professorship of the Institutes of Medicine was kept open, by various means, till 1778, when Dr. Gregory, then only in his twenty-third year, was appointed to the vacant chair. Although young, he was eminently qualified for the situation, from the extent of his acquirements and his own natural talents. Of this we need no better proof than is afforded by his text-book, " Conspectus Medicinæ Theoreticæ ad usum Academicum," which he published a few years after obtaining the professorship, and which procured for its author a high professional character throughout Europe.

In 1790, on the death of Dr. Cullen, Dr. Gregory was elected Professor of the Practice of Physic, and successfully maintained the reputation acquired by his predecessor. His success as a teacher was great; and his class was, during the long period he filled the chair, numerously attended by students from all parts of the world. He also held the appointment of first Physician to his Majesty for Scotland.

Dr. Gregory was distinguished for his classical attainments, and especially for proficiency in the Latin language, to which his thesis, " De Morbis Coeli Mutatione Medendis," in 1774, bore ample testimony. His talents for literature and general philosophy were of a high order; and that he did not prosecute these to a greater extent was no doubt owing to the pressure of his professional duties, which scarcely left him an hour to himself. In 1792, he published two volumes 8vo, entitled " Philosophical and Literary Essays," in which he combated the doctrine of fatalism maintained by Dr. Priestley in a work previously published by that author under the title of " Philosophical Necessity." He forwarded the manuscripts of his essays to Dr. Priestley for perusal prior to publication, but the Doctor declined the honour, on the ground that his mind was made up, and that he had ceased to think of the subject.

Respecting Dr. Gregory's extensive practice, and the numerous patients who, attracted by his fame, came from great distances to consult him, several anecdotes have found their way into books of light reading. The scene in his study with a guzzling, punch-drinking citizen of Glasgow, is amusing, and must be familiar to almost every reader. No man possessed more gentlemanly manners than Dr. Gregory; yet, in such cases as that of the Glasgow merchant, or of the lady who came from London to consult him against the infirmities of age, he expressed himself with a brevity and bluntness the reverse of gratifying.

Dr. Gregory was likewise the author of a " Dissertation on the Theory of the Moods of Verbs "—a paper read to the Royal Society, of which he was a member; and he published an edition of Cullen's " First Lines of the Practice of Physic," two vols. 8vo.

We have now to allude to a series of publications, commenced in

1793, which but for the extraordinary degree of local excitement created by them at the time, we should willingly have passed over without comment. The first of these was a pamphlet by Dr. Gregory, in which he endeavoured, by *internal evidence*, to fix the authorship of a book, entitled "A Guide for Gentlemen studying Medicine at the University of Edinburgh," upon the two Doctors Hamilton, father and son. The author of the "Guide" had been somewhat severe in his strictures in regard to some of the professorships of the University; while, in the opinion of Dr. Gregory and his friends, an undue degree of praise had been bestowed upon the midwifery classes taught by Drs. Hamilton. To this Dr. James Hamilton, junior, replied in a well-written pamphlet, in which he calmly, yet with spirit, urged the groundlessness of the accusation, and the unprovoked asperity of his opponent. In the meantime law proceedings had been instituted against the publisher of the "Guide," in order to discover the author, while Dr. Hamilton commenced counter-proceedings against Dr. Gregory, for the injuries his character had sustained by the manner in which he had been traduced.

In 1800, another paper warfare occurred, in consequence of a memorial addressed by Dr. Gregory to the managers of the Royal Infirmary, complaining of the younger members of the College of Surgeons being there allowed to perform operations. This was replied to by Mr. John Bell, surgeon; and a controversy ensued, which for some time engrossed the whole attention of the Edinburgh medical profession.

Again, in 1806, the Doctor entered into a warm controversy with the College of Physicians, owing to some proceedings on the part of that body which he considered derogatory to the profession.

In 1808, he printed, for private circulation, a small volume in 8vo, entitled "Lucubrations on an Epigram:" also, in 1810, "There is Wisdom in Silence"—an imitation from the Anthologia; and "The Viper and the File"—an imitation of the well-known fable of Phædrus, "Vipera et Lima." As a specimen of his epigrammatic talents, we give the following—

"'O give me, dear angel, one lock of your hair'—
A bashful young lover took courage and sighed;
'Twas a sin to refuse so modest a pray'r—
'You shall have my whole wig,' the dear angel replied."

Dr. Gregory was of an athletic figure, and naturally of a strong constitution. He had enjoyed good health; and, from his abstemious mode of life, might have been expected to live to extreme old age. The overturn of his carriage, whilst returning from visiting a patient, by which accident his arm was broken, proved injurious to his constitution. He was afterwards repeatedly attacked with inflammation of the lungs, which ultimately caused his death. He died at his house in St. Andrew Square, on the 2nd April, 1821, in the sixty-eighth year of his age.

Dr. Gregory was twice married. By his second wife—a daughter of Donald Macleod, Esq. of Geanies, and who still survives—he left a numerous family. His oldest son was educated for the bar, and was admitted a member of the Faculty of Advocates in 1820. A younger son, Donald, who died in October, 1836, in the prime of life, was for several years Secretary to the Society of Antiquaries of Scotland ; and in this situation he highly distinguished himself by his zeal, assiduity, and agreeable manners. In his late work, entitled the "History of the Western Highlands and Isles of Scotland," brought down to the year 1625, he has fortunately left us a permanent memorial of his learning and accurate research—not the less valuable that it is, in fact, one of the first attempts to investigate the history of that portion of the British Empire, not by reference to vague traditions and idle reveries, but by the most careful examination of original documents, and the various public records. This work, indeed, forms part only of his contemplated scheme, for, had his life been spared, he intended to have followed it up with another volume relating to the other great division, or the Central Highlands, which could not have failed to have proved of even greater historical interest, independently of what he purposed to have prefixed—"A Dissertation on the Manners, Customs, and Laws of the Highlanders," at an early period ; and for which, we believe, he had collected very important materials.

When the Royal Edinburgh Volunteers was formed, in 1793, Dr. Gregory entered warmly into the spirit of the design, and was among the first to enrol himself in the ranks. He never, however, attained eminence in his military capacity. The well-known Sergeant Gould used to say, " he might be a good physician, but he was a very awkward soldier." At drill, he was either very absent or very inquisitive, and put so many questions, that Gould, out of temper, often said—"——— it, sir, you are here to obey orders, and not to ask reasons : there is nothing in the King's orders about reasons!"

Aware of his deficiency, the Doctor was not only punctual in attending all regimental field-days, but frequently had the Sergeant-Major at his own house to give him instructions. On one of these occasions, the Sergeant, out of all patience with the awkwardness and inquisitiveness of his learned pupil, exclaimed in a rage—"Hold your tongue, sir, I would rather drill *ten clowns* than *one philosopher!*"

Small parties of the volunteers were drilled privately in the Circus (now the Adelphi Theatre). On one of these occasions, while marching across the stage, the trap-door used by the players having been inadvertently left unbolted, the Doctor suddenly disappeared to the "shades below;" upon which a wag belonging to the corps exclaimed —"Exit Gregor's Ghost!"—an allusion to a popular Scotch ballad called "Young Gregor's Ghost."

ALEXANDER OSBORNE, ESQ.,

Of the Edinburgh Royal Volunteers.

MR. OSBORNE was right-hand man of the grenadier company of the First Regiment of the Royal Edinburgh Volunteers. His personal appearance must be familiar in the recollection of many of our readers. It was not merely his great height, although he was probably the tallest man of his day in Edinburgh, but his general bulk, which rendered him so very remarkable. His legs, in particular, during his best days, were nearly as large in circumference as the body of an ordinary person. He was a very good-natured and well-informed man. Shortly after the Volunteers had been embodied, Lord Melville introduced his huge countryman, dressed in full regimentals, to his Majesty George III. On witnessing such an herculean specimen of his loyal defenders in the north, the King's curiosity was excited, and he inquired—"Are all the Edinburgh Volunteers like you?" Osborne, mistaking the jocular construction of the question, and supposing his Majesty meant as regarded their status in society, replied—"They are so, an' it please your Majesty." The King exclaimed—"Astonishing!"

Mr. Osborne was frequently annoyed by his friends taking advantage of his good nature, and playing off their jests at the expense of his portly figure. One day at dinner, the lady of the house asked him if he would choose to take a pigeon? He answered—"Half a one, if you please." Bailie Creech, who was present, immediately cried—"Give him a whole one; *half* a one will not be a seed in his teeth."

In his youth, Mr. Osborne is said to have had a prodigious appetite; so much so, as to have devoured not less than *nine pounds* of beef-steaks at a meal. He was no epicure, however; and in later times ate sparingly in company, either because he really was easily satisfied, or more probably to avoid the observations which to a certainty would have been made upon his eating. On one occasion, the lady of a house where he was dining, helped him to an enormous slice of beef, with these words—"Mr. Osborne, the muckle ox should get the muckle winlan"—an observation which, like every other of a similar import, he felt acutely.

On another occasion, he happened to change his shoes in the passage of a house where he was dining. Mr. Creech, of facetious memory, having followed shortly after, and recognizing the shoes, brought one of them in his hand into the drawing-room, and presenting it to another of the guests, Mr. John Buchan, Writer to the Signet, who was of very diminutive stature, said to him—"Hae, Johnny, there's a *cradle* for you to sleep in."

The personal history of Mr. Osborne affords few particulars either peculiar or interesting. His father, Alexander Osborne, Esq., Comptroller of Customs at Aberdeen, and who died there in 1785, was a gentleman of even greater dimensions than his son.

After having filled an inferior appointment for some years at one of the outports, Mr. Osborne obtained the office of Inspector-General and Solicitor of Customs. He was subsequently appointed one of the Commissioners of the Board; and, latterly, on the reduction made in that establishment, retired upon a superannuated allowance.

Mr. Osborne was never married; and, being of frugal habits, he amassed a considerable fortune, and made several landed purchases. Besides a pretty extensive tract of land in Orkney, he was proprietor of a small estate in Ayrshire. Gogar Bank, a few miles west of Edinburgh, belonged to him, where he had a summer house, and a very extensive and excellent garden. Here he often contemplated building a handsome villa, but the design was never carried into execution.

Mr. Osborne died only a few years ago, at the advanced age of seventy-four; and it is understood the bulk of his property was bequeathed to a gentleman of the west country. He lived at one time in Richmond Street; but latterly, and for a considerable number of years, in York Place.

FRANCIS RONALDSON, ESQ.

Of the Edinburgh Royal Volunteers.

MR. FRANCIS RONALDSON of the Post Office was one of the least men of the regiment, but a very zealous volunteer. He is placed in the same Print with Osborne, in order to record an anecdote of Sergeant Gould. In forming a double from a single rank, at a squad drill, Francis became Osborne's rear man. Poor Francis was never seen; and Gould, addressing the next man, continued to call out—" Move to the right, sir; why the devil don't you cover?" Little Francis at length exclaimed, with great naivette—" I can't cover—I do all I can!"

Mr. Ronaldson was Surveyor of the General Post Office, which situation he held for upwards of forty years. He was a most active, spirited little personage, and remarkably correct in the management of his official department. He kept a regular journal of his surveys, which, on his demise, was found to have been brought up till within a few days of his death.

In private life, Ronaldson was exceedingly joyous, full of wit and anecdote, and was withal a man of rare qualifications. He had also some claims to a literary character. He was a votary of the muses, and a great collector of fugitive pieces. He left upwards of two dozen volumes of *Scraps*—culled principally from newspapers—consisting of whatever seemed to him valuable or curious. He was also deeply versed in divinity; and, strange as it may appear, several well written sermons were among his manuscripts. As illustrative of his talent for the pulpit, it is told of Mr. Ronaldson, that on one occasion he invited an acquaintance, a clergyman, to take a drive with him in his carriage on a short official journey. The day being the last of the week, his friend declined on the ground that he had "a sermon to study for to-morrow." "O never mind," said Ronaldson; "if that's all, step in—I'll assist you with it." The clergyman afterwards acknowledged the aid he had received; and expressed his astonishment at the extent of information, and the fluency of language displayed by the Post Office Surveyor.

When the duties of the day were over, Francis delighted to hurry home to his literary labour. There you were certain to find him—his coat off, and "in his slippers"—busily engaged with scissors and paste-brush, while armfuls of dissected papers, spread out on the table before him, sufficiently attested to his rapacity as a gleaner.

We have glanced over several sheets of his sermons, and have seen his scrap-books, which are indeed curious. Several of the volumes are in manuscript, and contain original as well as selected pieces, both in prose and verse. As a specimen of the poetical department, the following may be taken :—

"LINES ON SEEING, IN A LIST OF NEW MUSIC, A PIECE ENTITLED 'THE WATERLOO WALTZ.'

" A moment pause, ye British fair,
 While pleasure's phantoms ye pursue,
 And say if sprightly dance or air,
 Suit with the name of Waterloo !
  Awful was the victory—
  Chasten'd should the triumph be:
  'Midst the laurels she has won,
  Britain mourns for many a son.

" Veil'd in clouds the morning rose;
 Nature seem'd to mourn the day,
 Which consign'd, before its close,
 Thousands to their kindred clay.
  How unfit for courtly ball,
  Or the giddy festival,
  Was the grim and ghastly view,
  Ere ev'ning closed on Waterloo !

" See the Highland warrior rushing,
 Firm in danger, on the foe,
 Till the life-blood warmly gushing,
 Lays the plaided hero low.
  His native pipe's accustom'd sound.
  'Mid war's infernal concert drown'd,
  Cannot soothe his last adieu,
  Or wake his sleep on Waterloo !

" Chasing o'er the cuirassier,
 See the foaming charger flying;
 Trampling in his wild career,
 All alike, the dead and dying.
  See the bullet, through his side,
  Answer'd by the spouting tide;
  Helmet, horse, and rider too,
  Roll on bloody Waterloo !

" Shall scenes like these the dance inspire ?
 Or wake enlivening notes of mirth ?
 O ! shiver'd be the recreant lyre
 That gave the base idea birth !
  Other sounds I ween were there—
  Other music rent the air—
  Other waltz the warriors knew,
  When they clos'd on Waterloo !

" Forbear!—till time with lenient hand
 Hath sooth'd the pang of recent sorrow;
 And let the picture distant stand.
 The softening hue of years to borrow.

When our race has pass'd away,
Hands unborn may wake the lay;
And give to joy alone the view,
Of Britain's fame on Waterloo!

"*April 23, 1817.*"

In Mr. Ronaldson's collections are to be found many very amusing and humorous articles, strongly indicative of his relish for the ludicrous. The following may serve as a specimen:—

"[*Taken from a Church-door in Ireland.*]

"RUN AWAY FROM PATRICK M'DALLAGH.

"Whereas my wife, Mrs. Bridget M'Dallagh, is again walked away with herself, and left me with four small children and her poor old blind mother, and nobody to look after house or home, and I hear has taken up with Tim Guigan, the lame fiddler, the same that was put in the stocks last Easter for stealing Barney Doody's game-cock, This is to give Notice, that I will not pay for bit or sup on her or his account to man or mortal, and that she had better never show the marks of her ten toes near my house again.   PATRICK M'DALLAGH.

"*N.B.—Tim* had better keep out of my sight."

Mr. Ronaldson belonged to the right centre company of the Volunteers, but was occasionally drafted to other companies; in consequence of which he was sometimes brought to cover Mr. Osborne. In this position little Francis, from his convenient height, was of important service to his gigantic friend, by helping him to his side-arms, when ordered to fix bayonets—Osborne, owing to his immense bulk, finding great difficulty in reaching the weapon.

The regimental firelocks being rather too heavy, Mr. Ronaldson had one manufactured specially for himself. One day at a review, General Vyse, then Commander-in-Chief, happening to observe the difference, remarked the circumstance—"Why," said Ronaldson, with great animation, "if my firelock is light, I have weight enough *here!*" (pointing to his cartridge-box). The General complimented little Francis on his spirit, observing—"It would be well if every one were animated with similar zeal."

Although in the Print allusion is made to the "game-laws," Mr. Ronaldson was no sportsman; that is to say, he was not partial to roaming through fields with a dog and a gun; but he affected to be a follower of Walton in the art of angling. On one of his fishing excursions on the Tweed, he was accompanied by a gentleman, who was no angler, but who went to witness the scientific skill of his friend. Francis commenced with great enthusiasm, and with high hopes of success. Not a leap was observed for some time; but by and by the water seemed to live as it were with "the springing trout;" yet, strange to say, all the dexterity of the angler could not beguile even a single par from its element. After hours of fruitless labour, Francis was perfectly confounded at his want of success. In vain he altered his flies—all colours and sizes were equally ineffectual; and at length the closing day compelled him to cease from his labours. On his way home he was accosted by an acquaintance—" Well, what luck to-day, Mr. Ronaldson?"   "Very bad," he replied; plenty raised, but not a single take."   This apparent plenty, however, did not arise from the abundance of fish, as Mr. Ronaldson supposed—his friend, who always kept a little to the rear, having amused himself by throwing small pebbles into the water, in such a way as led to the deception.   The gentleman kept the secret, and Francis for years puzzled his brains in vain to find out the cause of his extraordinary ill luck in the piscatorial exploits of that eventful day.

Mr. Ronaldson was a native of Edinburgh.   He was married, but had no family.   He resided in a house at the Calton Hill, where he died in 1818, his widow surviving him only a few years.   The most of his property was bequeathed in various sums to the different charities of the city.

THE REV. ROBERT WALKER,

Of the High Church.

THIS much esteemed clergyman was for upwards of twenty years a colleague of the celebrated Dr. Blair, whose memoir has already been given.

MR. WALKER was born in the Canongate of Edinburgh in 1716, his father being minister of that parish.   He studied at the University of Edinburgh; and, in 1737, was licensed by the Presbytery of Kirkcudbright.   In 1738, he received a unanimous call to the parish of Straiton, situated within the bounds of the Presbytery of Ayr, to which he was ordained; and, for nearly eight years, continued zealously to discharge the duties of the pastoral office among the parishioners, by whom he was much beloved and respected.   He has been frequently heard to declare, in after life, that he looked back upon the years passed at Straiton as the most happy and satisfactory period of his life.

From Straiton, in 1746, he was called to the second charge in South Leith.   Being then in the prime of life, he appeared in the pulpit to great advantage, and became very popular.   Here he remained till 1754, when he was appointed to one of the collegiate charges in the High Church, where he continued during the remainder of his life.

Mr. Walker maintained a high character, both as a man and as a preacher.   He published two volumes of Sermons, which long retained their popularity, and are yet so much admired by preachers, that, with a few alterations, they are frequently adopted by some in the pulpit as their own!   With his colleague, Dr. Blair, notwithstanding a difference of opinion on some minor points, he lived on terms of the closest friendship and intimacy; and although he did not aspire to the literary fame of that divine, his eloquence as a preacher was not less commanding, nor his local popularity inferior.   The celebrity of the one existed principally among the higher classes in the city; while the more evangelical discourses of the other endeared him to the less opulent, yet equally, if not more, devout portion of the community.

The congregations of the two incumbents were thus very dissimilar in character. Dr. Blair's was less numerous than that of Mr. Walker, but the church-door collections of the former were much greater. Hence the elders were wont to remark, that it took *twenty-four* of Mr. Walker's hearers to equal *one* of Dr. Blair's.

In private life, Mr. Walker was certainly more *generally* esteemed than his colleague. This probably arose from a familiarity on the part of the one, which was in some measure foreign to the character and manners of the other; and there was at least one virtue—liberality in money matters—which he possessed to a greater extent than his literary colleague. One day, during the repairs of the High Church, while the two ministers were looking on, the workmen importuned Mr. Walker for some money to drink their healths. To this Mr. Walker jocularly replied—"apply to my colleague," whom they knew to be not remarkably generous—at the same time quietly giving them five shillings.

Mr. Walker was highly Calvinistic in his religious views; and, where he conceived it to be his duty, no man could be more firm in denouncing any derelictions of a public or private nature. He was an enemy to many public amusements. During the early part of his incumbency in the High Church, the celebrated case of Home, the author of Douglas, called in an especial manner the attention of the clergy to the stage, and brought down their severest denouncements. On reading the admonition of the Presbytery of Edinburgh from the pulpit, on the 30th of January, 1757, he entered warmly and fearlessly upon the subject of theatrical representations. On another occasion, which caused no inconsiderable degree of excitement in the city, some thirteen years afterwards, he spoke out with equal boldness; and although, at the present day, there may not be many who will coincide to the full in his opinions with respect to the stage, all must admire the manly tone of his sentiments, and the eloquence with which they were expressed. The circumstance to which we allude occurred in 1770, when the comedy of the *Minor*, under the management of Mr. Foote, was performed on the Saturday evening. The occurrence gave rise to severe remarks in the periodical works of the time; and called forth a sermon from the Rev. Mr. Baine, which he published and dedicated to Mr. Foote. The following account of the affair is from one of the London journals—the article having been forwarded from Edinburgh:—

"On Saturday, November 24, Mr. Foote gave us the *Minor;* that piece of his which has made so much noise. The play for that night was bespoke by the Lord President of the Court of Session [Robert Dundas of Arniston], in justice to whom, however, it must be observed, that he did not fix on the particular piece that should be acted; and when it was known to be the *Minor*, a very proper message was sent to Mr. Foote, not to exhibit the ludicrous epilogue. Some of our thoughtless bucks, however, were determined to frustrate the decent and becoming resolution of their superiors; and, having planted themselves in the pit, they, with much vociferation, roared out for *Dr. Squintum*. After a pause, to see if the storm would subside, Mr. Foote, who was by this time dressed for the character of *Major Stur-*

geon, came forward, and made an apology, putting the audience in mind of the old proverb—*De mortuis nil nisi bonum*—which ought never to be violated. A distinguished buck cried, ' That won't satisfy us.' ' Sir,' said a noble peer, ' if you have a heart it should satisfy you.' Nothing, however, would do but Mr. Foote's speaking the epilogue—which he accordingly was obliged to do. Next day the Rev. Mr. Walker, one of the ministers of the High Church, having had occasion, in the course of his lecturing on the Scriptures, to mention the doctrine of *regeneration*, he took an opportunity of censuring what he called the gross profanation in the Theatre the preceding evening. He delivered himself with dignity, propriety, and spirit; and, though we could not go so far as he did in our notions of the stage in general, we could not but admire him for speaking his sentiments with an earnest firmness. He happened on that day to lecture in course on 2 Cor. v. 14—21; and, when he came to verse 17, before expounding it, he said—

" ' I cannot read this verse without expressing the just indignation I feel upon hearing, that last night a profane piece of buffoonery was publicly acted, in which, unless it hath undergone very material alterations, this sacred doctrine, and some others connected with it, are introduced to the stage for no other purpose but to gratify the impiety, and to excite the laughter of thoughtless, miserable, dying sinners.

" ' I had occasion some years ago to deliver very fully, from this place, my opinion of theatrical entertainments in general—an opinion then supported by the laws of my country. And as my sentiments in that matter were not formed upon such fluctuating things as the humours, or maxims, or decrees, of man, it is impossible that any variation in these can alter them; though perhaps I should not have thought it necessary to remind you of them at present, had not so gross an outrage upon the very passage that occurs this day in my course of lecturing challenged me to it. When I say this, I do not mean to make any sort of apology for using my undoubted privilege to walk with perfect freedom in the King's highway—I mean in the highway of the King of kings. If any jostle me in that road, they, and not I. must answer for the consequences. I here speak upon oath; I am bound to declare the whole counsel of God; and *wo is to me if I preach not the gospel*. If men are bold enough to act impiety, surely a minister of Christ may at least be equally bold in reproving it; he hath a patent for doing so more valid and authoritative than any theatre can possess, or any power on earth can give.' "

Such is a specimen of Mr. Walker's pulpit oratory, and of the manly independence of his spirit. The Lords of Session, the Barons of the Exchequer, and the Lord Provost and Magistrates, were present on the occasion.

Mr. Walker possessed a sound constitution, and enjoyed almost uninterrupted good health till 1782, when he was seized with apoplexy. He recovered so far, however, in the course of the year, as to resume his ministerial labours. On Friday, the 4th of April, 1783, he preached in the forenoon, apparently in his usual health; but on leaving the pulpit he complained of headache, and no sooner reached his own, house, which he did with some difficulty, than he was instantly seized

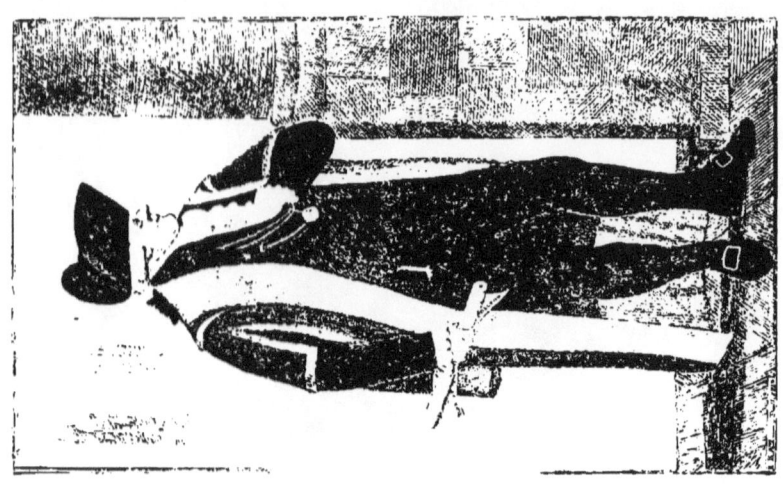

THOMAS ELDER

DAVID DOWNIE

with a stupor, and died in the course of two hours. Funeral sermons were preached, on account of his demise, by the Rev. Dr. Erskine, and by his own colleague, the Rev. Dr. Blair.

Mr. Walker resided at the Castle Hill, nearly opposite the Water Reservoir.

DAVID DOWNIE,
Tried for High Treason in 1794.

TOWARDS the end of 1793, several meetings of the British Convention were held in Edinburgh. At one of them (5th December) the Magistrates interfered, dispersed the Convention, and apprehended ten or twelve of the members, among whom were several English delegates; but who, after examination, were liberated on bail. The Magistrates at the same time issued a proclamation, prohibiting all such meetings in future; and giving notice to all persons " who shall permit the said meetings to be held in their houses, or other places belonging to them, that they will be prosecuted and punished with the utmost severity of the law." Notwithstanding this proclamation, another meeting was summoned by the secretary, William Skirving, to be held in the cockpit, Grassmarket, on the 12th of December. On this occasion the Magistrates again interfered, and apprehended several of the members; some of whom were served with indictments to take their trial before the High Court of Justiciary. It was about this time that Watt and Downie became deeply involved in those transactions for which they were condemned. After the dispersion of the British Convention, they became active members of a " Committee of Union," designed to collect the sense of the people, and to assemble another Convention. They were also members of a committee, called the "Committee of Ways and Means"—of which Downie was treasurer. In unison with the sentiments of the London Convention, it appears, the " Friends of the People" in Edinburgh had abandoned all hope of, or intention of further demanding, redress by constitutional means; and the more resolute of them began to entertain designs of an impracticable and dangerous nature. Of these wild schemes Watt was a principal and active promoter.

The first attempt of the Committee was to gain the co-operation of the military, or at least to render them neutral; for which purpose they printed an address, and circulated a number of copies among the Hopetoun Fencibles, then stationed at Dalkeith. The regiment was about to march for England. The object of the address was to excite the men to mutiny, by persuading them that they were sold to go abroad; and that, if they revolted, they would get thousands to assist them. John Geddes, a witness, and one of the soldiers, said he read the address. Some of the words it contained were—" Stay at home! O! dear brothers, stay at home!" A plan was also formed, by which it was expected that the city, together with the Castle, would fall into the hands of the " Friends of the People." The design was as follows:

"A fire was to be raised near the Excise Office, which would require the attendance of the soldiers, who were to be met on their way by a body of the "Friends of the People;' another party of whom were to issue from the West Bow, to confine the soldiers between two fires, and cut off their retreat. The Castle was next to be attempted; the Judges and Magistrates were to be seized; and all the public banks were to be secured. A proclamation was then to be issued, ordering all the farmers to bring in their grain to market as usual; and enjoining all country gentlemen unfriendly to the cause to keep within their houses, or three miles of them, under penalty of death. Then an address was to be sent to his Majesty, commanding him to put an end to the war—to change his ministers—or take the consequences."

Before this extraordinary project could be carried into effect, it was necessary that arms, of some description or other, should be procured. Another committee was consequently formed, called the collectors of "Sense and Money," whose business it was to "raise the wind," in order to procure arms. Two smiths (Robert Orrock and William Brown), who had enrolled their names among the "Friends of the People," were employed to make four thousand pikes; some of which were actually completed, and had been delivered to Watt, and paid for by Downie, in his capacity of treasurer.

Meanwhile the trials of William Skirving, Maurice Margarot, and Joseph Gerrald had taken place; but it was not until May that Watt and Downie were apprehended. On the 15th of that month, two sheriff-officers, while searching the house of Watt for some goods which had been secreted, belonging to a bankrupt, discovered some pikes, which they immediately carried to the Sheriff's Chambers. A warrant was then given to search the whole premises, and also to apprehend the parties. In the cellar, a form of types, from which the address to the military had been printed, as also an additional quantity of pikes, were discovered; and in the house of Orrock, the smith, thirty-three pikes, finished and unfinished, were likewise found.

True bills of indictment having been found against Watt and Downie, the trial of the former took place before the Court of Oyer and Terminer, on the 14th of August, 1794; and of the latter, on the 7th of September. The facts set forth in the indictments were fully proven against the prisoners. A letter from Downie—as treasurer to the Committee of Ways and Means, to "Walter Millar, Perth"—acknowledging the receipt of £15, in which he gave an account of the riots in the Theatre, was produced and identified; and Robert Orrock stated that Downie accompanied Watt to his place at the Water-of-Leith, when the order was given for the pikes. William Brown said he made fifteen pikes by Watt's order, to whom he delivered them; and that, on a line from Watt, Downie paid him twenty-two shillings and sixpence for the fifteen. Margaret Whitecross, who had been at one time a servant of Mr. Downie, on being shown one of the pikes, "declared that she saw a similar one in Mr. Downie's house one morning when she was dressing the dining-room: that Mr. Downie had come home late the previous night: that Mr. Downie's son, Charles, came out of an adjoining closet, where he slept, as soon as he heard her in the room, and took it away; and at this time he had only part of his clothes on, and did not seem to have any other business in that room : that she remembers hearing Mrs. Downie ask her husband what he had done with the large *dividing-knife* which was found in the dining-room?—to which he answered, that he had locked it by : that she never heard her master speak of having such weapons to defend himself; and when she saw it, she thought she never saw such a dividing-knife before." A verdict of guilty was returned on both occasions ; and sentence of death passed upon the prisoners.

Watt suffered the extreme punishment of the law, according to the form usual in treasonable cases. Previous to his execution, he made a confession of the extent and purport of the measures contemplated by the Committees.

The execution of Watt, which took place at the west end of the Luckenbooths, was conducted with much solemnity. He was conveyed from the Castle on a black-painted hurdle, drawn by a white horse, amid a procession of the magistracy, guarded by a strong military force. The prisoner, who was assisted in his devotions by the Rev. Principal Baird, exhibited a picture of the most abject dejection. He was wrapped in a great-coat, a red nightcap (which, on the platform, he exchanged for a white one), with a round hat, his stockings hanging loose, and his whole appearance wretched in the extreme. He was about the age of thirty-six, and was the natural son of a gentleman of fortune and respectability, in the county of Angus, but, as is usual, took the name of his mother. At about ten years of age he was sent to Perth, where he received a good education ; and, at sixteen, he engaged himself with a lawyer; but, from some religious scruples, took a disgust at his new employment; and, removing to Edinburgh, was engaged as a clerk to Mr. E. Balfour, bookseller, whose shop is now occupied by the *Journal* Office, and with whom he lived for some years, without any other complaint than the smallness of his salary. Being desirous of becoming a partner of the business, he, by the influence of some friends, prevailed on his father to advance money for that purpose ; and then made proposals to his employer; but his offer was rejected. Having money in possession, he entered into the wine and spirit trade, and for some time had tolerable success; but was ruined, it was said, on the commencement of the war with France.

Downie was pardoned on condition of banishing himself from the British dominions, and he died in exile. He was married, and had a family. He bore a respectable character as an honest and industrious tradesman, and had been twenty-four or twenty-five years a member of the Corporation of Goldsmiths, during a considerable period of which he held the office of Treasurer to the Incorporation. His shop was in the Parliament Square.

Reference has been made to the riots at the Theatre. These riots commenced on Monday night, the 8th of April, 1794, when the tragedy of Charles I. was performed. At the end of the second act several gentlemen called to the band in the orchestra to play " God save the King," during the performance of which a few individuals did not uncover. Some of the more loyal portion of the audience insisted that they should ; and from words the matter came to blows. On the next night of performance (the 10th) some attempts were made to create a disturbance, which was speedily got under; but on Saturday, the 12th, the democratic party mustered in greater numbers; and preparations had been made on both sides for a trial of strength. The play— "Which is the Man"—was allowed to go on to the end without interruption. A few minutes of ominous silence followed, when a voice at last called out for "God save the King," and "off hats." This seemed to be the signal for attack. A general melee ensued, which put an entire stop to the business of the stage, and created the utmost alarm. "It is difficult to say," observes the *Courant* of that period, "which party made the first attack; it was furious beyond example; each party had prepared for the contest, by arming themselves with bludgeons; and while the affray lasted, the most serious consequences were apprehended, as both parties fought with determined resolution. Many dreadful blows were given, which brought several individuals to the ground; and the wounded were in danger of being trampled to death in the general confusion. The party, however, who insisted on keeping on their hats, being at length overcome, left the house, and the wounded were carried out. The pit was the principal scene of action." A considerable mob were congregated out of doors anxiously waiting the result.

THOMAS ELDER, ESQ., OF FORNETH,
Lord Provost of Edinburgh.

THIS gentleman held the office of Chief Magistrate of Edinburgh at the following different periods:—First, from 1788 till 1790; again, from 1792 till 1794; and, lastly, from 1796 till 1798.

Great responsibility was attachable to the office during the second period of his provostship, in consequence of the disturbed state of the country and the measures of agitation resorted to by the "Friends of the People." Provost Elder exerted himself vigorously to check the inroad of democracy. Although the troops then scattered over Scotland were under two thousand, he ventured, assisted by a few only of the more respectable citizens of Edinburgh, to suppress the meeting of the memorable British Convention, held on the 5th December, 1793, taking ten or twelve of the principal members prisoners; and, in a similar manner, on the 12th of December, he dissolved another meeting, held in the cock-pit at the Grassmarket.

On the 13th January, 1794, an immense crowd had assembled, on occasion of the trial of Maurice Margarot, for the purpose of accompanying him to the Court of Justiciary. In anticipation of this, the Magistrates, city-guard, and constables, with a number of respectable inhabitants, met at an early hour in the Merchants' Hall, and sallying forth, with the Chief Magistrate at their head, about ten o'clock, they met Margarot and a number of his friends walking in procession, under an ornamental arch, on which the words "Liberty, Justice,"

&c., were inscribed. The canopy was instantly seized and thrown over the east side of the North Bridge, and, with the assistance of the crew of a frigate lying in Leith Roads, the crowd was dispersed, and the two arch-bearers captured.

At a meeting of the Town Council on the 9th September, immediately previous to the annual change in that body, they "unanimously returned their thanks, and voted a piece of plate to the Right Hon. the Lord Provost for his spirited and prudent conduct while in office, and especially during the late commotions."

On the formation of the Royal Edinburgh Volunteers, in the summer of 1794, Mr. Elder intended, on retiring from the provostship, to enter the ranks as a common volunteer; but this resolution was rendered nugatory by a mark of distinction emanating from the members of the association. For obvious reasons, the commission of Colonel was to be invested in the Chief Magistrate for the time being; and it was the wish of the volunteers that the commissions should, as far as possible, be held by gentlemen who had served with reputation in his Majesty's regular forces. An exception, however, which at once testified their estimation of his character, was made in the case of Provost Elder, for the volunteers unanimously recommended him to his Majesty to be their First Lieut.-Colonel.

In 1797, the Principal and Professors of the University requested him to sit for his portrait, to be preserved in the University library. Mr. Elder accordingly sat to the late Sir Henry Raeburn, who finished an excellent likeness in his best style—from which a mezzotinto engraving was afterwards published. Provost Elder merited this compliment, which had previously only been conferred on men eminent for learning or science, by being, in addition to his general usefulness as a magistrate and a citizen, prominently instrumental in maturing the design of rebuilding the College, which probably would have been finished during his lifetime, had it not been for the exigencies of the war.

In 1795, Mr. Elder was appointed Postmaster-General for Scotland an honour which testified that his services had been highly appreciated by his Majesty, and which was considered by his fellow-citizens as no more than a proper reward.

Throughout the whole course of his life, both in public and private business, Mr. Elder displayed "great and persevering activity in all his undertakings, inflexible integrity in his conduct, and perfect firmness in what he judged to be right. These talents and virtues were exerted without pomp or affectation; on the contrary, with the utmost openness and simplicity of manners; and it was often remarked of him, that he could refuse with a better grace than many others could confer a favour." Under his guidance, the political measures of the city were regulated with much tact and propriety; and the interest of the ruling party was never more firmly or honourably maintained.

Mr. Elder's acceptance of the Provostship the third time, was looked upon with a degree of uneasiness by his friends. His health had been visibly impaired by the harassing nature of his duties while formerly in office; and they were afraid a renewal of the anxiety and fatigue inseparable from the situation of Chief Magistrate, even in the quietest times, would prove too much for his weakened constitution. Mr.

Elder was himself aware of the danger, but he could not " decline the task consistently with his strict notions of public duty."

The fears of his friends were too well founded. His strength continued gradually to decline; and, before the end of 1798, his health was altogether in a hopeless state. He died at Forneth on the 29th May, 1799, aged sixty-two.

Mr. Elder was the eldest son of Mr. William Elder of Loaning, and married, in 1765, Emilia Husband, eldest daughter of Mr. Paul Husband of Logie, merchant in Edinburgh, by whom he left a son and four daughters. The eldest was married to the late Principal Baird; the second to the late John M'Ritchie, Esq. of Craigton. He carried on business as a wine merchant in the premises opposite the Tron Church, presently possessed by Mr. James Hill, grocer, where he realised a considerable fortune. For some time he resided in the house in Princes Street, afterwards occupied by Mr. Fortune, and long known as Fortune's Tontine, and subsequently at No. 85 Princes Street.

THE RIGHT HON. LORD VISCOUNT DUNCAN,
Admiral of the Fleet.

ADAM LORD VISCOUNT DUNCAN, one of the most celebrated names in the annals of the British navy, was born at Dundee on the 1st July, 1731. He was the younger son of Alexander Duncan, Esq. of Lundie and Seaside, in the county of Forfar, by Helen, a daughter of John Haldane, Esq. of Gleneagles and Aberuthen.

He entered the navy at the age of sixteen, as midshipman in the *Shoreham* frigate, in which he served for three years, under the command of his maternal relative, Captain Robert Haldane. From thence he was transferred to the *Centurion*, which then carried the broad pennant of Commodore Keppel. While on the Mediterranean station, he had the good fortune, by his intrepidity, steadiness, and seamanship, to attract the notice of the Commodore; and, in 1755, when Keppel was selected to command the transport ships destined for North America, he placed the name of Duncan at the head of those he had the privilege of recommending for promotion. He was consequently raised to the rank of Lieutenant, in which capacity he was present at the attack on the French settlement of Goree, on the coast of Africa, where he was wounded, and distinguished himself so much by his bravery, that, before the return of the expedition, he was promoted to be first Lieutenant of Keppel's own ship, the *Torbay*. Shortly after, he was raised to the rank of Commander.

In 1760, Duncan was appointed Captain of the *Valiant*, of seventy-four guns, on board which Keppel hoisted his flag as Commander of the fleet destined for Belleisle, where the newly promoted Captain had the honour of taking possession of the Spanish ships when the town surrendered. In the same ship, he was present, in 1762, at the reduction of the Havannah.

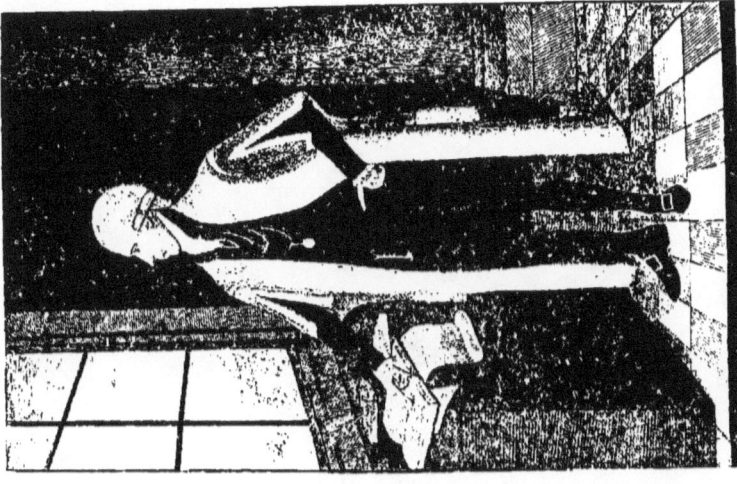

SIR JAMES STIRLING

LORD VISCOUNT DUNCAN

[To face page 242

In 1773, Captain Duncan had the singular fortune of sitting on the court-martial held on his friend and patron Admiral Keppel, who was not only honourably acquitted, but immediately afterwards received the thanks of both Houses of Parliament.

Having obtained the command of the *Monarch* seventy-four, the Captain's next expedition was with the squadron sent, under Sir George Rodney, to the relief of Gibraltar, in which they succeeded, and also had the good fortune to capture a fleet of fifteen Spanish merchant-men, with their convoy. Immediately afterwards, on the 16th of January 1779, a Spanish squadron, of eleven ships of the line, hove in sight off Cape St. Vincent. The British fleet directly bore down upon them, when Captain Duncan was the first to come up with the enemy. His daring conduct having been observed by his no less resolute Commander, he was warned of the danger of rushing into a position where he would be exposed to a very unequal contest. "Just what I want," he coolly replied; "I wish to be among them." The *Monarch* dashed on, and was instantly alongside a ship of larger size, while two of no less magnitude lay within musket-shot. A desperate engagement ensued, but the Captain soon succeeded in disabling the latter, when, directing all his fire against the *St. Augustin*, that vessel struck in less than half-an-hour; then pushing into the heat of the engagement, the *Monarch* contributed materially towards the victory which was that day obtained over the Spanish flag.

In 1782, Captain Duncan was appointed to the command of the *Blenheim* of ninety guns, and was present at the engagement with the united fleet of France and Spain in October, off the mouth of the Straits of Gibraltar. For several years after this, during the peace, he remained in command of the *Edgar* guardship at Portsmouth; and, on the 14th September, 1789, was made Rear-Admiral of the Blue. When the late Earl Spencer came to the Admiralty, he inquired for "Keppel's Captain," and, in February, 1795, appointed him Commander-in-Chief of the North Sea Fleet.

It is needless to follow him through his arduous services while holding this important command. When the fate of Ireland hung upon the balance; when a powerful fleet was concentrated at the Texel, for the invasion of that ill-fated country—torn to pieces by internal faction—Admiral Duncan suddenly found himself deserted by his fleet, and left, in the face of the enemy, with only one line of battle ship besides his own. The veteran Admiral, in spite of these disheartening circumstances, maintained his post undaunted. He continued to menace the Texel, by keeping up signals, as if his whole fleet were in the distance; and thus prevented the Dutch from attempting to leave their anchorage.

To give a detailed account of Admiral Duncan's memorable conduct during the mutiny at the Nore, would lead us beyond our limits. Suffice it to say, that by a judicious blending of firmness and conciliation, he entirely quelled the first symptoms of insubordination in his own ship, the *Venerable*, and also in the *Adamant*, Captain (now Sir William) Hotham—the only ship which remained with him to the last. His speech to the crew of the *Venerable* is to be found in the naval history of the country. We may, however, mention the following anecdote, for the authenticity of which Sir William Hotham has vouched. When told, on one occasion, that the Dutch fleet was getting under weigh, he directed Sir William to anchor the *Adamant* alongside the *Venerable*, in the narrow part of the channel, and to fight her till she sank, adding—"I have taken the depth of water; and, when the *Venerable* goes down, my flag will still fly."

On the termination of the mutiny at the Nore, Admiral Duncan was immediately rejoined by the rest of his fleet; and, after cruising for four months, he left a small squadron of observation, and set sail for Yarmouth Roads. He had scarcely reached the Roads, however, when he received intelligence that the enemy were at sea. He instantly gave signal for a general chase, and soon came up with them between Camperdown and Egmont, where the well known and decisive naval combat of the 11th October, 1797, ensued, in which De Winter, and two other Dutch Admirals, were taken prisoners, and the Dutch fleet annihilated. Admiral Duncan's address, previous to the engagement with Admiral de Winter, was both laconic and humorous: "Gentlemen, you see a severe *Winter* approaching; I have only to advise you to keep up a good *fire*."

Immediately after the victory, Admiral Duncan was created a peer, by the title of Viscount Duncan of Camperdown and Baron Duncan of Lundie; and a pension of £3000 a-year was granted during his own life and that of the two next succeeding heirs to the peerage. He was presented with the freedom of the city of London, together with a sword of two hundred guineas' value, from the corporation. Gold medals, in commemoration of the victory, were also given to all the Admirals and Captains of the fleet, while the public testified their respect by wearing certain articles of apparel named after the engagement. The cloth worn on this occasion was a species of tartan, of a large pattern, intended as emblematical of the species of tactics pursued by the British Admiral.

On this occasion the inhabitants of Edinburgh were not to be satisfied with any cold or formal expression of esteem; they resolved upon a public and special demonstration in honour of their gallant countryman. The animating scene is thus described by the Edinburgh journals of the period :—

"The tribute of gratitude and respect universally due by every Briton to the gallant Lord Duncan, was yesterday (7th February, 1798) paid by his fellow-townsmen, the inhabitants of Edinburgh. The whole brigade of volunteers were called out in honour of the day; and the muster was a very full one, between two and three thousand. The different corps, having assembled in Hope Park, and other places of rendezvous, about two o'clock, soon after entered George's Square, by the north-east corner, through Charles Street, and proceeded through the Square in slow time, passing Lord Duncan's house, before which his lordship stood uncovered, saluting them as they passed. Here the procession was joined by a naval car, on which was placed the British and his lordship's flag, flying above that of Admiral de Winter, attended by a body of seamen; then followed, in carriages, Lord Adam Gordon and his Staff—Lord Viscount Duncan—Captain Inglis of Redhall—the Lord Provost, and the eldest Bailie. The troops marched round the Square, filing off by Windmill Street, Chapel Street, Nicolson Street, across the South and North Bridges—the infantry leading, and the cavalry closing the procession. At the end of the North Bridge the populace took the horses from Lord Duncan's carriage, and drew it during the remainder of the procession, which proceeded through the principal Streets of the New Town. The arrangement of the military procession, which in beauty and grandeur was far beyond any ever seen in this country, did honour to those who planned it. It was one of those happy, but rare instances, in which expectation is exceeded by reality. An elegant entertainment was given to his lordship, in Fortune's tavern, by the Lord Provost and Magistrates, at which he was presented with the freedom of the city in a gold box of elegant workmanship."

Lord Duncan retired from the command of the North Sea squadron in 1800, being desirous of spending the remainder of his days in private life; but he did not long enjoy his retirement. He died of apoplexy at Cornhill, on his way from London, in 1804.

In a brief sketch such as the present, it would be out of place to dilate on the character of one so generally known as Admiral Duncan, or to advert to the importance of those services which his superior genius enabled him to perform. As a naval officer, he is entitled to every credit, both for the soundness of his tactics, and the novel daring and decisive nature of his movements; while in domestic life he was remarkable for those amiable qualities which ever accompany true greatness.

His lordship married, in 1777, Henrietta, daughter of Lord President Dundas, by whom he had four sons and five daughters. Robert, the second son, in consequence of the demise of his elder brother, Alexander, succeeded to the titles and estates, and was created Earl of Camperdown in 1831. He married in January, 1805, Janet, daughter of the late Sir Hugh Hamilton Dalrymple, of Bargeny and North Berwick, Bart., by whom he has issue. The third son, Henry, afterwards Sir Henry, entered the navy and rose to the rank of Post-Captain. He died suddenly on the 1st November, 1835. He was considered a bright ornament to the navy, and one of the most promising officers. A magnificent monument to his memory has recently been erected in the neighbourhood of London by those who served with him during the war.

The widow of Admiral Duncan survived him many years, and died in her house in George Square, November, 1832, lamented by all who knew her. She was a lady of the most bland and attractive manners, and of eminent piety. The house, which is now occupied as the Southern Academy, still remains the property of the Earl. The celebrated painting of "The Battle of Camperdown," by Copley—which cost £1000, and to which the inhabitants of Edinburgh had access annually for many years on the anniversary of the victory—has since the death of the Dowager, been removed to Camperdown House, Forfarshire.

THE REV. DAVID JOHNSTON, D.D.,
Minister of North Leith.

It may be said of this excellent man, that he inherited the virtues of the clerical character by descent. His father was minister of Arngask, in the county of Fife, and his maternal grandfather, the Rev. Mr. David Williamson, of the parish of St. Cuthbert's, Edinburgh, was a celebrated clergyman in the days of the persecution.

Mr. David Johnston was born in 1733. His early years were sedulously devoted to the study of those acquirements necessary for the important office which he was destined so long and so honourably to fill. After attending the usual academical courses, and having obtained authority to preach, his character and talents soon procured for him the parish church of Langton, in Berwickshire, to which he was ordained in 1759. He remained there, however, only about six years, having been then called to the more important charge of North Leith, the population of which, though at that time only seven hundred, had increased to as many thousands before his death.

There are seldom any striking incidents to record in the biography of a parish clergyman. "The even tenor of his way" is less liable to be disturbed by those ruder shocks which frequently assail men in other spheres of life. This observation is peculiarly applicable to the subject of the present sketch. If we except the frequent alarms experienced by inhabitants of Leith during the early part of the last war, when the country was threatened with foreign invasion, and the interesting yet arduous duty which he faithfully discharged in consoling the fears and animating the courage of his people, no occurrence very peculiar falls to be narrated within the scope of his history; but it would require a volume of no ordinary dimensions to note down all the acts of genuine Christian philanthropy in which he was engaged almost every day of his existence. In the pulpit he inculcated, with earnestness and power, those principles and doctrines which all feel to be the very basis of the moral structure; while, in his parochial visitations, he sedulously laboured to carry the precepts of religion home to the firesides of his parishioners. On one of his catechetical rounds among the cottages of the fishermen of Newhaven, the curious version of *Adam's fall* was given, which, as the anecdote is illustrative of that peculiar class of people, will be found related in our notice of a "Newhaven Oyster Lass." Many still alive remember with what diligence their venerated pastor continued, even in old age, to visit the humble dwellings of the poor, and to attend the bed of sickness and of death, carrying along with him that consolation which the mission of peace never fails to bestow. Neither was his solicitude confined to the spiritual welfare of his people. In their temporal affairs he took a lively interest, and felt for their misfortunes as if they were his own. "To the widow, he was as a husband—to the orphan, as a father—to the destitute and helpless, a steward of Heaven's bounty; their protector, patron, and support."

Dr. Johnston's philanthropy was of the most active description. He was no sentimentalist, to weep at the recitation of a well-told tale, and yet turn his eyes away from actual misery. In a maritime district such as North Leith, where a great portion of the inhabitants are engaged in the precarious and dangerous occupation of fishing, casualties are of frequent occurrence. The moment he heard of a case of distress, he could not remain satisfied without instantly doing something to assist the sufferers; and, while he was no niggard of his own means, he was indefatigable in his endeavours to procure aid from others. Whether his charity was exerted in behalf of individuals, or of institutions, he was equally unremitting in his endeavours; and whenever a benevolent project was pointed out to him, he entered into the scheme with the most ardent enthusiasm, and prosecuted it with untiring energy. Perhaps there was no one of whom it could more truly be said, that "he went about continually doing good."

The only dilemma in which the good old Doctor is known to have been placed with a portion of his parishioners, occurred when the old church of North Leith—abandoned to secular purposes—was, in 1817, supplanted by the present building, with its handsome spire, surmounted by a *cross*. Some of the out-and-out Presbyterians saw in this emblem an alarming approach to Popish darkness; and, not infrequently, when in the course of his visitations, he found himself in the *place* of the *catechised*. On this subject the Doctor held only one opinion; but, in deference to the zealous declamation of two old women whom he one day encountered, and who had fairly borne him down by strength of lungs, if not by strength of argument, he at last exclaimed—"Well, well, what would ye have me to do in the matter?" "*Do!*" replied one of them; "what wad ye do—*but just put up the auld cock again!*"

With the establishment of that benevolent institution—the Blind Asylum of Edinburgh—the memory of Dr. Johnston is affectionately associated; and so deeply and actively did he interest himself in originating and promoting funds for the undertaking, that he might with justice be designated its founder. So much were his feelings bound up in the success of the institution, that he regularly devoted a portion of his time to give it his personal superintendence, and watched over its progress with all the fondness of a parent. This surveillance he continued every day in the week, except Saturday and Sabbath, walking to and from Edinburgh; and, at the extreme age of ninety, gave proof of the wonderful degree of muscular activity for which he had always been remarkable, by performing the journey as usual. He disdained the modern effeminacy of the stage-coach; and, in going up Leith Walk, generally got a-head of it.

Both in person and in features, Dr. Johnston was exceedingly handsome; and in dress and manners he was a thorough gentleman of the last century. He died at Leith on the 5th of July, 1824, in the ninety-first year of his age, and sixty-sixth of his ministry, leaving behind him one daughter, the only survivor of a large family, who was married to William Penney, Esq. of Glasgow. Some years prior to his death he had been assisted in his parochial duties by the Rev. Dr. Ireland.

The remains of this much respected and patriarchal clergyman were followed to the grave by upwards of five hundred persons, among whom were many of the most distinguished citizens of Edinburgh and Leith. The inmates of the Blind Asylum, who had been so much an object of his care, lined the access to the churchyard; and, by their presence, added much to the melancholy interest of the scene. The Rev. Dr. Dickson, of St. Cuthbert's, preached the funeral sermon on the Sabbath following.

SIR JAMES STIRLING, BART.,
Lord Provost of Edinburgh.

THIS gentleman, whose father was a fishmonger at the head of Marlin's Wynd, had the merit of being the architect of his own fortune. Marlin's Wynd, which stood east of the Tron Church, was demolished to make way for the South Bridge. Mr. Stirling had for his sign a large, clumsy, wooden *Black Bull*, which is preserved as a relic in the Museum of the Scottish Antiquaries. In early life he went to the West Indies, as clerk to an extensive and opulent planter, Mr. Stirling of Keir, where he conducted himself with such propriety, that, in a short time, through the influence of his employer, he was appointed Secretary to the Governor of the Island of Jamaica, Sir Charles Dalling.

Having in this situation accumulated a considerable sum of money, he at length returned to Edinburgh, and was assumed a partner in the banking concern of " Mansfield, Ramsay, & Co." (lately Ramsay, Bonar, & Co.), whose place of business was then in Cantore's Close, Luckenbooths. Not long after he had entered into this concern, Mr. Stirling, naturally of an irritable temperament, became uneasy at the extent and responsibility of a banking establishment, and proposed selling his estate of Saughie, which he had recently purchased. Old Mr. William Ramsay, having been apprised of his intention, addressed him one day after dinner in his usual familiar manner—" I hear, Jamie, that ye're gaun to sell the Saughie property. If that be the case, rather than let you advertise it in the newspapers, and thereby bring suspicion on the stability of the concern, I'll tak it frae you at what it cost ye." Stirling instantly agreed to the proposition; and scarcely had the property been transferred to Mr. Ramsay when that gentleman had the offer of nearly double the purchase-money. The value is now more than quadrupled. In this copartnery he was very prosperous; and his good fortune was increased by obtaining the hand of Miss Mansfield, the daughter of the principal partner.

Mr. Stirling first became connected with the Town Council in 1771, when he was elected one of the Merchant Councillors. During the years 1773-4, he held the office of Treasurer; and, from 1776 till 1790, was frequently in the magistracy. At the annual election of the latter year, he was chosen Lord Provost, and held that office during the city riots of 1792.

At this period politics ran high. The Reform of the Royal Burghs of Scotland had been keenly agitated throughout the country for some time previous; and a motion on the subject, by Mr. Sheridan, in the House of Commons, on the 18th of April, which was negatived by a majority of twenty-six, had incensed the public to a great degree. Henry Dundas Lord Melville, then Principal Secretary of State for the Home department, by his opposition to the motion, rendered himself so obnoxious to the people, that in various parts of Scotland he was burnt in effigy by the mob. The Pitt administration had become unpopular, by a proclamation, issued at the same time, against certain publications—a measure which the people viewed as an attack upon the liberty of the press. In this state of excitement the authorities of Edinburgh contemplated the approaching King's birth-day on the 4th of June, with much uneasiness; but the measures of precaution adopted by them were imprudent, and tended rather to irritate than conciliate the populace. The disturbances which ensued are thus recorded in the journals of the day:—

"The Magistrates of Edinburgh, having got information by anonymous letters and otherwise, that, on the King's birth-day, many persons who had taken offence at the parliamentary conduct of Mr. Dundas, in the opposition of the Scottish Burgh Reform, were determined to burn his effigy, in imitation of the burghs of Dundee, Aberdeen, &c., in consequence of this information, they took the opinion of the high officers of the Crown, with regard to the conduct which it was proper to pursue, when they resolved to prevent, if possible, the designs of the populace, by bringing in some troops of dragoons to overawe and intimidate them. Accordingly, in the afternoon of the King's birth-day (Monday, 4th June, 1792), the dragoons made their appearance in Edinburgh, riding furiously through the streets, with their swords drawn. This behaviour, instead of having the desired effect, provoked the indignation of the people, who saluted them with hootings and hisses as they passed along. In the afternoon, when the Magistrates were assembled in the Parliament House, to drink the usual healths and loyal toasts, the populace also assembled, and were indulging themselves, according to a custom which has prevailed in Edinburgh for many years, in the throwing of dead cats, &c., at one another, and at the city-guard, who are always drawn up to fire vollies as the healths are drunk by the Magistrates. At this time some dragoon officers, incautiously appearing on the streets, were insulted by the rabble. This induced them to bring out their men, who were accordingly directed to clear the streets. Some stones were thrown at them; but at last the mob retired without doing any material mischief.

"On the evening of the next day, Tuesday, a number of persons assembled before Mr. Dundas's house in George Square, with a figure of straw, which they hung upon a pole, and were proceeding to burn, when two of Mr. Dundas's friends came out from the house, and very imprudently attempted to disperse the mob by force. Their conduct was immediately resented. The gentlemen were soon obliged to retire again into the house; and the mob began to break the windows. Not content with this, they proceeded to the house of the Lord Advocate (Dundas of Arniston), whose windows they broke. It then became necessary to bring a party of the military from the Castle to prevent farther mischief. The Sheriff attended and read the riot act; but the mob not dispersing, after repeated intimation of the consequences, the military at last fired, when several persons were wounded, and some mortally. This put a period to the outrages for that night.

" On Wednesday, in the evening, the mob assembled in the New Town, with an intention of destroying the house of the Chief Magistrate. A fire was lighted on the Castle, and two guns were fired, as a signal to the marines of the *Hind* frigate, stationed at Leith, and the dragoons, quartered about a mile east of the town. On their appearance the mob finally separated."

During the prevalence of these riots, Provost Stirling prudently sought shelter in the Castle. In so doing he acted wisely, as, if the mob had laid hands on him, there is no saying what might have followed. It was at this time that " Lang Sandy Wood," whom the crowd mistook for the Provost, narrowly escaped being thrown over the North Bridge.

The Magistrates, naturally alarmed at what had occurred, thought it best to lay the whole facts of the case before their fellow-citizens. With this view, a public meeting of the inhabitants was called, in the New Church aisle, on the Thursday forenoon following. The Lord Provost in the chair. Of this meeting the following account is given in the journals:—

" The Lord Advocate, Mr. Sheriff Pringle, the Lord President, Lord Adam Gordon, Commander-in-Chief, Mr. Solicitor Blair, and several others, declared their sentiments. The meeting unanimously expressed their full approbation of the measures pursued by the Magistrates and the Sheriff, for suppressing the riots; and published resolutions to that effect.

" A proclamation was issued the same evening, recommending to the people not to assemble in crowds, or remain longer on the streets than their lawful business required, as the most decisive measures had been resolved upon for quieting the least appearance of any further disorder; and offering a reward of one hundred guineas for discovery of the ring-leaders. Fifty guineas were also offered by the Merchant Company, who, and all the incorporations, voted thanks to the Magistrates for the measures taken to suppress the riots. It is said, that certain attempts to procure a vote of thanks to the Magistrates for introducing the military into the town, *previous to any riotous act,* proved abortive."

Perhaps the zeal displayed by Provost Stirling, in support of the existing administration on this occasion, may have recommended him as a suitable object for ministerial favour; however this may be, on the 17th of July following, " the King was pleased to grant the dignity of a Baronet of the kingdom of Great Britain to the Right Hon. James Stirling, Lord Provost of the city of Edinburgh, and the heirs-male of his body lawfully begotten."

The irritation of the populace against Sir James gradually subsided;

and latterly vented itself entirely in pasquinadoes and lampoons, in which the humble origin of the Baronet was not spared.

The satirical allusion of a second Print will be best understood by reference to the debate in the House of Commons in the month of May prior to the distubances. The subject of discussion was the King's proclamation (already alluded to), which the Whigs opposed as tyrannical and unnecessary. After several speakers had delivered their sentiments, *Mr. Courtenay* said—" The proclamation was a severe censure on ministers for not having discharged their duty—in not having prosecuted the libels, which they said had existence for several months. He declared his misbelief of the proclamation having been intended for insidious purposes by one of his Majesty's cabinet ministers, the Home Secretary (Mr. Dundas), whose good nature and civility had always induced him to accommodate himself to every minister ; which good nature and civility called to his mind the *old man in Edinburgh*, who used to go about with a pail and great-coat, calling out—' Wha wants me ? ' The honourable Secretary, upon every change of administration, had imitated the old man, by calling out—' Wha wants me ? ' This readiness to oblige, therefore, did away with all suspicion of malice."

To this sally of humour, Dundas of course made no reply. He was impenetrable to all such assaults. It did not fail, however, to excite the notice of his opponents north of the Tweed ; and we have seen by the " Patent of Knighthood " how the artist improved upon the suggestion.

Notwithstanding his temporary unpopularity, Sir James was subsequently at the head of the magistracy in 1794-5, and again in 1798-9. During the latter warlike period his conduct was truly meritorious. Scottish commerce had suffered considerably from the attacks of French and Dutch privateers, even on our very coasts, which had been left in a shamefully unguarded condition. By the representations of Sir James, and his judicious applications to Government, proper convoys were obtained for the merchantmen, and due protection afforded to our bays. He zealously forwarded the plan of arming the seamen of Leith and the fishermen of Newhaven, by which a strong body of men were organised in defence of the harbour and shipping.

So highly were the services of Sir James appreciated, that at the annual Convention of the Royal Burghs of Scotland (of which he was preses), held at Edinburgh in 1799, the thanks of the Convention were presented to him in a gold box, " for his constant attention to the trade of the country, and in testimony of the Convention's sense of his good services in procuring the appointment of convoys, and in communicating with the outports on the subject."

Sir James Stirling died on the 17th February, 1805. In private life, he was very much respected : of mild, gentlemanly manners, but firm in what he judged to be right. His habits were economical, but not parsimonious ; and the party entertainments given at his house were always in a style of magnificence. In person, he was tall and extremely attenuated. It is related of Sir James, that on being pointed out to a country woman while walking, attired in his velvet robes, in a procession, she exclaimed—"Is that the Lord Provost? I thocht it was the corpse rinnin' awa' wi' the mort-cloth."

At one period Sir James resided in St. Andrew's Square, the first house north from Rose Street; and, latterly, at the west end of Queen Street, not far from the Hopetoun Rooms. He acquired the estate of Larbert, in Stirlingshire, which, with his title of Baronet, descended to his son, the present Sir Gilbert Stirling, then a Lieutenant in the Coldstream Guards. He left two daughters, Janet and Joan, the former of whom was married to Admiral Sir Thomas Livingstone of Westquarter, near Falkirk.

END OF VOL. I.

www.ingramcontent.com/pod-product-compliance
Lightning Source LLC
Chambersburg PA
CBHW031952060726
47497CB00016B/1458